Passage
Into
Light

BOOKS BY JUDITH PELLA

Beloved Stranger
Blind Faith
Heaven's Road
*The Stonewycke Legacy**
*The Stonewycke Trilogy**
Texas Angel

DAUGHTERS OF FORTUNE

Written on the Wind

LONE STAR LEGACY

Frontier Lady
Stoner's Crossing
Warrior's Song

RIBBONS OF STEEL†

Distant Dreams
A Hope Beyond
A Promise for Tomorrow

RIBBONS WEST†

Westward the Dream
Separate Roads
Ties That Bind

THE RUSSIANS

*The Crown and the Crucible**
*A House Divided**
*Travail and Triumph**
Heirs of the Motherland
Dawning of Deliverance
White Nights, Red Morning
Passage Into Light

*with Michael Phillips   †with Tracie Peterson

The Russians

7

Passage Into Light

Judith Pella

Bethany House
Minneapolis, Minnesota

Passage Into Light
Copyright © 1998
Judith Pella

Cover illustration by Dan Thornberg
Cover design by Sheryl Thornberg

Published by Bethany House Publishers
A Ministry of Bethany Fellowship International
11400 Hampshire Avenue South
Bloomington, Minnesota 55438
www.bethanyhouse.com

Printed in the United States of America by
Bethany Press International,
Bloomington, Minnesota 55438

ISBN 0–7642–2527–8 (Mass market)
ISBN 1–55661–869–7 (Trade paper)

To Tracie Peterson,
whose enthusiasm is so very refreshing,
and whose friendship is a true blessing!

JUDITH PELLA began her writing career in collaboration with Michael Phillips on several major fiction series. THE RUSSIANS was begun as a team effort, but eventually they mutually agreed that Judith would continue the series on her own. These extraordinary novels showcase her creativity and skill as a historian as well as a writer of fiction. An avid reader and researcher in historical, adventure, and geographical venues, her storytelling abilities provide readers with memorable novels in a variety of genres. She and her family make their home in northern California.

CONTENTS

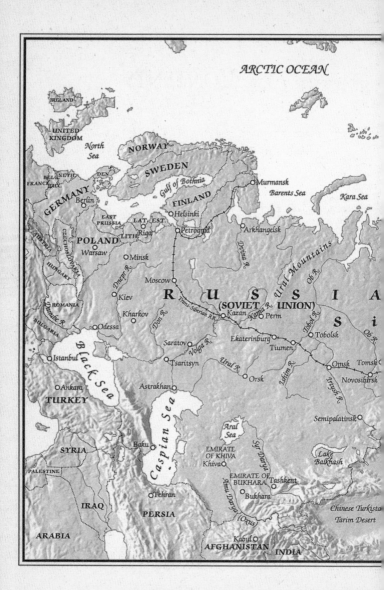

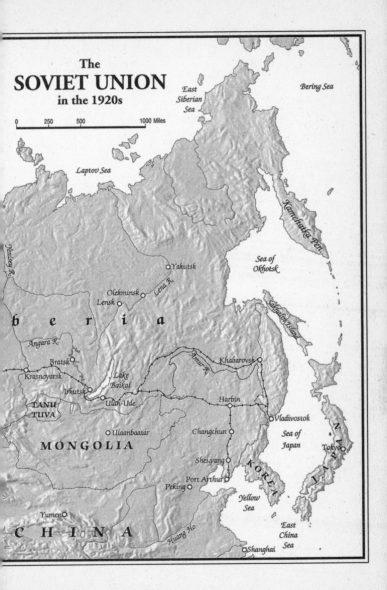

The
SOVIET UNION
in the 1920s

0   250   500   1000 Miles

East Siberian Sea

Bering Sea

Laptov Sea

Kamchatka pen.

Yenisey R.

○ Yakutsk

Sea of Okhotsk

Olekminsk
Lensk ○   *Lena R.*

b   e   r   i   a

Angara R.

Bratsk ○

Amur R.   Khabarovsk ○

Sakhalin Island

Krasnoyarsk

Irkutsk ○   *Lake Baikal*

TANU TUVA   Ulan-Ude ○   Harbin ○

○ Ulaanbaatar   Changchun ○   Vladivostok ○   *Sea of Japan*

MONGOLIA

J   A   P   A   N

Tokyo ○

Sheisyang ○

K   O   R   E   A

Port Arthur ○
Yumen ○   Peking ○

Yellow Sea

C   H   I   N   A

Huang Ho

East China Sea

○ Shanghai

CAST OF CHARACTERS

(in order of appearance)

Andrei Sergeiovich Fedorcenko—a.k.a. Andrei Christinin, Malenkiy Soldat, Ivan. Son of Anna and Sergei, younger brother of Yuri.

Sonja Morozovna—Andrei's friend.

Rudy Gruenwald—Andrei's friend.

Anna Fedorcenko Grigorov—nee Burenin. Mother of Andrei, Yuri and Mariana. Widow of Sergei, wife of Misha.

Raisa Sorokin—Anna's roommate and close friend, and mother of Talia.

Daniel Trent—American reporter, husband of Mariana.

Mariana Trent—nee Remizov. Wife of Daniel, adopted daughter of Anna.

Children of Mariana and Daniel—John, Katrina, Zenia.

Yuri Sergeiovich Fedorcenko—son of Anna and Sergei, brother of Andrei.

Cyril Karlovich Vlasenko—relative and nemesis of Fedorcenkos, one time member of the Imperial Ministry.

Katya Fedorcenko—wife of Yuri.

Nicholas Romanov—former tsar of Russia.

Alexandra Romanov—former tsaritsa of Russia.

Children of the Romanovs—Olga, Marie, Tatiana, Anastasia, Alexis.

Bruce McDuff—a.k.a. Lord Findochty and "Finkie." British aristocrat and supporter of Russian monarchy.

Paul Burenin—brother of Anna, revolutionary, associate of Kerensky.

Alexander Kerensky—a.k.a. Sasha. Minister of Justice, later Minister of War and finally, Prime Minister of the Provisional Government.

Stephan Kaminsky—Lenin's bodyguard, formerly a friend of the Burenins and one-time suitor of Mariana.

Vladimir Ilyich Lenin—leader of the Bolshevik Party.

Dr. Eugene Botkin—physician to the tsar, friend of Yuri.

Prince Viktor Fedorcenko—grandfather to Yuri, Andrei, and Mariana. Father of Sergei.

Lev Trotsky—leader in Bolshevik Party, Lenin's right-hand man.

Sergei Viktorvich Fedorcenko—deceased father of Yuri and Andrei.

Lt. Boris Soloviev—head of a monarchist organization involved in rescue of the tsar.

Monarchist soldiers assisting Daniel—Melink, Sedov, Pitovranov, Karloff.

Count Wilhelm Mirbach—German ambassador.

Yakov Sverdlov—president of the Central Executive Committee of the All Russian Congress of Soviets.

Vasily Yakovlev—Soviet Commissar and head of military unit sent to move the tsar.

Misha Grigorov—husband to Anna.

Dmitri Remizov—birth father to Mariana.

Yakov Yurovsky—head executioner.

I

ASHES TO ASHES
Spring 1917

1

The cold clamped down upon Andrei's fallen form as insistently as the pain and fear that gripped his soul. He had been drifting in and out of consciousness, but he knew the next time oblivion struck would be the last. He literally felt the life ebbing from his body.

"Mama . . ." he murmured, not even certain if sound accompanied the word.

"I'm here now, my dear one," came an ethereal voice out of the dark shadows surrounding him.

Was he only imagining that voice as he'd thought he'd imagined Talia calling her kitty? Then hands began to jostle him. Had his attackers returned? Would they kill him now by manhandling his pain-wracked body? It certainly felt as if that were their intent. He cried out when a particularly sharp movement wrenched his side where the gunshot wound had penetrated.

"Stop! Rudy, we are only making it worse for him."

That was the same voice Andrei had heard soothing him a moment ago, a female. Was it the voice of a rescuer rather than an attacker?

"You fetched me out in this wretched storm to save this man," answered a male voice. "Let's get on with it."

"But every movement pains him so."

"Better for him to suffer now than to lie here and freeze to death. And I tell you, Sonja Morozovna, though he may die from his injuries, he certainly will perish if left in this storm any longer."

"Oh, but my Ivan cannot die. . . ." The woman brushed gentle fingers against Andrei's cheek.

"He isn't Ivan. . . ."

"What . . . ?"

"Never mind that, Sonja, let's just get him moved. I'll grip him under the arms and try to drag him as much as possible. You mind his feet. I don't know how we'll get him up two flights of stairs to your flat, but even if we leave him in the entryway of the building, it will afford him some protection from the elements."

"His bed is all ready for him with fresh, clean sheets. I knew he'd come home soon. I am ready for him. I have a nice ham in the oven baking. . . ."

"Ah, Sonja," sighed Rudy, "if you have a ham in these times, or even clean sheets, I will give up my atheism and consider the possibility of a God."

Sonja made no response but to whisper words of encouragement to Andrei. "Dear boy, it will hurt for a bit. It can't be helped . . . be brave and strong, then you will be safe in your mama's home."

"Mama . . . you are here, then. . . ?" breathed Andrei.

"Always, child. I will not leave . . . and you will not leave me again."

The two rescuers began again the difficult and excruciating process of moving Andrei. Mercifully, he blacked out after a few minutes.

———

It took a lot longer than it would have in normal conditions to traverse the alley, round the corner, and cover the few yards to the building's front entrance. But Rudy was not a large man, and he was a scholar, not a laborer, so he was hardly conditioned to move two hundred-plus pounds of dead weight even a short distance. Once they left the shelter of the alley, the wind and falling snow impaired their vision, and the icy ground caused them to slip and slide several times before they reached the steps to the building. And those five steps up might just as well have been a mountain. At least the doorman, who had disappeared when the revolution began, was not there to question them. Everyone knew all doormen in Russia were agents of the Okhrana.

By the time Andrei's body was deposited in a corner of

the inside entryway, as far from the door as possible, Rudy felt certain they were merely transporting a corpse. He had completed three years of medical school before he had been expelled for political reasons, but he did not need those years of instruction to tell him that no one in this man's condition could survive such treatment. He was shocked when he bent over the body and felt Andrei's chest rise and fall. True it was only a slight movement, but unmistakable nonetheless. The man was still alive!

"Well, he made it this far, Sonja!" said Rudy, clasping his frozen, gloved hands together to warm them.

"Of course," Sonja replied. "Did you ever doubt it? Now the stairs—"

"Hold it! I will die if I have to lug this bear to your flat. Leave him here for the night, and in the morning we can get more help. It will be easier, anyway, to transport him to a hospital from here."

"A hospital. . . ?" Sonja shook her head. "I will not let my Ivan leave me again. Besides, I can nurse him better than any stranger in a hospital could."

"You may be right there," said Rudy, "especially in these times. But still it can wait till tomorrow—"

"No! I will get help now. He has come so far to get home." She spun around and rushed up the stairs.

Sonja Morozovna was about fifty years of age, though she looked much older. Her frame was petite and slightly bent in the shoulders, but she moved with amazing speed and agility. If only her mind were as quick and able as her body. But the last few years had taken a terrible toll on her. Rudy remembered her in happier days when her family filled the flat on the second floor and there was always laughter and life in her home. Though working-class folks, they were never as poor as most because her husband was a skilled weaver. Sonja, a hardworking, industrious woman, brought in additional income by selling fine handmade lace items. She was generous, though, with her bounty. Rudy and many of the other neighbors had often enjoyed her fresh bread or the sweets she loved to bake.

Three years of war destroyed all that. Her husband and two eldest sons were killed in the first year of fighting. Her youngest son, Ivan, overcome with grief, ran away and joined the army against her wishes. He was killed in the fall of 1916, less than six months ago. Sonja's sanity had already begun to deteriorate. She simply did not have the stamina to face a grim, dark, lonely world with a future that promised only more heartache. Ivan's death sent her completely over the edge. Perhaps that was a mercy. In her clouded mind the world had not changed. Why, she even continued to bake bread for her neighbors—not real bread, of course, for there was not enough flour for that. Wearing a smile that was an empty shadow of her former happiness, she would offer a dish just as empty.

To ease his mind of Sonja's sad story, Rudy focused his attention on the wounded young man. He loosened the clothing, a difficult process because the blood-soaked areas around the wound were frozen and stuck to the broken skin. When Sonja returned he would have her boil water in her flat so he could pack the area with warm compresses. The cold had stanched the bleeding a bit, a fact that might well have saved the fellow's life. The wound appeared to be the result of a gunshot, which raised many questions in Rudy's mind. It was not surprising with all the violence and chaos in the city now. But it did cause Rudy to wonder what side his "patient" was on to have ended up in the line of fire. The dirty red armband tied around the young man's coat sleeve meant he supported the revolutionaries. However, there were many who had donned the armbands only in hopes of traversing the city safely.

Rudy Gruenwald himself was a revolutionary, though he could claim no membership in a specific party. At the beginning of the war his German heritage had caused him to be ostracized at the university. He was already accustomed to harsh treatment because of his Jewish ancestry, but it nevertheless encouraged him to become more deeply involved in revolutionary activity. He finally got himself expelled from medical school for marching with a group of strikers at the Putilov Steel Works about a year ago. After that he had immediately been drafted into the military. His German name no longer seemed to matter. Not fancying the "underground" life, he did his duty—that is until about three months ago when he deserted along with droves of other disillusioned Russian soldiers. The senseless carnage, due almost entirely to the inept leadership of bungling Russian generals, had become too much. Rudy could not stand by and watch a moment longer. Under normal conditions it would have been unwise to return to his old home, but with no place else to go, he took the risk. He found his old room let out to other tenants, but there was a vacant attic room that proved quite suitable. And, as it turned out, the country was in such disorder that he was never pursued.

In a few minutes Sonja returned with two old men at her side—strong, young men were hard to come by these days. Between the four of them, they managed to carry the unconscious man up the stairs to Sonja's flat. Unfortunately, the jostling caused the man's wound to start bleeding again.

"You must patch him up, Rudy," Sonja said. The young man had been laid upon her own bed, which for warmth's sake was in the main room of her two-room flat.

Rudy shrugged. Even with three years of medical school behind him, he felt far from competent to treat such a wound. Still, under the circumstances, he might be the young man's best hope of survival. He certainly couldn't harm him any further.

"I'll need some water boiled," he told Sonja. "And gather whatever you can find to use as bandages. I will also need instruments—a good, sharp knife will have to do. And vodka—someone in this building must have some

19

hidden away. Get all you can."

Sonja jumped up and hurried to the door, but she paused before opening it. "You must save him, Rudy... he must live."

Rudy nodded and tried to offer a reassuring smile. Too bad God did not exist, for the young patient had little hope but that.

2

A huge red flag dominated the top of the Winter Palace. Images of double-headed eagles lay in piles of rubble on the streets. The monarchy was gone. The tsar no longer ruled. But Russia was still Russia. All was completely changed, yet eternally the same.

The *khvost*, or bread queue, was a seemingly eternal fact of life in Russia. Anna Fedorcenko Grigorov had come to think very little of waiting hours in a *khvost* for bread, meat, or a few beets for borscht. Instead of complaining about the inevitable, most Russians just made the most of such an ordeal, turning the *khvost* into a social experience. It became the main source of news and gossip, and of many of the most fantastic rumors imaginable. Anna once heard that the Germans had surrendered, then five minutes later that the Allies had been driven from Europe altogether.

The only thing Anna knew without doubt was that the future of Russia, and indeed her own future, was as uncertain now as when she had been a young girl embarking on a journey from her peasant village to the frightening big city.

She let her thoughts wander wistfully back forty-one years to that day she left her family's *izba* in Katyk. Her papa used to call her his little "snow child," after the old fairy tale about the childless couple who after years of longing for a child were finally given a daughter formed out of the snow. But when the child had to leave them before the winter snows melted, they were greatly grieved until she assured them she would return with the first snowfall of winter. That was Papa's way—always finding joy in difficult circumstances. No doubt he would quip now that waiting in line for bread for hours wasn't so bad, because it gave him a chance to visit with his neighbors.

Oh, Papa, Anna thought with a sigh, even you would find it hard to rejoice in the midst of the grief that weighs upon me.

For days after Andrei had been shot, Anna kept hoping he would show up at her door. Yuri might have miscalculated the seriousness of his brother's wounds and the hopelessness of his survival. But after two weeks, even Anna had to accept the fact that her son was dead. It would drive her insane to keep on hoping. Yet there were times when Anna wondered how she kept her sanity. Despite everything she still could not shake the image of the snow child returning when all seemed darkest. There was a part of her, passed down from her father, Yevno Burenin, that made hope impossible to shake entirely. Although each day she recognized there was a very thin line between hope and lunacy.

She had to go on—as she had been doing all her life. It was the same for Russia, too. The Motherland would go on, limping at times, full of despair, but it would continue. If there was one thing Russia—and Russians—knew, it was how to go on.

Anna shivered as a gust of wind swept down the street, seeming effortlessly to penetrate her threadbare coat. It was almost April but winter still gripped the city, as it would for several more weeks. The coming of spring would only slightly ease the hardships of war and revolution. There were still few men to plant spring crops. Anna had heard from her son-in-law Daniel that Russian loss of life in the war had thus far amounted to millions, so that even when the war ended, laborers would be in short supply. Who could tell when food would again be plentiful in Russia?

Anna's thoughts quickly skipped to Misha—the one person, besides Andrei, who was most on her mind these days. How desperately she longed for him, for his dear friendship, and for the marriage that had been allowed so little time to be enjoyed. He was a prisoner of war, and there was no telling where he was or how he was. Anna prayed for him daily and, perhaps selfishly, for his speedy return. Secretly, she hoped the revolutionaries who wanted the war ended had their way, even if it meant Russia pulling out prematurely and leaving the battle against the Germans solely to their allies. She didn't care what it took, if only it brought Misha back to her. Misha himself would probably be the first to chide her for her disloyal thoughts, but he would understand, too. Maybe by now he had also had enough of war and separation. Before he left he had promised her that after the war he would resign his commission with the Cossack Guards so they could be together always.

Anna was jarred from her thoughts by a stirring in the queue. She was several yards from the door to the bakery, but the grumbling voices, rising in discontent, filtered back to her quickly.

"This is unjust!" yelled a woman.

"We have waited all morning."

"We must have bread!"

Even as the voices rumbled back, the queue itself suddenly surged forward. And Anna remembered how this Russian institution, *khvost*, could very quickly turn from a social gathering into something else entirely. Caught in the tide of the erupting queue, Anna stumbled forward against her will. As the crowd opened up momentarily before her, she caught a brief glimpse of a sign in front of the bakery:

NO MORE BREAD.

The door was shut, yet several men lunged toward it like a human battering ram. A crashing sound, as of breaking glass, reached Anna's ears, then the crowd closed back in and Anna was jostled roughly, first one way then another. She fought to stay on her feet.

In all the time of food shortages, she had managed to avoid the riots that sometimes broke out in the queues. Mariana had been caught once in a riot last week and had come home bruised and disheveled. Now it seemed as if Anna's luck was at its end. Her hatred of crowds had begun that awful day at Khodynka Field at the time of Nicholas the Second's coronation. Hundreds of people had been killed during a picnic when they feared there would not be enough food to go around. Sergei and Misha had been there for her then, but now she was alone. Her heart quickened with dread and fear.

"Please . . . this won't help," she struggled to get the words out. Her breathing felt strangled as if she might suffocate.

No one heard her small voice. The yelling of those around her continued. Even in her panic Anna noted how the anger of the mob lacked focus. The tsar was gone. Who could they blame now for their woes? But Anna spent little time philosophizing. She had to concentrate on the situation at hand and get away before she was hurt or even killed. And her fear made her struggle with a strength she had forgotten she possessed. She held up her arm to fend off a stick being wielded wildly in the hand of a man who under normal conditions would never think to harm a woman. Then she turned and made one final, desperate, push to extricate herself from the mob. She pushed hard at a body that had suddenly come tripping into her path. The person stumbled and grabbed Anna for support, causing them both to tumble to the ground. Anna used the momentum from the fall to roll away from the crowd. When she finally came to a stop a few feet from the angry queue, she was not alone. The person she had pushed had rolled with her and now bounced on top of her.

It was an old woman.

Anna gasped, realizing that in desperately thinking only of herself she had done the very thing that appalled her in others. "Oh, Matushka!" she exclaimed, gently taking the woman's arm and helping her up. "Are you hurt?"

The woman shook herself and appeared like a brittle leaf about to fall from a half-dead tree. "No worse than I was when I woke this morning," said the woman. "And you?"

"Nothing to speak of."

"We are Russian women, eh? It would take more than a mere bread riot to defeat us."

"I . . . hope so," Anna replied, feeling as shaky as the shy girl she had been forty odd years ago.

The woman parted her thin, dry lips in a toothless grin. "Never doubt it . . . never, deary. Tsars come and go, but matushkas like us will always be."

They moved away from the mob even as its initial burst of anger began to ebb. Anna still wanted to get as far away as possible.

"Good day to you, Matushka," Anna said.

"And to you, also."

As Anna hurried home, she tried to be encouraged by the old woman's words, but the empty basket on her arm made her think instead of the proverb, "We do not eat the bread, it eats us."

At the door to her building, she met Raisa Sorokin, who had been foraging for food in another part of town. Her luck had been better—she had brought back a pound of dry fish. But without bread it would make a spare meal for the many mouths they had to feed. For a time there had been sixteen of them crammed into the flat, but soon after the tsar's abdication, Paul and Mathilde Burenin had gone to a friend's place near the Tauride Palace where

Paul was spending a great deal of time. It was still a full household with Daniel and Mariana and their children occupying the big bedroom; while the single women, Anna, Raisa, Countess Zhenechka, and Teddie wedged into the other bedroom. Yuri, Katya, and Irina shared the little cubbyhole room, but Yuri was gone most of the time at his hospital and took all of his meals there to ease the burden on supplies. He also pilfered what he could from the hospital larders for the household, but there was less and less available for that purpose. Daniel also brought back what food he could, using contacts at the American Embassy.

And so they managed from day to day. No one was starving yet—that was something.

Raisa gave Anna a quick appraisal. "Your coat sleeve is torn," she said with concern.

"How can you tell on this ragged coat?"

"I mended every tear yesterday. This is definitely a new one."

Anna shrugged. "There was a bit of a row in the queue today. Nothing serious, thank God."

"Oh, what a sad time we live in." Raisa opened the door to their flat. "I wonder how—"

But she was cut off by an exuberant childish yell.

"Grandma! Auntie Raisa! Look what Papa brought!" It was little Zenia, Mariana's youngest, as always full of boundless energy. Her mop of yellow curls danced wildly as she bounced toward them.

"What can it be?" Anna forced herself to catch the child's excitement. "The Crown Jewels perhaps?"

"A loaf of bread would be far better," said Raisa.

Zenia clasped Anna's hand and fairly dragged her into the kitchen. Raisa followed close behind. They found Daniel and Mariana and the other children, all full of excitement and chattering merrily.

"Ah! Mama and Raisa, you've returned just in time," said Daniel. "Look here." He gestured with his hand toward the table on which two newspapers were prominently displayed. Russian papers were rare to come by these days, but Anna quickly noted these were in English. One was the *London Times*, the other the *New York Register*, the paper Daniel worked for.

"Word at last from the outside world," said Daniel. "I've managed to get dispatches out, but receiving anything has been next to impossible."

"I've felt we have been on a desert island for the last weeks," said Mariana.

"No more." Daniel grinned. "And the biggest news is confirmation of the rumors that the United States has recognized the Provisional Government. Now many Americans, including President Wilson, are turning the war cause into a struggle of democracy against absolutism. It won't be long now before the U.S. enters the war."

"Thank God!" said Anna. "That can only bring the end that much closer. But, Daniel, as much as the newspapers are exciting, I can't imagine them causing Zenia to bubble so."

"Not newspapers, Grandma," said Zenia. "Show her, Papa."

Daniel chuckled and picked up an opened parcel lying next to the papers. "My friend from the embassy who brought the papers also brought a few small delicacies— peppermint sticks for the children and real coffee for the rest of us."

It had been months since there had been such treats for the children. And as for coffee . . . Anna preferred tea, but real anything would be a delight after months of ersatz brews that had long ago lost their marginal appeal.

"Can we have one, Papa?" pressed Zenia.

"I'll tell you what, you can each have one now. But take them out to the other room so we grown-ups can have a few minutes to talk."

When the children exited, each holding a piece of candy, Daniel continued, "I have a bit of other news to pass along. The fellow who delivered these newspapers is planning to return to the States in a couple of days. Mariana, he has assured me he can escort you and the children out of the country."

"But, Daniel, I'm not ready to leave."

"I know, we have discussed this before, but who knows when a chance like this may arise again. It is getting harder and harder to come and go. Your papers are about to expire, Mariana, and since you are still a Russian citizen, you will be at the mercy of the Russian Emmigration Department."

"Yes, but—" Mariana glanced at Anna.

"I don't expect you to stay," said Anna. "In fact, I would feel so much better if you were safely away from here."

"Then I would go crazy with worry," Mariana countered. "I would rather we suffer together than be cut off from one another. Besides, I am certain things will settle down soon. Now that the new government is official, they will begin to regulate and alleviate many of the problems." She looked to Daniel with imploring eyes. "Let's give it a while longer. *You* certainly don't plan on leaving now that so much is happening. I want us to face whatever comes together. Please, Daniel."

He shook his head with defeat. "All right. I really didn't expect to win this battle, anyway. But I intend to keep closely attuned to the political situation, and at the least sign of things going awry, I will insist upon you and the children leaving."

Mariana gave her husband a slight smile. "And I will obey, my dear, as always."

This brought a smattering of knowing chuckles from all the others, including Daniel. Then Anna, not wanting this lighthearted moment to end, said, "Why don't I fix us all some of that wonderful coffee?"

3

Yuri Fedorcenko had grown accustomed to death and dying. He was even used to the shortages of the most basic medical supplies. But what he would never become hardened to—at least he hoped it would never happen— was the despair that daily surrounded him. The wretched stare of a mother who knew she was completely helpless to prevent her family's starvation, or the forlorn eyes of a child who has lost his innocence, along with the childish concept of his parents' invincibility. And, worse yet, the abject misery of men broken by war and famine and total loss of control over their own destinies.

It was, of course, the men to whom Yuri most related. Some days he felt as broken as the worst of them. He felt as if he were being carried along by a raging river, clinging to a thin chunk of bark—that alone keeping him from being sucked under the relentless current. If only he could staunch the wild flow, or at least climb, even for a brief moment, to the muddy shore.

Just a moment's rest—

Then he reminded himself that rest was the last thing he wanted. Not a night had passed since Rasputin's death, and especially since Andrei's death, that had not been shattered by nightmares. He dreaded sleep, and only his exhaustion at the end of fifteen-hour days—and many nights on call in the hospital—forced him to face his bed at all. The fact that his days were often waking night-mares did not help.

He wanted desperately to find hope, a small primrose among the ashes of a dying world. He longed for even a fraction of his mother's faith. He did not know why he could not find in God the comforter she had surely found during these days of grief. His faith had never been as strong as that of his parents, but now the gulf separating him from God was nearly insurmountable. Only *nearly*...? Then perhaps he was able to concede some hope after all. Perhaps if he prayed harder or went to Mass more often. He had tried to talk to Daniel a few times, but Yuri had a hard time accepting his brother-in-law's simple assurance of God's grace. Absolution could not be that simple. One must suffer. But perhaps that was only the Russian way. What if the way to God was indeed as unencumbered as Daniel, and even his own mother, tried to tell him? What if—

"Dr. Fedorcenko!" A nurse hurried up to Yuri, who was standing at the nurse's station making notes in a patient's chart.

"Yes, Sister."

"There is a man in Ward Three asking for you. He is quite agitated and insistent—"

"A man? A young man? Who—?"

"I don't know. I didn't see him. The head nurse just sent me to fetch you—"

Before she could finish, Yuri was hurrying down the corridor. He bypassed the elevator that was slow and often malfunctioning, like most machines in Russia these days. He went instead to the stairwell, flung open the door, and raced up the steps two at a time. He knew it was irrational but he could not help himself. All reason and medical knowledge told him Andrei could not have survived the blizzard that night with his wounds. Yet Yuri still found himself hoping—ah, maybe he wasn't as dead inside as he feared! He scrutinized anyone coming into the hospital who even vaguely resembled his brother. Even on the street his heart would leap at the sight of a large man. It was possible Andrei might have been found and taken to another hospital in the city as an "Ivanov," an unidentified indigent. Daniel had revealed that after entering Russia Andrei had given his travel papers over to Daniel. He had feared being caught on the streets teeming with revolution carrying the diplomatic documents Daniel had arranged for him and being mistaken as an envoy of the tsar. As far as Daniel knew, those had been the only identifying papers Andrei had.

Yuri rushed into Ward Three, then slowed in order to collect himself. He was still the Chief of Surgery and must at least make an attempt at decorum.

Sister Elizabeth came to him as he entered. "Thank you for coming so quickly, Doctor. It really wasn't an emergency, however—"

"Where is he?" Yuri broke in, eyes anxiously scanning the ward.

The nurse nodded toward a curtained bed. Yuri now noted two guards, wearing the insignia of the Provisional Government, standing in front of the curtain. Yuri strode to the bed and pulled aside the curtain.

"I said I wanted privacy!" came a harsh, vaguely familiar voice from the bed.

Yuri saw that it was indeed a large man on the bed— but not the man he hoped for. It was instead his grandfather's cousin, Count Cyril Vlasenko.

"Oh, it's you, then," said the count. "It's about time."

Yuri swallowed his disappointment and tried hard not to replace it with ire toward this man, his family's perpetual enemy. He reminded himself that Vlasenko was now a fallen man—a prisoner of the Provisional Government, which explained the guards. It was a miracle that Vlasenko was still alive.

"So, Count Vlasenko," Yuri said coolly, "what brings you to this humble hospital?"

"They wouldn't take me to my son's hospital. The idiots feared it would be too easy for him to aid my escape. Little do they know my son. If I did intend to escape, he'd be the last person I'd rely on for assistance. Anyway, if I had to come here, I wanted to be certain I received decent care."

"So, you requested me?"

Vlasenko shrugged. "You had the confidence of the

tsar. That's good enough for me."

Rather than attempt to discern the count's possible ulterior motives, Yuri decided to take the man at face value. He really didn't care about Vlasenko's motives, anyway. "What seems to be the problem, Count—the medical problem, that is?"

"Chest pains."

"Have you experienced them before?"

"Occasionally. Nothing to speak of, though. My son diagnosed them as indigestion."

"I see." Yuri listened to Vlasenko's heart with his stethoscope and detected a slight arrhythmia. "Tell me about the pain."

"Like a blow to my chest, right here." He laid his fist over his sternum. "I could hardly move my left arm as well, and I had a devil of a time breathing. It has subsided a bit now."

"Your symptoms are classic angina pectoris."

"Angina—what?"

"Simply put, it is a disease affecting the arteries of the heart muscle. They become clogged. It is sometimes referred to as fatty heart."

"And I suppose you will now browbeat me about my diet and weight," groused Vlasenko.

"You no doubt have far greater things to worry about now, Count," Yuri replied with just a hint of sarcasm. "And it is most likely those very worries that brought on this attack. Your weight and diet are, to be sure, contributing factors."

"So, what can you do about it? I don't like my accommodations at the Tauride Palace, locked into a basement room, but I like even less this bed and this hospital."

In such cases morphine was often prescribed for relief of the pain, but Yuri did not intend to waste even a quarter grain of the precious medicine on Vlasenko, especially since he was obviously over the extremes of the seizure.

"I'm going to prescribe nitroglycerin." Yuri picked up

Vlasenko's chart and wrote as he spoke. "This is only to be taken during an attack. One tablet by mouth. Let it melt slowly under your tongue. But I must tell you, Count, that there is little else to be done for you. I've known patients to live for years with such attacks. On the other hand, the next attack might well be your last—that is, it could kill you." Yuri did not relish these words as much as he thought he might. "You must do what you can to reduce stress—"

"Ha! Then I am a dead man for certain."

"You have survived this long, Vlasenko. Only those whom the gods love die young."

"I am hardly young."

"My point exactly!" Yuri smiled. "I'll have the nurse make up a prescription for you, then you can be on your way."

"So soon?"

"I thought you didn't like this place."

"Well . . . listen here, Fedorcenko—" Vlasenko crooked his finger, motioning for Yuri to lean closer to him. When Yuri did so, Vlasenko continued in a whisper, "Our families may have our differences, but the truth is, Yuri Sergeiovich, that our political sympathies are not all that far apart. You were a physician to the tsar, and, rumor has it, you were an accomplice in the assassination of Rasputin, which even I realize was done in an attempt, however misguided, to save the Crown. You took a great risk in the interest of the tsar."

"What are you getting at, Vlasenko?"

"There is still hope of putting the tsar back on the throne—"

"You are a dreamer, Count."

"There is a large contingent of loyal monarchists out there who need but a leader to rouse them. If I were free, I could be that man. We could mount a counter-coup against that ruffian Kerensky and his gang."

"And you want my services in assisting your escape?"

"Why not? You had the courage to kill Rasputin. You are loyal to the tsar—"

"Really, Count, I believe the blood has not only been cut off from your heart, but from your head as well. The monarchy is gone, and the sooner we accept that, the better off Russia will be."

"I will never accept it. And it is because of apathy such as yours that Russia crumbled in the first place."

"I take full responsibility," Yuri said dryly. "Now, I will be discharging you, Count. My medical advice to you is to abstain from counter-coups and the like. They would not be good for your health."

Followed by a loud disgruntled curse from Vlasenko, Yuri stepped around the curtain and, pausing before one of the guards, said, "Citizen Vlasenko can leave the hospital as soon as the nurse gives him his prescription."

Yuri left the ward feeling almost amused at the encounter with his relative. Counter-coup indeed! Vlasenko's mental facilities must be one kopeck short of a ruble. Yuri did feel a bit sorry for the man, too. Vlasenko had lost everything in the revolution. Besides his position, his power, his ambition, there was nothing else to Vlasenko. Though he still blustered and bullied, he was a very broken man, as much as any other man Yuri might lament. As much as himself—more so, really. And that revelation was quite astounding to Yuri. Though Yuri had lost much, suffered much, he had not lost all. He still had a supportive family, a loving wife, and his own personal honor and integrity. The essential person he was, even if he might at times fear otherwise, was still alive. At least he had to believe that. He had to!

"Yuri!"

For a moment he thought his imagination was playing tricks on him. The voice calling his name was one he loved above all. But she never came to the hospital.

"Katya! Whatever are you doing here? What's wrong?"

"Nothing, dear," she quickly assured him as she hurried close to him.

He reached out and took his wife in his arms, not caring that he was the Chief of Surgery and was standing in the middle of a hospital corridor. His arms trembled with a passion that surprised even him. If he had been praying just then, he would have known her to be the answer to that prayer.

"Well, well," she teased, "if I'd known I'd receive a reception like this, I would have come here more often."

"I realize now, you are the primrose—"

"What's that?"

"I'll tell you later. But first, why have you come? There must be something amiss."

She smiled that mysterious, childish, petulant smile that had won his heart three years ago. "I have been sent to take you away from all this." He gave her a puzzled scowl and she continued, "Your mother told me to pry you from this hospital even if I had to gag and bind you. It's time for a holiday."

"I still don't understand."

"The family is having a bit of an outing, and it would not be complete, especially for me, if you were not there."

"Where? Why?" He felt foolish. These days "outings" and "holidays" were about as foreign to him and most Russians as apple pie and those American hot dogs Daniel was so fond of.

"It's the children's fault, really," said Katya. "They get a little candy in their tummies and suddenly think there should be a party. They wanted to go ice skating. And your mama said, 'Why not?' And to all of our surprise, none of us could think of a good reason not to go. No one has skated all winter, and soon the ice will melt and the chance will be lost. So, everyone has gone to their favorite ice pond, and I was sent to fetch you."

"It sounds wonderful, but I can't just . . . leave." He

paused and suddenly caught his wife's enthusiasm. "Can I?"

"You must because I don't know where this secret family ice pond is, and I need you to guide me there."

"Well—"

She looked at him with beguiling, imploring eyes. She was probably more beautiful now, seasoned as she was by adversity, than when he had first met her at Felix Youssoupov's engagement party. The depth of character she had tried so to hide back then had now been allowed to flower and grow. She was now all the woman he had desired then, and she was certainly far more than he probably deserved.

"I suppose I could get away for a couple of hours. But my skates—"

Katya triumphantly held up a shopping bag he had only vaguely noticed before. "I'm prepared."

"Then let me tell someone and we can be off."

<hr />

4

Anna watched as Yuri and Katya approached, waving as she glided past on the ice. It seemed like a dream really, a happy family skating upon the Neva in the middle of a revolution. Mariana and Daniel were skating ahead of Anna with little Zenia between them holding their hands. John and his sister Katrina were trying to make figure eights in the middle of the pond, while Teddie was holding the hand of her little four-year-old charge, Irina. Even Countess Zhenechka had come and was seated with Raisa Sorokin on a bench at the edge of the pond watching the skaters' performances that ranged from Mariana's skilled grace to Teddie's shaky stance, barely keeping upright.

Anna's skill ranged somewhere in between those. She

could do an adequate figure eight, but hardly the spin that John was now executing to impress Irina, who was watching him with awe. Ten-year-old John landed on his feet, much to his obvious delight, since it was only his second attempt at the spin. The viewers on the side and those on the ice all applauded. And truly, the dreary recent times and the even drearier prospect for the future faded for a short time at least.

Yuri and Katya had finished putting on their skates and were now stepping onto the ice. Anna was struck suddenly with how much Yuri resembled his father. Of course, she'd always known that, but here, in happy, pleasant surroundings, it was so much more evident. It took no more than that for Anna's mind to wander back over the years to when she had first met Sergei—the young prince, scion of a family that for generations had closely hobnobbed with royalty. And Anna—the shy handmaid who barely had the nerve to look at him, much less speak.

———

"I've just realized I don't yet know your name," said Sergei.

"It's Anna, my lord Prince. Anna Yevnovna Burenin."

"Well, I am Sergei. Sergei Viktorovich. Now, until my father is dead, which I don't anticipate for a very long time, I will always think of him as the prince, not myself. I suppose I am a prince, after all, but somehow it never sounds right to my ears when I am called one. And as for the rest, well, to tell you the truth, I'd be much more comfortable if you just called me Sergei."

Anna did not reply.

"Do you skate, Anna Yevnovna? I think you were about to tell me what you did at home a few moments ago."

"No, sir," answered Anna. "At least not like you skate here. We used to fasten sticks to our boots, but it did not always turn out so well."

"Sticks? It must have been rather awkward."

"Yes. Sometimes my papa carved pieces of wood for us with his knife, and they worked better. But even sticks could be no more difficult than standing on those thin blades of metal."

"Have you ever tried it with skates, Anna?"

She shook her head.

"It's really much easier than it looks. Let me show you. My sister has an extra pair of skates that should fit you well enough." He rose to leave the sleigh.

"Oh no, sir, I couldn't. It wouldn't be right."

"Come, come, Anna. I thought we had all that settled about separation between the classes. Or at least between you and me!"

Still she sat, pondering what to do. Olga and Nina would be scandalized at the way this day was turning out!

Sergei's thin, sensitive lips twitched into a genuine, reassuring smile. "Come, Anna," he said, kindly this time rather than sternly, "the fate of the Motherland does not hinge upon your decision."

"But . . . but what will Princess Katrina say? I am supposed to attend her if she needs anything."

"I will tell my slave-driving sister I needed a partner and that I insisted that you join me . . ."

A few moments later, when the skates were firmly in place, Sergei took Anna's hand, helped her to her feet, and led her to the edge of the ice. He stepped onto the river, then, as her blades met the ice, gently tugged at her hand to pull her into motion.

Before Anna could catch herself, suddenly her feet flew out from under her and she was on her back.

"Ouch!" she cried, looking up to where Sergei towered above her.

"It may take a while," he said, "but you will get the feel of it."

"It's already far different than with sticks," she replied,

reaching up for his hand while rubbing her sore bottom with the other. "That hurt!"

Sergei laughed. "You can depend on the ice for two things," he said. "It's cold, and it's hard!"

Timidly Anna crawled to her knees, gingerly putting one skate under her weight, then the other, hanging on to Sergei for dear life, propriety all but forgotten.

"Up you come . . . there! Now if we can just get moving, it will be easier."

Again Sergei began slowly to ease his way across the ice; this time, however, grasping Anna's left arm firmly while his right stretched around her waist for support.

Steadily their speed increased, Anna's two feet wobbling back and forth uncontrollably. Her legs started to split apart . . . wider . . . wider . . .

"I can't—!" she cried, but it was too late.

Clutching desperately at Sergei's arm to keep from falling, Anna toppled sideways, pulling him along with her. The next moment they were a tangled mass of legs and scrapes and bruises.

Sergei was laughing so hard he could not speak.

A smile crept across Anna's lips. What a day that had been. She and Sergei had certainly broken all the rules of social propriety. But what a grand time she'd had once she had forgotten about her fear. She had even managed to laugh over her frequent spills and her completely graceless performance. That Sergei could have fallen in love with her after that day was always quite incredible to her.

"It's good to see you smile, Mama." Yuri had skated up beside Anna.

"I'm glad you came, Yuri."

"I needed to get away from that hospital."

"Perhaps I should call for a holiday once a week—at least."

He linked arms with her and they skated together

around the ice. Yuri was an accomplished skater like his father. Katya was up ahead of them with her daughter and Teddie. They were laughing because Teddie had nearly lost her footing and only Katya's appearance and quick response had kept the older woman from a painful meeting with the ice.

"You'll never guess who I had for a patient today," Yuri was saying. "That old snake, Cyril Vlasenko."

"Poor Cyril. They say he is now a prisoner of the Provisional Government and may face execution."

"The bullets would probably bounce off him. He has an uncanny way of defying his just deserts. Even now with heart trouble that could prove serious, he is plotting his escape. And I wouldn't be surprised if he succeeded."

"All must answer for their deeds eventually, Yuri," said Anna simply.

She did not hold as much malice against Vlasenko as perhaps she had a right to. After all, Vlasenko had been a nemesis to the Burenin and Fedorcenko clans for years. He tormented the peasants in Katyk as one of the local promieshik and seemed to bear a special grudge against Anna's family. Anna always wondered why this was and could only speculate that Vlasenko simply could not abide a peasant like Yevno who was so obviously ten times the man Vlasenko, with all his titles and power, could ever be. The problems with the Fedorcenkos were more straightforward. His grandfather and Viktor's grandfather had been brothers. Cyril's grandfather had mismanaged his inheritance and lost it, although he claimed the reason for his financial decline was that he had been cheated in his inheritance, that Viktor's grandfather had received the lion's share, leaving worthless scraps for the next son. He passed this resentment on to his heirs, including Cyril.

Seventeen years ago Cyril had usurped the Fedorcenko St. Petersburg estate. His means of doing so had been totally dishonest, but since there was no way of proving that, the estate was lost. But that very loss had miraculously brought about the recovery of Viktor's mental stability, and had also been the catalyst for the emotional reunion of Viktor and his son, Sergei. No one much regretted the loss of property because of all they had gained in its place. And now the estate lay empty and in ruin. Half had been burned down during the early days of the revolution, and the remaining parts had been plundered. Anna had not had the heart to visit the place since then. She would rather remember it in the days of its glory and splendor.

"Mama, I'm afraid I've made you sad," said Yuri. "I should never have said anything." He shook his head dismally. "Leave it to me to ruin a happy day."

Anna tenderly patted her son's arm. "Not at all, Yuri. Actually, what you said reminded me of a very fine thing. We have so much, son. Imagine, with all our sad losses, we are still surrounded by so many who love and care for us. What we have as a family simply cannot be touched by all the discord and chaos on the surface of things. I was thinking about when Count Vlasenko took away your grandfather's estate. Nothing but good came of that. It's how God always seemed to care for us."

"And you think good will come out of all that is happening now, Mama? The collapse of our society? Andrei's . . . death?"

"I must believe that, Yuri."

"If only I could . . ."

"First you must be able to trust the one who gave that promise."

"I think it is more a matter of being a worthy recipient of that promise."

"It doesn't help for me to tell you otherwise, son, does it?"

He shook his head. "I want to believe what you've always told me about God. But even God must draw the line somewhere in His vast forgiveness. I know . . . I know what you will say to that. He even forgave His own murderers. In a way, I can think of no more cruel act. I think His forgiveness is sometimes more painful than to be beaten and tortured."

"I remember how Andrei used to chide you for analyzing everything too much. You are a thoughtful, sensitive man, Yuri, and that is a fine thing. But sometimes I think a little simplicity might not harm you."

"Believe me, you don't know how often I've prayed for that myself. But it's not easy to change who I am." He paused and took a breath, seeming reluctant but resolved to say what was on his mind. "Mama, you often say how much I am like father, and I realized recently that Papa had a similar experience to mine. He killed a man, too."

"That is true. He killed his commanding officer in order to save some prisoners the commander was about to execute."

"Similar to why I . . . did what I did to . . . the monk. Not that I am trying to justify my actions. I don't. I can't and that's where my problem lies."

"Your father did what he did in the heat of passion and later never could justify his actions either. It nearly destroyed him."

"Mama, what did Papa do to get over that? The father I knew was not destroyed, or even burdened by his deed."

"Oh, a small part of him was always burdened by what he had done. A man of conscience can never truly get over taking a human life, no matter what the reason for it. What is it you want to know exactly, Yuri? You know very well it was your papa's faith that made him the man you knew."

"I know, but . . . it's not enough. I mean, the things he said to me are—I am ashamed to say—dim in my memory. I thought I'd never forget but—"

"Gamma! Look!" Zenia yelled exuberantly as she skated—or rather careened—toward Yuri and Anna. "I can do it myself!"

Anna glanced at Yuri, then at Zenia, torn. "Yuri, I—"

41

"Never mind, Mama. I am spoiling this wonderful day. We'll talk again another time."

"That is a binding promise."

"Upon my word!" He grinned and let go of her arm as they both applauded Zenia's accomplishment.

The moment was never recaptured that day. But perhaps it was just as well. There had been such a hollow aspect to the grin arranged on Yuri's face that it made Anna ache for her son. She would indeed take up that conversation again with him, but she decided this time of pleasure was just as necessary as a soul-searching discussion. And truly, after two hours of frolicking with his family, Yuri seemed to have shed a great deal of the tension that had lately become such a part of his bearing.

Of course, he was not really changed—*a changed man*, as it were—but she had faith that would come in time, too. And before the day was over, Anna remembered something that would be better for Yuri than either a discussion or a day of ice-skating. Somewhere she had Sergei's journals put away. She would find them and give them to her son.

5

The shovel sliced through the thick snow with a practiced ease. The man who wielded it was not unaccustomed to hard work, though he had lived most of his life with hordes of servants to wait on his every need. He was glad for the diversion brought by this labor of clearing the freshly fallen snow from the sidewalks. The exercise was good for his constitution, not to mention his mind. People might well wonder how the once mighty tsar of all the Russias could endure his downfall with such patience and restraint. Of course he had wept in his Alix's arms that first night when he had returned to Tsarskoe Selo a virtual prisoner. But the days that followed brought such rest and peace to him that he was almost content with his lot. There were no detested reports to read or momentous decisions to make. He had all day to do nothing but walk about the gardens, play with the children, smoke a good cigarette, and read for pure pleasure. Even Nicholas had to admit that this was really the life he had been cut out for.

True, it wasn't completely idyllic. He still agonized over the fate of his beloved country. And occasionally there were moments of personal shame when a guard would treat him with contempt. Once a particularly loathsome guard had ordered him to do a menial task in the presence of his son Alexis. But on the whole the guards treated him and his family with respect, some even with awe. No one called him Your Highness anymore except for the most loyal of servants—and never within earshot of the guards. He was the ex-tsar of Russia. He tried to joke about his new title—Ex-Tsar—hoping to ease the pain of what had happened.

It was hardest on Alix, perhaps even more so than on him. She was bitter and angry. But then, she had borne the brunt of the people's venom over the whole Rasputin matter. She now spent more time than ever in her bed and seemed to have aged ten years in the last month. She had worn herself out nursing the children and Anna Vyrubova from their bouts with the measles. Marie and Anastasia were the last to contract the infection and were still quite weak. There had been secondary infections and ear abscesses—it had been harrowing. At least Baby had not had any serious bouts of his terrible bleeding. They had been worried about that when Alexis had first contracted the measles.

Then there had been the loss of her friends who had been a great source of comfort to Alix. Shortly after Nicholas's abdication Anna Vyrubova had been arrested and taken to the Fortress. Lili Dehn, who had been with Alix almost constantly, had been banished from the palace. It seemed such a cruel and senseless act, which had even further embittered Alix. Nicholas was doing all he could to bolster her, comfort her, and lighten her heavy emotional load. Thank God they both hadn't fallen into a depression.

Nicholas adjusted the gloves on his hands, then gave the shovel another push. Besides concern for his family, the worst of his plight was the uncertainty of their future. They were now confined to the Alexander Palace, which had always been their main residence anyway. At first they had been locked inside, and Nicholas had been kept apart from his family. After a few weeks he had been reunited with them, and they had been given the freedom to walk in the gardens.

The new Minister of Justice for the Provisional Government, a man named Kerensky, seemed to be quite committed to treating the royal family civilly and protecting them. He was determined that this revolution be conducted honorably and as bloodlessly as possible. However, in the newspapers he was allowed, Nicholas could see that the present government was not entirely stable and for the most part operated by the will of the people, of whom a large number wanted to see the Romanovs imprisoned in the Fortress, or worse.

Kerensky had opened negotiations with King George of England over asylum for the deposed Romanovs. This had offered a gleam of hope until recently when the news had arrived that George, Alexandra's cousin, had to refuse them entry. Apparently the prime minister, Lloyd George, a liberal who took no pains to hide his dislike of Nicholas, convinced the king that there would be a serious backlash from the British people if the Russian monarch was let into the country. The merely symbolic British monarchy had to guard its own future. Nicholas bore no animosity toward King George for his decision.

Nicholas finished clearing the walkway. The feel of the chill air against his sweaty brow was refreshing. He was carrying the shovel back to the work shed when a servant hailed him. They were still permitted servants, though certainly not as many as in the past.

"Your . . . ah, that is . . . ah . . . Citizen Romanov," the man said, "your luncheon is being served."

"Thank you. I shall wash up and be there directly," Nicholas replied with the practiced formality that remained always with him.

The family was gathered around the table for the meal—all except Marie, who was still in her bed with a severe cough and congestion. Nicholas took such pleasure from his family that he was certain all would be well with him as long as the new government did not deny him their presence.

A maid came to the table carrying a platter of meat. "May I serve the empress now?" she asked with all the diffidence of the old days.

Alexandra raised an eyebrow, then, with a coy glance at her husband, replied, "Ta, ta, Marta, I'm not an empress any longer, but an ex-empress!"

There were chuckles around the table. Even the children realized what a victory it was for Alexandra to actually make light of their situation.

The maid served the meat to all, and when Nicholas received his, he poked it suspiciously with his fork. It was rather strange-looking with a peculiar discoloration.

"This may have once been ham," he said. "But I do believe it is now ex-ham!"

Everyone burst out laughing, a sound that was better than music to the deposed tsar's ears.

6

The gardens looked fine in the full flower of spring. Bruce MacDuff was pleased with the results of the landscaping done last year, although it was Louise, his wife, who alone could take credit for that. Bruce had opposed the changes, which had included an archway of miniature roses and a fountain graced by statues of a merry fawn and a chubby fellow who was purportedly a likeness of Bacchus. It was not only a bit too whimsical for his taste, but he would have preferred to maintain the essence of the garden as it had been for the last two hundred years.

Bruce, styled Lord Findochty, was the first to admit that he tended toward stodginess if he was not downright retrogressive. Change always came hard, even if he understood that it was necessary. Louise, on the other hand, was a modern woman who relished change and new things. He loved her for it, truth be known.

He had his Scottish blood that, according to Louise, kept him down-to-earth enough. But it was hard for a man with flaming red hair such as his to be too awfully conservative. The patch over his right eye also gave him an air of derry-do. And, in truth, he was a man of action, if his war record was any proof.

Coming to the covered gazebo just past the fountain, Bruce paused. The servants were nearly finished setting the table for afternoon tea. A white cloth covered a round table that showed places for five. The maid placed a vase of daffodils and white iris on the table.

"Very nice," said Bruce.

"Thank you, m'lord," replied the maid, pleased.

Bruce climbed the two steps that led to the gazebo. He straightened a misplaced fork and repositioned a fluted serviette that had fallen over.

"Have Hanley bring the guests directly out on their arrival. I shall greet them here," he said.

"Yes, m'lord."

The maid left and the other servants followed directly.

Bruce seated himself, not at the table but on a wrought-iron bench adjacent to the table, and mused briefly about the gathering soon to commence. Besides himself there would be four other gentlemen taking tea that afternoon. Louise had chided him that there were no women on the list, but she herself had opted to visit London to shop rather than spend the afternoon with a bunch of "stuffed shirts." "Present company excluded, of course, my dear," she had added with a laugh.

Yes, by all appearances the gathering might seem staid and stodgy. Yet, they represented a great deal of power—power that might well ignite some very important actions.

Fifteen minutes later, they were all there—a bank president, a retired and much-decorated general, a cousin of King George, and a shipping magnate. They, like Bruce, were all titled and very wealthy. They were also all old friends, school chums—Eton, of course—except for the general who was Bruce's father-in-law. Bruce was the youngest, at thirty-three, and the general was the oldest at sixty-two.

Tea was served, and after a time of trivial pleasantries, the men got down to business.

"So, has everyone heard the latest about the situation in Russia and specifically our king's response?" asked Bruce, feeling it was his place as host to get the ball rolling.

"It's utterly scandalous!" said the general, not one to mince words. "His Majesty really ought to be ashamed of himself."

All eyes turned to the king's cousin.

"Don't look at me," he said with a chuckle. "I fully agree. That's why I'm here, I daresay. I believe my cousin made a grave error in rejecting the tsar's request for asylum."

"But, Charlie," said the shipping magnate, "did he really have much choice? My word! A revolution has taken place in Russia! A monarch has been toppled from his throne. That would have to be sobering even to the monarch of a stable government such as ours. Not only do we have a strong Socialist element, but there is also a viable antiroyalist movement here as well."

"There has always been an antiroyalist movement— nothing but piffle, I say," said the general.

"At any rate," put in Bruce, "the purpose of this gathering is not to defend or rebuke the king, but rather to respond to his actions."

"Respond, Finkie. . . ?" said the banker, using Bruce's nickname.

"Come now, Gus, you must know we are gathered here to do more than talk."

"I simply don't see what *can* be done," said Gus. "That is, more than what's already being done in Russia itself."

"Don't be so dense," chided the general. "The king's hands are tied, but ours are not. We have at our disposal wealth and power enough to remove seven refugees from an embattled country. Those Ruskies may have their faults—heaven knows their commanders have all but bungled the Russian war effort. But I have personally met Nicholas and judge him to be a man of honor who certainly doesn't deserve the fate those pesky revolutionaries have in mind for him. And his wife and five little children certainly don't."

"I concur with you, General," said Gus, "though I have never met the man myself. I trust your judgment in it. However, as I see it, the Provisional Government appears to have nothing sinister planned for the tsar. It was they who initiated proceedings with our ambassador, after all. It would appear they are committed to a bloodless transfer of power."

A butler approached with a fresh pot of tea and another plate of cakes and sandwiches. He refilled the cups.

Bruce plucked a lump of sugar from a china bowl with silver tongs, dropped it into his cup, and, stirring thoughtfully, said, "It would appear . . ." He glanced around at his companions. "I suppose it all depends on how stable that Provisional Government is . . . and remains."

"I agreed to join this gathering," said Gus, "because I support the idea of giving asylum to the deposed tsar. However, as long as he is not in mortal danger, I believe we ought to allow the situation to take its natural course. No doubt he will soon be put on a boat and sent into exile. If our government refuses him, certainly he will find succor in the United States. They will take anyone."

"Freddie"—Bruce turned to the shipping magnate—"we haven't heard much from you."

"Oh, you know Freddie," said the king's cousin. "The great observer."

Freddie nodded, not in the least offended by the statement. "That is a stance we would all do well to take in this situation. Watch and wait. That's what I say."

"What we need," suggested the general, "is a pair of eyes in Russia—eyes we can trust—to keep us apprised of the situation, which I am certain will remain volatile for some time."

"My take exactly," agreed Bruce.

"You are not saying one of us should go to Russia?" Gus was appalled at the idea. He preferred the comforts of his West End flat to adventure any day.

"The idea is enticing," replied Bruce with a gleam in his left eye.

Before taking on the duties of his title after his father's untimely death in 1910, Bruce had experienced a few adventures—big game safaris in Africa, excursions to India, and other uncivilized places. His assumption of the title along with his marriage had ended his adventurous life. His stint in the army at the start of the war had provided an outlet for him, though it was cut off when he was wounded six months ago and sent home. He truly did not believe that things like war and the misfortune of a tsar were merely vehicles for his thirst for adventure, yet he had to admit that he had been eager to fight in the war, and he was just as eager to come to the aid of the tsar.

In times like this, Bruce's conservative side served him well, for it kept a level head on him and made him acutely aware of the ramifications of events beyond their ability to provide adventure. His interest in Russia was personal, beyond adventure or even concern for the tsar.

"However," Bruce continued, "I doubt that even if one of us was able to get into Russia now, we'd be able to gather the kind of intelligence necessary. None of us speaks the language, we have little knowledge of the customs, and beyond the embassy officials and minor business dealings, we have few contacts."

"So, where does that leave us?" asked the king's cousin.

"I do have a contact in Russia who could be quite valuable to us," offered Bruce.

"Who would that be, Finkie?"

"An American newspaper reporter."

"Is that the Trent fellow you told me about?" queried the general.

"That's the man. Daniel Trent—"

"Not Archibald's son?" asked Freddie.

"The very one," said Bruce.

"Tell them how you met," prompted the general.

"At the front," said Bruce, "not long before I was wounded and sent home."

"Bruce is too modest," put in the general. "He saved Trent's life. That's how Bruce lost his eye. Tell them my boy."

Bruce gave a depreciating shrug, genuinely uncomfortable. "There's really not much more than that to it. Anyone would have done what I did in the same position, including, and especially, Trent. I heard the incoming artillery shell before he did, shoved him out of the way, and caught some shrapnel in my eye. But all that aside, Trent visited me nearly every day in the hospital before I was shipped out. I believe in that short time we forged a friendship that transcends a sense of obligation. He is a man of honor and a man of deep faith. I would trust him with my life."

"Ah," ruminated the king's cousin, "I see now where your interest in Russia comes."

"That certainly is part of it. . . ." Bruce replied vaguely.

"And this Trent is in Russia as a member of the press?" asked Freddie.

"Yes, however his wife is Russian. She, in fact, has personally met the royals. Her mother's family were members of the nobility and at one time were advisors to tsars dating back to the first Romanov."

"I should think, then, that Trent would be more worried about getting her out of the country than the tsar," said Gus.

"There are some rather complicated limbs in the family tree. At any rate, she was raised a peasant and thus her ties to the nobility are a bit clouded, as it were. Interestingly enough, her stepbrother, or cousin, depending how you interpret her family tree, was involved in the assassination of the Mad Monk."

"So, Trent has no intention of leaving Russia?"

"Not while it remains breaking news. Shall I contact him, then?"

"How will you do that?"

"We all have friends in the Foreign Office. I'm sure something can be arranged via diplomatic pouch."

It was agreed that they would establish and maintain contact with Trent. Bruce would have desired more than just the "wait and see" posture, but if they were to accomplish anything, they had to remain united as a group. Perhaps Gus was right about the Provisional Government. It did seem early enough in the game to give the matter some time and thought. If a rescue of the tsar did become

51

necessary, it would require a great deal of thought and planning.

Content for the time being, Bruce served his guests sherry while they discussed the stock market and the latest rugby scores.

7

Somehow, Yuri felt that in attending the long-delayed funeral for those killed in the first days of the revolution, he might find a kind of closure within himself. There had never been a funeral for Andrei because, of course, there had been no body. A brief memorial Mass had been said for him, but both Anna and Talia had insisted it be performed in a manner that did not put Andrei completely "to rest." Perhaps the mass funeral this day at Mars Meadow would help him to at least put Andrei to rest in his own heart.

He was more than happy when his uncle Paul Burenin suggested they attend together. As agreed, he met his uncle at Tauride Palace about an hour before the service was to begin.

"Ah, you are early," said Paul as he greeted Yuri at the door of his office. "Perhaps you would like a glass of warm tea before we go out and face the elements again."

It was freezing outside, and there was a fresh snowfall.

"I would like that very much." Yuri continued as Paul drew the tea from the samovar, "It's a bit quieter here than I remember from the last time I came."

"Yes, but no less confused. I am sorry to say the hold of the Provisional Government is shaky right now."

"Andrei used to talk about the theory that a democratic period must precede a final socialist victory. I hope that's not what we are experiencing now."

"Between you and me, I don't think socialism would be a bad thing—a democratic socialism, of course. Unfortunately, a few minutes in a Duma session, with its pure mayhem, is proof that Russia isn't ready for democracy of any kind."

"Not to mention that the majority of our population is illiterate and uneducated peasantry."

Paul sighed. "But my heart still lies with the peasantry. It always will."

"Is that why you gave up your seat in the Duma?"

"The Duma has come to be too closely associated with the bourgeois and privileged classes. The Executive Committee of the Petrograd Soviet considers itself the watchdog of the Duma and vice versa. But the Soviet is where I belong, and I am fortunate they offered me a seat. They forbid holding duel positions."

"Except in Kerensky's case."

Paul smiled. "I don't doubt they would give Sasha the world."

Alexander Kerensky was not the leader of the Provisional Government, that position being held by Prince Lvov, but he was still one of the few leaders the *people* revered and trusted. Yuri remembered hearing how Kerensky had solidified his position at a meeting of the twelve hundred members of the Petrograd Soviet. Yuri could almost picture that wiry little man with the sallow complexion, whose flair for the dramatic was becoming legendary. Kerensky stood before the crowd, wild-eyed and passionate, defending his choice to accept a position in the new government as Minister of Justice. He had screamed at the gathering that his motives had been to protect the will of the people among the representatives of the old regime. And incredibly, the crowd had cheered him on.

Kerensky had then attempted to resign his post in the Soviet, but, again, incredibly, the people had shouted for him to remain in both positions. Kerensky's final response was surely what endeared this fiery politician to the people. "I cannot live without the people! If there ever comes a time when I lose your confidence, kill me!"

Yuri and Paul talked for a few minutes more, then Paul suggested they make their way to the funeral. Luckily, it was only a short walk to the Meadow because, as was so often the case these days, the public trams were not functioning.

"Did you know," Paul said as they walked, "that the people had been clamoring to have the common grave located in the Winter Palace Square in defiance of the monarchy?"

"It would have been a shame to spoil one of the most beautiful locales in the city," Yuri replied.

Perhaps one of the most amazing things to happen following the revolution was that wholesale vandalism and destruction had been averted. There had been several fires, one destroying half of the old Fedorcenko estate, and mobs had pried double-headed eagles and other Imperial emblems from buildings and wrecked a few statues. But that had been the extent of it. Perhaps the people, in the end, had heeded pleas from such as Maxim Gorky, who had written that the beautiful palaces and works of art now belonged to the people. These things were their national pride, "the soul from which will grow your new national art."

The funeral service began around noon. Over a million mourners lined the icy streets that day, but amazingly, it was an orderly gathering, full of reverence. No religious ceremony was to be permitted. But Yuri knew many citizens were privately lighting candles and saying novenas in honor of the dead. The procession of coffins, all painted red, was a moving sight even if they were bereft of crucifixes and icons.

Yuri had come to Mars Meadow that day in hopes of honoring Andrei, and perhaps even to find the strength to accept his brother's death. Andrei was as much a victim of the revolution as any in the dozens of coffins carried that day. But Yuri could not keep from thinking of the many others over the years who had died in the cause of revolution. His own father had been killed in the Bloody Sunday massacre. How many hundreds of other lives, perhaps even thousands, had been sacrificed since that first major rebellion, the Decembrist Uprising in 1825? No one would ever know the real toll of lives, but the common grave consecrated this day would surely hold the spirits of them all.

Yuri and Paul were subdued as they departed the Meadow after the service.

"I wonder," Paul murmured, "if these people realize that the road to freedom has only begun."

"Do you think so, Uncle?" But Yuri knew it to be true. Still, he hated to think of how many more such funerals there would be before the end.

"There is still so much work to be done," Paul was saying, interrupting Yuri's momentary reverie. "The union of Provisional Government and the Soviet is tenuous at best. A mere spark could cause it all to blow apart."

"A spark . . ." mused Yuri. The Bolshevik newspaper Paul used to contribute to was called *Isrka*, the spark.

"Are you thinking what I am thinking?" Paul asked. "I have been pondering it a great deal lately. There was a time, Yuri, that I believed a revolution would not happen in Russia without my old friend, Vladimir Ilyich Lenin."

"But it did happen without him."

An ironic smile flicked across Paul's solemn face. "I don't think we have heard the last of old Ilyich. He has applied for entry back into the country, but the Provisional Government is doing all it can to keep him out."

"Does he even have much of a power base left in Russia?"

"The Bolshevik Party is small. Its present leaders, Stalin and Kamenev, are returning Siberian exiles. They are not enthusiastic about Lenin. Against his wishes, they are supporting—if halfheartedly—the Provisional Government."

"There you go. He doesn't have a chance."

A slight arch to Paul's brow and that lingering ironic slant to his mouth said it all. Paul knew Lenin as well as anyone. And Yuri knew Russia. And he had to agree with his uncle. The struggle had only begun.

———————

No one could deny that the ragtag band of Russian Bolsheviks had come through marvelously. Stephan Kaminsky was duly impressed with the large turnout at Petrograd's Finland Station that Monday morning, especially in view of the fact that it was the day after Easter and a holiday.

As the train approached the station, Inessa Armand sidled up to Stephan and they both stood on the platform at the back of the car.

"He pulled it off, didn't he?" said Inessa with unabashed admiration. She was intensely loyal to Ilyich, and Stephan knew that loyalty came from more than the fact that she was Lenin's mistress.

"Even I was beginning to wonder if this day would come." As Lenin's bodyguard, Stephan enjoyed a close association with the Bolshevik leader. Like Inessa, he'd been at Lenin's side the entire time in exile. He had fought the other Party members who had cast doubts about Lenin's ability to pull off the coup now being realized.

True, there had been good reason for the reluctance of the Party leaders, especially when Lenin first proposed the plan to travel back to Russia through Germany. They had no guarantees Lenin would not be arrested as a traitor the moment he stepped onto Russian soil. There had been little communication with Russia since the revolution had begun a month ago. Both Lenin and Stephan were disappointed that even Andrei Christinin had failed to communicate. But Stephan was hardly surprised. No doubt the minute Andrei had set eyes on his bourgeois family, he forgot all about his Party loyalties.

Thus, Lenin had no way of gauging the mood of the people. The Proletariat had lost millions of their number defending Russia in the imperialist war with Germany and might not think kindly of a leader who had, by all appearances, "fraternized with the enemy."

But Lenin made certain it was all set up so that he was as distanced from the Germans as possible. He insisted that no conditions be imposed on the travelers. And none would have any direct contact with the Germans even en route. They would travel on a "sealed train," in essence having the extraterritorial status of an embassy. The Germans had scoffed at all the conditions.

"I was under the impression that it was not I but rather Mr. Lenin who was requesting permission to travel through *my* country," Romberg, the German liaison, had sneered.

But in truth, the Germans were just as anxious as Lenin for the journey to proceed. With the United States on the verge of entering the war, the Germans were more desperate than ever to eliminate the Russian threat any way they could, even through instigating a socialist uprising.

"Inessa," Stephan said, "can you believe we are actually back in Russia?" Stephan had been in exile for seventeen years. One brief visit on Party business about five years ago had been his only and last contact with his beloved Motherland in all that time. It felt good to be back. He felt a surge of hope and anticipation within. This time they would truly set the world on fire. If the people thought that paltry excuse for a revolution in March was the end of it, they were mistaken.

The rousing sounds from several military bands reached Stephan's ears and seemed to confirm his thoughts. The strains of the "Marseillaise" caused chills to course through him. The sight of triumphal arches of red

57

and gold cloth made him more proud than ever to have stuck by Lenin even when opposition within their own Party had plagued them.

The train screeched to a stop, belching steam and noise that nearly drowned out the music. Stephan and Inessa stood back as Lenin and Krupskaya approached the exit where they stood. Lenin gave each of his faithful associates an embrace before debarking the train. He was obviously stunned and pleased at the reception. All fears of immediate arrest that they had entertained even on the seven-day journey were dissolved in a dazzling note of victory.

As Lenin, now forty-seven, stepped off the train, he clearly looked older than he had ten years before when he was forced into exile. Older, yes, but in no way was his essential strength diminished, nor the aura of power emanating from him. The bouquet of flowers someone thrust into his hand looked incongruous indeed in the grip of the stern-faced, resolute man.

Chkheidze, the president of the Petrograd Soviet, stepped up to Lenin to offer the official welcome. Rumor had it that the Soviet had been more or less coerced into participating in the event. They must appease the people at all costs. But he managed to convey his displeasure in his stiff, even gloomy appearance. His voice was rather monotone during his speech, but he wasted no time in driving home his most important point.

"Comrade Lenin," he said, "in the name of the Petrograd Soviet of Workers and Soldiers, we welcome you to Russia. We hope you will pursue with us the goals of the Soviet—the defense of the revolution from any encroachments from either within or *without*."

Stephan cringed as the man paused to allow the effect of his words to sink in. He well knew of Lenin's desire to end the Imperialist war by any means possible. Chkheidze was drawing up battle lines that conflicted glaringly with his final rhetoric.

"The success of this glorious goal requires unity among us all, the closing of democratic ranks."

Lenin seemed to hardly notice the Soviet president. During the speech, his eyes roamed over the crowd and even focused on the sky for a while. When he delivered his own speech, he deliberately turned his back to the president and addressed his words to the throng.

"Comrades, I greet you, the vanguard of the worldwide proletarian army. Remember this, when the Provisional Government delivers its sweet speeches and makes promises, they are deceiving you. The people need peace. The people need bread, and the people need land. Yet they are given war and hunger and poverty. It is time to fight for the revolution and for the victory of the Proletariat. Long live the worldwide socialist revolution!"

As the throng responded with wild cheers, Stephan, too, shouted out his praises. He even rubbed his hands together in anticipation of Lenin butting heads with that upstart, Kerensky. And he had no doubt it would be Kerensky, not a nobody like Chkheidze, who would be Lenin's major adversary.

But in the end Lenin would win. This was his destiny. He would wrest power into his hands even if it meant plunging Russia into civil war. And Stephan would stand at his side the entire time. It was his destiny, too—finally achieving the kind of status he had longed for since those days he had been a naïve peasant boy in Katyk. What would that snooty Mariana Remizov Trent think then, to find *him* lord over her? Like Lenin, Stephan Kaminsky would stop at nothing to achieve that triumph.

II

JULY DAYS
Spring–Summer 1917

8

It was the cold that woke Andrei. He felt it through the thick layers of covers; it seemed to cling to his bones, making him feel as if he would never be warm again. Only when he tried to move did he feel the pain. But though it was intense, it still did not let him forget the cold. There was a stabbing ache in his side and a throbbing numbness in his hands and feet.

Despite the pain it caused, he lifted his hand so he could pull the covers away from his face in order to glimpse his surroundings. Moving away the tattered edge of a blanket, he saw a simple room with dingy walls and old, worn furnishings. It was not a peasant hut, though for some reason he thought that's where he ought to be. A peasant izba had figured often in his dreams. Across the room was a stove, and he wondered why his bed wasn't atop it as in many peasant homes. Perhaps then the cold would go away. Then he realized there was no heat emanating from the stove, no flicker of flames inside. This must be a very poor house if there was no fire on such a cold day.

A few simple icons hung on the wall and he saw a "beautiful corner," and as his eye moved around the room, he noted that it was also the kitchen, for there was a cookstove and a washbasin and a row of cupboards on the wall.

That's when he saw the woman. Her back was to him and she was bent over the washbasin. She was tiny, almost wraithlike, with a slight stoop in her back visible under the worn crocheted shawl draped over her narrow shoulders. Her hair was iron gray and knotted into a bun at the nape of her neck.

"Hello," he said in a soft, brittle voice that felt and sounded as if it hadn't been used in a long time. He vaguely wondered how long he had been lying in this cold bed. He felt as if he had only slept for a night, but he instinctively knew that his legs would not function if he attempted to rise.

The woman turned and her thin, wrinkled visage lit up into a smile that was far too large for her narrow, almost emaciated face. "The dear boy speaks at last! Praise be to God!" She hurried to him. "My darling Ivan! You have returned to me at last."

"Ivan?"

"Yes, my son. Do you not know your own name?"

All at once a horrible panic gripped him. The name Ivan sounded completely strange to him yet he could not think of anything to replace it with. "Ivan. . . ?" he said again as if repeating it might make it sound more familiar. She nodded with a warm, loving smile and he wanted that to be his name if for no other reason than to please this woman. Instinct told him that she cared for him and would help take away the pain.

"My mind is so foggy. . . ."

"You've been asleep for a long while."

"I have?"

"A whole month. Oh, you've slipped in and out, but you were never very clearheaded. I can tell now, though, that the long sleep is finally lifting."

"What . . . happened . . . to me?" A month! How had he come to be here? Why was he in such pain? Was he dying? Why couldn't he remember?

"You were shot, my child. In the War."

"The War. . . ?" Yes, he did remember that. There was a war on, with Germany. Was he a soldier then?

"You were gone such a long time," she was saying, "but you finally came home to your mama . . . so I could nurse you properly."

"You are my mother?" She had seemed to be a stranger to him. If she was his mother, why could he not recognize her? He ought to know his own mother. But even more

64

disturbing was that he could not say for certain that she was not his mother. His panic did not abate.

"Your mind is still a little sleepy," she said confidently. "It will all come back to you."

"I feel as if a cloud is clinging to my brain."

"Oh, Ivan, you always did have a way with words! Now, do you feel like you could eat something?"

"I . . . I don't know. Perhaps . . ."

"A little soup to start with. Some chicken broth. You always did like Mama's broth. But there is not as much meat as usual, and only a few pieces of potato. The War, you know . . ."

At least he could remember the War, but not whether Russia was winning or losing. If there were such food shortages, then it must not be going well for Russia. He wanted to ask the woman—his mother?—but she had already turned back to the kitchen area and was stoking up a fire in the cookstove.

"I am sorry there is so little heat," she said as she worked. "There is not enough fuel for the main stove, and I must keep the fire in this stove as low as possible to conserve. I borrowed blankets from friends for you. But don't worry, I have not told any except those I could trust that you are here. Rudy said you might be a deserter and could get in trouble if the police found out. He said the fewer people who knew about you the better. I do not believe you are a deserter—" She paused and turned a plaintive look upon him. "You're not, Ivan, are you—? But it doesn't matter. If you are, I know you would have had good reason. The world is so confusing these days . . . to some, deserters are heroes—and soldiers are . . . who knows? I am just glad you are home. That's all I care about."

In a few minutes she brought a bowl of broth to Andrei. It was lukewarm and watery, but Andrei let her feed it to him because she seemed to enjoy doing so. She propped a folded blanket behind him, and he tried to work his way into a better position, but the effort produced little effect except to exhaust him. When he finished the broth, she set aside the bowl and began fussing with his covers.

"Rudy says I must check your wound frequently," she said. "You bled so much at first we thought we'd lose you. It still bleeds if you move about too much, but I know it will heal. Rudy says there is a bit of an infection and I must keep it clean, too. Oh, but even when you were unconscious, it pained you so for me to tend it."

She pushed the covers away and lifted his nightshirt. Andrei raised his head so as to view his wound. The bandage, which appeared to be nothing more than rags torn in strips, was splotched with red. Suddenly his head began to swim, and he felt the blood drain from his face as clammy perspiration beaded on his brow. Groaning he let his head fall back.

"What is it, dear?" the woman asked.

"I don't know. I felt dizzy and sick."

"But I was not even touching you."

"The blood . . ."

"I will ask Rudy about it later." She replaced the nightshirt and the covers.

To distract himself from his nausea he asked, "Who is Rudy? My father? My brother?"

"Heaven's, no! He is our neighbor, but a good friend. Your brother and father are still in the War." She looked at him with concern. "You really can remember nothing?"

He shook his head. The cloud persisted.

"We will ask Rudy about that, also."

———————

A few hours later Andrei had a chance to meet Rudy. He was a man of medium height, about twenty-four or five. He was thin, lanky, and rather gawky in his movements, like one who has never quite come to terms with his body. He had a head of thick, black, curly hair that was allowed to have its own way. His thin face sported a bushy beard and a large nose on which was propped wire-rimmed spectacles. His eyes were black like his hair, sharp and sad, yet oddly warm, too.

After knocking on the door, he strode into the room casually as if quite at home here.

"He's awake," the woman announced.

"Good news!" Rudy replied in a soft yet intense voice. He turned toward Andrei's bed. "You really awake?"

"Yes," said Andrei.

"How do you feel?"

"All right, I suppose. Alive, at least. There's some pain . . . my head is . . . rather foggy."

"Foggy?"

"He can't remember things," put in the woman. "But that's normal after such an illness, isn't it, Rudy?" She paused then added, "Ivan, Rudy is a medical student—"

"*Was* a medical student," interjected Rudy with some rancor in his soft tone. "My surname, which by the way is Gruenwald, was too German-sounding for those bourgeois masters at the university, and so they put me out of the school. I was in my last year, too. I was born in Russia, as were my parents, but that doesn't matter in these times."

"You have been caring for me?" asked Andrei.

"I have been helping Sonja here. She has done the lion's share, even giving up her bed for you."

"I . . . I didn't know," Andrei said apologetically. "There could never be enough thanks—for both of you."

"And what else do you expect a mother to do for her son?" Sonja clicked her tongue, then smiled. "Now, I will fix tea for us."

Rudy pulled a chair up to the bed. He felt Andrei's forehead, then checked his wrist for a pulse. "Your pulse is fast and still a bit weak, and you are warm. I've been worried about an infection. If you don't mind, I will check your wound."

When Andrei gave his leave, Rudy lifted the covers and

Andrei's nightshirt. Andrei could not help a groan or two when Rudy gently pried away the bandages, and when the bandages were removed, he could not resist raising his head long enough for a glimpse. But one glance at the angry red wound, with blood still seeping from unhealed areas, made Andrei fall back against the bed with nausea and lightheadedness.

"Ooooo," he moaned. "I'm going to be sick!"

Sonja was at his side in an instant with a small bowl that was put in place just in time to receive the little that was in Andrei's stomach.

"Rudy," said Sonja, "this happened before when I tried to look at his wound. What is wrong with him?"

"Perhaps the pain is too much."

"I had not even touched him before."

Rudy addressed his next statement to Andrei. "You afraid of blood or something?"

"I don't know. . . ." said Andrei.

"Never seen any blood before?"

"I . . . I don't know. . . ."

"You can't remember?"

Andrei nodded.

"What's your name?" Rudy asked.

"The woman . . . Sonja . . . says it's Ivan."

"What do you say?"

Andrei swallowed and his voice shook as the panic returned. "I . . . I can't remember." He gazed at his two caregivers. "I can't remember anything! But if Sonja says so, I must be Ivan her son. Yet . . ." He finished his helpless statement with a shake of his head.

"Sonja," Rudy said, "I have a couple chunks of wood in my room. Would you get them to help warm our tea. I want to have a little talk with our patient. You know . . . man to man."

"Yes, I see," said Sonja and she hurried from the flat.

When he and Rudy were alone, Andrei asked, "What's wrong with me that you did not want her to know?"

"I thought it would be easier for me to clarify things without Sonja around. She is a dear, dear woman, and you may not have noticed yet, but she is, ah, not completely right in her head. But I will get to that. Let me first explain a few things and see if we can jog that lazy memory of yours."

Andrei nodded, but hesitantly. He was wounded. Maybe he didn't want to remember some things.

Rudy continued, "We found you a month ago—just a day or so after the revolution had begun—"

"Revolution? In Russia?"

"You don't remember that either? Hmm . . ." Rudy paused thoughtfully. "This may be worse than I thought. There has been a revolution in Russia and the tsar has abdicated. You do remember Russia and the tsar, don't you?"

"Yes, and the War. There is a war with Germany."

"Good. Now we're getting somewhere. You were in an alley, here in Petrograd, with a bullet in your side. You have no idea how you got there?"

Andrei shook his head, and Rudy went on asking Andrei a series of questions about Russia such as the name of the tsar during the Crimean War, the name of the largest Russian province, the name of the longest river. Then he asked questions about math and science, progressing to questions about the world in general. Andrei answered nearly all intelligently. He was uncertain about some of the mathematical questions, and he wasn't sure who the current President of the United States was. Rudy went on to ask some more personal questions. How old was he? Where was he born? Was he married? Andrei had no answers.

"It appears as if you have selective amnesia. That is, it seems to be confined only to personal memory." Rudy sighed. "But then that's the most important thing, isn't it?"

"Is it temporary?"

"That's hard to tell. I would say the trauma of your

injuries brought it on. And we must hope that it will go away as you become stronger."

"Is . . . is Sonja my mother?"

Rudy smiled, obviously with affection for Sonja. "No, I am sorry to say she is not. You are not Ivan, though she believes you are. Poor Sonja has not been right in the head since the war began. You see, her husband and oldest son were killed early on. Her youngest son, Ivan, did not go to war because the law permitted him to remain home to provide for his mother. But when his father and brother were killed, Ivan enlisted. By then Sonja was already losing touch with reality, unable to accept her losses. But six months ago, when word came of Ivan's death, she lost whatever sanity she had left. You are about Ivan's age, so is it any wonder that when she found you, she decided that you were her dear son returned at last to her?"

"I'm almost sorry that I am not."

"She is a wonderful woman. Before the war she was a happy person with such a cheery nature. She made all who knew her happy. When I came here to live several years ago, estranged from my own family, she took me in practically as another son. Her husband was a weaver and brought home a good income. And Sonja made sure no one she knew went without. She was always baking for her neighbors—a loaf of bread to this one, a sweet cake to that one. She found joy in giving others joy. She still bakes for her neighbors—imaginary loaves and cakes. And everyone takes her empty baskets and they thank her, hoping in that way to return to her some of the happiness she once gave them. Sonja simply could not survive in the world Russia has become, so she made her own world. And now 'Ivan,' you are part of that world."

"I owe my life to her."

"Will you be her son, then?"

"I suppose I have a real mother somewhere who might be grieving over me."

"Perhaps. Maybe you are an orphan."

"Do you think I should be Ivan—for Sonja?"

"Don't you want to find out who you really are?"

"Yes, of course. But how do I begin?"

Rudy smiled benignly. He was only a year or so older than Andrei, but he now wore an indulgent, fatherly expression. "We must work with what we know. For instance, your answers to my questions indicated you are an educated man. I can put this knowledge together with a few items we found in your pockets and come up with some answers. You interested?"

"My pockets, of course! I must have papers." Andrei started to sit up, then wincing, he fell back again.

"Relax, Ivan. I suppose that will have to stand in for a name, if you don't mind. Let me help you."

Rudy did most of the work, frequently telling Andrei not to fight it, but to relax. Eventually Andrei was propped up in bed, and though he was breathing heavily from the exertion and the pain, it was not nearly as bad as it would have been if he had done the task alone. Nevertheless, if he knew nothing else about himself, he did know he did not like being helpless. He wondered how long it would take him to get on his feet again.

But Rudy was now going to a dresser in the room. "What we found are only pieces to the puzzle." Opening a drawer, he removed a handful of things, brought them to the bed, and spread them out on the blanket in front of Andrei.

It was an odd assortment. Several newspapers, all of the same issue and only a few pages each; a few chunks of charcoal, the kind that would be used for drawing; a fountain pen; some coins, mostly Swiss but also a few French and Polish; and a folded paper that, upon opening, appeared to be a handbill for "The Ballet Russe."

Rudy picked up a newspaper. "These were tucked into your belt under your coat. They are all copies of *Pravda*. Interesting, don't you think?"

Andrei frowned, having no idea what Rudy was implying.

"*Pravda* means nothing to you?" But Rudy didn't have to wait for a response to know the answer. "This is the official organ of the Bolshevik Party. Had you but one copy, we might conclude that you had merely picked it up, perhaps casually, or been handed it innocently. But there are ten copies here. It appears as if you were distributing them. Quite significant, yes?"

"Are you saying I might be one of these Bolsheviks?"

"You know what a Bolshevik is?"

"A Social Democrat—one of two splinter groups, the other being Mensheviks." Andrei smiled, but he didn't know why. Perhaps it just felt good to know something, anything.

"Very good. Are you one?"

"I don't know. It doesn't strike any chord in me."

"Well, put it together with the foreign money, eh? And the fact that you have no identity papers. Perhaps you are a returning exile. Many have returned since the revolution. Lenin himself returned a few weeks ago—after we found you, of course—but if you were an exile, and a Bolshevik—"

"Lenin. . . ?"

"You've heard of him?"

"Yes . . ."

"Did you know him?"

"I . . . don't think so. I couldn't have."

"I saw something in you just now." Rudy studied Andrei's face as if hoping to discover a truth. "There was a flicker of . . . something."

"I'm tired, Rudy. I need to rest."

"Rest? Or run away, Ivan my friend?"

"I can't remember! Don't you think I would if I could?" Andrei retorted. "Blast it! I'm not running away. I want to find out who I am! It's just . . . I'm so very tired."

Rudy shrugged. "You deserve to rest. You will remember when you are ready. Would you like to lie back again?"

"No, this is good for now. Thank you, Rudy." As Rudy rose, Andrei grasped his arm. "And, Rudy, I know I owe my life to you also, and I am grateful."

"Sonja had to practically twist my arm to get me to help. And speaking of Sonja, I had better go see what has become of her."

Andrei wondered if Rudy had left his belongings on the bed on purpose. These were his things, yet they might as well be refuse from the streets. He leafed through the newspaper, pausing occasionally to browse an article. Mostly political rhetoric. There was an interesting cartoon of a world globe with German soldiers on one side and Allied soldiers on the other, each pushing with all their might against the other. But crushed under the globe were a mass of people and the words, "The proletariat of the world bear the weight of the imperialist war." The cartoon was signed by a "Malenkiy Soldat"—Little Soldier. Andrei shrugged and laid the paper aside. He decided he was too bored with it all to be a Bolshevik.

Then his eyes wandered to the handbill. He spread it open before him. Besides the words announcing the appearance of the Ballet Russe in Paris in May of 1914, there was an abstract drawing in ink, tinted with pastels, of a dancer. It was quite nice. He picked up the handbill and, as with the mention of Lenin, felt a stirring. Of what, he could not tell. Perhaps he had been a patron of the arts, or simply loved the ballet, not unusual for a Russian. Perhaps . . .

But beyond that final "perhaps" was a complete blank. Nothing but a vague sense that there was *something*. He folded up the handbill and impulsively tucked it under his pillow. He must have carried it with him for some reason. Maybe if he continued to keep it close, it would stir the dead embers of his memory.

9

Yuri did not often have visitors at the hospital. The last time was when Katya had come to take him ice-skating. Thus when he saw Daniel approach, he was both puzzled and concerned. Katya's visit had been good, but Yuri was too much of a pessimist to believe he could have two such visits in a row.

"What's wrong?" he said without preamble.

"I'm sorry, Yuri—"

"Dear Lord! It's Mama."

"No, no—please, there is nothing wrong, honestly!" Daniel flashed a smile to punctuate his earnest words.

Yuri gave the chart he was holding to the nurse he had been talking with. "I wonder if I'll ever become an optimist again?"

"You never were, Yuri," Daniel said good-naturedly. "Do you have some time to talk?"

"There *is* something wrong."

"No. It's just that I so seldom find you home that the only way to corner you was to come here."

"All right." Yuri turned to the nurse. "Keep up the warm compresses for another twenty-four hours. Cleanse the wound three times a day with the iodine solution. I'll look at it again tomorrow."

"Yes, Doctor."

The nurse left and Yuri turned back to Daniel. "I have to be in surgery in an hour. Will that be enough time?"

"I'll make do. Is there some place private we can go?"

Yuri led Daniel to the elevator, which for once was functioning. They rode to the sixth floor, exited, and walked down a corridor to Yuri's office.

It was a small room packed with a desk, several filing cabinets, and a couple of metal chairs. The furnishings were shabby, and there was no carpet on the floor nor curtains on the single small window that looked out on the wall of the next building. A pungent musty odor pervaded the cramped quarters. It was hardly the kind of appointments one might expect the Chief of Surgery of a large metropolitan hospital to have. Besides this, the room was quite messy with stacks of charts falling all over the desk and books and other miscellany piled on the floor.

Daniel glanced around, a bemused look on his face.

"I'm lucky to have an office at all," Yuri said apologetically. "The hospital is so overcrowded. And there is no money for an assistant, so the paper work piles up on me." He motioned Daniel to a chair. "I didn't want the job as Chief of Surgery in the first place, and said I would not sacrifice direct patient care to the tyranny of paper. The board of directors really didn't care. Someday, I suppose, there will be a new and efficient bureaucracy in Russia, and I will probably be tossed into the Fortress for not filling out forms in triplicate. But for now, the disorder of society is my ally." He dropped into a seat adjacent to Daniel, not behind the desk.

"You look tired, Yuri."

"As do you."

"I suppose we are both slaves to our work."

"Do you think we'd be that way if there wasn't such a huge need?" Yuri realized it had been so long since he'd had a friendly chat with anyone that he found himself relishing it and wanting to prolong it. He knew Daniel must have a special purpose for this visit but saw no harm in taking advantage of the moment.

"I fear we would be," Daniel replied. "My hardest task is to force myself to stop and spend time with Mariana and the children."

"They seem well-adjusted enough, so you must have found a proper balance. My only salvation is that Katya is wonderfully understanding. And Irina never had a father, so she is content with anything I do."

"Well, we must be thankful for the small things." Daniel paused.

After a minute of silence, Yuri chuckled. "Have we run out of things to talk about already?"

"Only if we want to avoid talk of the news and medicine."

"What else is there in our lives? Perhaps we ought to take up a hobby. Can you picture us lolling by the side of a lake, fishing?" Yuri paused, but only for a brief moment before he added, "Are you sure you didn't have something specific to talk about?"

Daniel smiled. "Yes, but friendly conversation happens so little these days."

"I was thinking the same thing. How about when this cursed revolution is over, and life returns to normal, you and I buy a couple of fishing poles, find a lake, and see what we can catch?"

"I'll look forward to it, Yuri." Daniel tapped his lips thoughtfully. "Now, about this 'cursed revolution' . . ."

"Yes, how is it going, Daniel? You probably know more about it than anyone I know besides Uncle Paul."

"Lenin is stirring up things—and just when the Provisional Government was beginning to get a handle on the situation. Before Lenin arrived most Bolsheviks were content to take the part of the peaceful opposition party. When Lenin published his April Thesis in *Pravda*—which uncompromisingly denounced the war, calling for an immediate peace, and which also called for the Proletariat to oppose the Provisional Government any way it could—the editors quickly informed their readers that those were the personal opinions of Lenin and were in general unacceptable to them."

"If his own party doesn't support him, he doesn't have a chance."

"Lenin does not give up that easily. I have seen the man in action. He can bend the will of even the most obstinate adversary. But I didn't interrupt you from your important work to discuss Lenin, though he might well have an effect on everything in the future. I really wanted to talk to you about the royal family."

"I have recently spoken to Dr. Botkin, and he tells me they are holding up well."

"I'm glad to hear that. You must know, of course, that there are those who are especially concerned with their safety—"

"According to Uncle Paul, Kerensky is one of those."

"Yes. He is committed to their protection. But what if someone rises to power who is more easily swayed by the oft-heard cries of the people to make the tsar stand trial and answer for his crimes?"

"As Mama would say, Daniel, why borrow trouble?"

"True, but your mother would be the first to be *prepared* for trouble should it come."

"What are you getting at, Daniel?"

"Sorry for being so cryptic. Been around too many politicians lately. Here it is clearly. I have been contacted by a small group of men in Britain who are interested in preserving the safety of the royal family. They were especially appalled by King George's refusal to grant asylum. They would be prepared to mount a rescue."

"That's quite noble, but why them? There are many monarchists in this country who talk of the same thing—and they are Russian."

"Yuri, you know I love the Russian people as I do my own people. But they are a notoriously disorganized and disjointed lot. One look at the way the revolution has been run is proof. Many groups talk of a rescue, but few are able to agree on a single plan. I think my British contacts believe a little Anglo order might be called for."

"All right, then, I applaud them." Yuri leaned back in his chair, shaking his head, puzzled. "I still don't see what you are getting at."

"They—the Brits, that is, would . . ." He hesitated. "Well, they would like some inside intelligence."

"Inside Russia?"

"Inside Tsarskoe Selo."

There was a long silence as Daniel's intent began to dawn on Yuri. His brow wrinkled, and he just stared at his brother-in-law, waiting for him to continue.

"Yuri, you are the only man I can trust who can do this job."

"Even if I agreed to do such a thing, you know yourself I am at the hospital sixteen out of twenty-four hours. I haven't time for my own family. How would I find time to spy on the tsar?"

"You wouldn't have to go there on a regular basis. An occasional visit would suffice, bolstered by your communiqués with Botkin. You have already established yourself as a consultant in the care of the tsarevich—"

"That was before the abdication. In fact, I haven't been to the palace since . . . the monk died."

"Since your involvement in that matter never became known to the tsar, it would be far simpler for you to reestablish yourself there than it would be, say, for me to do so."

"True."

"That's all you need to do for now. If and when an actual rescue were to occur, there might be more—relaying messages in and out of the palace, that sort of thing."

"I don't know. . . ."

"Yuri, you once sacrificed a great deal to save the tsar. I know you thought it was all for naught when the revolution came and he was forced to abdicate. But what if this is a chance to redeem yourself, to make your former sacrifices mean something after all?"

Yuri shook his head. "It's too late for that, Daniel—" When Daniel opened his mouth to protest, Yuri raised his hand. "But there is another reason for me to do what you ask. I need to have some purpose in life that is more positive than the pain and death I face every day. It's a more selfish motive, to be sure, but then I never did wear altruism very well."

"I think it's a perfect reason," Daniel said, smiling. "I've heard too many platitudes from politicians lately to trust altruism much, anyway."

10

Getting back into Tsarskoe Selo was easier than Yuri thought it would be. He called up Botkin on the pretense of needing to consult with the older physician on a difficult case at the hospital. Botkin was permitted the use of the telephone at Tsarskoe Selo, but he had to go to the guardhouse to do so because all other phone lines in the house had been cut. Also, the conversation had to be entirely in Russian so the guards could monitor it. Yuri inquired about the health of the royal family and was told that all were well except for Marie, who, having contracted the measles after her brother and sisters, was still ill and appeared to have come down with pneumonia as well.

"Can I be of any assistance, Dr. Botkin?" Yuri asked.

"Well . . ."

"I would really like to lighten your load, Doctor," said Yuri with emphasis. "Please, let me come and see what I can do." He felt rather the fool, sounding as if he could do more than the older man who was his mentor and a far superior and more experienced physician than he. But Yuri hoped Botkin would, by the very irregularity of the request, catch the hint of an ulterior motive and consent.

Botkin hesitated and Yuri groaned inwardly.

Then, surprisingly, the older man said, "I will see that a special pass is sent to you and the guards are notified."

Yuri took the train to Tsarskoe Selo the next day. He

stopped first at Botkin's home to greet his family and inquire if there were messages they would like him to deliver to the doctor. But because the doctor was not technically a prisoner, but rather had chosen to stay with the royal family, his own family was able to see him on a regular basis. So Yuri went on to Tsarskoe Selo and the Alexander Palace where the royal family was "imprisoned."

The "Tsar's Village" was quite changed from the last time Yuri had been there, and even if he expected it to be so, the changes were unsettling. The guards were a motley group, a far cry from the fine Cossacks that had once proudly guarded the tsar. These new sentinels were dressed in shabby, mismatched clothes, with uncombed hair and unshaven faces. Boots were caked with mud and weapons were held like sticks in grimy hands. The guard at the door of the Alexander Palace was seated in a gilded chair he had dragged from the palace. His feet were propped up on brocade cushions, and his rifle was carelessly lying across his knees. And he was reading a newspaper!

Yuri had to loudly clear his throat to get the man's attention.

The guard lowered the newspaper and looked up, not even trying to conceal his displeasure at being interrupted. "Yeah? What d' you want, and who might you be?"

"I'm Dr. Yuri Fedorcenko. I have a pass." Yuri held out the official paper. "I'm here to see Dr. Botkin."

"On what business?"

"Medical business."

"Someone sick?"

Incredulous that the guard was not better informed about the status of his captives, Yuri answered, "One of the tsar's children."

"You mean *ex*-tsar."

"Yes, of course."

The guard took the pass and scrutinized it, but Yuri doubted the man could even read. Then the man demanded to search Yuri's medical bag. Every item was carefully examined, including the lining of the bag. When he determined there were no weapons or other items he deemed dangerous in it, he said, "All right. Go ahead."

Yuri reached for his pass, but with a sly, toothless smile, the guard said, "I'll keep it, Doc, till you leave."

Shrugging, Yuri entered the palace and was received by Count Benckendorff, the elderly Grand Marshall of the Court. The count bore himself with the same regal formality as he had prior to the revolution. It was both heartening and dismaying.

Fingering the monocle in his eye, the count said, "Come this way, please."

Yuri followed him to a receiving room. On the way, he noted that the interior of the palace was not much changed except for a few pieces of furnishings out of place, and a couple of blank places on the walls where paintings had once been. Yuri waited there five minutes before Botkin entered.

"So sorry to keep you waiting, Yuri Sergeiovich."

"It was no problem at all, Doctor. How are you doing?"

"Quite well, thank you." But Botkin's normally robust figure seemed to have thinned, and his hair was peppered with more gray than Yuri recalled. "It was very kind of you to offer your assistance. You would think that with only a handful of patients I ought to be quite at my ease, but . . ." He shrugged, perhaps unable, or unwilling to finish his statement. "I should talk, eh? I understand the hospitals in the city are filled to bursting. But I have also heard that you are acquitting yourself quite admirably as Chief of Surgery. Not that I had any doubt you would."

"I do what I can and what I must," Yuri replied. "But I know better than anyone that I should never have been promoted to that position at such a young age."

"Never mind that. You are doing the job and doing it well. Would you care to have tea with me, Yuri?"

"Very much, sir."

Botkin spoke briefly with a servant, then led Yuri to a small drawing room. On the way they encountered two or three of the guards roaming, seemingly, idly about the corridors.

Botkin shook his head sourly and said in a low voice to Yuri, "They have made themselves quite at home here. One of the ladies-in-waiting awoke last night to find a guard standing over her bed. They are especially fascinated with the young heir and are constantly trying to get into the nursery to have a look at him."

"Do you get any privacy?"

"Oh, yes we do, I suppose."

"It appears to be a pretty slipshod operation they run here."

Sighing, Botkin, shook his head. "Appearances are not everything. Let the tsar try to take a mere walk about the grounds and there is one guard or another right there to bully him. It's disgraceful."

They reached the drawing room and went in, but Botkin was careful to leave the door ajar.

"No sense *inviting* their curiosity as a closed door is sure to do," he said.

They seated themselves, and in a few minutes a servant brought a tray of tea. She put it down with a careless clatter, making it quite obvious she thought such work was beneath her. The water in the pot was lukewarm, and there were no cakes or other edibles to go with it.

"There are still some loyal, respectful servants," said Botkin after she left. "But many would rather be doing something else—though who knows what they would do, since serving is all they know. The only reason many have stayed is because the new government has commissioned them to be spies for the government and report all suspicious activity here in the palace."

Understanding the impossibility of talking freely, Yuri took a notebook from his pocket and jotted a brief message: "My purpose for coming has to do with *more* than the medical welfare of the royal family."

A slight smile on his weary face, Botkin took the message, read it, then rose and walked casually to the hearth, where he casually tossed the small paper into the fire. "Yuri Sergeiovich, I am in need of some fresh air. Would you mind accompanying me on a brief walk about the grounds before we look in on my patients?"

"Certainly, Doctor."

They walked for about ten minutes. There were still patches of snow on the ground, but the sun was shining and the temperature was practically warm enough for shirtsleeves, though both Yuri and Botkin wore jackets. Two guards kept a close watch on them but remained several paces behind so that the two doctors could converse, if only in "coded" sentences and whispers. Yuri was, however, able to communicate the true purpose of his visit.

"This will be very encouraging to the tsar," said Botkin.

"It's only in the early stages—information gathering, that sort of thing. I will keep you posted while you keep me apprised of the situation here."

"We must be careful. All mail is read and packages and such are carefully searched." Botkin rubbed his beard thoughtfully. "I'll continue to have you consult on the children—"

"Hey there!" interrupted one of the guards. "What's all the whispering about?"

"We are merely consulting on a confidential matter regarding a patient," Botkin replied with affront.

"Well, no whispers around here." The guards now drew closer.

"Dr. Botkin," Yuri said in a loud voice, "I have never seen the like of it. When I opened up the patient, such an odor rose from the bloody cavity as I have never before experienced."

"What symptoms indicated a gangrenous lung?"

"The sputum sample for one. Besides a fetid odor it had three distinctive layers—a rather frothy layer on top of a more translucent, serous one containing strings of pus. The bottom layer was of a reddish-green purulent material—"

"All right!" yelled the guard. "You've had enough air. Back to the house."

When Yuri and Botkin turned and saw the two guards looking decidedly greenish, the two doctors barely restrained their grins. They became more serious when, once inside, they met Alexander Kerensky in a corridor.

Yuri had never met his uncle's friend and colleague before but had heard much about him and seen him from a distance. He was dressed as a common workingman in a collarless blue shirt, coarse gray trousers, and heavy boots. He had the small, darting eyes of a man who is in motion even when standing still. Those eyes now gave particular scrutiny to Yuri, instantly aware that he was a stranger to the palace.

"Dr. Botkin, I don't believe I have had the pleasure of meeting your companion," he said.

"This is Dr. Yuri Fedorcenko. I have asked him to come and consult regarding young Marie."

"I see." He held a hand out to Yuri. "I'm Kerensky."

"Yes, I know," said Yuri. Then he played his trump card. "My uncle speaks very highly of you, sir."

"Your uncle. . . ?"

"Paul Burenin."

"Ah . . . Pavushka. Well, I think very highly of him also. A good man. You should be proud."

"I am, sir."

"Well, then, I must go now to meet with the ex-tsar."

"Kerensky, sir," said Botkin. "Might I have a brief word with you first?"

"What is it, Doctor?"

"I wish to request, sir, on behalf of my patients, that you seriously consider transferring the family to the Crimea for their health. They are recovering much too slowly from their illness, especially Marie, who has contracted pneumonia. The air in the south would do them a world of good, I am certain."

"I am sorry, Doctor. That is simply impossible at this time."

"I cannot see what difference it would make—"

"For one thing, Doctor, public sentiment against the tsar in the south is quite strong. There would be a strong public outcry if the family were to be ensconced in the relative luxury of Livadia. And this could well impair their safety. So, I am afraid it is out of the question. Now, I must be on my way. Good day, gentlemen."

Kerensky hurried away and Botkin shook his head. "Well, it was worth a try."

"Is Kerensky really as concerned for the tsar's safety as he says?" asked Yuri.

"I believe so. And I will tell you another thing. The man has changed markedly in his assessment of the tsar since his first visit here a few weeks ago. He, like everyone who comes face-to-face with Nicholas, has seen the man's humanity and his genteel nature. Kerensky, in fact, has dropped his judicial investigation into the tsar and tsaritsa's activities before the revolution."

"Perhaps he might be willing to assist our little venture," said Yuri wryly.

Botkin chuckled. "An interesting thought. But I'm afraid Kerensky has too much to lose by collaborating. He will free the tsar through proper, legal channels, or not at all."

After examining the royal children, Yuri departed the Alexander Palace. He rode the train back to Petrograd in deep thought. He had no idea what he could accomplish. And, unfortunately, if health broke out among the tsar's family, he might not be able to accomplish anything. He hated to wish ill health upon them, but at this juncture, it might be in their best interests. For once, Yuri made a concerted effort to be more optimistic. He had taken on this task in order to have a positive purpose—and there was absolutely nothing about his visit that proved otherwise.

11

The snow and ice had melted before Andrei was well enough to venture from the haven of Sonja Morozovna's poor flat. At first it was all he could do to negotiate the three flights of stairs down to the street. It took, with Sonja's help, a quarter of an hour down and a half hour back up with a lengthy rest in between. A walk partly around the block was his next feat. It was quite a sight, the tiny Sonja, who looked as if she might crumble like a dry leaf at a mere touch, bracing the man who was at least a foot taller than she. Andrei had lost weight, and because of the shortage of food, he might never return to his former size that Sonja had described to him as well over two hundred pounds when they found him in the alley. Yet he was still a towering figure, and no skeleton at about one hundred and eighty pounds.

He took his recovery slowly, having no problem obeying Sonja's admonitions not to overdo. He told himself he didn't want to risk a relapse, but down deep he wondered if he was, as Rudy had pointed out, running away. But would anyone blame him? If his real life were not terrible, why would his mind have blacked it out? Why not accept a loving mother who cared for him so tenderly?

Besides, from all Rudy said, the world was not a very inviting place these days. The war and civil unrest had brought about miserable living conditions in Russia, and especially in Petrograd. The prospects for the future did not look promising. April had brought yet another crisis to the new government, and it was no coincidence that this came shortly after Lenin's arrival. There had been renewed disorders in the streets and demonstrations sparked, according to Rudy, by a series of newspaper articles by Lenin, called his "April Theses." The main area of contention was Russia's continued support of the war—in Lenin's words, an "unconditionally predatory imperialist war."

Rudy said he knew some Bolsheviks who were shocked by Lenin's stand, yet his nearly superhuman force of will was influencing even the most recalcitrant. Eventually the workers took to the streets, declaring, "Down with Miliukov!"; "Down with the war!"; "All power to the Soviet!"

On May first, traditionally an international Socialist holiday, Miliukov, Prime Minister of the Provisional Government, blundered by sending a wire—the contents of which were subsequently leaked to the press—to the Allies assuring them that Russia intended to fight the war to its end. This brought a furor of protests from the people and forced the Provisional Government into an untenable position.

"Many believed Lenin would use this moment to seize power," Rudy told Andrei. "I'm not sure why he didn't."

"Lenin is many things, but he is definitely not impulsive—" Andrei, hearing his own words, stopped abruptly, mouth still hanging open.

"What is this, Ivan?" Rudy grinned. "A memory?"

"I don't know where that came from. But it's true, I know that."

"Maybe you did know Lenin."

"And so, should I just walk up to him and ask him who I am?"

"Why not?"

"Leave him alone, Rudy," Sonja scolded. "He wants nothing to do with the likes of this Lenin." Sonja turned toward an icon of St. Nicholas, kissed it, and crossed herself. "It is said he disdains faith in God."

"Well, I'm not sure about Lenin myself, however not

on grounds of faith, since I am an atheistic Jew," said Rudy. "But if I thought he could help me, I'd lower myself to seek him out."

"Men like that don't give without expecting something in return," said Sonja with a finality that seemed to put that part of the conversation to rest.

"So," Andrei asked, anxious to put the topic to rest also, "what happened next? That was less than a week ago."

"I'll tell you!" said Rudy. "The Provisional Government and the Soviet have formed a coalition government. Miliukov is out, and Prince Lvov is again the Prime Minister. Kerensky is the Minister of War, but if you ask me, he is really running things. The people will listen to him long before they listen to some prince."

"And Lenin?"

"He'll have nothing to do with it."

"Of course. No compromise for him."

Rudy gave Andrei an incisive glance but ignored Andrei's comment. However he did say, "I think it is time you had a little outing, Ivan."

"No, no," said Sonja quickly, fear in her small eyes. "It is much too soon. He can barely make it around the block."

"Sonja may be right," said Andrei. "I'm still so weak."

"You'll never get strong if you stay cooped up. I am the doctor, you know—well, almost a doctor. And I prescribe an outing, an evening of entertainment."

"I'll think about it. Perhaps tomorrow."

Rudy left, obviously disappointed. Andrei gave thought to their conversation about Lenin and wondered how he knew such things about the man. He tried to tell himself that he had probably picked them up reading the newspapers Rudy often brought him, but he knew that wasn't it. What he knew about Lenin went far deeper than that. Then, as Rudy suggested, why not go to the man and see if he could identify him? Yes, he would. Perhaps to-morrow . . .

———————

Andrei was seated in his bed a few days later, exhausted after a particularly grueling walk. He had gone out alone, lost track of distance, and ended up walking almost three blocks before he realized he would have to walk the same distance back. When he finally reached Sonja's building, he had nearly collapsed on the bottom step, and it had taken him an hour to work up the strength to climb the three flights to the flat.

Once back in his bed he began sorting through his possessions, as he often did, hoping that looking at them, touching them, would spark a note of recognition in his numb brain. But as usual there was nothing. He picked up one of the chunks of charcoal, wondering once again why he had them. This time, however, he thought he'd do more than wonder. He rose from the bed and looked about the room until he found some plain paper—actually all he could find was a blank leaf in one of the few books Sonja had. He sat at the old deal table and put the tip of the charcoal to the paper, almost as if he thought some magic would propel it along. In fact, it was a bit like magic as he began to make a sketch, astounding himself as a recognizable image appeared on the page.

First, he drew Sonja's "beautiful corner." It was a simple drawing, with the icons on the wall vague and only the pretty brass candle holder in focus, with as much detail as the charcoal would allow. He wished there was ink for the fountain pen, which would allow him to capture the engravings on the holder. Sonja would like the drawing because she had told him the candle holder, her most valuable possession, had been a wedding gift years ago.

Thinking of Sonja, he attempted a new sketch on another blank page in the book. This one he did from memory—what there was left of his memory. It was of Sonja.

She had a fascinating face with deep laugh lines and crow's-feet, sadly off-set by hollow eyes ringed with dark smudges. According to Rudy, she had once been a cheerful, laughing woman. But years of pain, grief, and hardship had left her bereft of not only her loved ones but of her joy as well. Even Andrei's presence had not brought back the laughter, as if, down deep, she knew he was but a substitute for her beloved son—a poor substitute at that who could not even remember her love and devotion.

Somehow Andrei captured all these things in the drawing—it utterly amazed him as the work unfolded before him. He knew it was good—very good—though he had no idea how he knew. He was so absorbed in his work he did not realize it when two hours passed. Only the opening of the front door made him pause and glance up.

Sonja came in after spending most of the day at the market. Her basket contained only a small loaf of bread and two chunks of dried fish.

"And I had to fight for these," she said, placing the basket on the sideboard near the basin.

"It is not right that you should be out foraging for our food while I take my leisure," said Andrei.

"I'll hear none of that. You have done more than your share, Ivan. You fought for your country and were wounded to boot. It is my pleasure to do for you now." She turned and smiled and was the image of the woman in Andrei's sketch. The smile did not bring the laugh lines to life, nor did it dispel the sadness from her eyes. "Let me have this pleasure, son." She removed the few items from the basket. "I only wish there was more. You are a big boy and must have more sustenance."

"I get enough." He knew she often gave him her share, and all the arguing in the world would not stop her.

"What are you up to?" she asked, walking up behind him. "Reading that old book? Your papa takes much pleasure in owning these books, though, of course, he cannot read himself. I think it is frivolous, but it gives him happiness and that's what matters."

"I'm not reading," Andrei replied. "I thought I'd see if I could do anything with that charcoal."

"You drew this?"

"Yes . . ." Andrei answered, suddenly shy, hoping it would not offend her.

"It is of me. Do I really look like that?" She paused and moved a bit for a better look. "Yes, I do, don't I? I didn't think I was that sad."

"It's not a good drawing—"

"No, it is a wonderful drawing. Where did you learn to do this, Ivan? In the war?"

"Well . . ."

"Of course, you don't know." She winked and gave his shoulder an encouraging pat.

"Do you really like it?" When she nodded, he turned over the page to the sketch of the "beautiful corner."

Sonja gasped with pleasure. "Oh, Ivan! My candlestick! It is lovely. And you truly made this picture yourself?"

"What's more, Sonja, I enjoyed doing it. I forgot all about the time. And it seemed so very natural."

"Did it?" Her tone now contained a hint of wariness.

"Whatever else I might be, Sonja, I am almost certain this is part of who I am. It gave me such pleasure, such a sense of completion. And I realize now that if this was part of my life—the life I have forgotten—then it could not have been an entirely terrible life."

"What do you mean?"

"I don't think I am afraid anymore to find out who I am."

"But we know who you are, son."

"Oh, Sonja." He rose from his chair and put his arms around her thin frame. Was there any way to discover his true self without hurting this dear woman? Sighing with frustration, he knew there wasn't. He would have to bereave one mother in order to restore a son to another mother. Yet it was this mother in his arms now that he cared for. The other woman would be a stranger to him.

Gently he released Sonja. There were tears brimming her eyes. She wiped them roughly away. "What a fool I am to carry on so, and with it far past dinnertime. You must be starved. Sit down and I will bring you your meal."

Andrei obeyed. It was the best way to diffuse the emotions of the moment. They spoke of trivial matters as they ate the dry fish and black bread. Sonja told of her day at market, waiting hours in various queues, leaving some empty-handed when supplies ran out. She told him how the final hunks of ice had disappeared from the Neva, and that many trees were already sprouting with a new growth of leaves. The Cheremukha trees along Nevsky Prospect were blossoming. For the first time since waking in Sonja's flat, Andrei wanted to get outside. He thought the signs of spring would be interesting to draw. He visualized just how he would capture a Cheremukha tree with its cherry froth of blossoms, perhaps juxtaposed against a sooty, gray building.

When Andrei finished his meal, he wanted to jump up and leave immediately. But he knew that would never do, for Sonja's reluctance about his leaving was quite clear. Instead he tried to sound casual. "You know, Sonja, I've been thinking that I haven't seen Rudy since the other night when I turned down his invitation. Perhaps I hurt his feelings."

"He'll get over it."

"I know, but maybe I should accept his offer. He's done so much for me, it's the least I can do."

"I still think it is too soon, son."

"I will take it easy."

Sonja shrugged and sighed wearily. Andrei rose and brushed her cheek with a brief kiss, then put on his coat—the same coat he had been wearing when they found him. Sonja had worked hard to clean it and had removed all but the worst bloodstains, patching the hole left by the bullet that had nearly killed him. He tried to shake away the sadness as he slipped into it. There was no way not to hurt Sonja. He could not prolong his search any longer. He had to discover the identity of the man who could take a piece of broken charcoal and turn it into a moving image.

12

The Imperial Ballet was no more, and with it had gone the financiers who had kept it in business. Many of the wealthy had fled Russia, taking their wealth with them; and those who remained were hoarding their possessions, or hiding them from possible confiscation by the new government. The pampered lives of dancers had thus changed dramatically. A glaring example of this was the ballerina Kshesinskaya's lovely oriental-style home on Petrograd Side, near the banks of the Neva, which had been taken over by the Bolsheviks and made their headquarters. How awful it had been for her to watch all those crude, dirty men tramping on the expensive carpets, carelessly bumping and jostling her fine things.

Talia Sorokin had not lost nearly as much, materially. In fact, she was still living in her flat near the Marinsky Theater on the Moika Canal that she shared with several other dancers. Her mother and Anna Grigorov had frequently tried to get her to come back to their place. They worried because she was so near the center of town and much of the revolutionary activity. But their place was crowded already. Talia did not want to be yet another mouth to feed. And the dancers Talia lived with needed her to help pay the rent. No more were the days when they could live off the fat of wealthy patrons. The dancers had to scrape and claw to find food just like everyone else.

Many, of course, had fled the country because even if they themselves were not part of it, their connections to the nobility were too strong for the new rulers—the Proletariat, as they had come to be called—to ignore. Talia had not reached such a level of notoriety to be forced into such a position. She did not have to flee.

Luckily, the Proletariat were Russians first, and they loved their ballet as much as the aristocrats. The tsar whom they despised and crushed had built for a fine people's theater, Narodny Dom. There the common man could be entertained at reasonable prices, which the tsar subsidized from his personal purse. Talia had performed there a couple of times before the revolution, prior to joining the Ballet Russe. However, without financial backers such places of entertainment were now struggling terribly or had closed completely. Many performers had literally taken to the streets, dancing or singing or playing instruments, living off the handful of coins passersby tossed their way. The people still wanted, and perhaps even needed, to be entertained.

Talia had done her share of dancing on street corners, but recently a dozen other dancers, including herself, had formed an informal troupe that traveled around, performing in the various theaters in Petrograd. For music they had but a skeleton orchestra, a mere handful of musicians. There was no scenery except what was left at the theater, and often it did not go with the stories, but it proved to be better than nothing. They also had managed to pilfer a few costumes from the Imperial Ballet closets. They frequently played to large audiences, which did not reflect accordingly on their income. Often, after expenses were deducted and the remainder divided between them, Talia came away with but a ruble or two for a night's work.

Talia was managing to survive, in body and mind, at least. Her heart was another matter. She still could not believe that Andrei was truly gone. It seemed just as it was when he was in Europe, that he was absent for a while, with hope for a reunion always present. Then she would remember that he was never going to return. He had died in an alley during a blizzard, all alone. Someone had probably carted off his body, and because Andrei had no papers—or so Daniel believed—he was no doubt buried in a common grave. His loved ones could not even have the comfort of a funeral service.

Talia still tried to conjure up hope, because Andrei's body had never been recovered. Perhaps that was just her nature, but she could not give up hope entirely that he might have survived. She tried to ignore the huge unanswered question this hope produced—a question Daniel and even Yuri would attempt to confront her with. If Andrei had survived, why, after two months, had he stayed away? Daniel said that Andrei had finally come to terms with his anger toward Yuri and his sense of shame. He had come home ready to reconcile with his family. So, if he was alive, there could be no reason for him to stay away.

They meant well in trying to make her face reality and accept her loss. To do otherwise might easily drive her insane. She ought to just accept the fact that her dear Andrei was gone. But acceptance did not fill the huge abyss in her heart resulting from the loss, not only of the man she now realized she loved, but also her best and dearest friend. It did not keep her from seeing his face in every crowd or hearing his voice. How many times had she stopped in the street, certain her name had been called, or that she had caught a glimpse of his broad shoulders disappearing into a building or around a corner? How many times had she chased after these phantoms, only to be miserably disappointed?

Talia looked in the mirror before the dressing table where she sat. The face that stared back at her was thin and pale—more so than usual. Even the theatrical touches of rouge and eye makeup did little to help. Her thick, dark brown hair, pinned up on top of her head with wispy tendrils framing her face, only emphasized the pallor, and her long neck made her seem even thinner than she was. What a fitting look for the "White Swan" of Swan Lake, the part she would dance tonight at the Narodny Dom.

It was said that she danced the part nearly as well as Pavlova, with artistry and passion. She knew this had nothing to do with her abilities as a dancer but rather because she had found a part she could truly relate to— Odette, the princess consigned to the body of a swan because of an evil spell that can only be broken by love. Robbed of that love by the deception of the cruel sorcerer who thus imprisoned her, Odette's only escape seemed to be death. It hardly mattered that Odette and her prince were finally united in death by the power of their love.

Even in her most optimistic moments, Talia did not expect such a bittersweet ending in her own life. She died a little every day, knowing that her love was never coming back to her.

————

It started raining just before Andrei and Rudy left for their evening of entertainment. Sonja tried to get them to call off the outing, but when Andrei insisted on going ahead, she thrust an umbrella into his hands instead. When he and Rudy were out in the street, Andrei glanced up just before opening up the umbrella. Sonja's face was pressed against the windowpane watching her "Ivan" fly from the nest. He waved up at her and she waved back, but even through the stained, dirty pane, he saw that she did not smile.

The walk that evening was tiring for Andrei. He could not remember a time when he had been fit and robust, but he knew there must have been such a time, and for more reasons than one, he wished for its return. Since his coming to terms with his fear a few days previously, and the accompanying increase in his desire to learn his identity, he had been consciously, and sometimes strenuously, working at accelerating his recovery. When Sonja was gone, which was often since marketing consumed so much time, he exercised on the apartment stairs, walking up and down, sometimes even trying to run. His wound still caused him pain, but it was healing steadily since the infection had been stanched by powders Rudy had somehow obtained from a hospital. Andrei's main problem now was loss of stamina, a problem he was determined to surmount.

When Rudy suggested they pause in their journey for a rest, Andrei gritted his teeth and shook his head. He knew the quest for his identity would be no task for an invalid. He had to get his strength back.

"By the way," Andrei asked, trying to get his mind off his shaking legs, "when are you going to tell me our destination?"

"I wanted to make sure we'd come far enough so you wouldn't want to turn back."

"I thought this was going to be entertainment, something I'd enjoy. . . ."

"I hope so." Rudy paused to run a finger across his glasses to clear the mist caused by the dampness the umbrella could not prevent. "Of course we have no idea what 'Ivan' would enjoy, do we?"

"No, but I'll bet you have something interesting up your sleeve."

Rudy smiled and they walked on. Crossing a bridge to the north side of the Neva, they eventually came to a large building of dull gray stone that had a vague Grecian look, except it was more severe than classical. Lettering on the front of the building identified it as Narodny Dom, the People's House. Andrei knew the building, just as he knew other public places in Petrograd. He even knew what it would look like inside. He had been there before, but that was no great revelation, for this building was a theater and many Russians came here. As always, it was perplexing to Andrei how some things were so clear when other things—the very personal things—were so very blank.

"I'm surprised the place is still operating," Andrei said casually.

"Well, people still want to be entertained. But it is not functioning in all its past glory, to be sure."

"And what are they showing?"

"Swan Lake."

"The ballet . . ."

Rudy smiled sheepishly. "You disapprove?"

"No, I think it is a good idea. The man I was probably liked the ballet. But I don't see how coming here will help."

"Don't worry about that. Let's just enjoy it. If it sparks something, fine. If not—well, nothing lost."

Andrei wondered if it could be that simple. At least it was something tangible, the only real link that he had to his lost past—besides the Bolsheviks. But he was still a bit nervous about taking that route, although he knew he would, sooner or later.

With a shrug, he entered the building, closed the umbrella, and shook off the excess rain. There were quite a few people milling about the lobby, but only a short line at the ticket window where he and Rudy purchased tickets for a couple of kopecks, much less than the pre-revolution prices, a fact that was tucked in Andrei's patchy memory.

Though there were two or three hundred in the audience, the theater was hardly full, and Rudy steered them to excellent seats ten rows from the front, in the center section. They sat down and had a fifteen-minute wait before the musicians filed into the orchestra's box. There were only a half dozen of them, but they were dressed in evening attire, though a close look revealed that their cuffs were frayed and the knees and seats of their trousers were shiny and worn. Rather than being saddened by the rather pathetic showing, Andrei felt a strange pride in this display of the indomitable spirit of the Russian people. Perhaps he was indeed a revolutionary, if not a Bolshevik.

But politics aside, he was inspired on another level as well. He took out a sketchbook Sonja had found for him—he was afraid to ask how she had come by it or how much it had cost her—which he now carried with him always, along with the bits of charcoal that had been in his pockets. Before the stage lights were dimmed, he was able to make a drawing of the "orchestra." Then the lights lowered and he was forced to tuck the sketchbook back into his inside coat pocket.

The opening scenes were hardly mesmerizing. The costumes were quite simple and the scenery was mediocre at best. Andrei reminded himself that the ballet had no doubt been hit as hard as anything by the revolution. The dancing was good, but it was not until the second act that he truly became caught up in the performance. That was when the White Swan came on the stage. He understood how the Prince Siegfried could fall so completely in love with her. The grace and beauty she emanated was only part of it. As the story progressed, one could tell this dancer somehow truly identified with Odette. Doomed to be lost forever in an evil spell, unable to grasp at love—the one thing that could save her.

In the end, as the swan was swallowed up in the lake formed by her mother's tears, fated to die with her prince, Andrei watched transfixed. He leaned forward in his seat, his breath held, as if the scene were trying to pull him to it, as if the dancer herself were a magnet, a force powerful in its frailty and delicacy. Yet, seeming to mock the death scene, his heart was pounding so hard he felt the throbs echo in his ears. The dancer's every movement only made it beat faster. He thought the sound of it could be heard all over the theater, like a drum. It seemed a sound such that could wake the dead.

But it did nothing to wake his dead memory. Andrei

was left with only a disturbing sense that his reaction had been due to more than the quality of the performance. Yet the void in his mind had changed almost imperceptibly. It was no longer just an empty void. Now it was like a large empty room, with a light in it, and a hollow echo, but nothing else. It was waiting, expectantly, to be filled.

13

Anna had searched the house over several times but could not find what she had been looking for. She was distressed not only because the journals were important, irreplaceable actually, but also because she had such high hopes that they would be the thing to lift Yuri from his melancholy.

"Dear Lord, what could have happened to them?" she murmured as she shut the lid of the old trunk.

They were Sergei's journals. In them were his account of his experiences in the Siberian labor camp, his escape, and his eventual journey to China where his true spiritual journey had begun. Of course, Sergei had recounted these things to Yuri and Andrei many times before his death. The boys had listened respectfully, but they had been young then and, as young people will be, rather cocky and disinterested in "ancient history" as they had perceived it. Anna was certain it would be different now. She was also certain it would have a far greater impact for Yuri to read these things in Sergei's own words rather than hear Anna's verbal rehash of things that were coming to be rather sketchy in her own mind.

But now the papers were missing. Yet she could not have been so careless with Sergei's things. Something must have been done with them. Perhaps Sergei had done something with them himself and had failed to tell her.

But no, Anna remembered reading them after his death, thankful for the comfort they had provided her. She remembered thinking how her sons would appreciate them when they were older. She remembered—

Yes, that was it! Her father-in-law, Prince Viktor, had come upon her once while she had been reading them. He had been quite emotional—after all, he had lost both his children and his wife to tragic, untimely deaths. Although his mental state had remained healthy through that latest tragedy, his grief for Sergei, with whom he was enjoying a wonderful renewed relationship, was deep. Anna had offered him the journals to take back to the Crimea and keep for a while. Viktor must have them still. But in these uncertain times, the Crimea was as far away from Petrograd as the United States. She would not trust such precious items to the Russian mail, nor could she herself travel south just to retrieve Sergei's journals.

Anna whispered another prayer, believing that God was as concerned for Yuri as she was, and that if the journals might be helpful to him, God would find a way for them to get to Yuri. In the meantime . . . well, Anna would do as she had always done—leave her loved ones in God's hands.

Nevertheless, when Yuri came home that evening, Anna wavered a bit in her faith. Pale and thin and as woebegone as ever, he practically ignored his little stepdaughter who wanted to snuggle next to him on the sofa. She had stayed awake far past her bedtime just to see him. When Katya tried to intercede for Irina, he snapped at her and finally shooed Irina away. He laid his head against the back of the sofa, rubbing his eyes. He hardly noticed Katya exiting the room, her lips quivering, nearly in tears.

"You look exhausted," Anna said, venturing into the parlor after she noted Katya's hasty departure.

"Yes . . ." he grunted in response, not opening his eyes or lifting his head. "I was called away at three this morning for an emergency."

It was now ten in the evening, and Anna had no doubt he had been working steadily since three.

"I never heard the telephone," she said just to keep up the conversation.

Yuri and Katya's room was near the phone, but Anna sensed that was not the only reason he was the only one to hear it. Yuri slept poorly if at all. Nightmares and anxiety haunted him day and night. Anna wanted desperately for him to find peace. She feared for his health, not to mention his soul, if he did not.

"Katya left a plate of food for you warming on the back of the stove."

"Yes, and for thanks I snapped at her." He sighed wearily. "Perhaps I should take a room at the hospital and come home only when I am in a more amenable mood."

"When do you think that will be, Yuri?"

He snorted with self-derision. "A good question, Mama. Maybe I should not come back at all."

Anna sat beside him and took his hand in hers. He lifted his head and looked at her, moisture brimming his eyes. "Dear Yuri . . . that would not be a good solution for anyone, especially Katya and Irina. They need you even if only part of you is here."

"I don't know. Sometimes I think I have this licked. Then everything gets to me and I collapse once more. I feel as if I am one of those tightrope walkers at the circus. I can never seem to keep my spirits up for any length of time. The thin rope I walk on is my sanity. I often wonder if this is what it is like to go crazy. Do you think I am, Mama—insane, that is?"

"Yuri, I am no doctor. But I need no medical training to see that you are as sane as anyone else in this confused world we live in. You are certainly as mentally stable as one can be who has suffered the things you have suffered in the last six months. And it *has* only been six months! In that time you have been through two very traumatic situations. Not to mention the traumas of society you have been involved in—war and revolution are no small things. And then every day at the hospital you must face the traumas of others."

"Working at the hospital is both the best thing and the worst thing I can be doing."

"Yuri, the worst thing you can do is isolate yourself from your family. Let us hold you up when you are weak. Let Irina give you the gift of her joy. And let Katya be the helpmate she so desires to be. Someday you will be able to give to us, but for now accept the gifts we have."

"When I married Katya"—Yuri lifted his head and turned pained eyes upon his mother—"I expected to be the one to care for her. I don't want to be needy, useless. It is hard to accept gifts when I have nothing to give in return." He paused, arranging an empty smile on his face. "How does anyone put up with me? I am even growing sick of myself. I whine more than all of the children in this house put together."

Sighing, Anna nodded her head unconsciously.

"So, you agree, Mama?" Yuri asked with mock affront.

"Well, I—" Anna began but didn't know how to respond because she did agree, but she didn't think it would be kind to admit it.

"You need say nothing, Mama. You have done wisely merely listening to me. You knew I'd eventually hear myself and be disgusted."

"I can't take credit for that, son." Anna smiled and said a silent word of thanks. It was a small victory, one that, as even Yuri admitted, might not last. But for the moment, Yuri had made some progress.

"Yuri. . . ?" It was Katya, and on hearing her voice, a hint of a smile bent Yuri's lips.

"I'm so sorry, Katya," Yuri said.

"Tut, tut, there will be none of that." And if Katya's cheerful tone was manufactured, Anna could tell it was welcomed by Yuri nonetheless. "Now, come and have something to eat before you waste away to nothing. And I would not like that at all."

Yuri leaned forward then rose. "Where is Irina?"

"She is in bed."

"I'll go tuck her in. Then I'll join you in the kitchen."

14

Lenin's increasingly militant stand against the Provisional Government was a surprise even to the Bolsheviks in Russia. Yet Lenin's influence grew where it mattered most. His promises of peace and bread and the communal sharing of wealth had great appeal among the masses. Thus, it was not long before he crushed Party opposition and became its undisputed leader.

Another "shot in the arm" came to the Party, and to Lenin, with the arrival of Leon Trotsky from America at the end of May. Trotsky had broken with the Party years before and was no longer an official member, yet he was a charismatic and well-known force and quickly rose in the ranks of the Soviet, eventually coming solidly in line with Lenin's philosophy. They made a formidable pair—the driven single-mindedness of Lenin and the tireless man of action who was Trotsky.

Andrei's patchy memory recalled nothing of Trotsky. But when he and Rudy attended a workers' rally at the Putilov Steelworks, where Trotsky was the main orator, Andrei was duly impressed. The man could stir a cold pot of borscht to a boil. It mesmerized Andrei even with the stock rhetoric about "power to the Soviets!" It was also more than merely Trotsky's fiery voice that captivated, for it was difficult to take one's eyes off his animated visage, the mane of thick, dark hair incongruously offset by narrow, intelligent eyes covered with sedate wire-rimmed glasses. He emanated fire and urbanity all at once. Andrei pressed closer to the front of the crowd.

"So, what do you think?" Rudy asked, elbowing Andrei to get his attention.

"He's a powerful force."

"I hear Lenin will speak to a public gathering tomorrow. You can compare them."

"I don't know. . . ."

"You must do this eventually, Ivan."

"Yes . . . yes. . . ."

"You may not need to confront Lenin directly," offered Rudy. "Perhaps one of his lieutenants will recognize you."

"Perhaps . . ."

Andrei felt pulled in so many different directions. Anxious to learn his identity, yet fearful and uncertain at the same time. But he had attended several political rallies lately in the hope that someone there might recognize him. Still, it felt rather foolish to boldly approach strangers with the question, "Who am I?" or, "Do you know me?" He had tried it a couple of times, only to be faced with blank stares or replies questioning his sanity.

Andrei turned his attention back to Trotsky, who was standing on a makeshift stage bellowing denouncements of the Provisional Government, the War, and anything else that conflicted with the Bolshevik doctrine. It occurred to Andrei that Trotsky had certainly changed his tune. Hadn't he previously embraced the Menshevik philosophy? Suddenly, Andrei realized he was having a flicker of memory. But the moment he tried to grasp it and squeeze more from it, the illusive flicker was gone. His head spun and he swayed on his feet. He must have bumped Rudy, for his friend turned.

"Are you all right?" Rudy asked.

"Yes, just a bit tired, I suppose."

"Do you want to leave?"

Andrei shook his head, not so much in refusal as in frustration and confusion. "Why can't I remember, Rudy?"

"Something happened, didn't it?"

Andrei nodded. "I belong here, I know that. . . ."

"Andrei, is that you?"

Andrei heard the voice coming from behind him but did not respond. Why should he? It was the name of a stranger being called. And the name was called again. Still he did not respond until a heavy hand grasped his shoulder. He started, then spun around, staring into the face of yet another stranger. A large man, as tall as he, hefty in weight and muscular development. His craggy features were rather stern and imposing, but his appearance at that moment was not entirely unfriendly in spite of the absence of a smile of greeting.

"Yes. . . ?" said Andrei.

"You look at me as if I am a stranger. It hasn't been that long."

"I . . . I'm afraid I—" He was too nonplussed to find a response.

Rudy interjected. "Please excuse my friend. He means you no disservice. Even if you were his brother, you would be a stranger to him."

"I don't understand," said the man.

Andrei finally found his voice. "I was injured a few months ago—"

"He nearly died," put in Rudy.

"In the process," Andrei continued, "I seem to have lost some of my memory."

"Lost your memory?" The man first looked incredulous, then he laughed. "Well, well! That's too fantastic of a story to be a lie."

"I assure you it's true."

"Some thought you were dead. Others, that you had perhaps rejected your Party loyalties. I, for one, hated to believe the latter."

"The Party. . . ?

"Perhaps I should start at the beginning."

"That's a marvelous idea," said Rudy, "but not here. My

friend is growing fatigued. There is a tea shop around the corner. Let's go there."

The three shouldered their way through the crowd, found the tea shop, and ordered tea before sitting at a table in the corner.

"Names first," said Rudy, and he followed his order by giving his own.

"I'm Stephan Kaminsky." The stranger paused, obviously confused at the peculiar looks on his companions' faces, then it dawned on him and he added, "You are Andrei Christinin."

If Andrei had hoped hearing his true name would open the floodgate of memory, he was greatly disappointed. The name proffered was just as foreign as the one he had been using these last months.

Andrei.

It meant nothing. And yet this was his identity. It was the key to who he was. It was the portal into the man he was seeking, into—hopefully—his own heart and soul.

"How do I know you?" Andrei said, trying to force logic instead of emotion into this monumental encounter.

"You were in exile with us—with Lenin himself. You are a Bolshevik. You remember none of this?" When Andrei shook his head, Stephan continued, "You don't remember *Malenkiy Soldat?*" Stephan reached into his pocket and withdrew a newspaper. Across the top was the name *"Pravda."* He pointed to the cartoon on the front page. It was of soldiers in the trenches. They were gaunt and hungry, garbed in ragged uniforms, some were holding broken weapons while others were merely throwing stones at the well-equipped and hardy enemy. Standing over the poor Russian soldiers was a Russian general, well fed and groomed, seated on a white stallion. The caption with the cartoon was simply, "Whose war?"

Andrei's first impression of the drawing was that it was terribly obvious. Hardly art even if the drawing was good and the characterizations vivid. "I drew this? But how?"

Andrei pointed to the current date on the paper.

"It is a reprint. You drew it in Switzerland. I watched you do it."

"You must tell me everything, Stephan."

And for the next hour as several pots of tea were consumed, Stephan Kaminsky did just that. Andrei learned of a young revolutionary, fervent and passionate in the cause. He had joined the exiles shortly before the beginning of the war and had quickly become an integral part of the propaganda machine. Stephan embellished his tale with much of his own propaganda, liberally interjecting Leninist philosophy into nearly every statement. Finally, he told how Lenin had sent Andrei back to Russia in order to distribute newspapers and to report on the status of the Bolshevik Party. That had been a mere handful of days before the revolution had begun.

"We heard nothing from you," Stephan said. "We weren't overly concerned until Lenin arrived in Petrograd and still you did not show up."

Several moments of silence followed before Andrei could ask the question most strongly on his mind.

"Do you know of my family, Stephan? My parents . . . anyone. . . ?"

Stephan sighed as if terribly regretful over what he must reply. "Andrei, it is our practice to speak little of our families—you know, for their protection. It is possible even the name I know you by is a pseudonym. I know nothing about your family, not their names, not even where they are from. You did mention your mother—but only in general terms, mind you. I believe your father is deceased." He shook his head sadly, then added with more enthusiasm, "But, Andrei, you must remember this if nothing else. Your Bolshevik comrades are your family now. You were part of us, and we will make you part of us once more."

"Yes, I suppose so . . ."

"What? Still reluctant?"

"What do you mean?"

"I . . . that is, I only meant that after all you have heard, you still wonder about your identity?"

"I'm hearing your words as if they are about someone else. Yet I must admit I do feel an affinity for the revolution. There is something inside me that knows the Russia of the past was not right."

"There you have it!" said Stephan with enthusiasm. "What is there to question? There can be no true revolution without Lenin. What we have now is a bourgeois sham, run by a prince no less! They are but a breath away from a monarchy."

"What about Kerensky?"

"Bah! He talks like a revolutionary, but in action he is still in awe of the monarchy. He treats the deposed tsar as if he is still royal. He would have the man exiled to live in luxury in England."

"And what would Lenin do with the tsar?"

"The tsar and his heir belong in prison. They are criminals."

Andrei decided to change the subject. "How will Lenin go about taking power?"

"A physical battle for power is the only way. Even now he is trying to find ways to arm the Proletariat. The question I would ask, Andrei, is will you be part of it? Will you take up the place you abandoned and continue the fight? And do not be fooled—the fight has only begun. We have yet to see the true revolution."

"You must understand—" Andrei began.

"I understand only that I have asked a simple question. Are you for us or against us?"

"It is hardly simple."

Stephan leaned back and studied Andrei for a long moment. Then he said in a quiet voice, as if he had decided upon a new tact, "You have been through a great trauma, I realize. Why don't you just come and have a look around our operation? It will all come back, I'm certain."

"Yes, that's a good idea. I'll come tomorrow."

15

Andrei tried not to think that he joined the Bolsheviks simply because of the sense of identity it gave him. And he did not let himself dwell on the disquiet he felt around many of the Bolsheviks. Often the hard-line rhetoric shocked him or amused him. He did tell himself that there was much to be admired in the Party, and that it especially needed level-headed, questioning men such as himself to keep the Party on an even keel. It didn't make him feel any better when Rudy joined the Party because, though it was never spoken, Andrei had a feeling his friend had done so merely to keep an eye on him.

At the Party offices, Andrei met others who had known him *before*. Some were able to add touches to the growing picture of Andrei Christinin, but none had enough information for Andrei to initiate a successful search for his identity. And none were able to jar his real memory. One said he had family in the city, but that Andrei must have been estranged from them, since no one had met them. Then again, it was probably as Stephan had said. The revolutionaries had been careful in not involving their families.

Andrei did attempt to find some Christinins, but the two families he located by that name did not know him. The name was probably a pseudonym, anyway, so it meant little. That was probably why it did not bother him that Sonja still called him Ivan. A rose by any other name was still just as confused.

Andrei was weary and frustrated with the empty void

in him. Sometimes the limbo of his life made him angry, but neither the anger nor his attempts to force his memory to ignite made any difference. He began to wonder what he would do if this was how he was fated to spend the rest of his life.

He spent most of his time at the offices of *Pravda*, which were separate from the Bolshevik headquarters. He let himself become absorbed in his work and, if nothing else, it did help him cope with life. It was quite time-consuming coming up with a fresh, new political cartoon every day. Moreover, he was also kept busy proofreading and doing other tasks necessary in the publication of the Party organ.

He did not dwell on the fact that drawing cartoons was not nearly as fulfilling as the drawings he had made for Sonja, nor the ones he did in his spare time in his little sketchbook.

The most unsettling experience of his new life as Andrei the Bolshevik was meeting his new superiors. He met Lenin only once, besides brief encounters in the course of his work. The Party leader welcomed him back but lacked any real warmth. Andrei had expected no more, for they had not been bosom friends by any means.

Andrei had hoped that his relationship with his editors at *Pravda* would offer more. He had at least hoped they could have been men who inspired loyalty and respect. But both Lev Kamenev and Josef Stalin were such bureaucrats by nature that they inspired little in anyone.

Kamenev was thirty-four and, with a thick, drooping mustache and goatee, looked uncannily like the ex-tsar—though the Bolshevik would have vehemently denied the similarity. He was married to Trotsky's sister. The fact that he was currently lining up with Lenin, while a couple of months ago he was among the moderates who backed the Provisional Government, clearly demonstrated his vacillating nature.

The same could be said of Stalin as well, but in his

case that was not the worst of his characteristics. Physically, he was a small man—Andrei towered over him by nearly ten inches—but he was powerfully built. His arms and legs were disproportionately long for his torso, and his left arm was rather stiff from—someone said—a bout with blood-poisoning as a child. His pock-marked face was the result of smallpox. His small eyes were cold, and indeed, nothing about the man emanated warmth of any kind. This probably contributed to the fact that he had few friends in the Party—few friends at all, according to some. Another factor most assuredly had to be his notable rudeness. He took no pains at all to be considerate of others, and, in fact, appeared to go out of his way to criticize and belittle.

Andrei immediately judged Stalin to be a highly vindictive man who hated, above all else, for anyone to excel him in anything. This was quite a problem, since Stalin was such an average man in so many areas that it was difficult *not* to excel him. He was a dull speaker, a mediocre writer, and a completely uninspired thinker.

Lenin had once called Stalin "that splendid Georgian." Andrei could only guess that Stalin had so impressed Lenin because he was such a workhorse, reliable and able to follow orders. As for being a Georgian, this was clearly something Stalin would like to underplay. It seemed to grate on him that he was not a true Russian and that he could not shake that pesky Georgian accent.

At least Andrei did not have to work closely with these men, for they were often assigned other duties. Stalin, for example, was frequently off to one factory or another organizing workers. But it was not only Stalin and Kamenev who raised Andrei's inner doubts and disquiet. He was constantly trying to bolster his Party enthusiasm, telling himself that the success of the revolution was foremost. Then, the apologist in him would argue that the revolution had already succeeded, and it was the Bolshevik Party that was trying to undermine it—not the revolution, of course, just the philosophies it pandered.

That's when Andrei became more confused than ever. He simply did not care about all the intricacies of philosophy that most of his comrades found so important. They could argue for hours over a tiny precept, putting Andrei soundly to sleep. If he knew nothing else about himself, he was certain he was no philosopher or intellectual.

He did have his opinions—who didn't? But too often they went counter to the Party line—Lenin's line. For instance, he believed the war was a matter of honor, and to back out would not only betray Russia's allies but also those Russians who had already sacrificed their lives to the war. He would, however, never voice this opinion to his Bolshevik comrades. He was beginning to feel as if he was leading a double life—quite an irony for a man who did not even know what his real life was.

He tried to keep a low profile in the organization, drawing his political cartoons, and doing whatever other inconsequential jobs were assigned to him—passing out leaflets and running errands, mostly. His greatest joy, however, was to go home, visit with Sonja and Rudy, and make his own private sketches. This, more than anything, made him see that even if he had once been a loyal Bolshevik, he truly did not belong now. Maybe losing his memory helped him see things in himself that he could never have seen otherwise. It was probably like stepping out of one's skin and observing oneself as an objective bystander. But even that thought was too deep for Andrei to want to ponder for long.

One afternoon when Andrei had been working at *Pravda* for about a month, he was asked to take some papers over to the Bolshevik headquarters—the mansion of the prima ballerina, Kshesinskaya, who had been the first love of the now deposed tsar. With coarse Bolsheviks tramping in and out, the expensive Persian carpets were now stained by the imprints of muddy boots. Many of the finer furnishings had been put into storage, but those things that remained had been moved about and replaced haphazardly. The chintz and brocade upholstery was soiled by the grimy clothes of the new proprietors. Shards of broken glassware and such lay where they had been carelessly bumped by peasants and workingmen who were not used to having such finery about. The arched, carved ceilings also were incongruous with the desks, file cabinets, and other office gear that had been brought in to accommodate the new purpose of the house. The palace now was always crowded with masses of workers, soldiers, and others on Bolshevik business. And there were frequently huge rallies in front of the palace where there was a fine balcony from which Lenin often addressed the gatherings. But essentially the aristocratic air remained, if rather askew.

Andrei got the idea of sketching the scene. It would make an interesting surrealistic subject. After he delivered his papers and received other papers in return, he decided to roam around the house in search of a good setting for his sketch. He looked in many rooms and made several quick drawings. But when he reached a parlor on the second floor, he forgot all about his initial mission.

He was suddenly captivated by a painting hanging in a corner of the room. He could not explain exactly why it drew him so because in itself it was not great art, which was probably why it had been overlooked when other valuables had been stored. Andrei could readily see that the famous ballerina had probably not purchased it because of its cubist style but rather because it was of a ballerina. Andrei could not tell if it was meant to be of Kshesinskaya herself, because not only was the face too muted to tell, but he didn't know what she looked like anyway. Nevertheless, it was clearly apparent that the artist had been highly inspired by the dancer. The passion of the work came through to him and nearly took his breath away.

"I wonder how my painting came to be here. . . ." he murmured.

A full moment passed before he realized what he had said. If his breath had been caught before, he was staggered now. Why had he said such a thing? And yet . . . he could explain his strange feelings about the painting in no other way. He walked up to it, within a few inches. And there it was. In the lower right hand corner was the signature—initials actually, A.C. He stared harder at the painting, trying to recapture the feeling he'd had when he murmured the words.

But it was gone. Like when a word you are trying to recall is on the tip of your tongue and just as you are about to speak it, someone interrupts and it is lost. Perhaps forever.

He reached up to remove the painting from its hook—he would not be the first revolutionary to loot a palace.

"There you are."

The voice jolted Andrei and he nearly dropped the painting, which he had just about liberated from the wall.

"Are you talking to me?" he asked, turning to find the fellow to whom he had delivered the papers.

"What are you doing?"

"I'm going to find a new home for this painting." Andrei lowered the painting to the floor.

"I don't think that's allowed. I mean you can't just walk off with what you wish."

"Why not? This is my painting—that is to say, I painted it."

"Still, you must go through proper channels."

Andrei pulled back his shoulders and stepped forward until he was within a few inches of the smaller man. "What channels would those be?" he asked with just enough of an edge to his voice to make the man pale slightly.

"Well . . . what do I care anyway? Take the stupid thing. Lenin says all things belong to the people."

"Exactly!" Andrei grinned and started to walk past the man, the painting tucked under his arm.

"Wait, I forgot to give you this." The man held out a folder. "Make sure it gets to Kamenev."

Andrei took the folder and walked from the room, no longer interested in his earlier mission of sketching the mansion in disorder.

Later that evening, Andrei showed the painting proudly to Sonja and Rudy. Sonja studied it very thoughtfully and somewhat sadly. Rudy examined it for any other identifying marks. He found none.

16

In the summer, the Provisional Government began a new offensive in the War. Tremendous pressure had been applied upon them by the Allies, and they had to show their commitment to the fighting despite the opposition within Russia. The United States, having recently entered the fighting, was pouring hundreds of millions of dollars into the Provisional Government, but there was one string attached—"No war, no money."

And, for a short while at least, it seemed as if the additional funds would be the trick to turn the tide for the Russian war effort. Troops went to battle well-equipped and advanced on the Germans with success. But as soon as German reinforcements arrived, the Russians were pushed back in a retreat that quickly turned into a rout.

Andrei heard the news with mixed emotions. While his comrades gloated, he felt sick at heart. He could not feel enthusiasm for the mounting agitation among the Bolsheviks to rush in and seize power. Zinoviev, Lenin's closest lieutenant, was pressing for action. But Lenin sharply opposed a premature seizure of power. "One wrong move could wreck everything," he insisted. He feared that even if the Bolsheviks were to seize power now, they would not be able to hold on to it. Lenin must have believed his cautions had been heeded, for he left Petrograd to spend a few days in Finland with friends.

By the first of July, Petrograd began to seethe with unrest like a kettle reaching the boiling point, ready to overflow. When one hothead, a Jewish-American anarchist, shouted, "Let the streets organize us!" many were ready to follow. Machine-gun regiments rushed to various factories to recruit more demonstrators. Twenty-five thousand workers at the Putilov Works, historically a hotbed of revolutionary ferment, joined the march.

With Lenin gone, the other Bolshevik leaders were frantically trying to decide what to do. In the boudoir of the ballerina Kshesinskaya, they wrestled with the dilemma for hours. Andrei went home that night hopeful that there would only be a peaceful demonstration, but even a casual observation revealed that arms and ammunition were everywhere, in the hands of workers and soldiers alike.

Late the next morning he made his way back to the Kshesinskaya Palace and found Lenin had only just arrived from Finland himself. They were greeted with the news that ten thousand sailors from the Kronstadt Naval Base, another revolutionary stronghold, had also arrived in the city that morning. The sailors joined sixty thousand other marchers on the Nevsky Prospect heading toward the Tauride Palace to have it out with the Soviet, which they believed was pandering too much to the Provisional Government and not giving enough heed to the people.

Andrei stayed at the Bolshevik headquarters waiting for news while halfheartedly drawing a couple of cartoons. But there was business to be conducted at the *Pravda* office. Others had articles that had to go to press, not to mention Andrei's cartoons. He was asked to take a sheaf of papers to the office. Perhaps his comrades had sensed that he was using the headquarters to take refuge from the chaos. But maybe he was better off outside, away from the constant debating of the Party leaders still trying to figure out how best to use this unexpected turn of events.

The minute Andrei reached the street he was swept into the throng, almost unable to move on his own volition. But worse than that was the nearly tangible sense of tension and frustration emanating from the mob. He could feel an undercurrent of violence throbbing through it, seemingly emphasized by the presence of military trucks traveling with the marchers, loaded with armed troops. Andrei wanted nothing more than to retreat back to the palace he had just left. He turned onto a side street to attempt to avoid the main thrust of the mob. But many others apparently had the same idea, and incredibly, even a couple of automobiles were trying to traverse the street.

Breathing hard, though he was hardly moving fast enough to exert himself, Andrei reached up to loosen his collar. He was perspiring but felt cold and clammy all over. He'd felt that way a couple of times when he was still recovering from his wound or when looking too closely at the bloody injury had made him feel faint.

But why should he feel this way now? Yes, the crowd was stifling, but he was certainly physically capable of taking care of himself. Yet something he was unable to define was sickening him. That was intensified when he chanced to glance in the direction of a child stumbling along behind his father. Their eyes met, the child's filled with fear and confusion. Andrei was certain his own eyes must have looked the same.

———

Talia had finished practice early, and she and Vassily, another member of her company, were exiting the studio. They had heard of trouble in the city, but there were always such rumors, and it was easy to think little of them. But when they reached the street and were confronted with the crowds—and they weren't even on a main thoroughfare!—Talia began to think this time was different. She could even hear distant sounds of gunfire. She glanced at Vassily. She was about to suggest they return to the studio, when two men stumbled toward them.

"Here's some bourgeois rats creeping from their nests," slurred one of the men who had obviously found some vodka and had helped himself liberally to it.

"We're no such thing!" said Vassily.

"Oh yeah! You're too pretty to be a worker."

"Get out of our way," demanded Vassily. Unfortunately he was a dancer, not a fighter, and he looked it. The thugs were not intimidated.

One of the thugs shoved him. "We'll see who gets out of whose way."

"Yeah," said the other as he too shoved Vassily.

Vassily swung his fist but missed both assailants.

"Please, stop!" cried Talia.

"I'll bet the lady can fight better than the pretty boy," taunted one of the thugs.

This incensed Vassily and he threw himself at the two men. One easily grabbed him while the other aimed a couple of punches at his stomach. Talia tried to stop them. She caught the thug's fist as he lifted it for another blow. He shook her away like a pesky insect but with enough force to make her tumble to the cobbled street. Even as she was falling, she silently wondered why someone didn't stop to help them. Had the whole city gone mad?

Then before she even remembered to pray for help, she saw a hand reach out to her.

"Are you all right?" the voice said. "Everyone's gone crazy around here."

"I . . . I'm all right, but my friend . . ."

The rescuer, a tall, brawny fellow turned quickly—too quickly for her to see his face—and grabbed the thug who was throwing the punches at Vassily. The attacker no longer looked ominous as the rescuer lifted him off his feet and sent him flying against the brick wall of an adjacent building. While that thug was lying dazed on the ground, the rescuer turned on the man holding Vassily. This man, thinking better of continuing his dirty deed, dropped Vassily and ran away.

"I could have taken him," panted Vassily, "if there hadn't been two of them."

"I'm sure you could have," said the rescuer. He then turned back to the woman. "Are you certain you are all right?"

Talia was on her feet now, but suddenly her legs felt as if they might give out on her again. She staggered back.

"Andrei . . ."

He looked at her, but there was something odd, and awful, in his eyes—they were the eyes of a stranger.

"Andrei . . ." she said again, unable to form any other words. She ran to him and threw her arms around him. She had been wanting to do so for so long, had even dreamed of doing so, though she had thought him long dead. Only when he did not return her embrace, or at least not with the enthusiasm she expected, did her rising panic fully grip her. "Andrei!" she cried.

"Yes," he said, his voice shaking. "That's . . . my name. Who . . . are you?"

"It's me. Please don't do this to me!"

"I'm sorry. I don't mean to be rude. It's just that I've been ill. I have forgotten things. My memory—"

"I thought you were dead—" Tears filled her eyes and choked further speech.

"Dear lord . . ." he breathed.

"You can't have forgotten me."

"I wish—"

But before he could finish, the chaos in the streets seemed to envelop them. Someone tugged at Talia's arm. She tried to shake the intruder away, then realized it was Vassily.

"Come on," he said.

"No, I can't."

But he wasn't listening to her. He kept pulling her until she found herself being shoved into an automobile.

"I can't leave him!" But the door slammed, and before she could try to reopen it, the vehicle pulled into motion.

She looked back, but the mob had suddenly swelled and she could not see him. No!—there he was, trying to fight his way against the flow of the mob toward the departing automobile.

"You must stop!" she cried to the driver.

"We'll be killed if we stop now," said Vassily.

The car turned a corner and, suddenly on a quieter street, it picked up speed. Andrei was no longer visible. Within minutes they were far from the demonstration.

Talia wept.

Not knowing where else to go or what else to do, she had the driver take her to Yuri's hospital, praying he would be there.

Yuri received her news with a mixture of shock, disbelief, joy, and dismay. Finally, when he was certain she had really seen Andrei, the joy overshadowed all other emotions.

"Amnesia . . ." he said. "That explains much."

"It was terrible, Yuri, to look at him, to know he was alive, but to have him stare at me as if I was a stranger. It was the worst experience of my life."

"Yes, I can understand how that would feel. But at least he is alive. Thank God, he is alive!"

"But how will we find him? I don't think I even told him my name so he could find me."

"Don't worry, Talia. I'll tear this city apart to find him. I won't let him get away from us again."

"We must go and tell your mother—"

Yuri felt his confidence of a moment ago begin to ebb. "I don't think we should tell her. What if something should happen? What if something keeps me from finding him? The city is so insane right now, I just don't want to risk getting her hopes up—"

"We *will* find him!"

"Yes, of course. But . . ."

"All right, we won't say anything to your mother. *But we will find him?*" The determination in her voice faded when the final words turned into a question.

17

Andrei tried to chase after the automobile, but the crowd thwarted him until the car finally disappeared from view. In a daze, not knowing what he was doing or where he was going, he wandered back toward the main street he had tried so hard to avoid before. His own safety didn't seem to matter now. All he could see was that pale, beautiful, devastated face—that lovely face that had no name. She had known him, and from the look in her eyes, perhaps she had even loved him.

Why couldn't he remember? What kind of man was he to forget such sweetness?

He grabbed his head, as if he could crush the hidden memories from it. But all the motion did was focus his eyes back on the present, making him realize he was once again back in the thick of the demonstration. For a brief time after he had encountered the woman, all his surroundings had receded, and only she and he had existed. It was only fitting for the awful crush of reality to coincide with her disappearance.

And the reality was indeed terrible. The palatable tension he had sensed before in the mob had now turned into full-blown anger. There were shouts and curses against all supposed enemies. *It wasn't like before when the marchers were singing hymns and imploring the tsar to hear their petition.*

Like before. . . ?

Andrei stumbled forward, or had he been pushed? He couldn't tell. His breathing was coming in labored gasps. He began to feel as if all the violence, all the boiling anger of the mob, was directed against him alone.

"Please," he murmured. "Forgive me. . . ."

Shots rang out—the staccato pelting of machine-gun fire. There were screams, and ahead of Andrei there was a sudden scattering of people. He didn't notice it in time and was jostled by people running in every direction seeking safety. Andrei stumbled forward, images bombarded his senses, but they weren't real, they couldn't be.

The mounted Grenadiers charged the crowd. But the people grasped one another's hands, still singing. . . .

But there were no mounted troops, they were in trucks. Andrei felt dizzy and sick. The burst of shots exploding in his ears magnified tenfold, causing his head to throb.

The foot soldiers broke through the opening the Grenadiers had made and started firing—not in the air this time, but directly at the crowd!

Blindly Andrei fought his way through the crowd, now in complete chaos. Screams, like the gunfire, echoed in Andrei's head. He was knocked to his knees and struggled to regain his feet, tugging on the arm of a nearby man. A moment later, he lost his balance again, this time tripping over something in his path. He fell over the obstacle and was kicked as someone ran past him. Then he saw what had caused his fall. A body was sprawled out before him.

"Oh, God!" Andrei cried. "Help me!"

He felt lost and weak like a child.

"Papa! Help me!" Andrei grabbed his shoulder. A sharp pain pierced it, but there was no blood, there was no wound.

What was happening?

"Papa!" Andrei cried again.

He reached for the body, but it was motionless. *Papa was dead. Killed by the tsar.* Andrei shook the body.

"Please don't be dead, Papa."

But his papa was dead, murdered twelve years ago . . . on Bloody Sunday. Andrei would never forget that day. He had so wanted to forget, to believe it had never happened. But in forgetting that, he had also forgotten his father altogether . . . and all those who loved him. How could pain and love be so deeply entwined?

But that is an idea too deep for me to ponder, Andrei thought. *It is more for the likes of Yuri. Let him fathom—*

Yuri . . . Mama . . . Talia . . .

"Andrei!"

He heard his name called and looked up, expecting to see his brother. But it was not. It was his friend Rudy. He started to acknowledge the man but had only opened his mouth when he felt a painful crack against his head. It knocked him over and all went momentarily black. He was only vaguely aware of an arm reaching down to lift him to his feet. He helped as much as he could, but his legs suddenly felt like limp rags, and with each movement he sensed his consciousness slipping away. That frightened him more than anything, for what if his memories left again? He struggled to keep his head, but the blackness was so strong, it enveloped him and he could not fight it.

––––––––––

When he awoke, he expected to look around and see Sonja's flat. But instead he saw from the cot on which he lay desks and chairs and file cabinets and several people. He was in the *Pravda* office. He tried to get up but his head throbbed when he moved it even a little. Reaching his hand to a particularly painful spot at the back of his head, he felt a lump. Removing his hand, he brought it forward and saw—blood. He felt woozy once again.

"Well, well, you are alive," came a familiar voice. Rudy.

"Yes . . ." Andrei replied weakly.

"You must start taking care of yourself, my friend. If I have to lug your hulk around again, I shall surely break my back." Rudy's tone was playful. In his eyes were affection and relief.

"I'm sorry—" But all at once the scene on the street returned to Andrei. And he remembered. "Rudy, I remembered!"

"You did? Everything?"

"All that is important, I think."

"I am happy for you, Andrei. Are they good memories?"

"Not all. My father was killed on Bloody Sunday. I think today's demonstration trigged those images from the past. I was shot, too, that day."

"No wonder you can't stand the sight of blood."

"But my mother and my brother are still here. And . . . Talia." Andrei paused as if savoring the truth. "The woman I love," Andrei said with a grin. "But I've never told her. And Rudy, I saw her—just before you found me. But I lost her again." He tried to get up once more, this time swinging his feet to the floor. But his head swam, though he resisted the urge to lie down again. "I've got to find her!"

"Of course you do, but I think it can wait until things quiet down out there."

"What's been happening?" The only reason Andrei did not persist in his desperate desire to find Talia was that he knew if he stood just then he would probably faint.

"The demonstrators reached the Tauride Palace. They actually arrested the president of the Soviet. Trotsky talked them into letting him go. But even then the Soviet would not support the demonstrators. They could have easily taken the power from the Provisional Government, but none were willing to make the decisive move. Then the Provisional Government played its trump card. They circulated rumors—"

"How long have I been out, Rudy?"

"Several hours. Time enough for the government to break up the demonstration. As I was saying, they circulated rumors among some of the key army regiments that were remaining neutral that Lenin is a German agent. They had some flimsy evidence made all the more believable when coupled with the rout in the recent war offensive."

"They are trying to blame that on Lenin? Ridiculous."

"Perhaps so, but it was enough to get the Preobrazhensky, the Semenovsky, and the Izmailovsky Guards to swing their support to the Provisional Government."

"And so it's over."

"Kerensky has issued warrants for Lenin, Zinoviev, and Trotsky's arrest, and any other Bolshevik leaders they can name. The Bolsheviks are being set up as scapegoats for the demonstrations. If only the government knew that it took Lenin as much by surprise as anyone."

"I still can't believe Lenin would betray Russia."

"It does not help his case that he traveled to Russia on a German train."

"No, it doesn't. Unfortunately, Lenin would do almost anything to gain power. But he is smart enough to know how even a hint of collusion with the Germans would hurt him in the long run."

"If he didn't, he knows now."

Suddenly, the front door of the room burst open. "We've got to get out of here!" the new arrival yelled. He was one of the *Pravda* staff. "Government troops have raided the Kshesinskaya Palace. Lenin escaped but many have been arrested."

Rudy turned to Andrei. "Can you walk?"

"I'll have to. Can I lean on you one more time?"

There was general mayhem in the office now as everyone began madly scurrying about, some trying to gather their belongings, others frantically pitching incriminating papers into the stove. Andrei got to his feet, using Rudy as a crutch. He tried to ignore the spinning room as he took a couple tentative steps.

He had barely moved a few inches from the cot when the doors crashed open once more. This time a dozen armed government troops stormed into the room. Shots were fired into the air and the frenzy of activity stopped short.

"All right!" ordered the leader of the troops. "Everyone against that wall."

The Bolsheviks complied, though they couldn't tell if they were about to be summarily executed. While three or four of the troops held rifles and machine guns on the Bolsheviks, the others ranged through the room smashing furnishings, dumping files, cutting upholstery with bayonets—in short, destroying all they could of the pesky little Bolshevik organ *Pravda*.

Andrei wondered if this was really the end. After all Lenin had been through over the years, could it really be over so quickly? But the worst of it to Andrei was that he really did not care. While his comrades looked in horror upon the destruction of their hopes and dreams, he could only think that this had never really been his dream. During the years of exile with Lenin, along with the more recent months, he had always been leading a double life. No wonder it had been so easy for him to succumb to amnesia. He had never in his life had a clear perception of who he was.

Except once.

"I don't hate the tsar, Papa. You taught me not to. That's why I'm asking to be part of this. When I grow up, I want to be able to say that I marched with the men who brought freedom to Russia. Please, Papa! Let me walk beside you."

That final talk with his father was clearer to him now than it had ever been before. That had been his dream.

The association with the Bolskeviks had, if anything, only muddled that dream.

And there had been one other important dream, one other thing that defined who he was—Talia. Only with her had he ever been the real Andrei. But his muddled perceptions had caused him to lose her, too. And now, staring down the barrel of a government rifle, he feared she would never be restored to him. His papa and mama had received a second chance when Papa miraculously returned from Siberia. But such miracles did not always happen. Life did not always have a happy ending.

"Move it," growled one of the troops, as if to confirm Andrei's fear. "You scum aren't going to stir up this city anymore."

He jabbed Andrei with his rifle, and with Rudy giving him support, they were herded outside and into a waiting truck. Within an hour, Andrei was processed into the Peter and Paul Fortress. He thought of the many great men who had spent time within those cold, dank cells— his own father had been one. He thought of rotting away in this prison and of life slipping away from him once more.

18

The July heat managed to penetrate the stout walls of the West End men's club where Lord Bruce MacDuff occasionally took his leisure when in London. The overhead fans turned lazily, stirring little, hardly even disturbing the haze of smoke from expensive cigars, pipe tobacco, and cigarettes. His companions seated around a card table had stripped to their shirtsleeves. Freddie had even unbuttoned his collar.

"If I can't open my collar here," he had defended himself when the others had taunted him, "then where, pray tell?"

"You are right, of course," chuckled Charlie. "No women, no collar buttons. It makes complete sense." He loosened his own button.

"Whose deal is it?" asked Gus. He was winning and did not not want his momentum broken.

"Perhaps we can take a bit of a breather," said Bruce. "And have a glass of sherry."

"That's all right for you, Finkie," said Gus. "You're losing."

"We're all losing, Gus," said the general. "None of us have a chance of gaining on you. I wouldn't be surprised if you had a card or two hiding up your sleeve."

Bruce signaled a waiter and in a few moments crystal glasses of fine sherry, along with a decanter, were placed on the table. Bruce struck a match and set it to a cigarette while the general and Charlie, the king's cousin, tamped tobacco into their pipes and lit them. Gus the banker and Freddie the shipping magnate lit up Cuban cigars. It was no coincidence they were all gathered together once more that warm summer day. Bruce had called them specifically, but saw no reason not to mix business with a little pleasure. However, after several games of faro, the time had come to get to the point of their meeting.

"So, Bruce, why don't you bring everyone up to date on our little pet project?" suggested the general.

"Perhaps we ought to have some sort of code name for this business," said Bruce.

"What?" said Charlie. "Something like 'operation blue blood'?"

"It's hardly an *operation*," said Gus, ever the conservative.

"I should think Bruce would like it to be otherwise," said Charlie sagely.

"I only want to do what is right," Bruce replied.

"For the moment, it appears there is nothing in Russia

to be alarmed over." Gus lifted his glass to his lips.

"I hope you're right." Bruce puffed his cigarette, then continued, "I have had word from my contact that others are attempting to pursue our same goals. The Dowager Empress is in the Crimea with some of the Grand Dukes, and they have apparently organized a rescue effort. But they are under as close scrutiny as the royal family. It is difficult to predict how effective they can be. Also I have been contacted directly by a Serge Markov who is with an organization called the Republican Center. They are interested in restoring Nicholas to the throne—of course a rescue would be part of this—and to that end are soliciting funds. Markov has been in contact with sympathizers in Madrid and Nice as well."

"Then the situation is well in hand," said Gus.

"For the time being it is status quo. Kerensky is still committed to protecting the royal family. We can as a group or individually funnel funds into these existing organizations. I plan to give a few thousand pounds to Markov, as I judge him to be sincere. However, I have yet to see any movement with real teeth in it."

"Then are you simply tossing your money into the trash bin?" questioned Freddie.

"I hope not. Markov will raise awareness of the situation, if nothing else. He is publishing and distributing leaflets in many European cities, and that will be money well spent. I still have not ruled out, however, a more personal part in the rescue—what was the name you used, Charlie?—Operation Blue Blood?"

A waiter approached the table. "Excuse me, gentlemen, but the evening papers have arrived." He passed one to each man.

The headline read: "New Russian insurrection barely contained."

The general was the first to look up after reading the article. "Incredible!" he breathed and took a long swallow of his sherry.

"I never dreamed the Bolsheviks could ever mount a viable opposition," said Gus. "Good heavens, if they take over the country I shudder at how it could affect the world economy. I am certainly no student of Marx, but his economic theses are frightening at best."

"Forget economics," said the general. "The Bolsheviks have leveled the loudest protest against Kerensky's mild treatment of the tsar. They would have the man tossed in their Fortress at the very least."

"They could never let the tsar live," said Charlie. "Nor the heir, nor even the tsar's brother. If the Bolsheviks usurped power, they could never live with the constant threat posed by a surviving monarch, even if he was exiled."

"But Lenin did *not* usurp power," said Gus. "The Provisional Government prevailed."

"Barely." Bruce tapped his cigarette on the edge of a brass ashtray. "Tens of thousands demonstrated against the government and even against the Soviet, which is supposed to represent the people. Even if the government won this time, they must realize their hold is tenuous at best."

"Still," said Freddie, "Lenin is in hiding, and several of the important leaders have been arrested. Do you really think Lenin can come back from that? Not to mention the accusations that he is in collusion with the Germans. That's what helped turn the tide against the Bolsheviks."

Bruce crushed out his cigarette. "I think it is time for me to go to Russia and see firsthand what is going on. It's the only way we will know for certain what to do."

"It's far too risky," said Gus. "I mean, I want to save the tsar, but is it really something any of us wants to risk his own life over?"

"You worry far too much, Gus," said Bruce, lighting another cigarette. "I can get into the country quite legitimately. I'll have no problem getting the proper papers. And even if everything isn't in perfect order, the country is so chaotic, I doubt anyone would notice or care."

The men all looked at one another. They realized now that since they had begun meeting and discussing a rescue of the tsar, they had been thinking mainly in terms of the *idea* of rescue. Actually going to the country, possibly sneaking about, or even physically removing the royal family from Russia had not really entered their minds. With the exception of Bruce. From the start he had known that he would do the thing, even if it meant by his own hand breaking into the palace, knocking out a guard or two, and leading the royals to safety. He would never have become involved in the first place if it had merely been a mental exercise.

He now faced his friends with a steely, determined gaze in his eye. And he prayed he had not misjudged them, and that in the end, these pampered gentlemen of British nobility would rise to the call and show themselves to be made of true British grit.

Freddie, the quietest of the lot, was the first to speak. He licked his lips nervously. He had not had to serve in the present war because of a slightly crippled leg. He had never fought a physical battle in his life. Not that he was in any way being called upon to do so now. Nevertheless, by supporting his friend he was taking on a burden that was for him as physical as might ever be expected of him.

"Listen here, Finkie. I ought to be able to get you a businessman's visa. I have a small office in Moscow, and couriers are coming and going all the time—well, not as often lately because of the difficulties, but it can be done. I should also be able to supply a vessel in the Baltic—for transport of the royals when and if that becomes necessary."

"Thank you, Freddie."

Everyone then fell in with their support, even Gus. Bruce thought he could be ready to go in a few weeks. Maybe in the meantime Kerensky would have found more legitimate means to get the tsar and his family away from Russia. But Bruce would be ready in any case.

19

After the July rising Prince Lvov resigned, and Kerensky took over the position of prime minister of the Provisional Government. He spent a great deal of his time visiting the Front and trying to bolster the morale of the troops, now seriously demoralized after the failed summer offensive. The rate of desertions rose to twelve thousand a week. The soldiers, many of them peasants, did not want to be killed before they could partake of the fruits of the revolution, specifically land ownership.

Those soldiers who did return home, however, quickly discovered that owning land in a time of huge food shortages and social and political chaos was hardly a boon. And things were only getting worse.

When Paul Burenin came to visit Anna, she listened halfheartedly to his account of how valiantly Kerensky was battling the tremendous obstacles facing him. She shocked him by commenting that Kerensky was making a huge mistake in keeping the war going.

"But, Anna, you don't understand," Paul tried patiently to explain. "Not only does it involve the honor of fulfilling our commitments, but the Allies are brokering large loans to us contingent upon our continued war effort. Our government, indeed our entire economy, might collapse without those loans. If you think there are shortages now—"

"Paul, even I can see that a huge percentage of those loans must go toward financing the war—manufacturing guns and such."

"And war production employs men, putting money in their pockets so they can buy bread."

"But there is no bread."

"Well, Anna, I won't argue the economic benefits of war when, in truth, I don't believe much in them myself. And Kerensky's motives are far less economic than moral."

An awkward silence followed as both tried to search for a new topic of conversation.

"How is Mathilde?" Anna asked finally. Shortly after the revolution, Paul's wife had been diagnosed with cancer.

"She has her good days and her bad. Yuri has increased her dose of pain medication. I fear she hasn't long."

"I am so sorry, Paul. You know that anytime you feel she needs more constant care, I would be more than happy to have her here. I know how demanding your duties in the government can be."

"I would rather she be close to me. I will resign my position if I must. I want to be with her at the . . . end." His voice became choked and sudden tears rose in his eyes. Anna reached out and took his hand in hers. "I love her so much. I don't know what I'll do without her." His voice trembled over the words. He had obviously been holding back his emotion over Mathilde's illness for a long time. "So much has been happening I haven't had time to let myself think of it."

At that moment, Daniel and Mariana returned home. They also did not bring good news. Mariana's travel papers were about to expire, and they had been haunting the immigration department trying to get an extension.

"There are literally thousands of others trying to get out of the country," Mariana said. "I'm on a waiting list, but it could take weeks, even months."

"One clerk had the nerve to suggest that I take the children and leave, with Mariana following later," said Daniel.

"I think you should," said Mariana, and a look passed between the couple, indicating this was a touchy subject.

"You only have a few months left on your visas."

"Why haven't you said anything to me sooner?" asked Paul. "I could probably get an approval from the prime minister himself."

"Until now we have wavered about leaving at all," said Daniel.

"I have wavered," corrected Mariana.

"I haven't helped," said Daniel with a conciliatory smile at his wife. "Russia has been a journalistic gold mine. I've done some of my best stuff these last few months."

"I can probably get you an extension, Mariana, at least until Daniel's visa expires. That would get you another few months with your mother, and Daniel a chance to see the revolution to its conclusion."

"A conclusion, you say. . . ?" queried Daniel.

"I have faith the government will stabilize soon."

"Even after the July business?"

"Kerensky is far more motivated than Lvov to implement the desires of the Proletariat. Kerensky is a man of the people, not a prince."

"What about the Proletariat's desires regarding the disposition of the tsar?" Without seeming even to realize it, Daniel was turning the conversation into an interview. He lacked only his pad and pencil in hand.

"If the people are appeased in other vital areas, I believe the new prime minister can convince them to support his commitment to protect the tsar. He does not want to become the Marat of the Russian Revolution, and I believe deep in their hearts the Russian people do not want another Reign of Terror."

"Can I quote you on that, Uncle Paul?"

"Now, now, gentlemen," said Anna. "Is there nothing else we can talk about?"

But it was hard indeed, in light of all that was happening in the world, in their country, and in their personal lives, to come up with much trivial discussion. Eventually

Paul took his leave and Daniel went to spend some time with his children while Anna and Mariana went to the kitchen to see what to do about dinner.

———————

In the midst of holding together a shaky government and overseeing an even shakier war machine, Kerensky had to also make some decision regarding the royal family. The government might have blocked the July uprising, but the fact that it had come so close to failing proved that the government, at best, was unstable. As the furor over the rumors about Lenin's German connections began to die down, it became apparent that the Bolsheviks were still a strong voice. They took any opportunity to spread their propaganda among the Imperial guards at the palace. Also, the nearness of Tsarskoe Selo to Kronstadt Naval Base, which was growing more and more rebellious, made the tsar's continued residence risky at best. It was imperative to get the royal family away from the center of activity. "Out of sight, out of mind," or at least Kerensky hoped so.

He made another appeal to England. A cruiser was requested to meet the royal family in Murmansk, and a promise was obtained from the German government not to attack the cruiser. But Ambassador Buchanan, in tears, had to deliver his government's refusal to Kerensky. The British Labor Party was in an uproar over the mere suggestion of offering asylum to the tsar, and there were still those in Britain who believed Alexandra was a German spy. At any rate, the British could not aid relatives of the German Kaiser—which the Romanovs were—no matter that half the royal houses in Europe were related in some way.

Kerensky again ruled out Livadia as a possible destination, though he knew the family greatly desired to go there. He simply could not guarantee a safe journey south, which would take them through many industrial towns that were heavily anti-tsar. Other possible destinations were also ruled out for similar reasons. He finally settled on Tobolsk in Siberia. The town was remote, without even a railway terminal. They would have to travel by rail to Tiumen, then by steamer on the Tura and Tobol rivers to Tobolsk.

"We must move you for your own safety," he told the tsar just a few days before the planned departure.

"I am mostly concerned for my family," said the tsar. "As you well know, Baby—that is, Alexis—is in a delicate state."

"We will take that into every consideration."

"Very well," said the tsar. "Do you have any idea how long we will be away?"

"I cannot say, but I feel confident that after the Constituent Assembly meets in November, you will no longer be under such constraints."

"We will be free?"

"I am confident of that fact."

"That is good news. Where are we going now?"

"I cannot say. Again, for your safety, I wish it to be kept in strict secrecy. I would suggest, however, that you pack plenty of warm clothes."

"I see . . ." It was obvious the tsar understood they would not be traveling south, but rather east.

"This is entirely for your safety," Kerensky repeated, perhaps more to convince himself than the tsar.

The tsar leveled an intense gaze at Kerensky. "I'm not afraid. If you say it must be so, then it must be so. We trust you."

It was quite a moment for Kerensky. Not long before, the tsar's wife had wanted him hanged. Now the tsar himself was placing implicit faith in him. He intended to live up to that faith.

Only four others in the government knew of this plan.

Seldom in Russia was a secret kept so well. Yuri certainly had no hint of it when he was called to Tsarskoe Selo to consult in the case of Countess Benckendorff, who was suffering from severe bronchitis. But he knew it was an illness that Dr. Botkin could have easily treated himself. Thus, when he asked Yuri to bring a variety of medications, few of which were standard in the treatment of bronchitis, he suspected something was afoot.

He arrived during the celebration of the tsarevich's thirteenth birthday. Alexandra had requested that an icon from a local church be brought, and it was carried through the village by a procession of priests to the chapel. There prayers were offered not only for the boy but also for a safe journey for the family. It was quite a moving sight, especially when even the soldiers came forward to kiss the icon.

Yuri also crossed himself in reverence. It moved him to tears when the young tsarevich embraced him and whispered in his ear, "We are leaving, and I want to say good-bye and thank you."

"It has been an honor to serve you, Your Highness," Yuri said simply. He did not ask all the questions that the boy's words raised in his mind. He would talk to Dr. Botkin later.

The tsar also shook his hand and thanked him, but the tsaritsa completely ignored him. It was the first time Yuri had actually seen Alexandra since the revolution, but her obvious snubbing made him wonder if rumors of his part in Rasputin's death had come to her. Or perhaps she just remembered Yuri's hostility toward the man when he had come to treat the tsarevich. He had heard how embittered she had become, and now he could see the truth of it in her pinched features and cold eyes. She appeared to have aged ten years in the last six months.

Yuri felt only pity for her. She might have made many mistakes as a woman, a mother, and a monarch, but Yuri was all but certain that her motivations had always been out of love and loyalty to husband, family, and country. He wanted to approach her and tell her he understood, but she was so unapproachable that he hung back. Perhaps one day he would be able to *show* her by helping to rescue her and her dear family.

When the tsar's family adjourned to their private quarters, Dr. Botkin took Yuri on a walk about the grounds, the only place they could be certain there were no unwanted listeners, although even then they had to be careful.

"The tsarevich mentioned something about leaving," Yuri said.

"We leave in a matter of days, perhaps hours," Botkin replied.

"You are going also?"

"I will not desert them now. My family understands, and I hope they will join me when I can give them a destination."

"So, you don't know where?"

"Kerensky is keeping it a secret for security. I'm all but certain it will be somewhere in Siberia."

"So, the Provisional Government is finally paying Nicholas back by sending him to where he sent so many revolutionaries."

"No, I'm certain that isn't the motivation. The tsar trusts Kerensky's motives and so do I. This can actually work to our advantage." Botkin smiled at Yuri's look of skepticism. "An escape would be next to impossible in and around St. Petersburg. That won't be the case in the outlands. You must tell that to your associates. We have not lost hope, so please, neither must you."

"How will we know where they have taken you?"

"I'm sure it can't be kept a secret much longer. I only hope we can get away before it gets out so that the radicals cannot attempt to waylay us. That's as much as anyone can hope for."

Yuri glanced around as they walked. It was a balmy

August evening, still very light because the White Nights were upon them. "We only have a couple of months before winter sets in, less in Siberia. That may make any attempts at rescue difficult until spring."

"How strong is your organization?"

"I really don't know. There is a group in England, but I don't know their size. Here in Russia there is only myself and another that I know of. I do know that money is no problem."

"That's good. Have you contacted other loyal monarchists? There are several groups working toward the same ends as you."

"I don't know, Doctor," Yuri replied honestly. "Thus far, I am merely a messenger."

"Before you leave I will give you a couple of names that may be of use to you."

After Yuri gave the countess a cursory examination and deposited his cache of medicines, which he now knew were for the purpose of bolstering supplies that might not be readily available in a remote town, he bid Botkin good-bye. The two doctors embraced, and as they did so, Botkin slipped a note to Yuri.

Yuri left the palace wondering when he would see his friend and the royal family again. He tried to match Botkin's hopeful mood but instead felt sad, as if the departure of the Romanovs from Petrograd was something very final. That with them would go an era never again to be revisited.

III

REVOLUTIONS AND REBIRTH
Fall 1917

20

Andrei was miserable. The fact that incarceration in the Peter and Paul Fortress amounted to a badge of honor among revolutionaries meant nothing. Not now. And it was also no comfort to know that the likes of Trotsky and Kamenev had also been imprisoned.

"Andrei, you are driving me crazy with that infernal pacing," said Rudy from where he lay on his bunk in the same cell as Andrei.

Andrei hardly even realized he was pacing, it had become second nature to him. He stopped and faced his friend. If only Rudy had gotten free, at least he could have somehow notified Andrei's family. But then, Andrei had not had time to say anything to Rudy before their capture, so there would have been no one—indeed, there *was* no one—to tell his family why he had disappeared once again. They must be going out of their minds. If they had not finally given up on him. Mama would never do that, but Yuri was, no doubt, furious with him. And Talia . . . what must she think? Perhaps knowing of his amnesia she would understand. She had no idea that he had recovered.

Still, it didn't really matter what they thought. What mattered was that he was stuck here unable to do anything about . . . anything!

"How long have we been in this place?" Andrei asked. Rudy had been keeping a meticulous record of the days by carving marks in the wall by his bed with a rusty nail he had found.

"A little more than two months. Oh, but do you want the exact count?" He started to count his marks.

"Never mind!" Andrei plopped down on his cot with such force it was a miracle the flimsy thing did not buckle in the middle. He ran his hand through his hair, which was getting quite long and unruly. "Rudy, this is the worst thing that has ever happened to me!"

Rudy laughed. "Oh yes. It is far worse than getting shot and nearly dying and having amnesia."

"What good does it do to have my memory back?" Andrei stopped, not really expecting an answer. Rudy had heard it all many times before in the last two months. "You know my father was imprisoned here." Rudy had heard that, too, but Andrei was running out of conversation. "I never told you the whole story about my father."

"Is that so? And why not, when I am dying of boredom?"

"I've always been ashamed—"

"That he died marching for freedom on Bloody Sunday? I can't believe that."

Andrei leaned back against the cold, damp stone wall. "No, I was never ashamed of that. You see, my father was an aristocrat—a nobleman of the highest order, actually."

"No!"

"Prince Sergei Fedorcenko . . . it actually feels rather good to say that name now. I abandoned it many years ago, and the heritage that went with it. I would have died of shame if my revolutionary comrades had discovered that I was a prince of Russia. Even now, the prince part makes my stomach feel strange. Because he was a fugitive, my father also gave up using his title, although I don't think he ever felt comfortable with it either. You know what, Rudy? I'm going to take back my true surname. What do you think? Andrei Sergeiovich Fedorcenko."

"It's a good name, Andrei," said Rudy earnestly. "I'm glad you left off the prince, though. It wouldn't go over very well at Party headquarters."

"Bah! I've very nearly had it with them. I'm still wondering about those rumors of Lenin's ties to Germany."

"You don't believe them, do you?"

"Lenin is definitely no German spy. But I wouldn't put it past him to cut deals with them in order to achieve power." Sporadic news came to the prisoners, and Andrei had heard that, though Lenin was still in hiding, anti-Bolshevik sentiment caused by the rumors had already begun to blow over. "I guess it doesn't matter either way. That isn't at the core of my discontent with the Party."

"Nor mine."

"Come on, Rudy. You've never admitted it, but it wasn't ideology that made you join the Party in the first place, was it? You joined to keep track of me, didn't you?"

"Do you mean you doubt that I am a true Bolshevik?" Rudy spoke with mock affront.

"You are no more one than I am."

"Then you are not?"

"I don't think so, not anymore. They have done nothing but cause strife since the revolution began. Because of it the government has never had a chance to get stable. And who suffers but the very people Lenin purports to want to help. When the revolution was all about philosophy and dreaming, Lenin's ways were tolerable. But now that they are being put into action, they leave a bad taste in my mouth. And now that I have my memory back, I know my family would not approve. Talia would not approve. And that means a great deal to me. I don't know why it didn't before. I suppose I was just stupid. I think losing my memory somehow made me smarter."

"Then what shall we do when we get out of here?"

"We are in a rather ironic position. While the Provisional Government remains in power, we are likely to remain right here. But if the Bolsheviks usurp power, we will be released. So, who do we cheer for?"

"I for one—"

But Rudy never finished. There was commotion and excited voices in the outside corridor. Andrei and Rudy jumped up and went to the door of the cell but could see little through the tiny barred window.

"What's going on?" Andrei called. Several others in the cell block were doing the same.

"Looks like there's been another coup attempt," a guard shouted so all could hear. "Backed by the Kadets and other moderates, and some on the right, General Kornilov tried to form a dictatorship. He wanted to destroy the Soviet and hang traitors like Lenin."

"Ha!" someone yelled. "Let him try."

"Oh, if that's going to be your attitude, maybe I won't be so generous as to give you the news."

Someone else yelled, "Never mind him. Tell us, was Kornilov successful?"

"Of course not! And you scum better be glad he wasn't. Word is, because the Bolsheviks helped mobilize the people against the general, the government is considering releasing you."

Andrei threw his arms around Rudy, fairly dancing with joy. "Did you hear? We're going to get out!"

"Yes, that's great." But Rudy did not seem as enthusiastic as he should have, in Andrei's mind at least.

"What's wrong?"

"Nothing. This is great news. Except . . . I don't know, Andrei. After what you just said, and what I have been feeling all along about the Bolsheviks, this doesn't set completely well with me. It's apparent that the Bolsheviks helped the Provisional Government—whom they have been ranting against for months!"

"Lenin must have seen something in it for himself."

"More than just the release of us poor prisoners."

"I must agree. I suppose one positive outcome of this entire affair is that it will pretty much silence the moderate voice in Russia."

"And that is a good thing, isn't it, Andrei?"

"I always thought so." Andrei went back to his cot and stretched out full length on it, his feet hanging over the edge at least ten inches. Crossing his arms under his head he stared up at the ceiling. "Do you want to know the truth of it, Rudy? I am burned out completely with politics. Moderates, socialists, right-wing, left-wing . . . they can all have it. I only want to get out of here and have a life with my Talia."

But it seemed, as with everything else in Russia, that the hoped-for release was not going to happen as quickly as Andrei desired. As more days and weeks passed, he became more and more disenchanted—with politics, and with life in general.

It only made matters worse when they learned that Trotsky and Kamenev and several others had been released. The minor Bolsheviks like Andrei had obviously been forgotten. Maybe they were doomed to rot within these dank, grim walls. He wouldn't be the first. But it seemed so very ironic that it should happen now when revolution and freedom had finally come to Russia.

21

The attempted Kornilov coup had an interesting effect on political alignment in Russia. For one thing, because of Kornilov's military ties, it put the entire army leadership into a bad light. The masses, including common soldiers, became far less tolerant of officers and anyone with even the faintest link to the tsarist regime. But more than that, it put the Bolshevik Party back in business, as it were.

Although the social revolutionaries, of which Paul Burenin and Alexander Kerensky were a part, were still the largest party, they were coming more to represent the petty bourgeois rather than the peasantry. The Mensheviks, too, were drawing support from a similar class. Thus the soldiers and the workers, by far the most vocal groups, were left to be exploited by the Bolsheviks. And gradually, these two groups began to send more and more Bolsheviks to represent them in the Soviets.

Shortly after Trotsky was released from prison, he managed to be elected chairman of the presidium of the Petrograd Soviet—the presidium being a sort of board of directors of the Soviet. And this trend continued throughout Russia, most significantly in Moscow, which also seated a Bolshevik chairman. But even this did not satisfy Lenin, who was weary with meetings and talk. From his hiding place in Finland he began pressing—indeed, hammering and raving would better describe his methods—for the Bolsheviks to organize an armed rising. "Delay means death," he urged. Now the time was right.

Kerensky's position in all this was becoming untenable. His stand against Kornilov turned the army officers against him while the army in general was completely demoralized. This in turn hindered the war effort and, as a result, made the Allies pressure and threaten the Provisional Government even more than previously. As if this were not enough, the Soviets withdrew their support of Kerensky as their leadership was increasingly dominated by Bolsheviks.

As the month of October came, Russia was, more than ever before, a nation ready to explode at the seams.

———————

It was a rare occurrence when anyone in the household arrived home later than Yuri. But he was sitting in the kitchen around ten in the evening having a cup of tea with Katya when Daniel came home and joined them.

"I'm exhausted," Daniel said as he gratefully cupped his hands around a glass of tea Katya had drawn for him from the samovar. "And not from actually *doing* anything. It's entirely from listening to yet another gathering of Russians endlessly debate the most minor issues."

"So, what gathering this time?" asked Yuri.

"The Democratic conference Kerensky called. It's obviously a desperate attempt of his to get support and to begin priming delegates to the Constituent Assembly next month. Tonight was the last day of seven, and I can see little that has been accomplished. On the first day, the Bolsheviks made sure to arrive *after* Kerensky's opening speech. But the biggest irony was that the naval guards Kerensky had brought in to protect the delegates from the Bolsheviks ended up being won over by Trotsky and protecting him instead! In spite of that, I heard Lenin was furious that any Bolsheviks attended the conference at all."

"How will it all end?" sighed Yuri, not really expecting an answer.

"I am more certain than ever that things don't look good for Kerensky," said Daniel. "And, if you are up for it at this hour, perhaps we can talk about the business with the tsar."

"Why don't I leave you two men to yourselves," Katya said, rising. "But, Yuri, don't be too long. You need your rest." She kissed her husband's forehead and exited the kitchen.

"The most peculiar thing about it," Daniel continued when they were alone, "is if you get away from these political meetings, life in Russia continues almost as usual. You can still get a good meal at Constant's or the Bear. The elite continue to have their dinner parties. The *khvosts* are still present. Workers go to their jobs and weave cloth or make war material. Mingling with common folk, I get the sense no one really wants another uprising. But, Yuri, it's going to come. I can practically feel it in my bones like an old man can feel the coming of a storm."

"And from what I hear you saying," said Yuri, "and indeed, many saying, Kerensky will probably not survive the next coup."

"At this point, I believe the workers, the soldiers, the people in general will support anyone who can guarantee peace."

"That won't be Kerensky, then."

"Not unless he makes a one hundred and eighty degree

turn—and that is not likely to happen. That is why we must begin to act more aggressively in our quest to free the tsar. I've had a note from Bruce responding to the information you gave me about the tsar's move to Siberia. He agrees it is time to act. He doesn't want to be like so many of the other rescue organizations—all bark, no bite. He is ready to come to Russia. And now that we know the tsar is in Tobolsk, I'm certain we will set up our organization there."

"Organization?" Yuri said. "There are only three of us, aren't there?"

"That is another matter Bruce would like to see remedied. We ought to be considering others to bring in with us. I've got some feelers out, but it isn't easy to find appropriate individuals, especially in the present political climate. If you speak to the wrong person, you are likely to find yourself in hot water."

"I'll give the matter consideration," said Yuri.

"We need to find people we can really trust. If only we could find Andrei," Daniel mused.

"We have looked everywhere since Talia saw him. I even ran into Stephan Kaminsky who said he wondered for months what became of Andrei."

"To be honest," Daniel said, "I'm beginning to think poor Talia had been seeing ghosts."

"She, too, is beginning to doubt what she saw. But, regardless, Daniel, what help do you think Andrei could be? He would be the last person eager to rescue the tsar. Wouldn't he see him as the supreme enemy?"

"Perhaps, but I've been thinking that if he is alive, and if he is suffering from amnesia as Talia reports, and if he does get his memory back—"

"Those are a lot of *ifs*."

"True, but I believe God can use such experiences to change men. I have been praying for that. Andrei was never a hardened Bolshevik, nor was he a hard man. He was certainly never dogmatic about politics—"

"I recall a few discussions with him that certainly bordered on the dogmatic." Yuri almost smiled. Such memories now seemed pleasant ones.

"He wasn't that way in spiritual matters." Daniel rose and drew himself another cup of tea. "He could never deny the existence of God entirely. The faith taught to him by your parents was just too integral to be ignored. And for that reason I truly believe God can and will work in him. Just as we can't give up hope that he is physically alive, we can't despair about his spiritual life. If Andrei were here, and if he thought innocent people were in danger, he would do what he could to save them."

"Well, he isn't here, so it is no use even discussing it." Yuri paused, then shook his head sadly. "I wish he were here. I truly miss him. We had our differences, but there was always a deep bond between us that nothing could sever." He glanced down at the fading scar on his index finger where he and Andrei and Talia had sealed a childhood pledge. "Oh, Andrei," he sighed, "come back to us. . . ."

"Amen," said Daniel reverently, realizing Yuri's words were also a fervent prayer.

At that moment, a knock sounded at the front door. The two men exchanged bemused looks. Could their prayers be answered so quickly? Saying nothing, Yuri jumped up and hurried to answer the door lest it wake the rest of the household.

On opening the door, he beheld not the face of his brother, but rather that of a stranger. At least he appeared a stranger on first glance, then there did seem something vaguely familiar about him.

"Forgive me for intruding at this late hour," said the man.

"What can I do for you?" asked Yuri.

By now Daniel had come into the foyer also and was looking on.

"Of course, I can't expect that you should recognize—"

"Peter!" Yuri exclaimed, finally realizing who it was. He was his grandfather Viktor's faithful servant.

It had been years since he had seen him, though it had only been two years since Yuri had seen his grandfather on that wonderful Christmas holiday in 1915. Only two years! It seemed so much longer. Viktor had been to the city again, but Yuri had been at the Front and had missed him. Since then, Viktor, now eighty-two, had not been up to much travel and had remained peacefully ensconced on his Crimean estate.

Suddenly the full implications of Peter's visit alone struck Yuri. "Peter, is Grandfather—?"

"No, dear boy. He is well. May I come in so that we can talk?"

"How thoughtless of me!" Yuri motioned the servant in as Daniel stepped forward and took his hat and coat.

As they went to the parlor, Peter said, "I know it is late. I just arrived by train and felt that with the uncertainty of life these days, I should not procrastinate my mission. However, would it be possible to wake Princess Anna?"

Yuri had not heard his mother referred to as princess for years. But Peter was from the old school. Yuri went to his mother's room and, as gently as possible, woke her. He tried to allay her alarm before he returned to the parlor while she quickly made herself presentable in order to join them. Within ten minutes they were all seated in the parlor, and Peter began to explain his "mission."

"There has been trouble at the estate down south," Peter began. "It is nothing more than what has been happening throughout the country, but in the past, Prince Viktor has remained somewhat immune, probably because he has always limited his household staff to a very few faithful servants. Recently there was an uprising among the local peasantry, and some hooligans who were totally unconnected to the prince raised havoc on the estate. The stable was burned, as was one of the older vineyards. Princess Sarah was caught in the melee and suffered a broken arm. Otherwise she is well, as is everyone else, thank God. The incident made the prince consider a move he felt he could no longer avoid. He and the princess have decided to leave Russia. An opportunity arose through a contact of Princess Sarah's who is with the British consulate in Yalta. They will travel to England, and, in fact, may be en route even as I speak."

"I think that is a wise decision," said Anna. "I wouldn't say this to Prince Viktor, but the hardships of life these days are far too difficult for the elderly. I am relieved they will be safe."

"He has not left without considering his family in the North—that is to say, you and your children, Princess Anna." Peter paused and held out a leather satchel he had brought with him. "This is for you. It contains several family papers, as much money as he could spare, and a letter describing the whereabouts of other valuables that he secreted in a hidden vault on the estate. Perhaps one day he will return and retrieve his possessions, but he realizes he is no longer a young man and will probably live out his last days in England. In that case, perhaps you or one of his grandchildren will someday be able to recover the items."

"How sad to think we may not see him again," mused Anna. "He is one of the finest men I have ever known. Even when he was a man of power and influence, he never lost his basic humanity. He was always kind even to a simple peasant girl."

"I believe he would say, Princess Anna, that he was kind to that peasant girl because he always held a great deal of respect and admiration for her."

Anna blushed but was pleased. "And what will you do, Peter?"

"I could not leave Russia, though Prince Viktor would have taken me with him. I have a sister in Moscow whom I would like to visit. Then . . . I don't know. I am too old myself to support revolutions and such. I greatly miss the old days. I suppose I will just live out my days feeding pigeons in a Moscow park."

"Do you have a place to stay tonight?"

"The prince gave me enough money to live quite comfortably for a long time, and he provided for my travel expenses here as well, including a hotel."

"You are more than welcome to stay here and save your money," said Anna. "But to be honest, I can only offer you a bed on the floor because all our other beds, and even some of the floor space, are quite full."

"Thank you, but I rather fancy the luxury of a hotel for a night."

They visited for a short time more, then Peter took his leave. Anna, Yuri, and Daniel sat in the parlor and just stared at the satchel for a few minutes. Then Anna pushed it toward Yuri.

"Why don't you open it, son?"

With a certain amount of reverence, Yuri fingered the fine leather for a few moments before lifting the clasp.

22

The first thing Yuri withdrew from the satchel was an ink drawing of a young woman. He had never seen her before in person, but he knew who it was from photographs and a large oil portrait he had seen hanging at Prince Viktor's Crimean estate. Yuri handed it to his mother.

Anna looked at the drawing and gasped with surprised pleasure. "How wonderful! It's Princess Katrina."

Daniel leaned forward to have a look. "She was beautiful, wasn't she? And so like Mariana."

Anna felt a paper attached to the back of the drawing and turned it over to find a letter. " 'The original oil is locked in my vault,' " Anna read out loud, " 'but I thought you might like this little sketch I made from the oil better than a mere photograph. However, I have also enclosed several family photographs for you.' "

Just then Yuri took a packet of about a dozen photographs from the satchel and passed them to Anna. She quickly looked at each photo, then handed them one by one to Daniel. Yuri looked over Daniel's shoulder. There was a formal photograph of Viktor and his first wife, Natalia, and one of them and their children at about ages ten and fourteen. Another was of Sergei alone in his army uniform, just as Anna remembered him when he went to fight in the Balkan war. There were also more recent ones, of weddings, babies, and one Anna had never seen of Andrei standing next to one of his paintings at his one and only gallery showing. Anna tarried over this one a moment longer than the others and ran a finger gently over the face of her youngest son.

Sighing heavily, she said, "How kind of Prince Viktor to send these." Her voice was shaky.

"Mama—" Yuri began.

"Yuri," Daniel interrupted, "what else is in the satchel?"

Yuri glanced at his brother-in-law and received a silent but cautionary look. He knew they had firmly agreed not to tell Anna about Talia's encounter. He reminded himself how awful it would be for his mother to have her hopes raised only to discover Andrei was lost to them again. Yuri was devastated himself, and he could only imagine how his mother might react.

He said no more and took another envelope from the satchel. Opening this, he found a thick bundle of rubles— easily several thousand. Another envelope contained a three-page letter written in Viktor's precise hand. This he gave to Anna, who set it aside to be read later.

The final item was quite large. Actually, there were four books bound together by a cord. On closer inspection

Yuri saw that three were bound diaries, and the fourth was a ledgerlike book. Opening this, he saw that inside were written diarylike entries. The handwriting was very familiar. He glanced up at his mother as he handed them to her.

"Your papa's diaries," she said. "I feel so bad that I lost track of these. You and . . . your brother should have had them long ago. Viktor took your father's death so hard—you know, it came just as they had renewed and deepened their relationship. I thought these might help him through the difficult time. Then I forgot about them and I suppose he did, too. Ah, well, they are back where they belong now." She gave them to Yuri. "These are yours, son. Your father always intended that when you were older he'd share them with you and Andrei. This must surely be the appropriate time."

Yuri lay the books in his lap. He wanted to open them right then but wanted to be alone when he did so. Yet he didn't want to be rude to his mother and Daniel. Anna must have sensed his dilemma.

"It is late," she said. "Tomorrow's visits to the *khvosts* will start early." She rose and kissed her son and her son-in-law each on the cheek before departing.

Daniel also rose. "What about you, Yuri? You must be beat."

"I'll be along in a few moments. I just . . . need to be alone a minute."

"Okay, see you in the morning."

———

Alone in the parlor, Yuri opened the books and arranged them in order by the dates written on the inside covers. The earliest one was the ledger. The opening date was January 10, 1882. The entry read:

> *I have been feeling a great need lately to set my experiences to paper. Writing has always helped me to put my*

emotions and ideas into better perspective. And now more than ever, I have many emotions I must sort through. I asked Robbie for some paper, and he found for me instead this old, blank ledger. He said, laughing in that infectious way of his, "We never have money in this mission, so we have no need of this ledger."

Ah, Robbie . . . meeting this man will surely change my life, but before I speak of him, I will write about my experiences before he came along. I will write about Siberia. In a way, I would like to forget that terrible time in my life, yet to do so would make it impossible to fully explain the progression of the changes that are beginning to take place within me . . .

For the next several pages Yuri read not only about his father's imprisonment in the hard labor camp at the Kara Mines, but also about the preceding months. Sergei wrote about the crime he had committed—killing his commanding officer in order to prevent the execution of supposed enemy prisoners—including old men, several women, and even a child.

I do not justify my deed. I was crazed at the time, completely unhinged by the stench of death and battle. Yet, I must say that faced with the same choice, I might well have still pulled that trigger even had I been in my right mind. I don't know. I'll never know. All I know is that I killed a man, and that act has forever changed my life, not only the direction of my life, but the state of my heart and soul. Even in receiving absolution from God for my deed, I still must carry with me the awful knowledge that I am capable of such a deed. I suppose the image of what I did will always dwell within me at some level.

Yuri nodded and his chest tightened. He understood painfully well what his father was saying. And if Sergei's crime sent him to the prison of Siberia, Yuri's had sent him to a prison just as well, not of snow and ice, but of despair. He forced himself to read on and found himself weeping as he read of his father's despair, accompanied also by such physical hardships Yuri could hardly imagine them. Yuri, of course, knew of his father's experiences, but Sergei never dwelt upon them. He never said to his children, "You're complaining about walking to school? I had to walk practically all the way across Siberia." Or, "You will not eat these vegetables? I had to eat insects and roots when I was in Siberia, and I was grateful for them."

No, Sergei would instead get a faraway look in his eyes and a slight smile on his lips. Once when Yuri was complaining about some silly thing, he recalled his father saying, "Ah, Yuri, my dear boy, I am so thankful we are here together, and I can listen to you, even if you are not exactly happy. I once thought I would never be so blessed as to hear the voice of my own son. And I cherish it. I cherish you."

The stories of Siberia, though they were few indeed, were always more like a soldier's old war stories. Sergei stripped away the terror and utter desolation. He always tried to find the good of it. But the diary was not written with a child's sensibilities in mind. Sergei must have felt the need to "pull no punches." He even wrote that he hoped in writing it all down it would purify his heart a little of the experience.

Yuri exhaled a relieved sigh when he came to the part about when Sergei came to the mission in China.

> I came to China as completely broken as a man could be. Even escape from Kara did not instill hope because I felt I had sunk so low that I could never be restored to my former life, not to mention my dear Anna. I had not exactly become an atheist, but rather I believed that if some Father in heaven existed to whom one might go for succor, what would it matter? The harsh realities of what my life had become would not change one iota. If there were some heavenly Savior, He would do better to expend His saving energies elsewhere. I felt that I was not only beyond saving, but that I did not deserve it. If only I were

an atheist it would have been so much better, because then I would not know what I was losing. But it shows my state of mind that I forgot, or would not let myself remember, the simple truths of faith that I heard often from Anna and Yevno and others like them. I considered myself a man without a scrap of manhood left within me. I was less than nothing. I had failed in everything—with my family, with my father, with the only woman I ever loved. I failed my country, my career . . . everything!

But now, after nearly two months at the mission, my eyes are at last being opened. In Robbie I have met a man whose own life could have sent him to the depths of despair. He lost a woman he loved to another man. Then, in running from his heartache, he found his escape to be fraught with hardships and betrayal. He came upon the mission just as I have done, a man filled with bitterness and frustration. There he met and fell in love with the daughter of the head of the mission. The bitter walls around him began to be softened by her sweet spirit and her strong faith. Then danger struck, and in a battle for this woman's life, Robbie lost an arm. Robbie admits that he had always been a man whose estimation of his worth had been wrapped up in his physical self. Thus the loss of an arm and the accompanying sense of dependency was a terrible blow for him. It was then that he could have truly abandoned hope, as I had done. If not then, he could have done so after the woman he loved and married died of a terminal illness.

Instead, by the example of the woman he loved and her wise father, Robbie began to see what it really meant to be a man. I see now that Robbie and I trod very similar paths, although I do not think I linked my manhood as much to the physical as he did. Rather, for me, it was bound up with honor and success (my limited concept of these things) and how others saw me. I had always viewed myself as a rebel of sorts, at least against the ways of my father. However, I see now that it still mattered very much to me how he and others perceived me. That I was essentially a failure even at my rebellion was an irony, to say the least.

At any rate, as with Robbie, my path led me to confront my manhood. And to do this it seemed only natural to look—as Robbie had done—to the prime example of manhood, Jesus Christ. Coming from a religious background that so emphasized the suffering Christ, the idea of Jesus as a man was quite a leap. But in a way, Christ's suffering was also the essence of his manhood. Here is a man who laid down everything usually associated with manhood. He became reviled, mocked, and suffered the most ignominious manner of death known in his time.

Yet Christ's response to all of this was not bitter rancor, but rather forgiveness. And surrender. To many men these are not the most manly of responses. Wholeness found in forgiveness? Strength found in surrender? It is so upside-down from what you would think. And I would doubt its validity if I was not faced daily with the results of such unusual thinking in the person of Robbie Taggart.

I spent much of my time at the mission studying this man Jesus, and also two of his sons—Robbie and his father-in-law, the head of the mission—whom I greatly respect. As I write this today, I am growing closer than ever to truly understanding these things. But I have never been a man of impulse. If I am to accept the things I am learning at the mission, and model my life after them, I will do so after much deep consideration.

Yuri read on until he came to the entry for March 5, 1882.

The official celebration of Epiphany was three months ago, but it was today, a mere hour ago, that I celebrated my personal epiphany—the day my Lord Jesus Christ was revealed to me in a personal way. Today my search, begun at a mission in China, came to a glorious culmination. I left the mission a couple of months ago after I found a berth as a seaman on a ship headed west. I could not sleep this evening, so I went up to the deck, as has often become my habit, just to think and enjoy the night sky. We were sailing along the west coast of Africa under full canvas. The sky was cloudy, so the reflection of the

moon was dulled a bit. But suddenly other far more im-
portant things became crystal clear to me. My bitterness
toward my father, my resentments toward God, and,
most sadly, my own self-denigration.

I fell on my knees there on the deck at the bow of the
ship, where, oddly enough, I was completely alone, as if
God himself had arranged this precise moment. I heard
myself cry, "I don't want to live like this anymore! Please
take away the anger and bitterness and unforgiveness in
my heart. I have not been the man I should have been—
not to my family, my country . . . not even to myself. But
I want to be, God. I want to be a MAN! I want to be
whole—"

But Yuri could read no more. His eyes had become so
full of tears the words on the page had blurred. How
could his father have known? For it was as if the words
his father had cried thirty-five years ago were identical to
the words Yuri himself had cried so often in the last year.

"I don't want to live like this anymore!"

But now, through his father's words and experiences,
Yuri knew the answer to that cry. Forgiveness and surrender. And like his father had in this Robbie Taggart, Yuri
also had an example to follow—his own father. That day
on the ship Sergei finally was able to forgive not only
those he thought had hurt him, but also the God he believed had forsaken him. And he had also forgiven his
worst enemy—himself.

All at once the journal slipped from Yuri's hands, and
he found himself kneeling in front of the chair on which
he had been sitting. Yuri decided then and there he was
going to do only one thing differently from his father. He
was not going to ponder this thing any longer. He was
ready. There was no need for him to suffer a moment
longer. He could be the man he longed to be, right now.

"Oh, God, forgive me for being so dense and so dull.
Help me to cease this wallowing in self-pity. Help me to
become a real man, a man my father would be proud of.

I surrender to you, for it is so very apparent I am incapable of success on my own."

Fifteen minutes later, a soft voice floated to Yuri's ears as he still knelt in the parlor.

"Yuri, are you alright?" It was Katya.

He glanced up and smiled, beckoning her to come to him.

"Yes, I believe I am," he said. "I believe I finally am."

"I haven't seen you smile like that in such a long time." She came close and lay a hand on his shoulder.

"Let me tell you about it, Katya."

And although it was the early hours of the morning and he had had no sleep since the previous morning, Yuri felt oddly revived. He and Katya talked until the first rays of the sun pierced the sky. By the time the first family member rose from bed, Katya had knelt down next to her husband and prayed a prayer similar to his. For even as Sergei had used the words "manhood," it was clear this was really a place a woman must find also. Surrender and forgiveness and wholeness, of course, transcended gender. And Katya had long been seeking these things, and especially so since the terrible debacle with the Monk. Now it seemed so very right that she should find them with her husband.

They rose when they heard some clattering in the kitchen. Anna was there preparing the morning meal. She took one look at the couple and dropped the spoon she was using to stir the kasha. She ran to them and embraced them both. It amazed Yuri that his mother could *tell*. Was it really so apparent in their faces? Or had she been expecting, hoping, this would be the result of reading Sergei's journal? Perhaps a bit of both. Nevertheless, Yuri did feel as if the new light in his heart must be positively glowing.

23

Though the political climate in the city was changing, there was still a warrant out for Lenin's arrest, and thus he still felt the need to reenter Petrograd in disguise. He shaved his beard and donned a wig, while Stephan Kaminsky did the reverse, gluing a theatrical mustache and beard onto his usually clean-shaven face. A cold and cloudy October day with intermittent rain greeted them in the city. This was not the first time they had come to Petrograd since going into hiding three months ago. The most recent such foray came a couple of weeks ago when Lenin made another attempt to ignite the sluggish Bolsheviks into an armed uprising. As usual he had met opposition. This time even Zinoviev, his closest ally, came out in open opposition to him. Stephan had to wonder if Zinoviev's defiance was mostly because his place as Lenin's second-in-command had been given over to Trotsky.

Lenin was demanding that Zinoviev and Kamenev, the most vocal against him, be thrown out of the Party. "I no longer consider either of them my comrades," he told Stephan.

Stalin, oddly enough, was urging Party unity, saying the exclusion of these two men would harm the Party more than help it. Personally, Stephan thought Ilyich was being a bit too hard on his comrades, but he held his tongue. He had decided early on to follow Lenin's course no matter what, partly out of loyalty but also because he intended on being in the right place at the right time when Lenin took power. Stephan was not going to let minor points of ideology or such prevent him from assuming as high a position as possible in the new government.

By the time Ilyich, accompanied by Stephan and a few others who had been in hiding with him, returned to

Petrograd in mid-October, the Bolshevik Party hardly seemed in any shape to mount a viable bid for power. Tensions were high as the Central Committee met in a member's apartment on the night of the twenty-third. It was perhaps ironic that this meeting of impassioned revolutionary leaders should take place in a setting so middle class with chintz-covered settees, heavy brocade drapes on the windows, tables topped with crocheted lace, and nice wool carpet on the floors.

"I tell you we will never be stronger than we are right now!" Lenin shouted, looking rather pale, no doubt because the debate had been raging for several hours.

"We would be fools to take such a risk now," countered Zinoviev.

Stephan thought Zinoviev was being kind in not mentioning that immediately after the Kornilov affair Lenin had preached compromise with the Soviet. But that was before the Bolshevik victories in the Petrograd and Moscow presidiums.

Lenin eyed his former friend with venom. "It would not be foolishness but courage and supreme insight. Kerensky is barely hanging on. Do you wish to wait until he plants himself firmly once again?"

"It's too soon after the July attempt." Zinoviev wiped moisture from his spectacles. The room was unbearably hot, but this no doubt came more from the flames of passion than the meager supply of coal. "If we fail, we will surely be destroyed, not only by Kerensky's forces but by the masses who will certainly lose faith in us. We need more time!"

"It would be to our eternal *shame* if we did not act! We can and will take power, if—and only if—we do not succumb to fear!" Lenin countered, the veins on his neck pulsating with his zeal.

Ten long hours later, after accusing the Bolsheviks of everything from being childish to outright betrayal, Lenin wrested a vote from the group and came out of it the victor with only Zinoviev and Kamenev dissenting. It was agreed then that "an armed uprising had become inevitable." However, no one, not even Lenin, put forth a definite plan for a revolt, much less a date.

A week later, in *Pravda* and other Party newspapers, Zinoviev recanted his opposition to Lenin, followed the next day by Kamenev. The Party was closing its ranks. The Bolsheviks in the Petrograd Soviet called for Bolsheviks throughout the city to make a loud but nonviolent show of strength. In answer to this there were demonstrations all over the city, and meeting places were filled to overflowing with supporters.

As Stephan exited the Smolny Institute, once an aristocratic girls' boarding school now transformed into the headquarters of the Petrograd Soviet, and by degrees more and more a Bolshevik center, he took special note of the atmosphere of the city. Was it just his imagination, or was there a heightened sense of tension, almost palatable energy, in the chill autumn air?

True, the life of the city was not at a standstill by any means. Nearly all the theaters were operating. A new ballet had opened at the Marinsky and played to full houses. Though most of the treasures of the Hermitage museum had been evacuated to Moscow, there were still frequent art exhibits. The Salvation Army, newly admitted to Russia under the Provisional Government, had plastered walls with handbills announcing Gospel meetings, a true rarity in the Orthodox country.

But life was growing more difficult, especially for the common man. There was talk of decreasing the bread ration from three-quarters of a pound to a half pound per day. Only half the children in the city tasted milk. All other commodities were ever more scarce and expensive, when they could be found. People were standing on street corners selling their possessions—clothing, jewelry, books, pots, crucifixes. Even former aristocrats were selling valuables, while some had been reduced to sweeping streets or other menial tasks to earn a few kopecks for bread. Fear of the coming winter could be read in the faces of people everywhere.

Walking down Shpalernaia Street toward the Alexander Bridge, Stephan, as never before, sensed a nation ripe for revolution. Of course he hadn't been there in February, but he was certain that now, after months of disenchantment, the country was about to explode. Any doubts Stephan might have had about Lenin's insistence on an imminent rising were quelled. It seemed more possible than ever that a relatively obscure party could rise up and take the reins of the Goliath nation that covered one-sixth of the earth's surface.

Stephan had been assisting Trotsky, who had taken control of the Military Revolutionary Committee of the Soviet. It seemed amazing that a man with no military experience could successfully take this area in hand. But Trotsky was nothing less than a wizard whose imprint could be seen in nearly all facets of the revolution. If it was Lenin's strength of will that sparked the Party into action, it was certainly Trotsky's incredible energy that kept it going.

Trotsky had already cajoled the garrison at the Peter and Paul Fortress to turn over their arsenal of weapons to the Proletariat. It would not be long before the prisoners incarcerated there would also be released. Stephan knew that Andrei was among those prisoners, and he might have been able to use his influence to get him released. But he had heard that Andrei's memory had returned and thus he hoped that a long stint in the gaol might reignite Andrei's revolutionary fervor.

Stephan was not exactly sure why he wanted to maintain a hold on Andrei. He had never quite forgiven Mariana Fedorcenko for rejecting him in favor of that American reporter. Oh, he wasn't pining away in love with her— perhaps he had never truly loved her in the first place. But he simply did not like to lose, especially to Mariana, who had flaunted her new aristocratic status in his face. It gave Stephan a sense of poetic justice that her brother was *his* comrade and was stirring up strife in her family. Stephan had always thought that the Burenin clan—Fedorcenkos included—needed to be knocked down a notch or two.

But this accomplishment was small indeed compared to the greater, far more glorious victory that awaited him and the Party he had served for so long. In the near future, bourgeois like the Burenins and Fedorcenkos would either bow to the victorious Party or be consumed by it.

Stephan reached the apartment in the Vyborg district where Lenin was hiding. Inside, Lenin paced, totally frustrated to have to remain holed up while revolution was flaming outside. Stephan reported on the progress being made. All but two regiments of the Petrograd garrison were behind the Bolsheviks. The commander of the government forces well knew something was brewing, yet he had taken no drastic measures to halt it. All he had done was send one of the Women's Death Battalions to guard the Winter Palace. These Women's Battalions had been formed by Kerensky months ago in an attempt to shame Russian soldiers into keeping up the fight at the Front. Whether they had been successful or not was open to debate. But it seemed impossible that they would be enough to hold back the tidal wave that was about to engulf Russia.

The following morning, Stephan woke from a fitful sleep to the sound of voices in the front room. Hastily slipping on his trousers, he hurried out to find a messenger from the Smolny headquarters excitedly reporting to Lenin.

"The government forces have cut the phone lines to the Smolny," he said. "They tried to occupy the printing presses but our men held them off. The cruiser *Aurora* was ordered to leave the Neva for the open sea."

"And?" said Lenin impatiently. The loyalty of the *Aurora* had never been entirely certain either to the government or to the Bolsheviks.

"Trotsky ordered them to stand—and they have!"

"What about Kronstadt?"

"A call has been issued for sailors at Kronstadt to come to the city without delay."

"Who made the call?" asked Stephan. The situation was extremely confusing, since both the government and the Bolsheviks were assuming command of the military forces in the country.

"Trotsky, of course. The government knows better than to rely on Kronstadt."

Lenin turned to Stephan. "It's finally happening," he breathed.

"What will you do, Ilyich?"

Lenin strode quickly to a writing table, grabbed a pen and sheet of paper, and scribbled out a note. "We must make our move this evening or tonight," he wrote. He gave the note to the messenger. "See that this gets to Trotsky. I will arrive there myself soon."

"Don't you think you should hold off, Ilyich?" asked Stephan.

"I will neither hold off my arrival at Smolny or the revolution. Tomorrow is the day, I feel it! The delegates to the Constituent Assembly will have arrived but will not have organized yet. The majority of them are Bolshevik, and if we present the opportunity to them, how can they refuse? They will give us the all-Russian backing we need for appearances' sake, if nothing else."

"There is still a warrant out for your arrest," Stephan protested.

"I'll see how things shape up through the rest of the day," Lenin conceded. "If things continue to go our way, the government will have more to do than keep track of me."

Stephan had expected no less. He also did not wish to be stuck in some apartment during the most crucial time in Russia's history.

Lenin waited until midnight, then donned his wig. As an added protection against being recognized, he wrapped a bandage around part of his face. He and Stephan went out into the rainy night.

At the Smolny, its doors pressed with crowds of demonstrators, the Red Guard blocked Lenin's entry. The Red Guard, a militia formed early in the revolution, drew its members mostly from the factory workers. Largely Bolshevik, it was ironic that the Guard was now in the position of blocking its leader's path even if they could not recognize him. But the soldiers were very adamant about seeing passes before admitting anyone, and rightly so, since the crowds were not all friendly.

Lenin had never before had need of a pass, and Stephan found that his own pass had somehow been left behind at the apartment. The faithful guards refused to admit them, and, of course, Stephan could not very well announce in public that it was Lenin himself who was with him. One simply could not be certain how many friendly members might be in the crowd. But Stephan thought of another way to use the throng milling in front of the Smolny.

"How do you like that?" he yelled loud enough to be heard by all. "I'm here for the Assembly and they won't let me in."

"We're only following orders," a guard protested.

"Let them in!" someone in the crowd shouted.

"Yeah!"

"Power to the Soviet!" another yelled.

"Power to the Assembly!"

Then with a united thrust, the mob helped propel Stephan and Lenin through the doors. Lenin was laughing at the experience as they continued through the corridors to Trotsky's office.

With Lenin's arrival, the activities at the Smolny took on an even more energized pace. By morning the Red Guard had captured the railway stations, telephone exchanges, the state bank, power stations, and several all-important bridges across the Neva.

24

October was easily the worst month of the Russian year. And all its worst elements were magnified in Petrograd. Dull, gloomy skies, which daylight did not penetrate until nine or ten in the morning, and which grew dark again at three in the afternoon. Bitter cold winds blew off the Baltic Sea. And when the winds ceased, it only meant a chill, oppressive fog would roll in. On top of all this, heavy rains came and turned the streets, which were frequently unpaved or in disrepair, into rivers of mud.

Daniel Trent had been trudging about in the mud and a steady, wet drizzle for most of the morning, circulating through the city and talking to common folk. He was gradually getting the impression that this day might well be the one to forever alter the history of Russia. But before Daniel sent his next news dispatch informing the world of the fall of the Provisional Government, he wanted to confer with someone in that government. When he went to Paul Burenin's apartment, Mathilde told him that her husband was at the Winter Palace.

Kerensky had moved his government to the palace after the July uprising. The ministers of the Provisional Government occupied part of the second floor and held their meetings in the Malachite Chamber, so named because it was lavishly adorned with the fabulous green stone from the Urals.

But the government was not alone in the huge structure of over fifteen hundred rooms. A hospital, which housed five hundred war casualties, also functioned in the palace with a full staff of nurses and doctors. Also, there was palace staff—holdovers from Imperial days, uniformed in royal livery. The task of maintaining the huge edifice, even at minimal levels, continued despite war and revolution.

Upon arriving at the palace, Daniel had expected to meet some resistance. But his press pass and a couple of packs of cigarettes got him easily through the Red Guard that loosely surrounded the palace grounds. He also met no resistance at all as he slipped into the palace itself through a back door that was completely unguarded! He supposed that with literally hundreds of entrances and exits to man, it was an impossible task for the government to keep tabs on them all.

Daniel made his way undeterred through the wide corridors of the Winter Palace, even asking directions of a couple of passersby. He noted that many areas had been turned into barracks for the guards stationed there. Mattresses were strewn upon the floors, and on some, off-duty soldiers were sleeping. Litter was everywhere—cigarette butts, food wrappers—and empty wine bottles indicated the truth of rumors that the vast wine cellars of the palace had been raided.

In spite of the disorder and the fact that this palace had been occupied by the Provisional Government for over three months now, Daniel could not keep from feeling a sense of awe at being in the mighty palace of the tsars. The vast rooms with their vaulted ceilings and gilded trim made the mere machinations of man—wars and revolutions and such—seem small and trivial indeed. Daniel's heels echoed on the marbled floors and made him think of all who down through the ages had trod upon these same floors. Not only tsars, but rulers from all over the world had come here to decide the fate of others.

Daniel wondered if there had been some poetic design in the Provisional Government's choice of this place for its—final?—retreat. Surely it was fitting even if it had not been intentional.

After asking further directions, Daniel found his uncle in the Malachite Chamber conferring with some of the ministers.

"What's it like out there?" Paul asked as he led Daniel to a chair.

"It really depends on who you talk to. Anyone with any political connections is in a state of high tension. But others are going about their day 'business as usual.' I spoke with a man on a streetcar who was shocked to hear a coup d'etat was being staged. He barely knew what a Bolshevik was. At least it hasn't spread to Moscow yet."

Someone brought warm glasses of tea, and Daniel gratefully cupped his in his cold hands.

"Every hour we get reports of one district after another going over to the Bolsheviks," sighed Paul.

"So, is that it, then?"

"What can we do? We have been hoping the Cossacks at least will defend us, but they have remained silent. And you know the adage, 'silence means consent.' "

"Then Trotsky's proclamation of a bloodless coup is true?"

"Trainloads of sailors have been coming in from Finland to support the Bolsheviks. We are powerless, cowering within these walls like trapped rats. I'm surprised you got in. Bolshevik troops are moving steadily in on us. You saw for yourself the armored cars and field guns they have outside. I wouldn't be surprised if we weren't soon completely surrounded. There is one positive note. General Dukhonin—"

"That would be. . . ?"

"Acting Chief of Staff for the army at the Front. We still have wire communication with him, and he has canvassed several regiments. All but the northern army indicate they will support the Provisional Government."

"The northern army . . . that's the one nearest Petrograd."

"Unfortunately, yes. But Dukhonin has promised to

send reinforcements of Cossacks and other troops."

"That could take time."

Both men instinctively glanced toward the window. They couldn't see it from where they were, but they nevertheless felt the ominous presence of the *Aurora* still anchored in the river. Worse yet, Daniel had noted as he entered the palace that the guns of the Peter and Paul Fortress had been aimed at the Winter Palace.

"Kerensky will be here in a few moments with an announcement of some sort. Perhaps he has a trump card to play. In any case, I decided to cast my lot with Kerensky and forsake the Soviet when they became so dominated by the Bolsheviks."

"What will you do, Uncle Paul?"

"Hold out as long as possible."

"I mean you—personally—when this is over?"

"You mean, of course, if it doesn't go well for us? I will no doubt be arrested by the new regime. I have not only been too closely associated with Kerensky, but you well know of my unfortunate dealings with Lenin. However, I have decided that if by some miracle I do avoid arrest, my first responsibility is to Mathilde."

"I saw Aunt Mathilde before coming here," said Daniel. "I noticed suitcases in the front room."

"We have been packed for a month now."

"Is she able to travel?"

"It won't be easy on her, but we have decided we will leave the country because that will be the only way we could remain together. If I can help it, I will not spend her last days in prison."

"I'll help you in any way I can. And if you can get to America my family will help you." Daniel paused, took a business card from his pocket and a pen, and wrote a few lines on the back of the card. "This will get you in to see my brother. He will be at your disposal."

"Thank you, Daniel. We haven't much money, so we will need much help I am afraid."

173

"You will not have to worry. If you contact him from some safe place in Europe using the code words I have written on the back of my card, he will send you passage—"

"That is too much—"

"Say no more, Uncle Paul. You are family. Besides, what else is all that Trent money good for?"

"Well, I am still full of hope that none of this will be necessary. We survived July. This is much the same—except that our military support has dwindled, but—"

Paul stopped as a stirring at the door of the chamber indicated Kerensky had arrived. He glanced at Daniel with a look that seemed to say, "Now, something will happen, just wait!"

Daniel hoped so. As a reporter he tried not to take sides in these types of affairs, but that was becoming more and more difficult as members of his family became involved. If Andrei was around, Daniel supposed his loyalties would be even more challenged.

Kerensky strode into the chamber with purpose. Except for added pallor to his complexion, he in no way looked like a man facing defeat. He glanced around the room to ensure all were present. He nodded toward Daniel, with whom he had spoken several times in the last months and thus knew fairly well.

"I believe we have been betrayed by the military commandant of the city," Kerensky said without preamble. "Even if not outright betrayal, he has proven himself unable to hold back the Bolshevik onslaught. Many key positions have fallen into their hands, and it appears they are backed by a majority of the military regiments in the city. Since telephone lines are cut, I have decided to attempt to leave the city in order to raise help from Gatchina. If need be, I'll go to Luga or even Pskov."

"But is there enough gasoline for such a long journey?" someone asked, practically enough, given the economic state of affairs in the city.

"We will manage somehow."

"Can you even get through the city safely?"

They debated that question for some time before it was finally decided Kerensky should make the attempt openly rather than try some covert mission. In that way he might deceive the Red Guard into thinking he was merely passing from one meeting place to another. Anyway, the risk must be taken, and Kerensky determined that he should take it rather than thrust it upon another.

Paul opted to accompany his friend, not only to offer moral support, he later told Daniel, but also because he was going stir crazy roaming the vast palace with nothing to do. At least attempting to raise troop support was something.

Daniel embraced his uncle. "Godspeed, Uncle."

"Thank you, Daniel. We will not get far without His blessing, I fear."

"And remember what I told you before—"

"Let's not act like this is a permanent farewell. Indeed, Sasha could raise water from a desert. He will get the help we need."

"Then, as we say in America, see ya soon!" Daniel wore an enthusiastic smile to accompany his words. But it was merely a front. He had been on the streets far more than Paul, and he had gauged the mood of the masses. They were not in a mood to trifle any longer.

Daniel and several ministers walked to the courtyard to bid Kerensky and his small party good-bye. Kerensky was giving last-minute instructions when a black Renault, flying an American flag, pulled into the courtyard. The driver stepped out.

"The American Embassy thought that perhaps it would help you to traverse the city under the protection of our flag."

"How did you know I was leaving?" Kerensky glanced at Daniel, who shrugged his ignorance. However the

Americans had gleaned their information, it had not been via Daniel.

The driver smiled. "We do have our ways."

"Well, thank you kindly," Kerensky said.

Kerensky threw Paul a final glance, as if to say, "I doubt it would help, but it was nice of them anyway." Then they ducked into the backseat of his Pierce Arrow touring car, and the small procession drove away.

Shortly after Kerensky's departure, Trotsky issued a proclamation to the effect that the Provisional Government had fallen and power had passed to the Military Revolutionary Committee—in essence, the Bolsheviks.

In the Winter Palace, there were more frantic meetings among the ministers, who, in the absence of their prime minister, were rather uncertain how to proceed. They tried to laugh at Trotsky's nerve. They told one another he was bluffing. After all, they were still a government. Weren't they?

Regardless, they tried to reinforce the guards at all the palace doors and hoped they could count on their main protection, the Women's Death Battalion. But as the day progressed, they were beginning to feel more and more impotent, while the Bolshevik forces were appearing, in the eyes of the people at least, much more *potent*.

Daniel had remained in the palace, deciding that if there was any resistance at all to the Bolsheviks, it would take place here. He continued to talk to ministers and soldiers. One soldier pleaded with Daniel to speak with the American consul so that he could obtain a visa to enter America.

"I want to be American soldier!" the fellow said. "A doughboy, you know! A real Yank."

Daniel tried to explain that visas were not easy to come by, but the soldier wrote down his name and address and pressed it into Daniel's hand.

An hour later when many in Russia were sitting down to their evening meal, the ministers received an ultimatum from Trotsky. They and their troops must surrender within twenty minutes or the assault on the Winter Palace would begin. A wire was dispatched to Dukhonin, who continued to give assurances of reinforcements. The ministers agreed to continue their resistance, but they moved to an interior room in the palace. Daniel knew then that resistance would be futile.

Daniel was interviewing one of the ministers when their conversation was ended abruptly by sudden bursts of explosions.

"It's started," said the minister dismally.

The *Aurora* shelled the Winter Palace from one end while the guns at the Peter and Paul Fortress did the job from the other. Actually the shells were mostly blanks and the assault was ineffectual at best, breaking a few windows, cracking some plaster. But that was enough for the Women's Battalion. They surrendered almost immediately along with several other guards. No doubt the women's politics were more questionable than their courage, and this was all it took to convince them of the Bolshevik propaganda they had been hearing day in and day out. Perhaps they had heard, as Daniel also heard later, that the Reds were reluctant to fire on the women, fearing the ire of the people.

At any rate, the exit of the main force of defenders was a signal for the Red Guards to "storm" the palace. It was, however, more a case of handfuls of Reds trickling in. Many became lost and confused in the vast corridors. Daniel witnessed a few hand-to-hand skirmishes, but nothing that was the substance of legends.

By one in the morning, after intermittent shelling, larger forces of Red Guards entered the palace. But there was essentially nothing in the palace left to *storm*. Most of the defenders had been neutralized, and the government—the ministers and their lackeys—had been reduced to a tremulous gathering of old men. The ministers were finally located by the Reds and all were arrested. With that, the coup was over. The Bolsheviks had won the day, if not far more.

When the news reached the Smolny, Lenin looked at Trotsky and with a bemused smile said, "We have gone suddenly from hiding and persecution to being in power. It makes me dizzy!"

25

With the Fortress under the control of the Red Guards, the prison doors were opened. Andrei walked out sometime before the shelling on the Winter Palace had commenced. Rumors had been circulating all morning in the prison. Thus he had heard, but still could hardly believe, that Lenin was claiming victory in this latest coup.

Outside, it was cold and gray and already dark, though only late afternoon. The rain of earlier in the day had stopped, but the streets were wet and glimmering under the streetlights. Andrei breathed in the air of freedom as if it were spring and the sky blue and balmy.

"Rudy, what will you do?" Andrei asked his friend as they approached the bridge that would take them from the fortress island to the island of Petrograd Side.

All around them many other released prisoners cheered their freedom and raised the call to join the Bolsheviks. Rifles had been thrust into the hands of several, and they jogged across the bridge with new purpose. Andrei and Rudy walked with far less determination.

"I'll go to see if Sonja is all right," Rudy replied.

"Then . . . I just don't know. I don't need to ask what you will do, Andrei."

"You are welcome to come with me, Rudy. My family would happily give you a home."

"Perhaps I will do that, but I'll let you have your time with them first."

They walked a bit farther, then Andrei paused. "Please tell Sonja I am well and that I will come to see her soon. I pray she is all right."

"Pray. . . ? That doesn't sound like you, my friend."

"Being locked up for as long as we have gives a man time for plenty of thinking. And I have thought a lot about the faith of my parents. I can't think now why I gave it up."

"Considering all you have been through, I don't see how you can think highly of God."

"I remember something my papa said once. I was young and had just suffered some little childhood tragedy. He told me, 'Andrushka, faith isn't some magic pill you take to have eternal good luck.' I asked, 'Then what good is it, Papa?' I haven't thought about his reply for a long time, but it came to me the other day. He said, 'You can have faith for the good things it does for you—'tis better than no faith at all. But don't measure faith by outward signs, not by what it does, nor by what the faithful *do*. Every man is different as is his measure of things. I see only one truly consistent reason for faith—because God is God. Only He is trustworthy.'"

"That is interesting. I always thought there must be more to it than blessings and good deeds."

"I can almost hear my papa say, 'If Russians based their faith on blessings, there'd be precious little of it.'" Andrei smiled. "He also said those who did base their faith on such tangible things usually had little else."

Rudy nodded thoughtfully. "It does seem odd that you would have turned your back on that kind of wisdom.

179

Had I heard such things I might never have become an atheist."

"Why did you become an atheist, Rudy?"

"My family was forced from our home in a pogrom when I was twelve years old. I guess I gave up my faith because of bad things happening, like you said. If Russians are beleaguered people, Jews are even more so. And Russian Jews! Oy! I don't even want to think about it."

"And that's when you refused your bar mitzva?"

"Yes. And my father has never spoken to me since." Rudy paused uncomfortably. Then, probably wishing not to be the subject of the conversation, he cast an incisive look at his friend. "So, Andrei, does this mean you have returned to the faith of your father?"

"It means I am thinking more about it than I ever have before. If only Papa were here to answer my questions now. The answers I remember were geared toward a child. My questions are different now, more complex."

They started walking again and reached the end of the bridge, where they would have to part company. Rudy would go to the right to the Trinity Bridge, which would take him into downtown Petrograd. Andrei would head to the left, where he would come to the Stock Exchange Bridge that would take him to Vassily Island—and home.

Before the two young men went their own ways they briefly embraced.

"I hope . . ." Rudy began, then paused awkwardly. "Well, I just want to say, I will understand if we don't see as much of each other now that you have found your family."

"You won't so easily be rid of this bear." Andrei grinned. "Once you rescue me from an alley, you are stuck with me. I expect to see you soon."

Rudy's thin face brightened. He grasped Andrei's hand and shook it vigorously. "I'm happy to hear that. I haven't had many friends in my life."

"Neither have I. Just my brother and Talia. But I am

honored to count you with them as a dear friend."

"After all you have said about them, I know I am in good company."

They were about to turn away when Andrei paused once again. "Rudy, as a friend, may I offer some advice?" When Rudy nodded, Andrei continued, "Go see your father. The whole world has changed, and it might well be that he has changed also."

"I might just do that. But first I will see to Sonja."

"Good. Tell her I will be along soon."

Once they parted, Andrei found his darkened route deserted. Most of the activity in the city was downtown where Rudy was heading. It suddenly occurred to him how strange it was for him to be walking *away* from the action—from the revolution. From practically his earliest memory the revolution had drawn him, captured him, dominated him. Especially after his father's death it had been *everything*, to the extent of pulling him from his family.

Now he was walking away from it—literally and, he believed, figuratively.

Out of the corner of his eye he saw a handbill tacked to a wall. He paused, tore it down, and though he had to strain a bit in the darkness, read:

TO THE CITIZENS OF RUSSIA!

The Provisional Government is deposed. The State Power has passed into the hands of the organ of the Petrograd Soviet of Workers and Soldiers' Deputies, the Military Revolutionary Committee, which stands at the head of the Petrograd proletariat and garrison.

The cause for which the people were fighting: immediate proposal of a democratic peace, abolition of landlord property rights over the land, labor control over production, creation of a Soviet Government—that cause is securely achieved.

LONG LIVE THE REVOLUTION OF WORKMEN, SOLDIERS, AND PEASANTS!

Andrei smiled ironically. What mad celebration there must be among the Bolsheviks. Lenin's Central Committee must be hysterical. And, in spite of everything, there was still part of Andrei that was glad for them. They had worked hard and suffered much for this day. He had been close comrades to them all—not in the way he felt close to Rudy or Yuri or Talia, but nevertheless, his life had been bound to them for a long time. He had worked and suffered, too, to bring about this victory.

Perhaps that was the true irony. To have worked half his life for something only to realize practically at the moment of final victory that he no longer cared about any of it. Well, he did still care on some level. He cared in the sense that one should always care about injustice. Tyranny was something he could never ignore. Russian freedom would never cease being a noble cause. Yet his amnesia had taught him that these causes were not what made him the person he was. And when he let them separate him from those he loved, he had cut off the most vital part of who he was. He was nothing without his family. His causes were meaningless without his family.

He glanced again at the handbill. "Ilyich, you have what you wanted." He crumpled up the paper and dropped it into the gutter. Then he reached into his pocket and took out the "Ballet Russe" poster that he'd always kept close to him. "Now I must go find what I want."

26

The old neighborhood had not changed. Even as he could hear artillery shells exploding in the city center, he approached his home with a sense of warm security. A new order was rising up in Russia. The old was about to be swept away—if Andrei did not misjudge Lenin—in a way that would be staggering. Yet the old babushkas still gossiped to each other on their doorsteps; children still squabbled in the street; the grocer was still yelling at his wife. Andrei almost expected to see Talia sitting on the doorstep of their building as she had many times in the past in order to catch him and fill him in on the day's events.

But Talia wasn't there. He wondered if she would even be inside. At least his mama would be there. Then Andrei hesitated. He knew his mama would never hold grudges against him for any of his actions. He was not so sure about anyone else. They must know about his amnesia and would no doubt forgive him for his disappearance since getting shot eight months ago. But what about before that? He and Yuri had had little chance to talk in the turmoil of their last meeting. He remembered his last words to Yuri were "I love you." But what had been Yuri's response? Andrei couldn't remember.

Of course his brother loved him. The wisdom Andrei had offered Rudy regarding reconciliation with his father was just as applicable to him and Yuri. The world had changed radically in the last several months. It was hard to believe that Yuri had not changed also.

And Talia. . . ?

Andrei could still see the devastation in her eyes when he did not recognize her. It must have hurt her terribly. Then for him to disappear again. Suddenly something occurred to Andrei. That look . . . had there been more to it than simply being rejected by a friend? *Could* there have been more?

"Andrei," he mumbled into the night air, "you are worse than Yuri standing here analyzing everything. You'll never know anything unless you *get moving*."

He took a steadying breath, then started toward his mother's building. He climbed the steps, opened the door, and entered. Even the smell in the entry hall had not changed—musty dampness mingled with onions and frying lard, and whatever else various tenants had cooked for dinner. He mounted the long flight of stairs to their floor. He met a woman he knew from years ago on the stairs, but she did not seem to recognize him, so he said nothing. It made him realize how long it had been since he had been home, not counting that brief stay when he came in March. He was acutely aware of how much *he* had changed.

When he reached the door, he felt stiff and awkward as he lifted his hand to knock. How many times had he burst through that door as an exuberant boy? What would he do now?

But when the door opened in response to his knock, he completely gave up his analyzing and followed his first impulse.

"Mama!" he cried and threw his arms around her, not caring about the past or the present. All he knew was that he really wanted to hold his mother close and feel her comforting embrace.

It took several moments for him to realize he was holding a limp, silent form in his arms.

"Oh no! Mama, what have I done?"

"What's going on—?" came a new voice.

Andrei glanced up to see Yuri several paces away. "I'm afraid I've shocked her," he said, his voice filled with the misery he felt.

At that moment, Anna stirred and opened her eyes. "It . . . it is you . . . Andrei. . . ."

"Forgive me, Mama . . ." said Andrei.

Anna reached up and touched his face as if she feared he was but an apparition that might fade away at any moment.

"Praise be to God!" she breathed, crossing herself.

"Mama, come and sit—" Yuri began.

"Yuri, do you see, it is your brother?"

"Yes, Mama. I see." Yuri now smiled and Andrei could see moisture glistening in his brother's eyes.

Together, the brothers helped their mother, who was still a bit shaky in the legs, to a seat in the parlor. As Yuri let go of his mother he lay a hand on Andrei's shoulder, gripping him with a trembling hand.

"So, you have returned to stir some excitement into our lives," Yuri said lightly, his voice nonetheless huskier than usual.

"There is a revolution going on outside," said Andrei. "Is that not enough excitement for you?" The brothers sat on either side of their mother. No one seemed to think to inform the rest of the household of the unexpected reunion.

"Don't you two boys start at each other so soon," said Anna with a smile. "Oh, on second thought, forget what I said. It is music to my ears." She put an arm around each of her sons and gave them a squeeze. "Andrei, you don't know how many times when I opened that door, I hoped it would be you."

"You too, Mama?" said Yuri.

"I did not want to say anything because I knew I had to be strong."

"Mama," said Andrei, "I put you through so much heartache. Did Talia tell you I had amnesia?"

"Amnesia? Talia? I don't understand." But Anna did not look too perplexed. She just gazed with wonder at her son returned to her from death.

"When I was wounded, I was found by a woman—"

"Wait a minute," said Yuri. "Unless you want to tell your story a dozen times, let me get the rest of the family."

It was another few minutes before everyone in the house was gathered in the parlor. Daniel was absent because he was somewhere in the city working, and Yuri was only home because he had been up all night with an emergency surgery. But Andrei did not get a chance to begin his story for several more minutes after many emotional greetings were exchanged. Raisa insisted that Andrei must have a hot glass of tea and something to eat.

Andrei did not mind the attention. In fact, he would have absolutely basked in it except that one important person was missing from the gathering. He desperately wanted to ask where Talia was, but the question was burning so intensely in him, he feared all would know his intent if he spoke it.

This somewhat distracted him as he told his story, but nevertheless he had a most attentive audience. Yuri laughed harder than anyone had heard him laugh in months when Andrei confessed that even with amnesia he nearly fainted when he first saw his wound. The children wanted to see his scar, but Andrei demurred because of the ladies present. What probably amazed everyone, and certainly amazed Andrei, was in all the telling of his story, he hardly mentioned politics at all. He did mention that he had a score to settle with Stephan Kaminsky for keeping the identity of his family secret. But other than that which pertained to events in his life, he said little about the revolution and made no mention at all of his opinions regarding it.

When he finished, Raisa determined that he needed to finish his meal. He had gained back some of the weight lost during his illness, but he was still much lighter than normal. Anna was reluctant to leave Andrei's side, and Raisa insisted it was not necessary. One by one all the others migrated to other parts of the house for various reasons, though probably mostly because they wanted to give Anna and her sons time alone. However, by now Andrei was growing restless. Being with his family was glorious, but he knew he would not be able to fully appreciate that until he could see Talia.

He had no idea what would happen between them. Perhaps she had fallen in love with someone else. Perhaps she was married, though no one had mentioned it, and he *felt* as if it could not be so. He did know that when he saw her again, he was going to let his impulsive nature have full reign. He was not going to risk losing her again.

He searched in his mind for a casual way to ask about her. There was none except to just do it.

"No one has mentioned Talia," he said, but his voice was stiff and much too high pitched to be casual. "She's well, isn't she?"

"I'm surprised it took you this long to ask about her," said Yuri dryly.

"Well, I—"

"I'll try to telephone her if you'd like."

Andrei wanted to scream, "Why didn't you do that an hour ago?" But instead, he just nodded and said with restraint, "Yes, I'd like that."

Yuri left and a few moments later returned. "The phone line is dead."

"Oh . . ." Andrei must have been wearing an extremely woeful expression because Yuri smiled sympathetically.

"Confound it, man!" Yuri finally exclaimed. "Why are you just sitting there? Go find her!"

"Do you think I should?" Suddenly all Andrei's determination was swallowed in self-doubt.

"Am I missing something here?" asked Anna, truly perplexed.

"Mama," answered Yuri, "Andrei is in love with Talia but has been afraid for years to tell her."

"Yuri!" Andrei protested, feeling like a love-struck child.

A slight smile of enlightenment bent Anna's lips. "She was so very upset when we thought you . . . were gone. I knew you were close friends, but it still seemed rather out of proportion to *friendship*."

"She was upset?" said Andrei, hope soaring.

"Of course she was, you dolt!" said Yuri. Then he shook his head with frustration, only partly in jest. "I see I am going to have to do what the two of you are simply too dull to do for yourselves." He jumped up and grabbed Andrei's coat, which he had shed earlier. He thrust it at Andrei, but when Andrei still made no move, Yuri grabbed his brother's arm and tugged him to his feet. He would have put the coat on Andrei had his brother not stirred into motion and done it for himself.

"All right, let's be off with you," Yuri said.

Andrei glanced at his mother. "Do you mind. . . ?"

"Do as your brother says," Anna replied. "Find that girl and tell her how you feel."

"I'll be back soon!" Andrei briefly kissed his mother's cheek.

Yuri told Andrei where Talia lived, then fairly shoved him out the door.

It had started to rain again, and a stiff wind drove it right into Andrei's face. But he hardly noticed. He was just barely aware, once he crossed the river to the Southside, of the armored vehicles barreling down the main streets with units of machine gunners crouched on top of the trucks. He couldn't avoid seeing units of troops on foot jogging east toward the center of town. Several almost ran him down.

But the heightened energy sizzling through the city could never match that within himself—his pounding heart, his tingling nerves, his mind racing to conjure every possible scenario in this long-awaited meeting.

It startled him and made him pause a moment when artillery fire caused the ground beneath his feet to quake. He glanced toward the Winter Palace whose spires he could barely see over the buildings nearer to him. Apparently the Reds had started shelling the palace again. The surrounding darkness allowed him to clearly see the bursts of light accompanying the explosions.

Then he turned and continued in the opposite direction. What mattered to him did not lie in the direction of the Winter Palace.

He crossed the Moika Canal, then found Talia's street. He was looking for numbers when he saw several women standing in front of one of the buildings about halfway down the street. They must have come out to see what the noise was about. All at once one of the women saw him and started down the steps that led to the street.

"Talia!" Andrei broke into a run.

She raced down the steps, hardly touching them as she descended. "Andrei!" she cried.

In another moment he had caught her up in his arms, literally lifting her light form two feet from the ground. Rain beat upon them, artillery shells burst in the background, but both felt only warmth and love and security.

"You remembered!" she said, her tears mingling with the raindrops.

"How could I ever have forgotten?" He was crying too. "It only shows what a fool I am and have always been. I wasted so many years with my stupidity."

"You were smart enough to love me." She was laughing and crying and panting. And he still held her in his arms. "You do love me. . . ?"

"I love you, Talia! I have always loved you. I will always love you."

"And I love you, Andrei! Ah, it feels so good to finally say the words."

"Like a weight lifted."

"Like a dream fulfilled."

He pressed his lips against hers as he had longed to do for so many years. And her hungry response was more than he ever could have imagined. She truly did love him!

A moment later he lowered her so her feet touched the ground. Still he did not let go of her, and she also clung to him. Only then did they notice the women on the doorstep pointing and giggling at them. The scene Andrei and Talia were making was far more entertaining than any revolution.

Laughing, Talia waved at her friends. "This is Andrei," she called happily to them. "The man I love."

"The one you thought was dead but only had amnesia?" one girl questioned.

"The only one I've ever loved!" Talia replied with conviction.

Andrei glanced down at her with a creased brow. Fleeting images of this very girl pining away for his brother threatened to mar his present euphoria.

She understood immediately. "I was a bit of a fool myself, Andrei. I wasted a good deal of time, too. How could I not have known all that time that it was my best friend whom I loved, not his brother?"

"Ah, well . . ." he said airily. "We know now and that's what matters." Then with an intense look, he added, "I truly mean that's what matters." He grasped her hand in his. "Let's walk and talk, Talia. For so long I have wanted to do that—almost as much as I've wanted to kiss you."

"But it's raining."

"Do you care?"

She laughed. "Not in the least!"

They walked for an hour—all the way back to Vassily Island and their mothers' apartment. They were drenched to the skin, but still they lingered on the doorstep and continued talking just as they had so many times in the past. They sat together on the step, and he clasped his arm around her shivering shoulders. The rain finally stopped and a few stars sparkled through cracks in the clouds.

Only when Talia's lips quivered so with cold that she could no longer form intelligible words did they finally retreat indoors. The family cheered when they walked into the apartment. And the two lovers glowed despite their wet, bedraggled appearance.

27

Alexis Romanov put his hands in front of him in the shape of a book. Tatiana called out, "Book title!"

Alexis nodded then, pausing only a moment to think, raised his arms, and clasped his hands so as to form an imaginary rifle. He jerked his hands energetically and managed to be quite animated, though he was seated in a chair. He then completed the picture by making guttural sounds in his throat.

"No sounds," said his sister Anastasia.

"Now, Anastasia," said their father, "let's not be too legalistic about this. Baby is doing his best."

"But it's not fair."

Alexis shrugged and silenced the sounds, still "blasting" away with his invisible machine gun.

The others gathered in the parlor to play "charades" began shouting out guesses. "Battle!" "Shooting!" "War!"

At the word "war" Alexis vigorously tapped his nose.

Mr. Gilliard, the children's tutor, called out, "War of the Worlds!"

Alexis silently indicated he would move on to the next word. He had barely laid his head on his hands in peaceful repose, when Tatiana shouted, "War and Peace!"

"That was too easy," whined Anastasia.

"Then you should have gotten it," said Tatiana with just a hint of smugness.

"Well, I was thinking of something harder," said Anastasia.

Nicholas said, "I shall put my mind to it later and try to come up with more difficult charades."

"But, Papa," said Alexis, "won't we perform our play tomorrow?"

It took a great deal of invention to keep five active adolescents and young adults entertained in the backwater village of Tobolsk, especially as winter began to clamp down in late October. They often played games such as this evening's charades. Sometimes Nicholas read aloud. But by far the most enjoyable event was the performance of various plays. This was one of Alexis's favorite pastimes. Everyone took part except Dr. Botkin, who said there needed to be an audience. Even Alexandra would take a small role now and then when she was feeling up to it.

"I think we need more practice," said Olga.

"I suppose so," conceded Alexis. "And there is still one part not taken." He cast an incisive glance at Botkin.

"Now, now," protested the doctor. "I am a far better spectator than actor. You would all agree if you saw me."

"But this part was made for you. A country doctor. You *must* do it."

"I assure you—" But the doctor was obviously wavering.

"It's only a couple of lines," persisted Alexis. "You could say them in your sleep."

The doctor threw up his hands and chuckled. "All right! But you will regret this, mark my words."

And thus one evening passed upon another in the modest home, once occupied by the governor, there in Siberia. The life of the deposed tsar and his family took on an air of peace and contentment—on the surface of things at least. Though the doctor and the royal tutors and other servants were free to come and go—Botkin had even set up a modest medical practice in town—the royal family themselves were still captives. They were comfortable, however, and able to receive some correspondence from their relatives. Colonel Kobylinsky, the head of the guard detail, treated them with civility, even respect. In fact, any guards that had direct contact with the family invariably ended up quite sympathetic to the royals.

Church services were held in the house, at least at first. But because there was no consecrated altar, there could be no Mass. This was hard on Nicholas and his family, for their spiritual well-being was very important to them. Eventually, they were allowed to attend Mass at the local church. They went to the early morning service and the public was prohibited. But when the Romanovs were out on the streets, the citizens of the village indicated their respect by bowing and doffing their caps.

It took nearly two weeks after the Bolshevik Revolution for the news to reach faraway Tobolsk. Nicholas had been avidly following events in Russia as much as possible. He had placed much hope in the attempted Kornilov coup and had been greatly disappointed at its failure. For the first time in months, he felt regret over his abdication. He had surrendered the throne only in hopes of benefiting his country, but now he was seeing how much in vain that act had been.

With the rise of the Bolsheviks, the national situation seemed more desperate than ever. Nicholas considered Lenin little more than an upstart ruffian, that is if the man wasn't an out-and-out German spy. It pained Nicholas greatly to see Russia fall into the hands of such a person. Other than this emotional strain, the Bolshevik takeover had little effect on the captives in Tobolsk. It was almost as if the royal family had been forgotten—and that, of course, was more a blessing than a curse.

Signs that the situation was changing came gradually. Finances were tightened and new guards of a younger, more revolutionary bent arrived. As Christmas approached, there was great excitement, even among the doctor and tutors and a few close servants who had come to feel very much a part of the family. Alexandra had knitted each of the loyal friends a special gift. Other gifts—handmade, of course, for gifts of Fabergé eggs and such were long in the past—were exchanged among the family. In this joyous time, all the cares and uncertainties of the outside world almost faded into the white snow-covered background.

On Christmas Day they all attended church together feeling a deep sense of contentment and camaraderie. Then the priest, Father Vassiliev, committed a great indiscretion. During Mass he invoked the once traditional "Prayer for the Long Life of the Imperial Family."

The young guards, full of revolutionary zeal, were outraged. Without even waiting for the service to end they protested.

"This is treason!"

"Long life to the Soviet only!"

One guard drew his weapon and, aiming it at Nicholas, demanded, "Revoke the prayer or we shall see how long the life of the ex-tsar is!"

The priest was placed under immediate arrest, but the harshest reprisal to the royal family was that their privilege of attending church was taken away. Not only were they deprived of spiritual comfort, but also of their only chance for a break from their confinement.

IV

NEW ALLIES, OLD ENEMIES
Winter 1917–1918

28

"I don't like the term 'ministers,'" offered Stephan Kaminsky. "It's been overused and smacks too much of bourgeois authority."

"I agree, we need something new," said Lenin.

Within two days after the Bolshevik Revolution, the Central Committee met to hammer out the policies of the new government. The first task was to assign positions for cabinet members, but the Central Committee was sidetracked on the issue of names.

"How about the Council of People's Commissars," suggested Trotsky.

"I like it!" Lenin replied enthusiastically. "It has a good revolutionary sound."

"Then, you will like this as a name for our nation," Trotsky continued, "Soviet of People's Commissars."

But finding a good name for the new government was far simpler than finding qualified individuals to run it. Many of the leaders of the revolution had spent the majority of their lives in prison or in exile, not running governments in any capacity. Even Lenin admitted in those early days that they were bound to make mistakes.

Inexperience, however, was the least of their problems. Their enemies were still many and viable and in no way ready to concede defeat. Within five days of the October revolution, Kerensky made an attempt at a counter-coup with several thousand soldiers he had managed to recruit. He failed and was forced into hiding, but others, both monarchists and moderates, continued to rally support. General Alekseev, one-time Chief of Staff under Nicholas, and later Supreme Commander of the Army under the Provisional Government, was called out of retirement to lead the White Army that had begun to form in the Don region where counterrevolutionary sentiment was especially high.

Establishing Bolshevik authority outside of Petrograd had to begin with Moscow, which proved to offer the toughest resistance to the new government. At first the pro-Bolshevik forces had been able to seize several important strongholds, including the all-important Kremlin. But counterrevolutionary forces rallied and eventually were able to siege the Kremlin. After three days the Bolsheviks were forced to surrender, but as they were exiting, the besieging army opened fire on them and dozens of Bolsheviks were killed. The Bloodless Revolution begun in Petrograd was turning out far differently in Moscow.

As the moderates claimed control of the inner city, Lenin called for Red Guard forces from other parts of the country to go to the aid of Moscow.

"Moscow is the heart of Russia," he said. "This heart must be Soviet in order to save the revolution!"

Stephan Kaminsky commanded a force of Red Guards from Petrograd. Even with his lack of military experience, he was certain no war could have boasted worse fighting than that which was waged in Moscow. The Reds fought their way back into the city from the outskirts, gradually squeezing the moderates into a tighter and tighter circle. Finally, after a week more of fighting, the Bolsheviks retook the Kremlin—and Lenin had his Soviet heart back.

But it was still anyone's revolution. Naysayers predicted Lenin's government would last only a couple of weeks. How could a quarter of a million Bolsheviks wield authority over a hundred and thirty million subjects? Hopes rose and fell with each successive battle.

And still the Bolsheviks hung on. Perhaps no one realized how years of exile, imprisonment, and hiding from the authorities had toughened these revolutionaries.

In January, Daniel received a message from Lord

Bruce inquiring about the status of their little "project." Daniel decided it was time to get a firsthand picture of the situation in Tobolsk. Also, he had been hearing via the "grapevine" of other rescue operations that he thought bore investigation. Besides being extremely busy with work, due to the volatile events in the city, little Katrina contracted pneumonia, and he could not consider any travel until she was well. He was not able to get away for several weeks.

In addition to observing "the lay of the land" in Tobolsk, Daniel wanted to investigate one rescue organization specifically because of the credentials of its leader. Called the Brotherhood of St. John of Tobolsk, the man at its helm was one Lieutenant Boris Soloviev. The peculiarity of his credentials was in the fact that he was Grigori Rasputin's son-in-law.

Having studied mysticism in India, Soloviev returned to Petrograd in 1915 and became involved in the spiritualist and occult groups surrounding Rasputin. Yuri's wife, Katya, had known him vaguely in those days. She was reluctant to speak of those confused times in her life and could make no judgments on the man's sincerity. She did say that she remembered Maria, Rasputin's daughter, mentioning that she did not care for Soloviev at all and wished everyone, specifically her father and Anna Vyrubova, would stop trying to match them.

Daniel thought Soloviev's marriage to Maria Rasputin in October, 1917, was terribly convenient. The connection to Rasputin gained Soloviev the immediate confidence of both Anna Vyrubova and the empress. And this quickly made him the final "clearing house" of practically all rescue organizations. All financial contributions were funneled through him, and since his return to Siberia following his wedding, all those interested in rescue operations reported first to him. Maybe it was Daniel's natural American independence, but he wasn't going to accede to Soloviev until he was absolutely certain about the man's sincerity. Though Soloviev's relationship to the late Rasputin had won the confidence of the empress, it had just the opposite effect on Daniel.

The normal three-day trip by train to Tiumen stretched to five arduous days due to several breakdowns and a strike by railroad workers. Finally in Tiumen it appeared as if Daniel's quest would end completely. He was supposed to make contact with a Lieutenant Melink, fiancé to Dr. Botkin's daughter, Tatiana. But the delayed train threw off their rendezvous. He had a photograph of Melink. The lieutenant was to identify him merely by the fact that he was a foreigner, a rare enough sight in Siberia. Daniel also had a code, something only Tatiana would know, to further identify him to Melink.

When he did not see Melink, he feared they had missed each other completely. Daniel waited another day before attempting to make his own way to Tobolsk.

In a waterfront tavern, he tried to hire transportation, a task that was made even more difficult by the language barrier. Daniel's Russian, because of his wife's tutorage, was better than many foreigners', with a solid command of the vernacular, but Siberian Russian was practically another language.

Ivan Rajbcov, a burly Siberian with slanted Mongol eyes and swarthy, leathery skin, shook his head. "Do you see the sky, American?" he said through an interpreter. "A storm could blow through at any minute."

Outside, ominous clouds hung heavy in the gray sky. In summer, one traveled by boat between the two towns. That, of course, was impossible now. The only way to Tobolsk in winter was via sleigh, and then only if the weather cooperated.

"I am willing to take the risk," said Daniel. "And I will pay you well for doing so."

"Bah!" scoffed the Siberian. "I don't care about your puny neck. It's my horses that worry me."

"There're a couple of villages on the way. If worse

comes to worst, we could hole up in one of them should a storm hit. I wouldn't wantonly endanger our lives or that of innocent beasts."

"So, what's so important in Tobolsk, American? Are you going to see the former tsar?"

"I'm an American newspaper reporter. I'd like to report on the situation there."

Rajbcov leaned close. "You put my name in your newspaper?"

The near proximity of the Siberian made Daniel wrinkle his nose, for the man smelled far worse than his precious horses.

"Sure," Daniel replied, quickly removing his notebook and pencil from his pocket. "Tell me how to spell it."

The man grinned, revealing rotten, uneven teeth. "If my horses die, you pay for them?"

"Of course, but—"

"But who pay for you or me if we die?" The Siberian laughed and tossed back a glass of vodka. "How much?"

Daniel took several bills from his wallet and laid them out on the coarse table. "Two thousand rubles now and two thousand more when we reach our destination."

"It could take five or six days. Only two by water. He grinned again and said, "But no water in winter." Rajbcov wrapped his hands around the rubles and stuffed them in his coat. "We go in the morning."

But in the night a blizzard struck and Daniel could go nowhere. As the wind howled outside, he began to wonder about the wisdom of his mission. If nothing else, it made him certain there could be no rescue attempt until spring. Even two healthy men would find it difficult to travel by sleigh in winter—and utterly impossible if, as it was doing now, the weather did not cooperate. But for a retinue of a dozen, including women—one of which was reportedly in frail health—and a handicapped boy, such a journey was impossible.

Late in the afternoon, Daniel returned to the same

tavern. Not only did he hope to find Rajbcov, but he also knew this was the best place to meet people and make contacts. Rajbcov was standing at the bar, his grimy hands clasped around a bottle of vodka.

"No sleigh ride today, American," grinned Rajbcov.

"Maybe tomorrow," said Daniel.

"After this storm, the pass will be blocked for . . . who knows how long."

"So, you're saying no one can get through?"

Rajbcov shrugged, sloshed a measure of vodka in a glass, and tossed it back.

"I suppose I'll take my money back then," said Daniel. "You can keep two hundred rubles for your trouble."

"What money, American?"

Daniel sized up the Siberian. He was at least six feet tall and weighed no less than two hundred and fifty pounds. He probably had been in more fistfights *that week* than Daniel had been in all his life—and he'd been in a few. However, Daniel had never been one to roll over in defeat.

"Listen, Mr. Rajbcov, I'm sure we can work this out reasonably." Daniel wasn't sure at all. "I don't have eighteen hundred rubles to throw around, and I am certain you don't need it to get around that you cannot be trusted as a businessman—"

Rajbcov suddenly dropped his bottle and savagely turned on Daniel, grabbing his shirt front and nearly lifting Daniel off his feet. "You call me a cheat, American?"

Daniel could barely speak because half his throat was clamped in Rajbcov's large fist. "No . . . of course not!" he gasped. "It's just that—"

"I kill men for far less affront!"

"We . . . don't . . . need to—"

He did not finish because the Siberian had raised his fist and was about to smash it into Daniel's face. But the man never completed the action. Two soldiers suddenly appeared behind Rajbcov. One grabbed the hand that was ready to strike, while the other soldier stepped between Daniel and the Siberian. Rajbcov struggled a moment but quickly saw that if he continued, he'd be involved in a three-against-one melee, something even he did not care to invite.

The soldier who had come between Daniel and his adversary spoke. "Give the foreigner back his money."

"It is not my fault there is a storm," Rajbcov countered.

The man behind Rajbcov twisted the Siberian's arm down sharply, causing him to gasp in pain.

"The money," said the soldier.

With his free arm, Rajbcov started to reach inside his coat. Quickly, the soldier pulled his side arm, aimed it at Rajbcov's cheek, and said, "Easy, Siberian."

Slowly, Rajbcov took the money from a pocket inside his coat and lay the crumpled wad of bills on the bar. With fastidious care, Daniel counted out eighteen hundred rubles, pocketed it, then pushed the remaining two hundred back toward the Siberian. As an afterthought he paused, took another twenty rubles from his wallet, and laid that beside the other money.

"A little extra," Daniel said. "Your drinks tonight are on me."

The Siberian took one more look at his opponents, then shrugged and scooped up the money. The one soldier let go of him and the other stood aside.

"No hard feelings, American," Rajbcov said expansively. "A man must do what he must, eh?"

"Most certainly, Rajbcov. Perhaps we will do business again sometime."

The Siberian laughed and gave Daniel a friendly slap on the shoulder that was so hard Daniel had to wonder what the man's angry punch would have been like.

Then he turned toward his rescuers. "Thanks," he said.

"We are happy to be of assistance," said the soldier who had thus far been the only one to speak. From his refined speech and the captain's signet on his uniform, Daniel knew he wasn't in the company of a common younker. "May we buy you a drink?"

"I should buy the drinks," said Daniel. "That's the least I can do."

Daniel paid for a round of Kvass, then the three went to a table. When they were seated, the soldier said, "I am Second Captain Oleg Sedov, and this is Lieutenant Georgi Pitovranov."

"Glad to meet you. I'm—"

"Daniel Trent, if I am not mistaken."

"How did you know?"

"Not many foreigners come this way. So, when I was told to look for a foreigner named Trent, I did not need a university degree to make the connection."

"You were told to look for me?"

"Lieutenant Melink was detained in Moscow and sent us ahead to make contact with you. He told me the code words to confirm identities."

" 'A white rose blooms in Kotelnikovo,' " Daniel quoted the code.

" 'The beauty of the white rose surpasses even that of diamonds,' " said Sedov. "The white rose is Tatiana Botkin's favorite flower, and Kotelnikovo is the location of Melink's dacha where they met."

"Very good," said Daniel. "So, now what? We can't get to Tobolsk."

"There is no need to go to Tobolsk. Soloviev has set up his headquarters here. I'm surprised you didn't know."

"It doesn't seem logical. Why here?"

"Here he is in a perfect position to watch all comings and goings to Tobolsk—you have to come through here to get there. And unless you are extremely careful you cannot pass undetected."

"It still doesn't make sense."

"There is much about Soloviev's operation that doesn't make sense. That's why we are here. Soloviev has made many claims and collected many thousands of rubles. For instance, he says he has mined every bridge into Tobolsk and that he has converted eight regiments of Red Guards. He also says he has a spy in the house of detention itself. Many are willing to accept him on the basis of his relationship to the Monk, and on the fact that the empress accepts him unreservedly."

"You know that for a fact—about the empress?"

"We have reports of investigators who have gone to Tobolsk and made contact with the tsar—brief words exchanged over the fence while the tsar was out walking in the yard. Nothing conclusive, but Soloviev set up these contacts."

"But you are suspicious?"

"There are irregularities, such as the fact that Soloviev's contact within the governor's house where the royals are being held is a parlor maid named Romanova. Why use her when Dr. Botkin would be a much better contact? He is allowed to come and go freely, and has even set up a medical practice in the town. And these Red Guard regiments—"

"Yes, I'd like to see them for myself. Eight regiments of Reds converted to monarchism? I'd have to see that to believe it."

"Soloviev took us last night to watch them drill."

"And?"

"They were there. And one of the officers even gave a prearranged signal to us. But how are we to know if it is only this officer working with Soloviev to deceive us? And Soloviev has informed the Petrograd monarchist organizations that they need not send more officers. He says it would be dangerous because more new faces would arouse suspicions."

"A valid claim," said Daniel.

"Perhaps. He asks only for money. And the money pours in. But it is difficult to see where the money is going."

"I'd like to meet Soloviev. Is that possible?"

"Yes. Hoping we would make contact with you, I arranged a meeting with him tonight. Now, Mr. Trent, may I ask you a question? It has nothing to do with trust, only curiosity." Daniel nodded for him to continue. "I am curious why a foreigner such as yourself would take an interest in the welfare of our tsar."

"First, I must tell you that my participation in all this was enlisted by a group of Brits who have come together for the purpose of rescuing the royal family. I am acquainted with one, and since I was already in Russia, he asked me to be their eyes and ears, as it were. I agreed to do so more on moral grounds than political. My wife is a Russian aristocrat of the house of Fedorcenko, but she was raised by peasants—that is a long story. At any rate, family political loyalties are stretched in many directions. Throw American politics into the pot and you have quite a brew. But in my mind none of that matters where the safety of an innocent family is concerned. Whatever the outcome of his actions, I believe the tsar acted with the best of intentions. I don't think he deserves to die for that, nor even spend the rest of his life in prison. And I especially don't think his children deserve to be punished for these things—as the young tsarevich surely would be."

Sedov eyed Daniel with respect as he spoke. "Well said, Trent. I pray to our God that He will honor such noble intentions."

29

Soloviev proved to be the kind of man whose looks were determined more by his personality than by actual physical features. He was not especially handsome unless he smiled, nor was he obviously ugly unless he grimaced.

He was not much taller than Daniel and of a slender build. His eyes were dark and keen, seeming to move constantly, taking in all aspects of his surroundings. His pencil mustache framed a smile that made up in charisma what it lacked in sincerity.

They met in the restaurant of Daniel's hotel, along with Sedov, Pitovranov, and another officer named Karloff whom Daniel had just met. Soloviev seemed not the least bothered by such a public meeting place, and in Daniel's wary mind that could mean but two things—either the man was drunk with confidence, or he had nothing to fear from the authorities because he was in collusion with them. And the man's behavior easily supported both theories.

"So, you are still not satisfied, Sedov?" Soloviev said. "And now you bring this foreigner to judge me also."

"This is Daniel Trent," said Sedov. "He is in a very good position to benefit our cause."

"And what position would that be?" Soloviev leveled an incisive look at Daniel.

Daniel replied, "I represent a group of very influential foreign personages with essentially unlimited financial resources."

Soloviev's dark eyes brightened considerably at this. "Unlimited, you say?"

"Yes, and they are committed to preserving the safety of the royal family. They would like to work with existing operations, realizing this would be the most effective way of attaining their goal. Of course, before contributing to an organization they would want to be assured of its credentials."

"Most certainly." Soloviev smiled and his eyes were bright and friendly, if not exactly warm. "And you will find the credentials of the Brotherhood of St. John of Tobolsk are faultless. Why, the tsaritsa herself named our organization. I am in close contact with Their Majesties. If you would like to see them for yourself, it could be arranged."

"But it is impossible to get to Tobolsk."

"Unfortunately, yes. But when the pass clears . . ."

"We have heard all this before, Soloviev," said Sedov impatiently. "We need more solid evidence of your work."

"You saw my regiments yesterday."

"We saw, yes. But I'd like to question some of them—"

"That would be impossible!" Soloviev exclaimed. "These soldiers are risking their very lives by their loyalty to us. If outsiders began questioning them, how long before their Bolshevik superiors became suspicious? No, no! I cannot allow it."

"Then what other specific plans do you have?" asked Daniel.

"What is your escape route?" asked Sedov.

"What about a time frame?" Pitovranov shot out.

Then followed a barrage of questions around which Soloviev danced like an expert performer. Gradually his patience wore as thin as his slick answers. He became ruffled and angered, and the angles of his features grew sharper and his charm darkened. Finally he jumped up.

"Enough of this!" he snarled. "You treat me like a criminal and I won't have it. I have the confidence of the tsaritsa, and you have nothing. See how far you get without me! All you will achieve by your suspicions is ruining our tsar's only chance of survival." He then turned on his heel and stalked from the room.

Daniel did not know what to make of it. Righteous indignation? Or, a man who feared his true motives were about to be found out?

Daniel retired to his room that night puzzling over the events of the evening. He still had no clear direction, but he did see more clearly than ever why no attempt to rescue the tsar had thus far been made. No one could trust anyone else. Even Daniel was becoming more convinced of the necessity of Lord Bruce's group working alone.

As he undressed for bed, there was a knock at his door. Before opening it, he slipped his shirt back on.

"Don't you even ask who it is before opening your door?" Captain Sedov asked, obviously agitated.

"I saw no immediate danger."

Sedov pushed his way into the room and quickly closed the door behind him. "Quickly gather up your things. You've got to get out of here."

"What's the problem?"

"Hurry! I'll tell you as you go." Daniel pulled out his small traveling satchel and began filling it as Sedov continued, "The Bolsheviks raided our hotel fifteen minutes ago. Because I was in the last room, I managed to get away. Pitovranov and Karloff were arrested. I would have stayed behind to help them but I knew you had to be warned."

"You don't have to defend yourself to me, Sedov. I appreciate what you have done." Daniel latched his bag. Then, as he threw on his coat, Sedov grabbed the bag.

The captain opened the door a crack and looked out. "Let's go, it's clear."

They hurried down the hall toward the main staircase but stopped suddenly as they heard loud footsteps on the stairs. Making an abrupt about-face, they sped, as quietly as their haste would allow, toward the back stairs. Reaching the stairwell they ducked inside. Daniel paused only for one brief backward glance to make certain their fears were well founded. In the hall, he saw half a dozen Red Guards heading directly for his room. Not taking another moment, he raced down the stairs behind Sedov.

Assuming the back entrance would be covered, the two fugitives did not go down the final flight of stairs to the exit but rather tried all the doors on the floor until they found one that opened. It was dark inside the room, and Daniel prayed it was vacant, or at the very least, that its occupants were sound sleepers. A brief inspection once his eyes adjusted to the dark proved the room unoccupied.

"Thank you, Lord!" Daniel murmured.

"What's that, Trent?"

"An answer to prayer."

"We're not out of this yet. Let's hope God continues to aid us."

They were able to climb out a window and shinny down a drainpipe the short distance to the ground. They saw the guards at the back exit before they themselves were detected and were able to slip past them, confirming to both men that they were indeed being assisted by a Higher Power.

They spent a cold, miserable night in a barn on the outskirts of town. In the morning, while it was still dark, they found some old clothes, apparently belonging to the owner of the barn. Donning these, Daniel stuffed their own belongings in his satchel. He left the owner a sizable sum of rubles to pay for the clothes. Then they made for the train station.

With the aid of their disguises, they eluded the Reds and boarded the westbound train.

————

Alexandra scraped a layer of frost away from the windowpane and gazed out. All was covered in snow and ice, and she felt a deep chill in her bones. It was warm enough in the house despite the fact that their new rulers had cut back on the fuel ration along with food and other comforts. Colonel Kobylinsky managed to continue to bring in the wood stumps for Nicky to chop—Nicky had requested this in order to have some form of physical activity. It was proving a valuable request.

No, what Alexandra felt was neither from the temperature in the room nor outside. It came from the inner desolation she feared would never go away. She tried to keep up her hopes, to trust in God's deliverance, but it was not always easy. How excited she had been several weeks ago when dear Grigori's son-in-law made contact with her and Nicky assured them that rescue was imminent. But now winter had clamped down harder than ever, and it seemed unlikely anything would happen until spring.

On top of that, life was becoming more difficult since those horrible Bolsheviks had taken over. The soldiers guarding them were getting far more demanding—uppity was another way of putting it. The other day they had made a search for weapons and had taken Mr. Gilliard's saber and Nicky's dagger—these were but ceremonial items, little or no threat at all. But a worse blow had come when they insisted that the officers, including Nicky, remove all epaulettes from their uniforms. Colonel Kobylinsky tried to talk them out of it, but it became sadly clear that he, their commander, had no real power over them. Nicky and Baby wore their epaulettes to church but hid them under their greatcoats. Kobylinsky had come to Nicky in great distress and said his nerves were falling apart and he wished to resign.

"Eugene Stepanovich, I ask that you stay," Nicky told him. "I don't know what we would do without you. Do you see that I and my wife and my children bear everything? You must bear it, too."

They did bear it. But for how much longer? Daily Alexandra felt as if the very life were draining out of her. She felt old and brittle. She tried to dwell on the good things. They had been allowed once again to attend church. The people in the village, when they had heard of the cut in rations, had started bringing them small items of food. And best of all, Baby had been doing so well lately. Not a single bleeding episode had occurred since coming to Siberia. That alone should have been enough to bolster Alexandra's melancholy.

"Mama, would you like a chair?"

"Ah, Tatiana, you are so thoughtful. I thought you were rehearsing *A Midsummer Night's Dream*."

"I wanted to see if you would join us."

"Perhaps later. I feel like lying down now."

Tatiana came to her and placed an arm around her

shoulders. "What were you looking at, Mama?"

"Nothing in particular." Slowly they walked to the bed, and Tatiana helped her mother recline upon it. "I can't help but wonder if soon the good Russian men will come to save us." Soloviev had assured her that three hundred Russian soldiers were standing ready to rescue them. She had gone so far as to discourage other monarchist groups from rescue attempts so as not to conflict with Soloviev.

"I don't know, Mama. It's been a while since we have heard anything."

"You mustn't lose hope, dear." Alexandra would never reveal her own inner doubts to her children. Hope and faith were all she had to give them these days. "Russia is a strong, noble country that is for a season in the hands of sinister forces. But the people are good and decent and will soon come to their senses and rise above it. God will not let this darkness reign upon us forever. He will deliver us."

Nicholas poked his head into the room. "There you are, Tatiana. We need you downstairs."

"Yes, Papa, I was just on my way down," said Tatiana. She bent down and kissed Alexandra's cheek, then went to the door.

"I'll be down directly," said Nicholas. Then, to his wife he added, "Are you not feeling well, Alix?"

"Just a bit tired."

Nicholas pulled a chair up next to the bed. "You should see the children. They are becoming quite accomplished thespians."

"They are growing so."

The girls were young women now. Olga had turned twenty-two just before Christmas. Tatiana was twenty, while Marie was eighteen. All three by rights could well be married by now. Anastasia, at sixteen, was still blossoming. But they were all four lovely girls, and Alexandra had no doubt that were they still at Court, they would be breaking many hearts. Even Alexis, though his parents continued to refer to him as Baby, was hardly that at thirteen.

"Marie and Tatiana," Alexandra went on, happy for some trivial conversation, "are worried they are getting fat with the lack of exercise."

"At least their hair is growing back."

The girls had lost handfuls of hair during the attack of the measles, and their heads had been shaved. They had been terribly self-conscious over this for some time. With all the troubles and upheavals in their lives, they were still young with all the normal angsts of youth.

Husband and wife chatted for a few more minutes, then Nicholas rose to leave. "It will be time for my lines soon. Do come and join us soon, Sunny."

"I will, dear Nicky."

He was about to bend down to give her a parting kiss when the door burst open.

"Mama! Papa!" It was Anastasia. "Baby has fallen down the stairs."

Apparently Alexis had become bored with the play rehearsal and, searching for something a bit more stimulating, had come across a small boat in a closet that he decided would be an excellent indoor sleigh. He carried it to the top of the stairs and had an exhilarating ride down until the boat hit the floor at the wrong angle and tipped over, sending him flying.

The injury to his groin was very similar to the one incurred at Spala six years ago. Only now it seemed far worse to Alexis. It had been such a long time since he'd had any serious flare-ups of his disease that he had been lulled into thinking perhaps it had been cured.

It seemed worse too for his mother, because there was no Father Grigori to offer help. Although in the last year hardly a day passed in which she did not miss her dear friend, now she was absolutely devastated by the loss. It was nearly as bad as that horrible day on which she had heard of his death.

As Alexis wept in pain and begged for death, Alexandra prayed for deliverance, begging God to show mercy upon them.

30

"I say, can you direct me to—"

But Lord Bruce was quickly rebuffed by the man who flashed him a suspicious glance before hurrying on his way. Even in spite of the fact that he was speaking English, Bruce had expected some sympathetic response. He knew Russians were more hospitable than this.

He stopped another passerby, a woman this time. "Madam, I am looking for—"

"Bourgeois! Bah!" she said before striding past.

If he'd known, really known, the true state of affairs in Petrograd, Bruce would have donned some manner of disguise. He could see now that the cut of his clothing—cashmere overcoat, expensive bowler, silk cravat—might be rather intimidating, or infuriating, depending on one's politics. Still, he had to find Daniel Trent's newspaper office. By phone they had arranged to meet this morning, and when Daniel had offered to come to his hotel, Bruce had declined. He wanted a chance to see a bit of the city and thought the ride to Daniel's office would be just the ticket. He hadn't counted on his cab driver leaving him at the wrong place, then driving away before Bruce could catch him. And he'd had no success at procuring another cab. They were apparently far more plentiful near hotels. His only hope now was to find someone who spoke English. But he felt rather like a panhandler standing on a street corner soliciting passersby. A gendarme was likely to arrest him soon, but perhaps that would be a blessing.

Bruce thought about his last visit to Russia some fifteen years earlier. It had been one of the last trips he took with his parents before they were killed in a boating accident. He had been a green boy of eighteen then, straining to be free—not knowing he would be free soon enough, and what a toll it would take on his life. But at eighteen he had resented his parents' control. He had been so rebellious that his father had often dubbed him "that little Jacobite."

His parents had gone to Russia both for pleasure and for business. His father was considering expanding some business interests to St. Petersburg. With Lord and Lady Findochty quite distracted with a vigorous round of social events at night, after consuming business negotiations all day, Bruce often found himself left to his own resources.

That's when Ella had come along. About Bruce's age, she was the daughter of one of the men who were attempting to woo Lord Findochty into investing in their firms. Although a countess, she was probably on a somewhat lower social level than Bruce. Bruce was not bothered at all by this. She was bright and beautiful and charming—and married. That did not prevent her from offering to escort Bruce about town and act as an interpreter. It was all innocent enough. Even her husband supported the idea. In fact, the man seemed hardly to care what she did with her time. Ella confessed it had been a marriage purely of convenience, arranged by their parents, and that there was no love in it at all.

It did not take long for Bruce and Ella to fall madly in love. They talked about her getting a divorce, or of simply running away together to some remote place, perhaps a tropical paradise. But down deep they both knew there was no future for them. Two weeks after the affair had begun, Bruce returned to England. He never heard from her again, and he never attempted to contact her, though for a time he had pined terribly for her. Then he met Louise, fell in love again, and married happily. But for some reason, he never told Louise about Ella—perhaps the only secret he had from her.

And he never did forget Ella. She had, after all, been his first love.

Nevertheless, it had been years since he'd thought about her—until the trouble in Russia had refreshed that dear but painful memory. Because her father and husband had been prominent, bourgeois types, it was possible they had suffered in the political upheavals. But Bruce refrained from contacting her. She had gotten on without him for fifteen years, so there seemed no sense in stirring up the past. However, when the general had voiced his own personal concerns about the fate of Russia, and the tsar whom he had met and admired, Bruce was easily recruited to take up the cause.

Now, here he was, back in Russia. He was tempted to look up Ella, but he resisted it. Despite the fact that he loved Louise, he still feared what might happen should the flames of youthful passion be stirred. On the other hand, it was quite possible Ella had aged into a fat old hag. Anyway, best to keep the memories sweet rather than destroy them with reality. Still, he could use Ella right about now to help him out of his present predicament.

He approached a few more persons until finally one took pity on him. At that point, all he could think to say that might be helpful was, "English! English!"

The young man, a student by appearance, took him in tow and led him around a corner to a book shop. Smiling, the fellow said, "English, eh?"

Bruce looked up to find painted on the shop window, "English Book Sellers." In short order, Bruce was set on his way. In fact the student, after getting directions from the proprietress, insisted on taking Bruce to his destination himself. Bruce's faith in the Russian character was restored.

Daniel wanted Yuri to be part of the meeting, so from the Register office, he and Bruce took a tram to Yuri's hospital, where they held their conclave in the hospital dining hall. Since it was between the breakfast and lunch hours, the place was practically deserted.

Daniel began the conversation by telling Bruce about his experiences in Tiumen.

"Rather an adventure, what?" said Bruce drolly.

"I believe I'm getting a bit too old for adventures like that," said Daniel. "I'm only glad I didn't know at the time just how close a call I had."

"What do you mean?"

"The two officers arrested by the Bolsheviks—they were executed."

"Good heavens!" exclaimed Bruce.

Misreading the Brit's expression, Daniel asked, "Do you still want to continue with this? It's more obvious than ever that the stakes are high."

"I am only more determined than ever to get on with it," assured Bruce. "I might have come sooner had I realized just how ruthless these Bolsheviks are. Anything could happen to the royal family at this point."

"I agree that we ought to move forward as quickly as possible. But one thing I learned from my trip east was that there is little we can do until spring. The tsar insists the family must stay together, and that makes travel in winter all the more impossible."

"I have also heard from Tatiana Botkin that the tsarevich has suffered a serious injury and is unable to walk," put in Yuri.

"How dreadful," said Bruce. "Even under the best of circumstances, I would think an escape of any sort, especially from the wilds of Siberia, would be physically demanding. Will they be able to do it when the time comes?"

"I think we ought to put the wheels in motion and worry about that later," said Daniel.

"The nature of the boy's illness would make him

always at risk," said Yuri. "But at least he would have a doctor with him at all times."

"So, it is your medical opinion that we move ahead?" questioned Bruce.

"Yes."

Daniel jumped in eagerly. "I propose we set up a head-quarters of sorts in Tobolsk—Tiumen, at the very least. But if we can get to Tobolsk, that would be the best locale because thus far it has no Bolshevik authority in place. And that is another reason to move quickly, because until the new government wakes up to that glaring gap in the chain of command, escape from the town will be far more manageable."

"What about the existing organization—you called it the Brotherhood of St. John of Tobolsk?"

"It is clear in my mind that Soloviev cannot be trusted," Daniel replied with conviction. "I have no con-clusive proof, but I am certain it was more than mere co-incidence that the Bolsheviks raided our hotel rooms the very night after we met with the man."

"So, you think he is in the pay of the Reds?"

"I'm not sure what his game is. He could merely have turned us in so he could have the 'corner' on all rescue attempts—and finances. But I would never risk trusting him. We have, however, gained a couple of valuable asso-ciates in this. The two officers I mentioned, Sedov and Melink, are behind us and will offer any assistance they can. And Dr. Botkin's daughter is in close contact with Yuri, which has proven a great help."

"You've laid excellent groundwork," said Bruce. "I only wish we had some insider in the Bolshevik organization itself. With the political situation so unstable and volatile, it could mean the difference between success and failure."

Daniel and Yuri exchanged looks, for this was a topic they had only recently discussed.

"Is there a problem?" asked Bruce.

"Not at all," said Daniel. "In fact, I believe we have just the man for the job."

But Yuri added, "I think I ought to temper that with my less than optimistic opinion. We know of a man who might be suitable, but it is still doubtful if he would agree to do this."

"Who is it? Have you spoken to him?"

"It's my brother," said Yuri. "He is a member of the Bolshevik Party—"

"You don't say! How extraordinary! I hope you don't mind my asking, since he is your brother and all, but . . . well, can he be . . ."

"Trusted?" Yuri finished for Bruce, saving him the awkwardness of the question. "He's had some rather extraordinary experiences himself in the last year and as a result has been having serious doubts about his affiliation. Nevertheless, I've been reluctant to broach the idea with him."

"If he does come on board," put in Daniel, "I have no doubt we will be able to trust him implicitly."

31

The months since his return home had been glorious ones for Andrei. For the first week he'd been pampered terribly. He found himself with three mothers who wanted to take care of him—not only his mother and Raisa, but he had also brought Sonja to live with them. Anna quipped that the big bedroom, already housing Raisa, Countess Zhenechka, Teddie, and herself, was becoming a regular girls' dormitory. Nevertheless, Anna was loving and accepting of the woman who had saved her son's life and did not seem to mind the fact that Sonja still called Andrei "Ivan" and thought him to be *her* son.

Andrei managed to distance himself from the Bolshevik

Party with a simple lie. Rudy told Stephan Kaminsky that the time in prison had wrecked Andrei's health and he'd had a relapse. None of his former Party comrades saw fit to visit his "sickbed" or even to verify his story. No doubt they were busy enough just trying to keep the government they had usurped from falling apart. Andrei did not mind their neglect in the least. It gave him a chance to fully sort out his feelings.

Never one to revel in long, drawn-out contemplation—he'd had plenty of that for the months in prison—Andrei quickly grew restless with his new and rather decadent lifestyle. He found a job loading freight in a factory. It was tough, physical labor, something he'd been sorely lacking in, but he enjoyed the work and the renewed physical fitness it gave him. He also liked being able to contribute to the household coffers, though he earned precious few rubles. He still had time to think and consider his future but not enough to unduly weigh him down.

His future . . .

There was so much confusion and uncertainty in his life at the moment, he hardly knew where to begin sorting it all out. First and foremost there was Talia, but before any commitments could be made with her, he had to work out many of the other things. They definitely wanted to marry, but he was in no position to support a wife and family. And he wasn't sure when he might be. He wanted to continue with his art, but few artists made enough of a living to support themselves, much less a family. Could he sacrifice his passion for art for Talia? He'd sacrificed it for the Party and had been miserable. Still he felt selfish even discussing it with her. Yet Talia made it clear she did not want him to sacrifice it. There must be a way to have their dreams and each other at the same time. In the meantime they contented themselves with being officially engaged. They saw each other nearly every day. Andrei arranged to work the night shift at the factory when Talia was usually performing, so their schedules did not conflict.

Then there was the matter of Andrei's political affiliations. He spent a great deal of his time with Talia mulling over those issues.

"Sometimes I feel so guilty lying to them as I have," he told her one day. The temperatures had warmed to about twenty-four degrees, and they were taking advantage of the sunny day by walking in the snow-covered Summer Gardens.

"I'm sure it's not easy to sever ties that have been so much a part of you for so long." Her arm was linked around his and it felt wonderful with her beside him.

"It's not that I agree with them anymore. I'm not sure I ever really did. I see now that I probably joined them merely as a rebellion against my family. I wanted to go as far in the opposite direction from Yuri as possible."

"But that wasn't the only reason for your beliefs, Andrei. They were always real and deep. When you expressed in your art the things you truly believed—not so much the *Pravda* cartoons, but the drawings of life, of oppressed peasants and workers—the passion you felt for freedom was so very clear."

"Yes, I don't deny that. But, Talia—" He stopped and turned to face her, his eyes afire with enthusiasm. "I've discovered something lately. I haven't talked to you about it yet because it is so revolutionary, I think it makes my former ideas seem tame." He gripped her arm closer to him and started walking again.

"Well, what is it?"

"I think my whole concept of freedom is—I won't say exactly *wrong*, but at least mixed up. You know I've been reading Papa's journals?"

"Yes, and you've said little about it."

"For once in my life I want to take it easy, not just jump in and ask questions later. I think this is going to be very important and I want to approach it with proper care." Talia smiled her support and he continued, "It's kind of ironic. The moment Yuri read the journals he said it changed his life immediately. He didn't have to think about it much at all. We've really changed places in this. He's frustrated that *now* I choose not to be impulsive." Andrei chuckled as he recalled his and Yuri's last discussion on the matter.

"You love driving your brother crazy," she said lightly.

"Yes, I suppose I do. But that's not my only motive. I truly want to do it right this time. I've made too many mistakes in the past with my impulsive nature."

"And so, what about your concept of freedom?"

"My father made mention of it when he escaped from Siberia and found himself in the mission in China. He was free in a physical sense but not in a spiritual sense. I began to examine my ideas of freedom. I believed the Russian people were in bondage to the tsar and that I must fight for their freedom. I believed that when the tsar was deposed, freedom would come at last. Finally, the tsar is gone, but are the Russian people free? It's just not as clear as I thought it would be—as I thought it *should* be. A grand utopia has not been realized. And I'm not sure it ever will be, not here or anywhere. I am beginning to think that political freedom, if it is valid at all, is merely a drop of water in a desert. Freedom means nothing if you are not free within yourself—"

"Spiritual freedom?" Talia said with a slight smile.

"You've known about these things all along haven't you?"

"Well . . ."

"I guess a person has to figure it out for himself. And, yes, spiritual freedom is definitely one of the things I am searching—and not making an impulsive decision about."

"I suppose if you must search, you must. But I'll bet your father said it was a very simple matter."

"He did. How is it so for you, Talia? Why does your faith never waver?"

"I can't say it never wavers. When I thought you were

dead, there were times I wondered if God was any use at all."

"But you didn't give it up—your faith, that is."

"A person's faith and their reasons for faith are not always simple to define. God feels far away at times, sometimes He feels very close. But I'm sure it's me that does the changing, not He. And that's just it. We are changing so much and, not surprisingly, our faith changes with us—but the object of that faith never changes, and that is why I cannot give it up even when God *feels* far away. He is still God, you see, and the *fact* of His mercy and love and redemption are always constant."

Andrei smiled. "I was thinking of something similar to that not long ago. Papa once said that very thing."

Talia returned the smile. "I know. I lived with your papa also, and learned from him."

"Why do I fight it so, Talia?"

"I just don't know."

"If only for you—"

"No, Andrei! I want more than anything for us to share a mutual faith. But I would never want you to put on faith just to please me. It wouldn't work, anyway. You know as well as I that it has to be real to be any good."

"I know. I appreciate your having patience with me."

"When it happens, Andrei, I know it will have been worth the wait."

"When. . . ?"

"Yes, *when*."

"Talia, have I told you today how much I love you?"

"I don't think you have, Andrei Sergeiovich." She mimicked a pout. "How very thoughtless of you."

"I do love you, Talia. I want so desperately for us to be together as husband and wife." He took her in his arms, but their heavy winter garments, gloves, hats, and scarves caused the embrace to greatly lack in the passion they both felt inside.

They laughed at how silly they must look.

"Now I know how two bears feel," Andrei quipped.

They started walking once again, and after a few minutes of comfortable silence Talia said, "Andrei, I must confess to you that I would marry a starving artist."

"And I must confess that I am almost selfish enough to say all right. But we will see what happens, Talia. I promise, I won't wait forever."

"At least we would starve together."

"I can think of worse fates."

———

Not long after that walk, another dilemma was to confront Andrei. He knew it did not bode well when both Daniel and Yuri approached him one evening after dinner. They were wearing very serious expressions.

"Can we talk to you privately?" Daniel asked.

When Andrei said, "Of course," they went in search of a private place, not an easy task in that house full of souls. They finally went to Yuri's room, and Katya and Irina busied themselves in another part of the apartment. Andrei, who was sleeping on the floor of the parlor, had seriously considered moving in with Rudy, who still was occupying his old room in the building where Sonja had lived. He'd be closer to Talia, but he knew it would be difficult for both Anna and Sonja if he left. Still, he often wondered how long fourteen people could continue to occupy the small apartment.

But he forgot all about that relatively insignificant concern when he and his brother and brother-in-law were settled in the bedroom and Daniel opened the conversation.

"Andrei, you have been home some time now, and I know you have been going through many changes," said Daniel. "The last thing we want to do is to make your life more complex than it is."

For a moment Andrei thought they were about to give him the boot. If only it had been that simple.

"We were wondering," Daniel continued, and Andrei could tell he was working hard to be diplomatic, "if you have made any decisions regarding your . . . uh . . . political affiliations."

Daniel would have been disappointed to realize his attempts at diplomacy were having the opposite effect. Andrei, still thinking they were about to ask him to leave because of the overcrowding, was put on the defensive. "Does that make a difference around here?"

"You don't understand," put in Yuri quickly. "Listen to what Daniel has to say before you fly off the handle."

"I'm not 'flying off the handle,'" Andrei rejoined, more defensive than ever, suddenly recalling all the old discord with his brother.

"I'm afraid I've gone about this all wrong," said Daniel.

"Why don't you just spit out what's on your mind?" said Andrei, making an effort to moderate his temper.

Daniel took a breath, glanced quickly at Yuri, then continued, "We need your help, Andrei. We need for you to get back into the Bolshevik circle. We need a . . . spy."

"What?"

"Your brother and I are part of an organization planning to rescue the tsar—"

"You? Both of you. . . ?" Andrei shook his head, completely mystified.

"It's a long story. We will fill you in completely if you decide to help us—"

"You want me to help you *rescue* the tsar?" Andrei rubbed his eyes as if to ensure that he wasn't imagining what he'd just heard. "I rejoiced the day he was deposed."

"And will you rejoice the day he is murdered?" Yuri asked harshly.

"How dare you!"

"Come on," said Daniel calmly. "Let's discuss this civilly. Andrei, I feel confident in approaching you with this because I *know* you don't want to see anyone murdered. I know you love justice as much as we do, and you honor mercy, not vengeance."

"Yes, I do," Andrei said tightly with a quick glance at Yuri.

"I'm sorry, Andrei," Yuri said earnestly. "I spoke out of turn."

"It's okay," said Andrei, then with a resolved sigh added, "What makes you think the tsar is going to get murdered, anyway? He has been in captivity for nearly a year, and he remains alive and safe—" He stopped, realizing it would help no one for him to play games. "All right, you are probably right to be concerned. The Bolsheviks have been shouting the loudest all this time for his death. Now that they are in power . . . well, anything could happen, it is true."

"What do you think about that?" asked Daniel softly, carefully.

"Thirteen years ago, I would have killed the man myself. For weeks after Papa was killed, I had dreams—nightmares, I guess—about killing Nicholas, about him blowing up into a million pieces, or of me aiming a rifle at him and blasting him full of holes. I never told anyone about those dreams. They scared me. I wasn't raised in a way that helped me to know what to do with such hatred."

"That's why you were so quiet after Papa died," said Yuri quietly.

"I knew you'd all think I was an evil person if I voiced such things, and they so filled me I knew they'd come out if I spoke. But, Yuri, didn't you have any such feelings?"

"I didn't let myself think that way," Yuri added quickly, almost defensively, "but I know now my reasons weren't entirely altruistic. I knew even then that my destiny was bound to the monarchy—that's what I wanted, to be of the aristocracy, the power structure—so it would have been self-defeating to blame the tsar."

"You had seemed so good and noble about it."

"I'm truly sorry . . ."

"Well, it's in the past. And my hatred dulled after time. I knew I wasn't going to murder anyone. I couldn't even try as Uncle Paul did." Andrei paused and chuckled, hoping to lighten things a bit. "I couldn't be a murderer because the minute I saw blood I'd faint and be instantly caught."

"There's always poison," countered Daniel, again lightly. But when he noted the grim look on Yuri's face his amusement faded. "I'm sorry, Yuri."

Yuri shrugged, trying to set him at ease. "Don't give it a thought. One can't turn around in this family without finding a painful skeleton or two in the closet. Anyway, Andrei, what are your feelings now about the tsar?"

"I think he was a misguided fool who was as caught in family history as we are—three hundred years worth for him! Does he deserve to die for that? It would serve no purpose. And certainly his thirteen-year-old son doesn't deserve to die."

"Yes. . . ?" Daniel prompted.

"Even if I do agree the tsar shouldn't die, you are asking that I spy on former comrades—betray them. I will be honest with you that I am no longer one of them in my heart, if I ever was. I have changed, perhaps become more pragmatic. Because I see both sides of many things now, I cannot muster my former passion for a particular political position. But that doesn't negate my past—I worked for the Bolsheviks to achieve power. I once thought I believed in them. I can't turn around and betray them."

"Even if what they are doing is morally wrong?" asked Daniel.

Andrei ran a hand through his hair and shook his head. "You know how I hate these mental conundrums."

"You can have time to think it over."

"No. That's the last thing I want. I'll do it." He then added in response to Daniel and Yuri's surprised looks, "It's the right thing."

32

Andrei met Stephan Kaminsky at the Smolny. They hadn't seen each other since Andrei's arrest in July, and the meeting was understandably tense. Only Andrei's desire to get himself back into the good graces of the Party kept him civil.

"You look well," said Stephan as they walked down a corridor to his office. "Gruenwald said you had pneumonia."

"Yes. I guess I hadn't regained my strength from my previous illness, then the time in prison—"

"Look here, Andrei, I hope you don't hold that against the Party."

"No, of course not. Why should I?" But it took all the discipline Andrei had not to confront Stephan with his worst offense—keeping the identity of Andrei's family from him when he had amnesia. But it would not serve Andrei's purpose to stir up grudges. This was the time to mend fences, not poke holes in them.

"Good." They came to a closed door and Stephan paused. "Come on in and let's talk. Perhaps we can see how best to use you in the new government."

Andrei restrained a relieved sigh as they entered the office. It appeared as if he had succeeded in being reinstated. There were three desks in the small, rather austere room, none of which were at the moment occupied. Stephan led Andrei to the desk by a window, drew up a chair for him, then took for himself the chair behind the desk.

"So, what is your position in the government?" Andrei asked.

"I am Second Commissar, under Dzerzhinsky, of the All-Russian Extraordinary Commission to Combat Counter-Revolution and Sabotage, known by its acronym of Cheka."

"What exactly is that?" Andrei didn't like the sound of it, whatever it was.

"I suppose it is best described as a security police force. The task of putting down counterrevolution and securing our success is perhaps one of the most vital in the new government. Sedition and brutality by our enemies must be met with equal and decisive force. You cannot believe the heinous acts the bourgeois are perpetrating against us—sabotaging food stores, murdering and mutilating Reds, not to mention inciting discord among the masses. Our survival depends on our unequivocal ruthlessness."

"Ruthlessness. . . ?"

"You always were a bit too squeamish, Andrei. But there can be no other way. We are trying to make a new world—a utopia, so to speak. Every day scores of decrees are issued from this office—that is, the Smolny. Every institution is undergoing dramatic restructuring. Private ownership of land has been abolished, and the banks have been nationalized along with private enterprises. Our entire justice system has been revamped. Women have been given equal rights with men. The power of the church has been greatly limited and all its lands—which amounts to an enormous quantity—have been confiscated by the state. Religious teaching in schools has been forbidden. Why, we have even adopted the Western calendar.

"So, you see, such changes cannot come easily, especially to the bourgeois who are most affected. All that we do is justified in the name of freedom. We must totally destroy the old world to prevent it from coming back to haunt us."

"I see . . ."

"We are a communist state now. Marx is our model. We cannot leave behind any remnant of the old, if for no other reason than that it would show our weakness."

"What about bread and peace, the rallying cries of the revolution?" Andrei had been reading the newspapers and knew about the changes Stephan was outlining. He also knew that the war continued, and hunger and privation were still rampant among the people.

"You must know that we have already increased the bread ration by half. Lenin has authorized raids all over the land and has found and confiscated tons of food stores, many that had been hoarded by the bourgeois for sale on the black market. As for the war, we cannot be expected to instantly clean up the mess left by the imperialist and bourgeois governments. The Allies have not recognized our government and have met all our efforts to include them in a peace initiative with silence. Trotsky, who is the People's Commissar for Foreign Affairs, has therefore entered into negotiations for a separate peace with Germany."

"That will not make Lenin's government popular with the world powers."

"No, but at least it will show them that we are not a force to be reckoned with lightly." Stephan shifted in his chair, obviously ready to move the conversation in another direction. "So, Andrei Sergeiovich, let's talk about where you want to fit into the Soviet of People's Commissars."

"I assumed I would continue with my old duties at *Pravda*. Surely the new government is in need of a vital propaganda machine."

"Indeed it is. But a man such as yourself might be better suited to a more—how shall I put it?—active role in the government. To tell the truth, I never have believed you well suited to the job of sedentary maker of pretty *pictures*." This last word Stephan said with such disdain, Andrei barely could keep from rising up in defense. "I propose taking you into the Cheka."

"I have no training as a policeman, Stephan."

"Not a single man in the government has training in the jobs assigned them. We are learning by the seat of our pants. Already, I have picked up a great deal I can pass on to you."

Andrei had hoped to secure his place in the new government in some mild, insignificant capacity such as his old job at *Pravda*. If he was thrust into an aggressive job like the Cheka, he might be forced to do things that conflicted not only with his newfound political stance but also with his sense of morality. However, he was just beginning to understand how naïve he had been. In order for him to be privy to the kind of intelligence necessary to save the tsar, he was probably going to have to worm his way into some security capacity. He should consider himself quite lucky that Stephan was proposing that very thing.

On the other hand, he knew Stephan, who had always been a little suspicious of his loyalty, was very likely testing him. He had to take care in his response. Stephan's suspicions might be raised if Andrei was too eager. Moreover, Andrei did not want to do anything that would tarnish his morals. Somehow Andrei had to show interest in the proposal without making a solid commitment.

"It is worth considering," said Andrei. "It would be rather difficult to sit in an office all day missing the real action. Still, I just don't know if I am physically up to such a job. My stamina has been greatly reduced since my most recent illness." Andrei was pleased with his ingenuity in his final statement. He could buy a lot of time by pleading his illness.

"We'll start you off slowly." Stephan smiled. "I have a small task I must perform this very day that could be an ideal initiation for you."

"What is it?"

"Our revolutionary tribunal has recently tried and convicted an old adversary of ours."

"Of ours. . . ?"

"Our old nemesis, Cyril Vlasenko."

"I wondered what became of him."

"The Provisional Government all but pampered and coddled those old tsarist leaders. While the Soviet government is trying to win world recognition, we are refraining from mass executions. But a special exception is being made in Vlasenko's case. His crimes against the Russian people are so well documented, even those squeamish Americans would not protest his execution."

"He is to be executed, then? Today?"

"Yes, and I'd like you to witness it with me."

Andrei swallowed back all his distaste at this prospect. Here was the perfect opportunity to increase his credibility with Kaminsky. "What perfect timing!" Andrei said with enthusiasm. "I'm glad you said something. That man has been a thorn in the side of my family for years. I would gladly watch as justice is served on him."

"I thought you might like that. We'll do it at sundown. Until then, let me show you around here a bit and let your comrades know you are back with us."

———

The cellars of the Butyrki Prison seemed especially dank and chilly as Andrei traversed its corridors on his gruesome mission. He tried to remind himself that of all people, Cyril Vlasenko deserved to die more than many. Not only for his spiteful crimes against the Fedorcenko/Burenin families. That alone was a staggering account—from his sadistic treatment of Uncle Paul, imprisoned as a youth in an Akulin jail, to his plots that financially ruined the Fedorcenko family. And who could tell how much Vlasenko was involved in the many other family tragedies. There was some hint that his plots had led to Sergei's banishment to Asia, which eventually propelled him down the path to Siberian exile.

But there had also come to light evidence confirming his part in many national crimes as well. As head of the Third Division, he had been instrumental in sending scores of revolutionaries—many of whom were now in power—into exile or to labor camps. During the tribunal, a substantial number had witnessed to Vlasenko's personal part in beatings, torture, and unjust executions of political prisoners. At least the Bolsheviks had given Vlasenko the benefit of a trial—a formality he had denied most of his victims.

Yet Andrei thought of his father's journal and the many references in it to forgiveness. Sergei, whose life had perhaps been most harmed by Vlasenko's evil machinations would have been the first to forgive the man. Andrei was somewhat comforted in the fact that he did not feel the depth of hatred and vindication he thought he might feel at this moment. Indeed, as he approached the room where the execution would be conducted, he felt deep loathing at what was about to transpire. He did not relish at all having to witness it.

At least, he thought, a greater good might come from Cyril Vlasenko's demise. And perhaps even the old reprobate might be comforted knowing that his death was contributing in a small way to bringing about the rescue of his tsar. After all, Vlasenko was as staunch a monarchist as there was.

Andrei, Stephan, and a handful of other spectators took their places at the back of the room, a good twenty feet from where the victim would stand. Then, five minutes later, the prisoner was brought in. The last time Andrei had seen Vlasenko was at his gallery showing not quite four years before. Vlasenko appeared to have aged twenty years in those four. His skin was pasty, his eyes ringed with dark circles, and great folds of skin hung from his face due to weight loss that probably amounted to some fifty pounds. Andrei recalled Yuri saying Vlasenko had a serious heart condition. He did appear to be having difficulty breathing.

But there was a certain defiance in the old man's eyes, especially as he glanced at the spectators' area. Andrei tried to avoid eye contact, but their eyes did lock for an instant, and he knew Vlasenko recognized him. Andrei wished at that moment he could tell Vlasenko that he did not want to be there, that his only purpose was to bring about the rescue of the tsar. He wanted to say, "I forgive you, Cyril Vlasenko." Instead, he had to stand there like Saul in the Bible, in essence holding the coats of the man's executioners.

To Vlasenko's credit, he waved away a blindfold and stood as straight as his old body could manage while he was tied to the post.

The head of the tribunal that had convicted Vlasenko stepped forward and read from a prepared statement: "In the name of the Soviet of People's Commissars, this day the sentence of execution by firing squad will be carried out against one Citizen Cyril Karlovich Vlasenko for heinous crimes against the people of the Soviet and against mankind. Citizen Vlasenko, do you have any last words?"

With an unmistakable smirk on his lips, Vlasenko merely shook his head.

The tribunal head then nodded toward the six riflemen, who took their places in front of the prisoner and lifted their weapons.

Until that moment Andrei had not given a thought to the actual execution. He had not considered what it might be like to watch a man die before his eyes, nor how this might affect his particular aversion to blood. And it was too late now to do anything about it. He just prayed it would have no affect at all. That—

Suddenly gunfire rent the air. Had Andrei been prepared he might have closed his eyes and kept them closed until he could escape that terrible room. But before he could do so, or even turn away, he saw the body jerk violently before it drooped against its bonds. He also saw the blood spray from the wounds.

And he was absolutely powerless to prevent his immediate physical response. He stumbled back against the wall as if he himself had been shot. And the next thing he knew he was doubled over, losing the fine lunch of cabbage and sausages Stephan had given him earlier in the day.

Had he had any capacity at all to think, he would have realized he had destroyed his chances of ingratiating himself to Stephan, and that the entire purpose in watching the execution had been spoiled.

Only with the help of Stephan and a few of the other spectators was he able to leave the room. His legs were trembling so, they had to support him all the way outside and into a cab that took him and Stephen back to the Smolny. It was in the cab that Andrei realized he hadn't spoiled his chances to help Daniel and Yuri after all.

Stephan was laughing at him, but in a good-natured way. "You are not the first man who has fainted at such a sight."

"I didn't faint," Andrei said weakly.

"No, that is true—to your credit!"

"I've never had much of a stomach for blood."

"This is only the first of many executions."

"I thought you said there would be no mass executions because of world image."

"It will happen eventually. It must. Remember what I also said about the old order being destroyed. Executions must be part of that. In fact it is our moral duty. Lenin has said that communist morality is what serves to destroy the old order that is exploiting the Proletariat. In doing this we are being morally and socially responsible. You'll have to get over your weak stomach if you want to work for me."

"Give . . . me time."

"What is it they say, 'the spirit is willing, but the flesh is weak.' " Stephan laughed again. "Don't worry, Andrushka, you'll get another chance."

Andrei wondered if that was a promise or a threat.

33

Nicholas knew it had been inevitable from the moment that Lenin usurped power. Yet he could not help reacting with overwhelming grief to the news in March of the Bolsheviks' peace treaty with Germany.

"And to think, they called my Alix a traitor! Those Bolsheviks are the real traitors!" he lamented. "And I can hardly believe that the Kaiser stooped to dealing with them."

He pressed Colonel Kobylinsky for all the details. "The Bolsheviks were stalling as long as possible trying to give the appearance of moving toward peace while at the same time creating whatever roadblocks they could."

"That scoundrel Lenin was just trying to buy time in hopes of fomenting a revolution in Germany!" said Alexandra bitterly. "Not that I care what happens to the Kaiser any longer."

"The Germans had reason to be worried," said Kobylinsky, gratefully accepting a glass of tea from Nicholas. "Their war effort is not going well either. Some say they are ripe for an uprising."

Nicholas gripped his own glass of tea in his hand, but he couldn't drink. His stomach was in too much of an uproar. "They'd want to move quickly, then. I heard also that they have poured upward of fifty million marks into the Bolshevik government. No doubt they feared it wouldn't stay in power long enough for them to receive a return on their investment."

"As it is, they got a very . . . good return." Alexandra's voice caught on her words as obvious emotion rose within her.

Nicholas, too, wanted to weep over the ugly results of the peace negotiations. Lenin had called for "peace at any price," and that he had received. The Germans were to occupy a quarter of Russian territory, comprising one-third of her population. That this territory included the Ukraine was even more devastating because Russia would lose nearly a third of its prime crop lands. With civil war looming over the battered land along with certain famine, it was difficult to see how Russia could survive.

Colonel Kobylinsky made mention of another aspect of the treaty, "I heard there is a clause in the treaty that demands that the royal family be handed over to the Germans unharmed."

Perhaps he thought he was delivering some hope to the Romanovs. He couldn't have been more mistaken.

"After this," Alexandra declared, "I would rather die in Russia than be rescued by those Germans!"

―――――

The peace treaty seemed to awaken Lenin to the fact that he still held a very hot property in Tobolsk. It was always possible he could use the tsar to improve the treaty terms. On the other hand, the Germans might also have use for the deposed monarch. The Kaiser had made noises to the effect that he wanted the royal family remanded to his custody.

Until Lenin decided how best to use the royal pawn he held, he felt it imperative that the guard in Tobolsk be strengthened.

Stephan told this to Andrei, who saw both disaster and opportunity in the news. Until now, Tobolsk had remained fairly untouched by the new regime, and according to reports Daniel received from a couple of soldiers he was in contact with, the present guards had grown rather sympathetic to the royals. Lenin's new directive would definitely impede rescue attempts.

On the other hand, Andrei saw the perfect opportunity to worm his way closer to the royal family. He quickly seized the moment without even discussing his actions with Daniel and Yuri.

"Stephan, I want to be part of the new guard regiment," he said emphatically.

"You?"

"Yes, why not? When will I ever have a better chance for vengeance?"

"You mean for your father's death?"

"Yes!"

"But this is not an execution squad."

"At least I will have the satisfaction of watching him totally debased. And who knows? Maybe it will be an execution squad soon enough. How much longer can Lenin skirt that issue? Since the revolution began, the masses have been crying out for justice."

"Believe me, Lenin wants justice."

"Please, send me. I don't want to miss whatever happens."

"I've never known you to be so passionate about such matters."

Andrei hoped he hadn't appeared too enthusiastic, but he felt he had to play out his move. "Since my father's death, I have dreamed of little else but the demise of the tsar, his killer."

"I suppose you have made mention of that." Stephan paused and rubbed his chin thoughtfully. "Tell me something, Andrei, would you take responsibility for such an act . . . the, how shall I put it . . . disposal of the tsar? Your weak stomach would not deter you?"

"Perhaps there will be some poetic justice to it," Andrei replied with a wicked smile. "I believe it was watching my father die that gave me my weak stomach in the first place. Perhaps watching his murderer die will restore it to normal."

"I'll see what I can do."

———

Andrei arranged a meeting with Daniel and Yuri. Since his return to the Bolsheviks, he had taken up residence with Rudy in his one-room apartment next to where Sonja had lived. The move had been hard on Anna, but he had felt it best to distance himself from his family, since Stephan had always been suspicious of Andrei's relationship with them.

Now, however, any meetings with his brothers had to be arranged clandestinely because it was almost certain they were being watched to some extent, especially Daniel, since he was a foreigner. Andrei selected Yuri's hospital as the meeting place, since it would be easily accepted that he had gone there for medical treatment because of his previous illness. And even Stephan would not think it too odd that Andrei would choose to be treated by his brother.

Daniel had the most difficulty getting there. He adopted a disguise—that of an old Russian worker dressed in threadbare clothes, a seaman's cap, and even a knotty old cane on which he hobbled masterfully. Any watchers only saw a worker, possibly a veteran, going to the hospital for treatment. He then slipped into an examining room next to the one Andrei had entered only moments before. Only Yuri and the hospital staff were aware that these two particular rooms had adjoining doors.

"I'm sorry I haven't been in touch this past couple of weeks," said Andrei once Yuri and Daniel had joined him. "But little has happened until now."

"So what—?" Yuri began but stopped instantly when a sound was heard outside the door.

"Dr. Fedorcenko," came a voice outside, "I am here for that consultation." The voice's owner spoke in very bad Russian.

To Yuri's and Andrei's puzzled looks, Daniel said, "I didn't have time to tell you, but at the last minute Bruce decided to attend the meeting. I gave him a lab coat and stethoscope that I found at home, Yuri. He appears quite authentic—except for his Russian."

While Andrei and Daniel stood away, out of sight, Yuri

opened the door. "Thank you for coming Dr., ah, Mitkov."

Bruce stepped in and Yuri quickly closed the door behind him. The Brit did indeed look like a doctor.

"I'm afraid I rather butchered the phrases you taught me, Daniel," said Bruce.

Andrei noted that the Brit might pass for a doctor, but never for a Russian. Not only because of his accent, but because he looked far too British to do so. And Andrei wondered how many doctors were blind in one eye. Even if there were some, the eye patch was the kind of identifying feature most spies would like to avoid. But the damage was done. Hopefully he and Daniel had been careful enough to have thrown off surveillance long before Bruce's arrival.

"We'll have to keep working on it, Bruce," said Daniel. Then he introduced him to Andrei. They conversed in English for Bruce's benefit, for although Andrei's English was worse than Yuri's, it was far better than Bruce's Russian.

Bruce shook Andrei's hand. "I hope you know how great a service you are doing for our cause. Your brother informed me of the sacrifice you are making. It has not gone unappreciated."

Andrei was truly flustered by the sincere formality of Bruce's words. "Spasiba—" he began, forgetting his English, then quickly corrected himself, "Thank you. It's . . . uh . . . that is, I—" but he could hardly think of a response in Russian, much less in English. He wished he'd been more attentive to his mother's lessons as a child.

Thankfully, Daniel came to his rescue. "Bruce, Andrei was just about to inform us of some new developments."

"Excellent! I hope they will benefit us. We do need a bit of a break."

It was slow going as Andrei made his report in English with much help from the others who prompted him when he couldn't think of the proper words.

"Well," Andrei began, "Lenin has finally taken notice of

his captives and is bolstering the guard in Tobolsk."

"We feared that would happen sooner or later," said Daniel.

"This is not good news," added Bruce, though it hardly needed saying.

"But I have managed to get myself assigned to the new guard contingent," said Andrei. "It was just made official a short time ago."

"What?" said Daniel and Yuri together.

Then Yuri said, "You are going to Tobolsk?"

"I will leave for Moscow in two days to join up with the regiment there."

"We must get to Tobolsk," said Bruce.

"You'll never make it in advance of the regiment."

"If we leave immediately, surely three of us can travel faster than a hundred soldiers," said Bruce, his left eye flashing with determination. "But my intent is not to try a rescue attempt before the troops arrive—that would be quite impossible. Nevertheless, we need to be there. Anything could happen with this change. We were only holding out here to allow you to do some good, Andrei. Well, I believe this is it. You have done very well. We won't have a better chance. It was one thing to have an informer in Petrograd. It will be far more to our advantage to have an informer in Tobolsk right among the guards themselves. We must grasp the opportunity!"

"We could be on the night train," said Daniel, catching Bruce's enthusiasm.

"I don't know," said Yuri, and all eyes turned to him. "I'm sorry, I don't mean to be a wet blanket, but . . . we weren't going to say anything until we were certain, and we only became certain yesterday."

"Certain about what?" asked Andrei.

"Katya is expecting."

Everyone momentarily forgot their mission as they offered happy congratulations to the expectant father. Daniel and Andrei knew what a momentous occasion this was

241

and how long Yuri and Katya had desired a child.

"Of course you can't leave her," assured Daniel.

"I wouldn't be so reluctant if it wasn't for the problems in the past."

"Don't give it another thought, Yuri," said Andrei. He smiled at his brother. "You're going to be a papa after all, and nothing is more important than that." He thought fleetingly of Talia and wondered if they would ever be in a place to know the joys of marriage and family. Andrei wanted more than ever for that time to come quickly.

Yet events seemed to be once again driving them apart rather than together. He had to go to Tobolsk, and he had to face the certain risks of being an informer among foes he now knew to be extremely ruthless against traitors.

34

Of course he played down the risks when he saw Talia in her flat later that day and told her of his impending journey to Tobolsk. It was late afternoon, and nearly all her roommates, six total, were present because they had finished practice for the day and had no other place to be until their various performances in the evening. The noise level and distractions were intense, and finally Talia took Andrei's hand and, after each donned a warm coat, led him outside.

A light snow fell upon them and the air was freezing. Andrei remembered that glorious day when they had declared their love in the rain. The elements would always be welcome to him. But Talia was shivering after a short walk, and finding an open tea shop, they ducked inside. Between them they could spare only enough money to buy a single glass of tea. Andrei was embarrassed by this circumstance. It made him all the more aware of the barriers that stood between them and marriage.

"I hate being always so poor," he complained.

"Please don't let it bother you, Andrei. We have so much besides money." The warm intensity in Talia's eyes spoke much more than her simple, almost trite words.

"And I have never been happier, Talia. Yet, here I am about to leave you again, and still I can make no promises for our future."

"I would like to talk to you about that."

"Our future?"

"No. I have complete confidence our future will work out. Instead, I wish to talk to you about leaving."

"I must, Talia. As much as I hate to admit it, all hope of success depends on my part in this."

"I know that, and I know you must go. I'm not going to stop you. But—" She looked up at him with her large doe eyes so full of warmth and love. "I am also not going to let you go alone."

"What do you mean?"

"I'm going with you."

His mouth fell open at the soft but firm declaration. "Talia—"

"Listen to me, Andrei. We wasted too many years separated, either by our stupidity or by circumstances or by actual miles. I won't let that happen again if I can help it—and I can help it now. There is no reason for me not to go to Tobolsk with Daniel and Lord MacDuff. Who knows how long you will be there, Andrei? Do you truly wish to be separated again for an indefinite period of time?"

"No, I don't, but—"

"But what? Will you tell me it is dangerous? I will share your danger as I share your love. Anyway, you are the one who will be taking the greatest risks. I know you have tried to downplay those dangers, but I know what they are. I know what could happen should you be discovered as an informer. Daniel and Lord Bruce are foreigners and would most likely be spared serious consequences. I am a woman and might be spared also. But you—" she paused, choking back sudden emotion. "Oh, Andrei! Please don't force me to be parted from you now! And I could very well be a help to you. There might be many uses for a woman in such a situation. I might be able to get into places and talk to people you or the others could not."

"I guess I am too selfish to refuse you," he said with a slight smile.

"It's not selfishness. You and I know too well how life can take unexpected turns."

"Talia . . ." Gazing at her he knew he should be happy, but just then he was suddenly sad. "Will we ever be free just to be together and love each other and . . ." He sighed. "I am so tired of all the twists and turns of life."

She reached out and placed her small, pale fingers over his large, strong hand. "I believe God will lift us from all this. If we trust Him, will He not give us the desires of our hearts?"

"If only I could have your faith, especially now."

"You can, Andrei."

"Yes, just by surrendering. My father wrote about surrender in his journal. Yuri has spoken of it also. I have no problem with surrendering to God. I suppose right now it is just a matter of timing."

He paused and reached for the glass of tea—his mouth was suddenly very dry. At the same moment Talia also reached for the glass. As their hands brushed, they chuckled. Talia nodded for him to go ahead, and he didn't argue as he brought the glass to his lips.

"It's not easy to talk about these things," he said when he finished and handed the glass to her. "Even to you, Talia."

"Don't you think I will understand?" She wasn't interested in the tea any longer.

"I know you will. And I'd have no argument to offer you."

"Why debate it then?"

"Christian faith is far too easy for a man like me. I'm afraid I will jump into it when life starts to get tough, then cast it aside when things are smooth—"

"When life *starts* to get tough?" Talia smiled. "Andrei, my love, look around. Life *is* hard. You have personally suffered much. Improvement seems distant at best. Maybe it will never change. How long will you wait in order to catch God at a good moment in life?"

"Do you think I am just making excuses?" He sighed.

Talia's silence was answer enough.

"Maybe I am, but I only wish to be certain."

"Andrei, let me ask you a question—and remember, I am not trying to push you, because I want you to be certain also. This is just something else to consider. Do you see yourself as the kind of man who would be the fickle sort, using God in bad times and forgetting Him in good?"

"I fear it."

"Then perhaps you don't know yourself as well as I know you. And I know you are not that kind of man. And even if you were, that is, even if your faith was more intense in low moments, what is wrong with that? Do you think, if your heart is sincere, God would reject you? Not my God, Andrei. Not the God your mother loves, the God your father loved all his life."

"Ah, I will tell you, Talia, I am growing weary running from God. All I have ever wanted was to be the kind of man my father would want me to be. Yet, I have shunned the one part of him that made him the man he was."

At that moment the tea shop door opened, and with a chill gust of wind, several customers breezed in. They were chatting noisily about a cinema they had just seen.

Talia took Andrei's hand. "Come."

They weren't far from the Nicholas Bridge, and at Talia's suggestion, they crossed the bridge to Vassily

Island. They did not pick up the dangling thread of Andrei's last comments. Andrei knew Talia wasn't ignoring it because she said she wanted to wait a bit before talking further on that subject. As they came to St. Andrew's market, Andrei began to perceive her motives. He made no protest.

The market was quiet that late in the afternoon. Most of the food to be sold was gone by then. Only a few sellers lingered, mostly individuals trying to hawk a few poor household items. Andrei and Talia crossed the marketplace and came to the entrance of Old St. Andrew's church. Andrei now recalled how his mother had once told him he had been named for the old church that she loved and still attended. Since the Bolshevik takeover, the Church was greatly frowned upon but, except for confiscation of lands and forbidding religious instruction in schools, no more far-reaching limits had been placed upon it. Andrei knew well enough Lenin's views on this subject and knew it was only a matter of time before the Church was suppressed more harshly.

Now, however, the doors were open and Andrei followed Talia inside. He was struck immediately with the close air and cloying fragrance of incense, such a strong contrast to the cold, crisp air outside. Candles burned on the front altar and a handful of worshipers milled about.

Finally, Andrei thought it was time to return to their conversation earlier in the tea shop.

"You know as well as I, Talia, that faith to Mama and Papa never had to do with a building such as this."

"I don't know why I wanted to come here," she replied quietly. "I have an odd feeling that one day soon a visit to a church will not be such a simple thing."

"I have more than an odd feeling about that."

Andrei looked about, his eyes pausing at the rich iconostasis on the front altar. The gold encasing the many icons was stunning even for a poor church such as St. Andrew's. He thought again of his father and of attending this church with him when he had been alive. The rituals of the Church were not everything to Anna, but they had definitely meant more to her than to Sergei. Andrei's father's faith always came so much more alive when he was relating to others in everyday life.

And that's how Andrei wanted to be. He truly did.

Perhaps all along his fear had not been that God would reject him, or even that he would be a mercurial Christian, a fair-weather type, but rather that he might never be able to measure up to his father's faith. The realization stunned him, and he must have gasped, because Talia looked up at him with concern.

"What is it, Andrei?"

"What would my father think if he knew he has been my greatest barrier to faith?"

"He'd be devastated."

"I'll never be as good as he—" Andrei shook his head with frustration. "That's just another excuse, isn't it?" His voice rose slightly and a woman nearby "shushed" him. He took Talia's hand and they moved to a corner far away from the other worshipers. He still wasn't ready to leave the church.

"Andrei, I read your father's journals, and I don't think he ever thought he was as good as he could be."

"Yes . . ."

"It accomplishes nothing to make comparisons. You don't have to be as good as *anyone*—that is the essence of Christianity. You don't have to be good at all—no one could be anyway. Daniel once told me about an American hymn called 'Just as I Am.' There's nothing else to it."

"Leave it to the Americans to be simple and to the point."

"But it is a true point."

"It is," he agreed with conviction. "And simplicity is what I want more than almost anything."

She smiled. "Indeed it is!"

"Talia, I think I would like to pray."

"Would you like to go to the altar?"

Her voice trembled a little, and he could tell she was trying with difficulty to suppress her joy and maintain proper decorum for a church.

"No, I don't need to. God will hear my prayer just as well back here. He will see my heart and know that I am finally ready to come to Him—like you said, 'just as I am.'"

V

PLANS AND DECEPTIONS
Spring 1918

35

In the Siberian region including Tobolsk, there were two rival Soviets. Omsk, the regional administrative capital, held the natural historic power. But the Ural Soviet centered in Ekaterinburg vied with Omsk for supremacy in the area. For years the Ural region had been the more fiercely radical of the two because of the concentration of Imperial mines and factories in the area. They were often referred to as the Red Urals. Thus, with the revolution, Ekaterinburg represented a staunch Bolshevik stronghold.

In the spring of 1918, both Soviets turned hungry eyes toward the little village of Tobolsk. Taking control of the illustrious prisoners housed there would go far in consolidating the power of one Soviet over the other. Both Soviets thus sent armed detachments to Tobolsk.

Alexandra, seeing the Ural troops march into town, mistook them for the long-awaited "good Russian men" promised by Soloviev who would rescue the family. She could not have been more mistaken.

The German embassy in Moscow was tucked away in Denezhny Alley. Count Wilhelm von Mirbach had recently taken up residence there as German ambassador.

"I tell you, Count Mirbach," said one of the men seated before him, "it would be a grave mistake to leave the Russian people to their own resources in fighting the Bolsheviks."

"Your indecision," said the second man, "places the Imperial family in great danger."

Sitting back in his leather chair behind an expansive mahogany desk, Mirbach briefly assessed the two Russians seated in front of him. They were both men of character and intelligence. General Gurko was a seasoned cavalry-man, tough and hot-tempered, but respected by his peers. He had served for a brief time as Chief of Staff at Stavka. Alexander Krivoshien, an urbane and intelligent man, had been Minister of Agriculture under Nicholas the Second, but had fallen prey to the Rasputin appointments and lost his job because of his outspoken criticism. Both men supported the idea of a constitutional monarchy and were committed to the rescue of the tsar and perhaps placing him back on the throne of such a monarchy.

These men and others like them had been making themselves quite a nuisance at the German embassy.

"Are you aware of the letter with similar complaints sent to me from Count Benckendorff?" asked Mirbach. Benckendorff, the Grand Marshall of the Imperial Court, had even gone so far as to suggest that Mirbach present the letter to the Kaiser himself.

"Then we do not need to remind you again, Count, that you Germans are the only ones who can save the tsar and his family," said Krivoshien.

"You must be patient," Mirbach soothed.

"We have sent an envoy to Tobolsk," said Krivoshien, "and he reports that the living conditions of the royal family are far from ideal. Their rations and income have been cut, and the young tsarevich is quite ill. How much longer can they endure this captivity?"

"If anything happens to the tsar, the cause will be due to your inactivity. Urgent measures are called for now!" demanded the general, as if browbeating a squad of raw recruits.

"Please calm yourselves," said Mirbach quietly, the picture of control and wisdom. "I assure you now, as I have in the past, the Imperial German government has the situation well in hand. You need not worry. When the time is right we will do all that is necessary." He then pushed back his chair and rose. "Now, gentlemen, I have a pressing engagement in a few minutes, so I must beg your indulgence." He reached his hand across the desk.

The gesture, as intended, left his two guests with little recourse but to rise and take their leave. When they were gone, Mirbach seated himself once again. He did not have another appointment for an hour, but he certainly wasn't going to reveal that to those nagging Russians.

"If there was ever a tangled web . . ." Mirbach murmured to himself as he shuffled through some papers on his desk.

What had Germany done in unleashing the Bolshevik scourge upon Russia? Mirbach was not the only German to regret that sad move. It had seemed such an inspired idea at its inception to introduce political turmoil into Russia and thus thwart their war effort. It was doubtful anyone truly believed that scrappy little Bolshevik, Lenin, would amount to anything more than a nuisance to the Russian government. Now *he* was the government! And he was bent on spreading his revolutionary ideas all over the world, most imminently in Germany.

It was Mirbach's task to try to extricate Germany from the political mess it had created. He, with the support of his government, was seriously considering the possibility of placing Nicholas back on the throne. With German backing, the White armies could easily overwhelm the Reds. And once the monarchy was restored—in a weakened form of course!—it would naturally be far more friendly toward its German benefactors. And Germany would need such friends if the war continued to proceed on its present course. Since the Americans had entered the war, it had taken a serious turn for the worse for Germany.

But first, those Bolsheviks had to be *handled*. And Mirbach would need to handle them delicately, but firmly— with just a touch of deception thrown in!

Mirbach picked up the telephone receiver on his desk and rang up Yakov Sverdlov, the President of the Central Executive Committee of the All-Russian Congress of

Soviets. How does one deal with people who insist on such unwieldy, impractical titles? Mirbach thought wryly as the phone rang at the other end.

"Comrade Sverdlov, please," he spoke into the receiver. "This is Ambassador Mirbach."

The secretary on the other end was obviously flustered to speak directly to the ambassador himself but quickly regained her wits and hurriedly got her boss on the line.

"Ah, Ambassador Mirbach, how very good to hear from you," said Sverdlov smoothly.

At thirty-two, perhaps Sverdlov had a right to his oily confidence. A close confidant of Lenin, he had, not undeservedly, attained a high position very quickly in the new government. His commanding presence, striking black beard, and tall, broad-shouldered figure was enough to make one overlook, even forget his youth.

Mirbach made sure to immediately assume the superior position with the man. After all, Russia was still very much at Germany's mercy.

"I have been in contact with my government recently," Mirbach began. "And we have decided that we would like Nicholas to be brought to Moscow."

"To Moscow, Ambassador? I don't see how—"

"This is *very important*, Comrade Sverdlov. It is imperative that my government interview the tsar—"

"You mean *former* tsar, of course."

"As you say . . ." Mirbach rolled his eyes. "At any rate, we want to speak with the man and assess for ourselves his present condition."

"I can assure you he is being well cared for."

"I have heard reports to the contrary."

"Nevertheless, Ambassador, moving the former tsar at this time would pose many difficulties."

"Come now, surely you can mount a guard regiment sufficient to protect the . . . ah . . . *former* tsar on such a journey."

"And to add to the difficulties," Sverdlov went on,

seeming to ignore Mirbach's statement, "the young son is quite ill and I doubt could be moved."

"We only want to see the ex-tsar. The others can remain behind if they wish."

"But—"

"At the moment, Comrade Sverdlov, I am making this a *request*. Please don't force me to make it more than that."

"What does that mean?"

"I think you understand me well enough. The German occupation forces are only an arm's length from Moscow, an even more ominous position now that Lenin has made Moscow the capital of Russia. Moreover, the peace treaty is quite fresh—I doubt the ink is even dry. . . ."

"I shall see what I can do."

"I am certain you can do more than that. Good-bye, Comrade Sverdlov."

Mirbach hung up the phone. That ought to spur some action, he thought with satisfaction. And once the tsar is in Moscow, anything can happen.

———

Yakov Sverdlov stared into the telephone receiver that had just gone dead. He cursed silently. But he was in a touchy situation, and no matter how it galled him to be pushed around by those Germans, he could not ignore them, or their "requests."

Stroking his thick, black beard he forced himself to remain calm. He had to give the situation some rational thought. One thing was certain, under no circumstances could Nicholas be brought to Moscow and within the clutches of the Germans. However, it was imperative that it *appear* as if Sverdlov were complying with the Germans. If some unavoidable mishap should happen enroute, there could be no way Mirbach could accuse Sverdlov or the Bolsheviks of wrongdoing.

Sverdlov's ties to the Ural Soviet would come in quite

handy now. Last year he had been sent to Ekaterinburg to direct the work of the Ural Soviet, and thus he was well-known and trusted by its present commissar, Zaslavsky. He would wire Zaslavsky immediately, but first he must set in motion his compliance to the German request. He lifted his phone, dialed up a number, spoke for a few moments, and soon was on the line with Commissar Vasily Yakovlev.

A half hour later Yakovlev was in Sverdlov's office.

"Thank you for coming directly," said Sverdlov. "Take a seat."

Yakovlev was similar in height and build to the tall Sverdlov. In fact they were also about the same age. Yakovlev, son of a peasant and born in the Ural region, was a seasoned revolutionary and Bolshevik and had served several years in European exile before his return to Russia after the February revolution.

"I am at your service, Yakov Mikhailovich."

"I know I can count on you Vasily. I have a very delicate operation I wish you to perform. The Germans want us to move the former tsar to Moscow so that they might interview him and learn of his situation—so they say. As you and I know, they cannot be trusted."

"And what is it you would like me to do?"

"We will move Romanov."

"To Moscow?"

"As far as the Germans are concerned, yes. And we will indeed move Romanov. Tobolsk is so full of monarchists plotting his rescue that the place looks more like Petrograd. So the timing for a move is right. I believe Ekaterinburg would make the former tsar the most inaccessible to the Germans."

"Ekaterinburg, Yakov? Could you really guarantee Romanov's safety there?"

"At this point, there is no better place. You should, however, imply, without saying as much, that you are going to take your charge to Moscow. The Germans must never believe otherwise."

"I understand perfectly."

"You will have complete authority in the matter, along with empowerment to shoot any who disobey you. You will also take a private telegraph operator so that we may stay in constant communication should there be any changes in this plan."

"Do you expect trouble?"

"Who knows? The Omsk and Ural Soviets have been making all manner of noise. I will telegraph them immediately and inform them of your departure and the *special importance* of your mission."

"How large of a detachment shall I take?"

"I should think a hundred and fifty ought to be sufficient. Include the special group that just arrived from Petrograd. You will leave in the morning."

36

Andrei, having never been to Siberia himself, had heard April was perhaps the worst possible time of year for travel there. The journey from Moscow took just under two weeks, and Andrei saw this fact for himself once his regiment, commanded by Commissar Yakovlev, left the railroad at Tiumen and trekked by horseback the hundred and eighty miles to Tobolsk. They were lucky when snow and ice still clung to the ground, because when it didn't, it meant knee-deep slush and mud, slowing their progress considerably.

Since Andrei had been in command of the small detachment from Petrograd, he found himself in a command position in the larger regiment—third under Yakovlev and his second, Guzakov. It was in this capacity that he learned about the true intent of the mission—that is, to move the former tsar to a destination as yet unknown.

Soon after arriving in Tobolsk, Andrei began to work on contacting Daniel about this new development. It had been decided before they left Petrograd that Bruce would remain in the background as much as possible, and Daniel would be the main contact. Talia was supposed to stay in the background also. It was also determined that the best place to make contact would be one of the local taverns. With the village now all but overrun with troops—not only the Yakovlev regiment, but also the detachments from Omsk and Ekaterinburg—the two taverns were busy places and contact would be easy. No one would notice a casual bumping of one customer into another, or the covert passing of a note. In this way, Andrei would pass word to Daniel of the impending move of the tsar.

But Daniel was not in either of the taverns. Much to Andrei's displeasure, as he entered the second tavern, it was Talia he saw instead. She had apparently secured employment there as a serving girl. He hated seeing her serve beer and kvass and vodka, moving in and out among the jostling soldiers, some casting her leering, unpleasant looks. He nearly lost all control when one of the soldiers grabbed her wrist and pulled her much too close for comfort.

But before Andrei could react, Talia laughed merrily and scolded the man. "Now we will have a riot on our hands if you keep me from serving these men their beer."

"Yeah!" yelled another man. "Let the girl do her job."

"Aw!" grumbled the first man as he let go. "Maybe later, sweetheart, eh?"

"I never socialize with customers," Talia replied lightly. "It would break too many hearts!" Giggling again, she moved away as swiftly and expertly as if she were dancing across a stage.

In another minute, she brought a glass of kvass to Andrei, who had ordered nothing.

"Well, soldier," she said with a smile, "you look very thirsty."

"I thought you didn't socialize with the customers," he said dryly. It was hard not to say more.

"This is just work."

"About that—"

"Tut, tut, soldier, no more talk. I must work."

"Wait!" Andrei was about to grasp her wrist, much as the other man had done, when she slipped adroitly out of reach.

Yakovlev came and sat at Andrei's table. "Forget about that, we have business to attend to."

"What are you talking about?" said Andrei testily. "I only wanted to give the girl a tip. She's taking a lot of abuse from these men."

"At any rate, we must go. We will meet with the Omsk and Ural detachments in a few minutes." Yakovlev drained the glass of beer he was holding, then rose to leave.

Shrugging as if it mattered little to him either way, Andrei rose also. "Let me pay for my drink. I'll be right along."

Yakovlev proceeded to the door, and as Andrei was heading to the bar to settle his bill, Talia approached him. "Oleg is busy," she said. "You can pay me."

Andrei took a ruble from his pocket and handed it to Talia. What no one but she noticed was that the ruble was wrapped around a small slip of paper on which he had written his message.

Talia smiled. "That's very generous of you, sir."

"I don't like this, Talia," he said under his breath.

"I don't either, my love, but what better way to gather information?"

Then she pranced away, and he could not even watch her for fear the longing in his eyes would have been all too obvious.

The tensions among the various guard factions were quickly illuminated at the meeting that night. Each faction had its own agenda, and because Yakovlev could not reveal the destination of the tsar's removal, half the men grew suspicious of the man from Moscow.

Yakovlev voiced his concerns later to Andrei. "I don't trust that Zaslavsky."

"In what way?"

"Many of those Ural Soviets would as soon see the tsar dead as moved. Zaslavsky and his bunch will bear close watching."

"As will the former tsar," added Andrei, noting that the commissar often used the word "tsar" without preceding it with "former." He thought Yakovlev would bear watching also but for different reasons.

"Yes," the commissar was saying, "we will visit him in the morning and inform him of our intentions."

———

"I am sorry that my wife is not yet ready," said Nicholas when Andrei and Yakovlev met him the next morning. "You were not expected this early."

"I hope I haven't inconvenienced you," said Yakovlev politely.

Nicholas shrugged. "I'm sure it couldn't be helped."

"I have come to inform you, Your Highness, that you must be moved from this place."

"On what authority?"

"I am a special emissary from Moscow. My orders come from the highest level."

"Well, I refuse to go."

"Your Highness, please, I ask that you cooperate."

"My son is quite ill and cannot be moved."

"I understand that, and thus my instructions permit

you to travel with me alone or with whomever of your retinue you choose."

"I won't be separated from my family."

Yakovlev cast a helpless look toward Andrei, who remained silent. It wasn't easy to order about a man who had once ruled one-third of the world. Andrei was quite impressed with Yakovlev's urbane, almost sympathetic treatment of the Romanovs. He was also relieved to note Yakovlev's rather awed, abashed demeanor before the deposed monarch. Andrei felt the same way in this his first meeting with Nicholas. He wondered what Nicholas would think if he knew that their grandfathers had been friends. For that matter, what would Yakovlev think!

Rather than pressing the issue with the tsar at that moment, Yakovlev took another tact. "Might I be permitted to see your son?"

"I suppose so, but you must not overly tax him."

Leaving his daughters behind, Nicholas led them to the tsarevich's bedroom. The boy was lying in bed with an elderly gentleman seated next to him. This man turned out to be Dr. Botkin. Andrei was struck again with the irony of his situation. If Botkin knew of his relationship to Yuri, it would no doubt open many doors. It would also very likely close the important connection to the Bolsheviks. It was unfortunate Yuri could not have come here. But it might be that he could have done no more good than Andrei because, as a close associate to the Romanovs, he would have been closely watched.

One look at the former heir, who was quite pale except for dark circles under his eyes, made it clear he was indeed ill. He also appeared to be asleep, and Botkin rose quietly, came to the door, and silently entreated the visitors to step outside.

Once the door was closed, Nicholas informed the doctor about Yakovlev's mission.

"Well, it is quite impossible," said Botkin firmly. "The child cannot be moved. Because he hasn't healed completely from his fall a short time ago, any movement or jostling could cause the injury to bleed again."

"I understand," said Yakovlev as they returned to a parlor. "I must speak with Colonel Kobylinsky. I will return in a few minutes." Turning to Andrei, he added, "Wait here, Christinin."

Shortly after Yakovlev departed, Alexandra came into the parlor. She walked slowly, using a cane, and she looked much older than her forty-six years. But none of this dulled the aura of pride she wore, which was especially noticeable as she shot a brief but haughty glance in Andrei's direction. She was every inch an empress.

Nicholas explained to her the purpose of Yakovlev's visit. They spoke in English and seemed to speak more freely because they assumed Andrei, a coarse, common Bolshevik, could not understand. But he did understand English, at least much better than he could speak it. He made no indication of this to the prisoners, however.

"This is outrageous!" Alexandra exclaimed. "You put your foot down, didn't you, Nicky?"

"I told him I wouldn't go. But will we have a choice? He said I would have to travel alone if necessary."

"But what would their purpose be in this?" puzzled Botkin.

"They are going to make me go to Moscow so I will sign that Brest-Litovsk Treaty."

"They want to get you alone like they did before—" The tsaritsa stopped suddenly and looked quickly at her husband, a flicker of apology on her face.

"I don't intend to sign anything."

"Nevertheless, we must not let them separate us and thus give them a chance to use your family to coerce you."

At that moment, Yakovlev returned with Kobylinsky. He nodded toward Alexandra, in a gesture that almost, but not quite, could be interpreted as a bow. Polite introductions were exchanged before Yakovlev continued with business.

"I am hoping that Colonel Kobylinsky can impress upon you the utter importance of your cooperation in this matter," said Yakovlev.

"Your Highness," said Kobylinsky, "the powers that be insist that you travel with them—"

"And where are they going to take me?" asked the tsar.

"I cannot reveal that at this time," answered Yakovlev. "It is for your own safety. Please do not refuse. I am under orders that I must obey. But be assured that I am bound with my own life to protect you. I ask then that you be ready to depart in the morning. If your baggage is not ready then, I will be forced to take you without baggage."

Although spoken with extreme civility, Yakovlev's meaning was quite clear. He then took his leave with Andrei.

As they crossed the courtyard to the street, Andrei took the opportunity to question the commissar.

"I'm unclear about the purpose of the move, Commissar. The former tsar seems to think he is being taken to Moscow in order to sign the Brest-Litovsk Treaty."

"How did you learn this?"

"Romanov said so to his wife."

"They spoke rather freely in front of you."

"They were speaking in English not knowing that I have a small understanding of the language."

"What else did they say?"

"Nothing else of import. But it seems the move will cause more problems than it solves. The tsar is extremely hostile about it and what he imagines its purpose to be."

"It doesn't matter what he thinks as long as he cooperates."

"But why the urgency?" Andrei hoped he wasn't pushing too much.

"You saw Zaslavsky last night. He has mayhem up his dirty sleeve. I truly fear for the tsar's safety if we don't get him away from those Ural men immediately. Not to mention the fact that there are scores of monarchists lurking about the village. Of course, where I must take him isn't much better—" Yakovlev stopped suddenly, obviously realizing he was about to say too much.

Andrei chose not to press the issue of the destination. It would probably get him nowhere and only make him appear too curious. Instead he asked, "Won't he be terribly vulnerable while en route?"

"We have one hundred and fifty well-armed and well-trained troops. Let anyone try to get to our prisoner. I meant what I said before. I will guard the tsar with my life."

"May I speak candidly with you, Commissar?" When Yakovlev nodded, Andrei continued, measuring his words, but taking a risk with each one. "That statement might, by some, be misinterpreted."

"In what way, Christinin?"

"It could almost be . . . well . . . considered sympathetic . . . to the tsar—I mean the former tsar." Andrei paused, his heart beating quickly. He prayed he had made a correct assessment of the man at his side. Yakovlev might be a Bolshevik, but he had seemed to Andrei to be a man of honor and sensitivity as well. His next words would tell.

"Are you offended by my treatment of the tsar?" asked Yakovlev.

"Only confused," said Andrei vaguely.

"Well, I will speak candidly with you, comrade. I don't think innocents should be harmed. Did you see his daughters? They are young women by appearance, yet if you look into their eyes, you can see they are but children at heart . . . pure and innocent. And the boy . . . a mere child also, and so helpless." He sighed sadly as they left the compound, crossed the street, and made their way back to the village. "Before this morning, I had but a detached duty to protect the family. Now it goes deeper. Even toward the tsar. I saw today a man concerned for his family, as you or I would be. I did not find a cruel, heartless autocrat."

"You are taking a risk in saying such things to me."

"You are no more like the others than I am," Yakovlev replied. "I saw from the beginning that you are a man of conscience and honor. I doubt you will report me."

"Believe me, comrade, that is the last thing I would do."

37

There was much turmoil that night in the House of Captivity. Alexandra was in great distress over the decision that had to be made, and it seemed that the responsibility for that decision was hers alone. Nicholas was absent during most of the debating, at times off by himself, or sitting with his son.

Alexandra paced nervously over the parlor carpet while her daughters and the tutor Gilliard mostly watched.

"I've always been so sure of what to do in the past," Alexandra lamented. "Or, I've been given some inspiration. But now I am at a complete loss. I don't know what to do. I fear so what might happen if I let him go alone. He is stronger with me at his side. Together we would be able to resist them."

"But, Mama," said Tatiana, "some decision must be made."

"Oh, what torture!" Alexandra wrung her hands.

The tutor interjected, "Your Majesty, the tsarevich has been improving. You can be assured that I and those remaining behind will give the child the best possible care."

"But what if I go and Baby has a relapse?"

"Mama, what are we going to do?" said Anastasia in a shaky, tearful voice.

Alexandra noticed for the first time that her daughters were in as much distress as she. All had been weeping.

"I will go with the tsar," she said at last. "I must place the benefit of Russia ahead of personal desires."

When the tsar came into the parlor a few minutes later, she informed him of her decision.

"If you wish," he said.

———

After receiving Andrei's message about the upcoming move, Daniel and Bruce met with Lieutenant Melink and Captain Sedov, the monarchist officers who had aided Daniel on his last trip to Siberia. The officers announced their intent to raise a force and attempt a rescue of the tsar on his journey.

Daniel was skeptical. He had seen the size of the force from Moscow and doubted there were enough armed monarchists in the area to mount much of a threat. But at least the officers were doing something.

The only useful task Daniel could think to perform was to circulate as much as possible to see what other information could be gathered. If he could learn the tsar's destination, they might not have to rush an almost hopeless rescue attempt en route. It might give them time to raise a larger force. But neither Daniel nor Bruce believed a frontal rescue by armed troops would work in any case. Their best hope, they felt, was to plan a covert operation.

Daniel went first to the tavern where Talia was employed to check up on her, since she could gather information as well as he. Daniel had not liked the idea of her working in the tavern, and he hadn't been surprised when she told him about Andrei's reaction. But Talia had pretty much overruled Daniel's protests. Daniel had not known just how stubborn the sweet, shy little Talia could be.

He felt compelled to keep close watch on Talia—motivated in no small part by the fact that his bear of a brother-in-law would crush him if he didn't. However, seeing that she was handling things well, he left the tavern after a few minutes and went to the other establishment.

When he entered, he noted that the place was occupied mostly by a couple of dozen men of the Ural contingent, all drinking pretty heavily—not at all an unusual circumstance among Russian soldiers. Daniel ordered a beer. He had become pretty adept at the art of making a single drink last an entire evening while giving the appearance of consuming as much as his companions.

He squeezed up to the bar between two burly soldiers. "So, do you have any idea when the thaw will start?" Daniel asked. The weather was always a good ice-breaker.

"You aren't from around here, are you, stranger?"

"No, I'm a fur trader from Vladivostok."

"I thought you had a strange accent."

"So, what do you know of the weather? I'm planning to leave in a couple of days and am afraid of getting caught."

"The thaw will make the river impassable for several days."

"I know. Perhaps I should forget the rest of my business and leave now."

"Thas up to you, friend." The man tossed back a shot of vodka. His voice was so slurred, Daniel had a difficult time understanding him. "We're gonna leave soon ourselves if ya wanna tag along with us."

"We. . . ? You mean the soldiers are leaving?"

"Soon as them Moscow blackguards try to move their prisoner. But when they do, we Urals are gonna make sure that cutthroat they got locked up don't get far. Who knows? Mebbe I'll be the lucky one to put an end to his miserabble existence! I'll drink t' that!" He banged his glass on the counter until the bartended refilled it, then he drank the contents in a single swallow.

"You're not talking about the former tsar—?" Daniel

began, then stopped suddenly and pretended to shudder. "Never mind, I don't want to hear anymore."

"Wha'? You got a weak stomach? Ha, ha!" He slapped Daniel on the back. "You need some courage. Hey, give my friend somethin' besides that sissy brew."

The bartender placed a glass of vodka in front of Daniel, who pushed it away. "Thanks, but I want to keep a clear head, especially if I am going to travel."

"Well, mind yerself on the road," offered the soldier, helping himself to the rejected vodka. "There's gonna be trouble or us Red Urals aren't worth our salt!"

An hour later, Daniel met Talia as she was leaving her tavern after her shift. They retreated to the shadows, and he told her what he had learned from the drunk soldier.

"Andrei will be in danger," she said.

"He's been in danger from the beginning," Daniel replied. "I am concerned for him, but our entire mission may be in danger—that is, the *object* of our mission."

"Yes, I see."

"We must get word to Andrei so at least he can be on his guard more than usual."

"It would be best if I contacted him," Talia said eagerly. Then, embarrassed, added, "Well, it would be less suspicious if he was seen with a woman, wouldn't it?"

"That's what I was thinking. But I want you to remember that I don't intend to trade the tsar's life for yours."

"Why not? The rest of you are risking your lives in this mission."

"Yes, but Andrei won't kill anyone if only Bruce or I are harmed."

Talia smiled. "I think you underestimate how much you mean to him."

"Nevertheless, *be careful*."

The regiment from Moscow had "liberated" a local estate on their arrival in Tobolsk and was bivouacked there.

Talia had little trouble finding it, but she had to be creative in finding a way in, especially at that hour of the night.

She found a basket and filled it with a loaf of bread, a cabbage, a few apples, and other food items she pilfered from the tavern. Then she walked by the estate gate as if on her way home from a hard day's work. She supposed it wouldn't matter if she was recognized from the tavern. When she was a few yards past the gate, she pretended to stumble—a perfectly plausible ruse, considering the numerous potholes in the road, not to mention the mud and patches of ice. She let out a cry as she crumbled to the ground.

"Miss, are you all right?" the guard asked as he jogged toward her. Her faith in Russian male chivalry had been rewarded.

"Oh, how clumsy of me," she said.

He held out his hand. "Let me help you."

"You are too kind, sir."

She clasped his hand, but as he lifted her, she let out another cry and fell against him. "I am afraid my ankle is sprained, or perhaps even broken."

"How far is it to your house?"

"Only a couple of versts."

"You will never make it."

"What shall I do?" She gave a shuddering sigh, as if very close to tears.

"I'll take you into the estate house. Our commander might give you the loan of a horse, or even a cart. Perhaps we will have to find a doctor. There is one who serves the former tsar, we will make him come."

"A doctor?" She shuddered again. "I can't afford a doctor."

"Don't worry. This is a socialist state now. All people, especially good proletarian women, are taken care of by the state."

He easily lifted her in his arms and carried her back to

the estate house. The soldiers were camped in a barn and a stable on the grounds, but the officers, even in the socialist state, had commandeered the house for their quarters.

The residents of the estate were huddled in one corner of the large main room, and Talia felt sorry for them. They were by no means aristocrats but were definitely rich moujiks and were not used to being pushed around in this way. At the other end of the room, several officers were gathered around a table playing cards. Talia was very relieved to see Andrei among them.

"What have you got there?" asked one of the officers, noticing the guard's entry.

"She fell and hurt herself in front of the gate."

At that moment Andrei looked up and saw Talia. He made no attempt to hide his instant consternation but luckily the attention of the others was focused on Talia and the guard.

The guard laid Talia on a sofa and the other men came forward, with Andrei at the front.

"It's my ankle," Talia said weakly. How she wanted to allay Andrei's worries, but she could say nothing, nor could she even make some silent gesture.

Andrei quickly knelt down beside her. "I know a little about these things," he said by way of explanation, mostly to the other men. He lifted her left foot.

"It's my right," Talia said.

He palpated the right ankle. "It doesn't appear to be broken."

"She can't walk," offered the guard.

"Probably a sprain," said Andrei.

"I must get home," Talia said.

"I thought perhaps we could spare a horse," said the guard.

"Yes, an excellent idea," said Andrei. "I'll see to it myself."

The guard was obviously not happy about this. After

all, he had discovered the prize. But even in a socialist army there was a chain of command.

"Don't be too long about it, Christinin," said one of the other officers. "We will depart in a couple of hours."

Andrei carried Talia to the stable where the regiment horses were being kept. The guard followed along to help with saddling. In a few minutes Andrei and Talia were mounted on the chestnut mare Andrei had ridden from Tiumen, with Talia comfortably in front. It was pure joy for Talia to be so close to the man she loved.

When they were well away from the estate, she said, "My ankle really isn't hurt, Andrei. I just had to get a message to you."

"I thought as much," he said stoically.

"Not at first from the look on your face. I feel so bad about that."

"I don't know what I would do if anything should happen to you." His arms held her tighter, and his lips gently brushed the back of her head. "I don't like you taking these risks, playing the secret agent."

"We're not playing, Andrei."

"I know. Why do you think I am so distressed?"

They rode for a while in the direction Talia indicated she had been going when she fell—ostensibly toward her "home"—because the guard was watching. Then Andrei circled back on an obscure muddy path he hoped would get them back to the village—it was going the right direction, at any rate.

"Do you want to hear my message?" Talia asked.

"Of course . . ." Pausing, he sighed. "I guess I was hoping we could just enjoy where we are for a while, as if dangers and rescues didn't exist."

"Ah, yes . . ." She snuggled closer.

After a couple more minutes, Andrei said, "Well, go ahead with it. Time is not ours at the moment."

"It will be someday, Andrei."

She turned in the saddle, facing him as best she could.

The moonlight glowed off his handsome face, and the pale hair sticking out from under his fur hat framed his boyish visage and nearly took away her breath. She would never cease to marvel at what she had found in Andrei, her dear friend, and now her future husband. To make the moment perfect, he bent down and kissed her yearning lips. For a time they forgot all about their mission. The horse ambled to a stop in the middle of the moonlit path.

But as Andrei had said, time was not theirs, and it was marching with cruel determination toward an uncertain future.

With great effort, Andrei moved his lips away from Talia's. "You . . . had a message. . . ?"

"What message. . . ?"

"I'm hoping you will tell me."

Talia shook away the unreality of the magical moment they had shared. "Daniel learned something tonight from a drunk Ural soldier. Are you leaving tomorrow with the tsar?"

"Yes, in a few hours."

"Well, it might be the Urals are planning to intercept you somewhere on the road in order to kill the tsar."

"Then they know we are leaving in the morning?"

"From what Daniel said, it didn't sound like they knew a specific time, but they are expecting it to be soon, before the real thaw starts."

"That's probably why Yakovlev has been so nervous tonight. He must suspect something. We'll just have to be extra vigilant."

"Andrei, do you know the destination yet?"

"No, but I am pretty certain it isn't Moscow. It might be Ekaterinburg. Yakovlev isn't happy about the orders he has and once accidentally admitted to me that the tsar would be in hostile surroundings in the new location."

Andrei urged the horse back into motion, and they rode in silence for a few minutes, then he said, "I ought to know something by the time we reach Tiumen. I will leave some kind of signal for you." He paused for a moment. "There are taverns by the waterfront. Daniel even mentioned going to one. I will start with the one nearest the train station until I find one I deem can be trusted."

"Even then, would it be safe to leave a message with a stranger?"

"It won't be a message, so to speak. I'll leave a package for my sweetheart. I'll give a sad tale of how I was to meet her there but was called to arms . . . no one can resist romance."

"And what will be in my package—I assume I am the sweetheart?"

"You are indeed. What sort of personal items do you have in your luggage? A scarf, perhaps? If that were in the package, it would mean we are going to Ekaterinburg. Now, what else. . . ?"

"I have some spare gloves—"

"Oh no, if you lost your only gloves, your hands would freeze. Something less important. A book, perhaps?"

"You are very good at this, Andrei."

"I learned all manner of 'secret agent' tricks when in exile—many from Lenin himself! So, you do have a book?" When she nodded he went on, "I will write in the flyleaf, 'In memory of our wonderful week in _____.' And I will fill in the blank with the destination."

All too quickly they reached the village and the hotel where Talia was staying. After Talia gave Andrei the book of poetry she had been reading, they said a reluctant good-bye, and as Talia watched him ride away, she said a silent but fervent prayer for his safety.

38

Commissar Yakovlev and his prisoners departed the house in Tobolsk at four in the morning. After hearing what Andrei had to say, he seemed more nervous than ever.

"*Pashle! Pashle!*" Yakovlev urged his charges in order to hurry them along.

Andrei knew that as soon as Zaslavsky and his bunch of Red Urals learned that the Moscow contingent had departed, he would be hot on their heels. Just the other evening, Zaslavsky had warned them, "When you move the debauched monarch, don't sit next to him if you value your hide." But they had to show some restraint so as not to arouse the royal family's fears more than they naturally were. All in the family showed the emotional strain. Alexis was in his room crying, and the girls' eyes were swollen from their recent tears.

Finally, however, the travelers were loaded into the carts. The group included Nicholas and Alexandra, their daughter Maria, Dr. Botkin, a valet, a maid, and a footman. There was an awkward moment when Nicholas started to get into his wife's cart, and Yakovlev asked him to go instead to the second cart. It seemed best that they be separated in case there was trouble.

The journey was difficult at best. They barely made it across the two major rivers in their path, the Irtysh and the Tobol, hampered by breaking ice and slush all the way. They changed horses frequently, which helped them make better time. Once they even stopped in Pokrovskoe, Rasputin's village, and the Monk's widow watched them from the window of her izba. Alexandra made the sign of the cross, her cold demeanor revealing a flicker of pain.

In Tiumen, they met their first resistance. On the station platform two dozen armed troops confronted them.

Andrei recognized several of them as the Red Urals they had seen in Tobolsk. Somehow they had managed to beat Yakovlev to the railroad.

"Stand down!" Yakovlev ordered.

"Never!" retorted the leader of the Urals, whose name Andrei did not know. "We have a duty to save the revolution!"

"I tell you, my orders come directly from the President of the Soviet," Yakovlev reminded the man as half of his own troops spread out on the platform. "If you interfere with me, *you* betray the revolution. I want no blood spilled here. But I will shoot anyone who tries to harm my charges."

"You are nothing but a monarchist dupe—"

"Then Sverdlov himself is a dupe. I only follow his orders." After a tense moment, Yakovlev added, "I give you one more chance to disband."

When nothing happened, the commissar nodded toward his troops and signaled them to prepare to fire. Only then did the Urals desist and, grumbling and cursing, begin to disband.

To Andrei, Yakovlev said, "I want a couple of prisoners to question."

Andrei took two of his men and went after the retreating Urals, grabbing two of them.

"What's this!" they protested. "We're leaving like we were told."

"And we are very happy about that," said Andrei, "but my commander would like a word with you two. No harm will come to you."

The interrogation did not take long. One of the Ural prisoners refused to talk, but the other was only too happy to spill all he knew.

"I didn't like the business from the beginning," he said. "We are not brigands who would kill our own comrades."

"What was their intent against our party?" Andrei asked.

"You know well enough. They want to destroy the *baggage* you are carrying. And don't think you've stopped them. They'll try again."

"Do you know when?"

"They'll do it outside of Ekaterinburg—that's our country there and they'll be able to marshal a larger force against you."

After they let the man go, Yakovlev turned to Andrei. "I was afraid something like this would happen."

"What are we going to do about it?" asked Andrei.

"I have my orders," Yakovlev said, but rather lamely.

"And that is to go to Ekaterinburg?" Andrei asked, reasonably enough, considering the present situation.

"I suppose you have a right to know."

"But," Andrei said, "surely Sverdlov would not send the tsar into that kind of danger!"

"I'm going to telegraph him now and let him know about these new developments."

"May I make a suggestion?" When Yakovlev nodded, Andrei continued, "Let's take the tsar east to Omsk. If things cool down we will be in an ideal position from there to go back either to Ekaterinburg or Moscow—or anywhere we choose, for that matter." Andrei carefully studied the commissar as he said his final words. There was neither shock nor rebuff in his eyes.

"Anywhere. . . ?" he said.

Andrei shrugged. "Who knows what might arise to change plans? Personally, I have my doubts that things will cool down. If they do, it will only be a temporary cooling. Now that the Ural men are roused, it won't be easy to hold them back."

"Which means the tsar will be in constant danger no matter where he is."

"In Russia at least."

"Andrei, are you suggesting what I think you are suggesting?"

"You said once that you would protect the tsar with

your life. Wouldn't it be easier to remove him from danger altogether?"

Yakovlev rose from where he had been sitting in the small room at the station they had commandeered for the interrogation. He began pacing in deep thought. Andrei was silent. He had already pushed it further than prudence suggested. But his gut told him Yakovlev was very much of like mind with him, and thus could easily be made into an ally.

"It is a moral dilemma, isn't it?" Yakovlev said after several minutes. "Here is a man—the emperor—to whom I have been opposed all my life. And now his life is in my hands. To sacrifice myself for him is far easier than being placed in a position of betraying my comrades. Do you understand this, Andrei?"

"Indeed I do, comrade. But there is a moral core within me that I must remain loyal to above all else."

Yakovlev paced a few more minutes, then went to the door. "I'm going to send a telegram to Moscow. In the meantime, commandeer a first class coach on the *eastbound* train and see to it that our charges are settled aboard."

"Yes, comrade," Andrei replied with enthusiasm.

Andrei did as he was told, then went in search of a waterfront tavern, with Talia's book, wrapped in newsprint, in hand. On the flyleaf of the book, he indicated the Omsk destination. Returning to the station after he had left the book with a suitable tavern keeper, he looked into the telegraph office, where Yakovlev was once again pacing. It had been nearly an hour since he had sent the message to Moscow.

"No word from Sverdlov," Yakovlev said to Andrei. He handed him the message he had sent. "Don't you think this would demand an immediate response?"

Andrei read the telegram, which was quite lengthy. One part in particular blared out at him:

THE EKATERINBURG MEN HAVE ONE DE-
SIRE, THAT IS TO DESTROY OUR BAGGAGE AT
ALL COSTS. THEY MADE ONE ATTEMPT HERE
IN TIUMEN AND BLOODSHED WAS BARELY
AVERTED. IN MY OPINION IT IS MAD TO GO TO
THE CENTER OF THEIR STRENGTH. I PROPOSE
TO TAKE THE BAGGAGE TO OMSK AND THENCE
TO A SECURE PLACE IN THE MOUNTAINS SUCH
AS SIMSKY GORNY IN THE UFA PROVINCE. I
AWAIT YOUR RESPONSE BUT TIME IS OF THE
ESSENCE FOR I CANNOT PREDICT IF THERE
WILL BE ANOTHER ATTEMPT HERE. YAKOVLEV.

Andrei handed back the paper. "How long will you
wait?"

"Come outside with me, Andrei," said Yakovlev. When
they were out of earshot of the telegraph operator, he continued, "I believe Sverdlov is ignoring me by design. He
wants the tsar in Ekaterinburg, but he wants to be absolved of responsibility should anything happen."

"Does he want the tsar dead?"

"I don't know. He wants him out of reach of the Germans."

"Vasily," Andrei said with emphatic familiarity, "we
must take the tsar east. We must. I have fought the emperor all my life. I have despised all he has stood for. Yet
I do not want his blood on my hands."

"Nor do I."

"Then we have no other recourse."

"I will give Sverdlov another half hour," hedged Yakovlev. "If I haven't heard anything by then, we will leave."

A half hour later, before dawn tinted the morning sky,
there was still no response from Moscow. The train pulled
out of the station heading east with Andrei, Yakovlev, and
their very important prisoners aboard.

———

Several hours later, in Moscow, Sverdlov received this

telegram from the Chairman of the Ural Soviet:

COMMISSAR YAKOVLEV, WITH HIS BAG-GAGE, IS AT THIS MOMENT ON THE EAST-BOUND TRAIN TO OMSK. OUR UNDERSTANDING IS THAT THE BAGGAGE IS TO BE TAKEN TO EK-ATERINBURG. WE DO NOT KNOW YAKOVLEV'S PURPOSE IN HIS PRESENT DIRECTION AND THUS CONSIDER THIS ACT TO BE TRAITOROUS. THE REGIONAL SOVIET HAS VOTED TO WAYLAY THE TRAIN AND ARREST AND DELIVER BOTH YAKOVLEV AND HIS BAGGAGE TO EKATERIN-BURG.

In response, Sverdlov sent this to the Ural Soviet:

YAKOVLEV IS ACTING ON MY ORDERS. TRUST HIM COMPLETELY.

Then he sent another message, this to the first station after Tiumen where he knew Zaslavsky of the Red Urals would be waiting anxiously for word from him.

WAYLAY BAGGAGE AT ALL COST AND CARRY TO ORIGINAL DESTINATION BUT DO NOT, I RE-PEAT, DO NOT HARM IT.

Sverdlov was careful to use a telegraph operator he could trust implicitly. After the message was sent, he burned the original; Zaslavsky was instructed to do the same. Sverdlov knew he was playing a tricky and danger-ous double game. And if all worked according to his de-vious plan, the tsar would be well out of the clutches of the Germans, while he, Sverdlov, would be absolved of any complicity in deceiving them. After all, what could he do if some renegade Reds overwhelmed his prisoners and took them in hand? If any harm came to the tsar, he would be absolved of that also. Personally, he felt the de-mise of the deposed monarch must come sooner or later. But there might still be some use for the man if he could prolong the inevitable just a while longer.

———————

In the flurry of telegrams speeding back and forth between several different geographic points, there was bound to be confusion. The Omsk Soviet heard only of Yakovlev's treasonous act and were thus convinced to join forces with Zaslavsky's Urals. So when the train made a brief stop at the Kulomzino Station some sixty miles from Omsk, they were surrounded by a large force of hostile troops.

A fleeting look was quickly exchanged between Andrei and Yakovlev, silently questioning the wisdom of putting up a fight. Words about protecting the tsar with one's life seemed far less prudent now when faced with the actual prospect of having to kill one's own people, or be killed oneself. And this time Yakovlev's forces were soundly outnumbered.

"There's got to be a way out of this," Yakovlev said. "I'm going to wire Moscow again," he said with resolve.

He left the train, returning an hour later wearing a defeated expression. "Sverdlov has told me to let the Urals take the tsar to Ekaterinburg. He says there is no way around it, and he has assurances from Ekaterinburg that the tsar will not be harmed."

"Do you believe that?" asked Andrei. There was a sick feeling in the pit of his stomach. He could tell that Yakovlev, never completely resolved to deceive his masters in Moscow, was going to capitulate, convincing himself that the Urals would honor their word to Sverdlov.

"I have done everything I could. I cannot jeopardize my men, nor can I ask them to kill their comrades."

The most difficult task was informing the tsar of the situation. Nicholas responded, "I would have gone anywhere but to Ekaterinburg. They are deeply bitter toward me there."

When Ambassador Mirbach lifted his ringing telephone later in the day, he could hear the smug satisfaction in Sverdlov's voice as he informed him of the unfortunate turn of circumstances.

"I did all that I could," said Sverdlov, his voice dripping with false regret. "But alas! The central government has not firmly established itself in Siberia. Thus we often must give the local Soviets their way."

Mirbach was furious. Not only had he lost the tsar, but he had been duped by that arrogant upstart in the Kremlin. Yet the ambassador was not ready to give up completely. Perhaps another ploy would work. There were still several royal relatives at large. One among them might be tempted to sign the Brest-Litovsk Treaty if offered the monarchy for himself. It was a tantalizing idea, at the very least.

39

Nicholas, who seldom made an astute judgment during his reign, was sadly right in his estimation of the citizens of Ekaterinburg. When his train pulled into the station, a mob greeted him shouting vicious epithets.

"Give us those dirty Romanovs! We'll thrash them good!"

"Let me spit in that scoundrel's face!"

"We have them at last!"

The train had to be shunted to a loading dock away from the crowd. Then the prisoners were unloaded and quickly transported to their new prison, one of the more substantial houses in town, requisitioned from a wealthy merchant named Ipatiev. The two-story house had received recent renovations in preparation for the new arrivals—an indication that it had been planned all along that they would end up here. One of the additions had been a tall, wooden fence around the entire perimeter of the house—officially called "The House of Special Purpose."

Not many among the Soviet members, a majority of whom were unschooled, knew of the small irony in the historical significance of the house they had chosen. But Nicholas, an avid student of Russian history, must surely have noted that it had been in the Ipatiev Monastery three hundred years earlier that the first Romanov had been installed as tsar of Russia. Now the *last* tsar was imprisoned in a house by the same name.

The Ural Soviet was placed in charge of guarding the Romanovs, and Andrei managed to get himself assigned to that duty, though his Moscow ties prevented him from ever being in the inner circle. Yakovlev faced several hours of intensive questioning by the Soviet but was eventually released when Sverdlov came to his support. Yakovlev then departed for Moscow to have a personal interview with the President of the Presidium.

Andrei hoped and prayed that Daniel, Talia, and Bruce would figure out that his message left in Tiumen was a mistake. They might end up in Omsk, but once there, Daniel's expert investigative skills would surely uncover what really happened.

In the meantime, Andrei took up his duties as guard. He learned as much as he could about the "House of Special Purpose." The family would be kept upstairs where all the windows were painted white so they could not see outside, and to prevent signaling for help. The downstairs of the house was for the guards, who were under orders to be especially vigilant. Guards were stationed both outside and inside the house. By now most of the original guards from Tsarskoe Selo had been replaced, but the remaining ones were now also replaced by locals and by men from the Cheka. Andrei felt as if he might be the only sympathetic guard left.

But worse than the extreme vigilance was the manner in which the guards tended to treat their captives. Their belongings, to Nicholas's vehement protests, were thoroughly searched; their walks in the garden were strictly limited; they no longer could carry their own money but had to ask their guards whenever they needed cash; and they had little privacy, with guards bursting in on them at any time with no notice. The celebration, if it could be called that, of the tsar's fiftieth birthday, on May sixth, was a dreary one indeed.

It would have made that birthday even more miserable had the Romanovs known that shortly after their arrival in Ekaterinburg, the Ural Soviet had voted unanimously for their execution. The only thing preventing this was lack of orders from Moscow. Apparently Trotsky was pushing for a public trial of Nicholas and Alexandra.

In the middle of May with the spring thaw, Nicholas and Alexandra were reunited with the rest of their family. The separation had been a terrible hardship on all of them, and so with the spring sunshine, the reunion brought a ray of joy for the Romanovs.

There was, however, a dark side. Two of their suite in Tobolsk, a general and a lady-in-waiting who had faithfully stayed with them during the entire captivity, were placed under arrest. Several others, including the tutor Gilliard, were released. Gilliard and two or three others remained in Ekaterinburg, even though they were not allowed to rejoin the family. There seemed to be no rhyme or reason to these moves by the Bolsheviks. Why arrest some, let others go free, while permitting still others to remain with the Romanovs?

For Andrei, May brought Talia, along with Daniel and Bruce. Soon Talia, who had left a pseudonym at the trade union hall, was called to assist the cook at the Ipatiev House. Since almost all the guards were new, she had no problem with being recognized from Tobolsk, but Andrei worried nonetheless. Still he was able to see her often and even talk on occasion. No one thought anything of a guard flirting with the pretty kitchen girl. Of course other guards also tried to flirt with her, which was unsettling to Andrei, but Talia handled herself well, as she had in the tavern.

Time alone, quality time when they could be themselves, was much harder to come by. But one night a few days after Talia arrived, they arranged a rendezvous at an abandoned barn Andrei had found about a versta out of town. The weather had started to warm up, but it was still a bit chilly at night. That particular night it was threatening to rain, so they took refuge inside the barn.

Andrei wasted no time in embracing Talia and kissing her, but wishing to avoid the temptation of her nearness, he did not linger long in this. He steadied himself by talking business.

"What are Daniel and Bruce up to?" he asked.

He spread his coat out on a mound of hay and they sat there as they talked.

"Daniel has made contact with Gilliard, the royal tutor," Talia replied. "And there are other monarchists in town with a view to rescue the tsar."

"I don't know why they can't get together."

"This group doesn't trust that group, or that group doesn't want to share the glory, or the other group doesn't want to share money. It's frustrating. Gilliard is willing to work with us but he is closely watched. He has been appealing to the French and British consulates. But, as you well know, there is little to be done."

"The guard is too tight," agreed Andrei. "I'm certain any attempt made now would result in a bloodbath—on both sides."

"But in time the guard may relax."

"Moscow plans frequent changes of the guard to prevent that."

"Then we just wait."

"Watch and wait." Andrei sighed.

Smiling, Talia reached up and fingered a lock of his hair. "Poor Andrei. Patience is not your best thing."

"And I have to be patient about so much these days." He brushed his hand gently against her soft cheek. "It's almost more than a man can bear."

"You are bearing it well, though I know it is hard. Andrei, when this is all over, what will we do?"

"Get married, of course. Right away!"

"No more worries about how you will support me?"

"We'll manage somehow." His old fears seemed so trivial now.

"Have you thought about what will happen . . . politically? Once the tsar is rescued, it won't look good if you quit the Party immediately. But for that matter, what if we—you—are implicated?"

"We'll all get shot and that'll be that," he replied lightly but instantly regretted his words when he saw Talia's face pale. "I'm sorry, Talia. I didn't mean to make fun of something so serious. We will come out of this fine, I know it. The worst that will happen is that we might have to leave the country for a while. How do you feel about that?"

"You and I have both lived away from Russia. We know how it is. But, Andrei, I love this country, I truly do. I would be sad to leave, and yet, if you and I are together, I could live anywhere."

"I love Russia, too," Andrei said thoughtfully, "but if things keep on the way they are, we would probably be better off someplace else. Perhaps we could go to America. I've always wanted to do that."

"Remember when we were children and we daydreamed about traveling? You and Yuri wanted adventures with pirates and treasure and such."

"And you wanted peace and tranquility." He smiled at her and wanted desperately to hold her again, but thought better of it in this dark, lonely place where they were so very alone. "I tell you honestly, Talia, I want only peace and tranquillity now, too."

"I always knew we were like-minded."

"Are you as afraid as I am that it won't happen?" He was embarrassed at the admission, yet he was so accustomed to telling her everything, he found it hard to hold it back. When she nodded, he added, "That's not all, Talia. It would be wrong to deceive you. I don't have confident hopes about our mission. Had we gone anywhere but here, there might have been a chance."

"Do you think we should disband?"

"I'm almost certain Daniel and Bruce won't give it up, and I am honor bound to help them. But I do wish you would return to Petrograd—"

"I won't do that."

"I know."

"I will be very careful, though."

Sighing, he put his arm around her and drew closer to her. He needed to feel her near. "Could we pray, Talia? For the mission and for our future when it is over?"

"Oh yes! What a perfect suggestion, and it is the best thing we can do."

They prayed for several minutes, mostly in silence, but Andrei said a few words aloud. Then they reverently crossed themselves and sat quietly for a few more minutes. Outside it had begun to rain, and the sound was so soothing and ordinary that Andrei felt sudden tears of longing rise in his eyes. He was glad Talia couldn't see, for she might be disappointed, thinking the prayer hadn't helped. Andrei himself wasn't sure if it had or hadn't. Only time would tell. And he prayed a final silent prayer before they departed that place that God would give him the patience he would need to give both time and God a chance to work.

40

Seldom had there ever been a more bedraggled procession. Russian soldiers, recently demobilized after the treaty with Germany, made their way along the muddy roads and paths hoping soon to reach a railhead that would take them home. Some wore bandages or hobbled on crutches. All were dressed in rags, the proud uniforms they had once worn now scored with years of battle.

Misha Grigorov looked little better than those around him. Nearly two years in a German prison camp had been as grueling as any battle he had ever been in. And he probably would still be there now, wading through red tape for his release, if he hadn't escaped a week before the treaty was signed.

His journey home had been slowgoing. First, he had walked through German-occupied territory. Once he entered Russian territory, he almost starved and encountered such disorganization he could not find his old unit. Finally, he had decided to head home, forgetting about trying to report in first. His wounded leg did not help matters. He'd been shot during his escape, and though the wound itself had finally healed, he still carried a bullet in his thigh as a constant painful reminder. He used a sturdy branch as a crutch and wondered if he would ever walk normally again. Perhaps Yuri would be able to fix it when he got home.

Home. Anna!

Those two words kept him going through the most difficult ordeal of his life. He desperately wanted to have a life with Anna. It seemed but a fading dream that they were truly married. He frequently had to remind himself of their wedding day and the brief few days that had followed before he had left for the war. He made himself reconstruct every detail of those wonderful days, but it was getting harder and harder to do.

Soon though, very soon, they would be together again. He prayed she had not changed her mind about her decision, or given him up for dead. But he knew Anna better than that. Her love and commitment were not things she gave away carelessly. She'd be there. The whole world in Russia had changed radically—news of the revolution had trickled into the prison camp. But Anna would never change.

"Captain Grigorov, is that you?"

Misha turned. "Lieutenant Kamkin!" The two men dropped the few belongings they were carrying and embraced. "I thought I'd never find anyone from the unit," Misha said. They parted, gathered up their packs, and began walking side by side.

"There are few of us left." Kamkin went on to name a long, grim list of casualties. And with each name, the lieutenant, who could not have been older than thirty, began to look older and older.

"So many," sighed Misha.

"And that was before I was taken prisoner. I suppose you and I are lucky."

"If it weren't for my family I would not agree. I would have counted it an honor to die with my comrades. But I have a new wife I have seen only a few days of the three and a half years we have been married. So, for her sake, I will count my blessings."

They walked for a few moments in silence, then Kamkin said, "If you hunger for more battle, Captain, the fighting isn't over yet." He glanced surreptitiously around and lowered his voice. "A White Army is gathering in the south, in the region of the Don—your country, isn't it, Captain?"

Misha had heard whisperings of the formation of an army to fight the Bolsheviks. There had already been battles in the south, though they had not gone well for the outmanned and outgunned Whites. Still, their ranks were growing, and hope for a final victory over the Reds was strong. Oddly enough, the Cossacks were most torn in their loyalties. In times long past, the Cossacks had been the traditional protectors of freedom in the land. More recently, however, the Cossacks had been the best tsarist defense against revolution. Misha still carried a deep shame over the actions of his people on Bloody Sunday.

The terrible and senseless debacle the Great War had become for Russia had turned many Cossacks into radicals—and their refusal to fire upon Russians in both the February and October revolutions was a huge factor in the success of both. On the other hand, there was still a large force of monarchist Cossacks, and thus both the Red and the White Army were counting on Cossack support. Although Misha had not become a Bolshevik by any estimation, he was among the many Cossacks who were torn in their loyalties.

"It has been so long since I have been to my home on the Don," said Misha, "that I can hardly remember it. For forty years, when I haven't been at war, I have been an Imperial Guard."

"And that is why I tell you of the army forming on the Don," said Kamkin. "I know where your loyalties lie."

"Look at me, Kamkin. I am sixty-one years old. I am covered with lice and filth; I can barely walk; my eyesight is weak and my hearing has been all but destroyed by gunfire. I doubt I would make much of a soldier any longer."

"At your worst, I'll wager you could outfight the best those Reds have to offer."

Misha laughed. "Maybe I could best Mr. Lenin, if I am lucky. But I don't feel very lucky right now."

"Go see your wife. Get that leg better. You'll start to feel like the soldier you are once again."

Misha shrugged noncommittally. Later, when he finally came to a train station and found a place among hundreds of other soldiers, he had forgotten all about

Reds and Whites. There was only one thing on his mind—Anna!

————

Anna and Mariana sat at the kitchen table as Mariana read a letter from Daniel. It mostly detailed trivialities—the weather, which was finally warming up; the various idiosyncrasies of the Siberian town of Ekaterinburg. Anna knew why he mentioned nothing pertaining to his mission. One, because of the chance the letter might be intercepted and read by the Reds; and two, because he and the others were able to do little at the moment to further the mission. At least the letter comforted the two women that their loved ones were all right. Both Andrei and Talia added short notes of greeting at the end of the letter.

"He leaves so much unsaid," sighed Mariana.

"We must try not to worry. They are in God's hands." Anna sipped her tea. The brew was so weak these days. She had been using the same leaves for several days now.

Mariana smiled. "And can you follow your own advice, Mama?"

"Of course not. I worry all the time. But they are still in God's hands."

"They are going to have to face so many dangers when the time comes for them to finally rescue the tsar."

"We will pray for them," said Anna. "But first, what does your father have to say?"

Mariana lifted the second letter. It was amazing to get two letters in one day when mail was so irregular and undependable. But since the letter from Dmitri Remizov had come by the hand of a friend who had traveled to Petrograd from Moscow, he had been able to write in much more detail as to his activities.

My dear Mariana,

I hope you get this letter and it finds you well. I have not even attempted to write before this because of the impossibility of the post these days. But there are certain changes coming here I wanted you to be informed about. First, shortly after the October coup, my family was forced from the Barsukov estate in Moscow—the only one left to us in town, since several other estates and palaces had already been confiscated. We have all fled to the Barsukov country estate near Riazan, a hundred miles south of Moscow. This estate has been parceled off and only a small plot of land is left to us, but we have retained half the house in which to live. The other half is occupied by the local commissar and his staff.

The whole family must contribute to the work—all the servants, of course, have fled. The children and I must work in the fields, and even Yalena, who has never done a stitch of work in her life, must labor in the kitchen preparing food, not only for us but for the commissar and his entire staff as well. It is an absolutely horrendous situation, but I suppose it could be worse. At least we have food. Many, as I am sure you have heard, have died of hunger—tens of thousands, in fact, all over Russia. At times I wonder if we should not have tried to get out of Russia earlier like so many other of the noble classes. But what would happen if all good, honest, and honorable Russians exited? Thus, Yalena and I decided that we must remain as long as our lives are not directly at risk.

And this brings me to the other major change I must tell you of. In a few days—in fact as you read this I will probably already be gone—I will be off to join up with the White Army. Yalena tells me I am too old for such adventures, but I do not look upon it as such. I feel it is my duty to defend my beloved Russia against these filthy usurpers that are trying to call themselves a government. The Whites desperately need experienced soldiers, and as I have said many times, that is the only real training I have in life. In times like these, age is no consideration at all. Even General Alekseev, one-time chief of staff under Nicholas, and commander in chief under Kerensky, has joined the fray. According to rumor, Alekseev, who is sixty—only a year younger than myself—also has an advanced case of cancer. So I am doing no more than any other man who longs to see order and peace return to our Motherland.

*With that, Mariana, I bid you farewell. I don't know
when I will see you again. I pray daily that you will find
a way back to America. But if not, and if I get to Petrograd, I will look forward to a good long visit with you and
with my dear grandchildren. Please convey a greeting to
Anna and to Daniel as well. My prayers are with you, as
I hope yours are with me. In these hard times, the faith I
took so lightly in the past has offered me great comfort.
You were right all along about that, dear daughter.*

> *With deepest love,*
> *Your Père*

Tears brimming her eyes, Mariana laid the letter on
the table and glanced up at her adopted mother. "Oh,
Mama, just when we thought the war was over."

"I wonder if Russia will ever see an end to war," said
Anna.

"I must say, I am proud of my father."

"You have a right to be." A faraway look briefly flick-
ered into Anna's eyes as scenes from the past rushed
across her mind like a motion picture. Dmitri had never
been her favorite person; he'd made many mistakes and
selfish misjudgments in his early years that unfortunately
had hurt many who loved him. She thought of her dear
friend, Princess Katrina, and her short, unhappy marriage
to Dmitri. But the death of Sergei and the influence of
Dmitri's young but kind wife, Yalena, had played a great
part in Dmitri's transformation as a man in his later years.

"Mama, let's pray right now," said Mariana. "For my
father, for Daniel and Andrei and Talia, for your Misha,
for Katya and her pregnancy. Oh, there is so much! And
we must also pray for our dear Russia."

"An excellent idea." Anna reached her hands across the
table and Mariana grasped them.

But as they bowed their heads, they heard a small
voice from the doorway.

"Mama, could you help me—" Eight-year-old Katrina

stopped as she saw her mother and grandmother obviously at prayer. "I'm sorry—"

Anna lifted her head and reached out her hand. "It's all right, my dear one. Would you like to join us?"

"Yes, grandmama, I truly would." Katrina came into the room and sat in a vacant chair at the table between the two older women. "What are you praying about?"

"Many things," said Mariana. "Everything that is on our hearts."

"For Papa?"

"Especially for Papa."

The three joined hands. At times they prayed aloud, and at times silently in their hearts. But Katrina took part and for a time seemed almost a woman herself. The deep joy Anna felt at this went far to balance the heaviness of a greater part of their prayers. Princess Katrina's granddaughter . . . so much like her it often made Anna's heart ache with joy and grief. Grief, in that the elder Katrina had never had a chance to experience the true fullness of life and that she could not be here now to participate in this wonderful melding of generations. But the joy was that Katrina's legacy would continue, not only in a more tangible sense by the physical similarities between the two Katrinas, but also in the deeper spiritual sense. And especially in that the faith Princess Katrina had acquired so near the end of her life would continue far into the future through her granddaughter.

Several minutes later, the prayer time was interrupted by the sound of commotion at the door. In these times such incidents could mean anything—a visit by the already feared Cheka, a riot in the streets, or any number of other bad tidings. It could also mean something good, but the sounds at the moment were rather discordant.

With Anna at the front, the three left the kitchen together to face whatever it might be.

Teddie, Katya's faithful nurse, had answered the door. To her, the bedraggled man standing before her was some beggar off the streets. Deeply protective of those in her new home, she would not allow just anyone to barge in.

"I will not let you in!" Teddie was insisting.

"Where are the people that used to live here?" asked the man desperately.

"I don't know, but—"

"Misha!" cried Anna. She broke into a run and hardly noticed Teddie's shock as she rushed into this filthy stranger's arms.

———

Anna did not leave Misha's side for the rest of the day except when a much needed bath was drawn for him. His clothes had to be burned, but others were found among Yuri's things. Yuri's were the only clothes in the house that came near to fitting him, and then would not have except that Misha had lost so much weight.

"I should have gone to one of the de-lousing centers first," he apologized, "but once I laid my poor tired eyes on Petrograd, I could not wait another minute to come here."

"I would have wanted it no other way," said Anna, happy now that he was clean to be able to properly snuggle close to him in the bed Yuri and Katya had given up for them so they could have a chance to be alone.

"Am I dreaming, Anna? I have dreamed of it for so long, it can't be real."

"Then our dreams have finally merged."

Misha leaned close to his wife and kissed her with deep passion. "I know I have aged terribly on the outside, but inside I feel like a youth."

"As do I. I think love is the true fountain of youth."

They had talked all afternoon, through dinner and into the evening, both between themselves and with the rest of the family. Misha had been completely filled in on the activities of the family since he had last seen them. He had listened avidly, asking many questions, but he had spoken little of himself. Anna understood that he didn't want to think of his years at war or in the prison, so she did not question him. She also glossed quickly over the hardships the family had experienced over the years. Next to Andrei's return from the "dead," this was the happiest time Anna could remember in recent years, and she was content to keep it that way as long as possible.

But she could also tell that something was on Misha's mind, though she avoided bringing it up. It was he, instead, who finally broached the subject.

"I still can't believe Daniel is off trying to rescue the tsar. Even more unbelievable is that Andrei is assisting in this!" Misha said. "I truly hope they are successful. I spent so many years of my life protecting the man, I would hate to see them wasted now. However, Anna, I must confess, I would not want to see Nicholas returned to the throne. I'm not sure I want to see a monarchy returned at all to Russia."

"I'm not surprised, Misha. You have always been torn in your loyalties."

"Yes, but I definitely don't care for those Bolsheviks either." He shook his head with disgust. "From what I have heard, they will remake Russia into a place that one day none of us will recognize."

"It's already happening."

"You must know that the White Army is starting to fight it."

"Dmitri Remizov has joined them, but they are not doing well."

"That doesn't surprise me."

He paused a long time, and Anna began to fear what he was thinking. "Misha, you want to join them, too, don't you?"

"Part of me does, yes. But I made a promise to you when we married—"

"Though it would nearly kill me to see you go again," Anna replied reluctantly but with loving resolve, "I also could not keep you from doing that which you feel honor-bound to do."

"I am honor-bound only to being a husband to you, Anna, my dearest love."

Anna smiled. "Are you sure?"

"With all my heart. And where my heart might waver at times, God has given me a lame leg to strengthen my resolve."

"I won't say I am thankful for your injury, but—"

"I understand, Anna. But even if Yuri can repair it and bring it back to normal, I am still not leaving your side. You have been left alone to face the terrors and uncertainties of these times far too long. You may have even come to a place where you don't need a man around—"

"I will always need you, Misha. Perhaps not as I did when I was a lost little servant girl in the palace of the tsar, but in a way that reaches so deeply inside me, I can hardly put words to it."

"Thank you for saying that!" He hugged her close.

Anna lay her head on his shoulder, basking not only in his nearness but in the completion she felt with him at her side.

VI

PASSAGES
Summer 1918

41

June loosened the grip of winter upon Siberia, but with the warm weather came even more uncertainty and disruption to the land of Russia. Lenin's government was starting to bend under assault not only from outside and the challenge of the Whites, but also from within, among rival socialist parties. As Lenin began to expel more and more critics from his government, he desperately began to look toward the Urals as a place of retreat for his beleaguered government should he still fail.

In the midst of this rose another unexpected threat that would not only cut off Lenin's hope of a retreat but which would prove most significant for the Romanov family imprisoned in Ekaterinburg. Before the end of the war, forty thousand soldiers of the Czech Legion had surrendered to the Russians. They had been coerced into the Austrian army and no longer wished to fight for the Imperialist nation. They now hoped to rejoin the Allies by getting out of Russia via the Trans-Siberian Railroad, east to Vladivostok. The Bolsheviks tried to induce them into staying and supporting the revolution. Eventually disputes flared between the two sides until finally the Czech Legion mutinied altogether.

With lightning speed, the Czechs began to overwhelm the disorganized Siberian Reds, taking town after town along the railroad and cutting off the flow of desperately needed supplies to Moscow and Petrograd. Ekaterinburg lay on a northern spur of the rail line, but because of its strategic importance, it, too, became a target of the invading Czechs. And inch by inch they began to close in on the city.

"What's that?" hissed Bruce, pointing toward a dim light.

"Maybe it's the one," whispered Daniel. There seemed no reason to speak in such hushed tones except the ambiance of the night invited it.

Tentacles of fog reached into the sultry air along the waterfront of the Miass River in Ekaterinburg. Daniel was thankful for the covering of the mist because there was little darkness to be had in this season of White Nights. All these weeks in Ekaterinburg, he and Bruce had managed to remain fairly anonymous. Luckily, the center of Russia's platinum industry, with a population of seventy-five thousand, was practically a metropolis compared to the sleepy little Tobolsk.

And there were many other more prominent figures for the Cheka to watch here besides the two quiet guests at the Palais Royal Hotel. Daniel continued to successfully pass himself off as a fur trader from Vladisvostok, while many thought Bruce was his mute secretary. It was under this guise that Daniel arranged to meet with the steamship skipper, Serge Plautin.

As Daniel and Bruce searched for the steamer *Ural Queen*, where Daniel had arranged to rendezvous with Plautin, he hoped what he had heard about the skipper was true—that he was a loyal monarchist. Daniel had been vague in his own introductory remarks when he met briefly with Plautin a few days ago, but the skipper was no fool and thus must have quickly surmised Daniel's true intent. If the man turned out to be a Red informer, he and Bruce would no doubt soon be walking into a trap.

The taverns along the waterfront were busy, testimony to the truth of the stories that Russia's peasants were distilling hundreds of thousands of tons of precious grain into moonshine vodka while people starved. But pulling his attention from that side of the street, Daniel continued to peer through the fog toward the dim light he had noticed.

They turned down a finger of the wharf where about half a dozen boats, mostly fishing scowls, were anchored. The area fit Plautin's directions and, sure enough, the boat with the dull light coming from a lantern in the cabin was the *Ural Queen*. Even in the foggy night it looked as if the fifty-foot steamer had seen several decades of hard service on the river hauling iron ore or coal from the many mines in the area.

"Plautin," Daniel called in a low voice.

A head poked out of the cabin hatch, and, illuminated in the eerie light, appeared to be just as hardened as the boat itself—leathery skin, scored with wrinkles, peppered with a dingy beard, with dull light coming from dark eyes.

"Come aboard," said the skipper in a discordantly refined voice. He came off as a man of culture in the skin of a derelict.

Daniel and Bruce scrambled aboard, and Plautin ushered them into the cabin, a cluttered, unkempt place with books crammed into every corner that wasn't filled with other odd debris. Daniel tried to picture the tsar of Russia and his proud tsaritsa traveling in these quarters.

"May I offer some refreshment?" asked Plautin. He reached for a bottle of vodka and three glasses.

"We'd rather not mix vodka with business," said Daniel.

With a shaky hand Plautin filled only one of the glasses. "I mix vodka with everything!" He grinned and sipped his drink. "So you intrigued me earlier when we spoke. What exactly do you want from me?"

"Passage out of Ekaterinburg for about a dozen passengers, as I said," Daniel replied. "Preferably in a very covert manner."

"Destination?"

"We would head north, eventually merging with Irtysh River and traveling north to the Barents Sea."

"A long journey. Who are your passengers?"

"Is it necessary for you to know?"

"If they were nobodies named Ivan Ivanov, it would mean nothing. But if the surname were . . . say . . . Romanov—well, you can see that it would make a great difference. The risks would be multiplied immensely."

"Then let's just factor in the maximum risks."

Plautin smiled, drained his glass, and quickly refilled it. "This will not come cheaply."

"Does anything in this land?" Daniel replied, then translated for Bruce.

"Tell him money is no object," said Bruce in English.

"That's all he needs to hear," said Daniel ruefully. "Let me barter just a little."

"I swear," countered Bruce good-naturedly, "you are becoming more Russian than American."

"It was bound to happen." Then Daniel turned back to the skipper, hoping that he could be just as canny as any Russian. "A thousand rubles," he said in Russian, "before we leave town and a thousand rubles when my party is safely at the destination." That was a total of just over two thousand dollars. Probably more money than the hapless Plautin had seen in years.

Plautin only laughed in response. "First, I want dollars—U.S. dollars. Nice new ones, no wrinkles. Twenty thousand of them—ten before we leave and ten when the job is done."

"You must be joking!" Daniel exclaimed. "Why, that's a king's—" But he stopped short of the word "ransom," realizing he was indeed bartering literally for a king's ransom. He interpreted the proposed deal to Bruce.

"I thought this man was a loyal monarchist," said Bruce.

"Loyal *capitalist* monarchist."

"Make the deal," Bruce conceded.

"I'm sure I can talk him down—"

"Don't bother. I am willing to pay a lot more."

Daniel hoped the refined skipper didn't speak English, for he might decide to raise his price upon hearing that.

Daniel said to Bruce, "It'll take time to get that much money in dollars."

"See if he will take pounds."

"You have that much?"

"Perhaps we can work something out with the British consul here. It would be faster and safer than trying to work through the American embassy in Petrograd."

Daniel made the proposal to the skipper.

"I'd rather have dollars," said the skipper obstinately. "I plan to retire to America after this job."

Daniel threw up his hands. "Never mind! We'll find another skipper."

"The only other decent skippers in this town are Reds," argued Plautin.

"I'll take my chances." In a huff, Daniel turned, nudging Bruce to follow him.

He had started to climb through the hatch when Plautin called out, "All right. I'll take the English money, but it must be good and new!"

With a victorious wink at Bruce, Daniel turned back. "Okay, when can we leave?"

"There is much to be done. Provisions must be procured, enough fuel to get us to the next port—and all in complete secrecy. This will not be easy."

"It had better not be, for twenty thousand dollars," Daniel grumbled under his breath in English. Then he added in Russian, "We'll take care of the provisions. You do the rest."

"Then as soon as you can get the money and provisions . . ." the skipper said casually.

And, of course, the skipper knew that would be the most difficult part of the deal, besides getting the passengers away from their present lodgings and to the boat.

Getting the money would be the most time-consuming. A backwater consul simply did not have that kind of cash lying around. Couriers had to be sent to Moscow. Because of this both the British and American embassies were contacted, and each was given written assurances by Daniel and Bruce for prompt repayment. The Trent and Findochty names hopefully would be enough to guarantee the loan. Whichever embassy came up with the money the fastest would determine if Plautin would be paid in dollars or pounds. Even at that, a departure in less than a week would be impossible. The Czech control of the railway also posed a problem. Some passenger trains were getting through, but there were long delays.

In addition to procuring the money, arrangements had to be made for the transportation of the Romanovs once they reached the mouth of the Irtysh. Daniel wished they could have begun the preparations long ago, but it was only recently that their final destination could have been decided. It had only been a couple of weeks since the British took control of the port of Murmansk, providing the perfect escape route for the royal family. A few coded telegrams from the British consul would get things rolling on that front.

Daniel decided to set an estimated time of departure for two weeks—July fourteenth. Not without a sense of irony did he note that it would be Bastille Day, the day that had launched the French Revolution.

42

When Andrei met with Daniel in the old barn that had become a regular rendezvous point, he seemed pessimistic about the feasibility of liberating the family from the heavily guarded house.

"I've been stewing over this since I arrived," Andrei told his brother-in-law. "I've tried to get assigned to duty inside the house without success. I've been lucky not to have been recalled completely—I suppose we must thank

Stephan for that. They are changing the guard frequently."

"But you are Cheka, aren't you, with authority from Moscow?"

"Yes, but I have no influence over the Ural Soviet, and apparently Kaminsky doesn't wish to press his influence any further than merely allowing me to stay here. Anyway, the Urals have been assigned the key posts inside the house."

"What about Talia?"

"I'd like her to be gone on the day of the escape."

"So would I, but you know she would never accept that. We need her, Andrei. But she doesn't have to be put in the line of fire, as it were."

"Well, she can pass messages and such. But there is still the problem of the actual escape. I'm thinking of staging some kind of diversion—a fire or something."

"That's good. They'd have to clear out the prisoners if the house caught fire."

"But we'd have to make a speedy exit from that point because we'll have Reds hot on our tails. How fast can that boat go?"

"That'll be a problem. I've talked to other prospective rescuers who have considered sneaking them out a window."

"Remember, the boy can't walk, and Talia told me that the empress's sciatica has flared up, and she can barely walk as well. We are simply not going to get them to *sneak* away from anywhere."

"Andrei, don't tell me this is hopeless."

"Nothing is hopeless, I guess. But anything short of a commando assault will be extremely difficult. And an assault . . . well, we all want to avoid bloodshed, and I have a feeling the tsar himself would veto blasting away fellow Russians in order to rescue him. But even if we should attempt this, there are ten thousand Red troops in town."

"Whatever we do will have to be clandestine."

"We could drug the guards. Dress the family in disguise . . ." It was obvious Andrei was clutching at fantasies. He'd probably read *The Scarlet Pimpernel* one too many times.

Daniel began to pace thoughtfully over the straw-covered barn floor. After a few moments he paused and asked, "Andrei, how safe is the tsar right now?"

"As I already told you, the Ural Soviet has voted for execution. But I've heard there has been more talk in Moscow about a public trial. That could buy time, but if there is a trial, I can't see any result other than a death sentence."

"All right," Daniel said with more decisiveness than he felt, "we have a little over a week. Come up with something. I hear the White Army is drawing closer. Maybe they'll save us a lot of trouble and rescue the tsar for us."

The grim expression on Andrei's face was unsettling. "Lenin does not want a live banner for his enemies to rally round. If the Whites get too close for the Ural Soviet's comfort, they will dispose of their captives rather than see them fall into White hands."

Silence fell between the two men. Nothing else needed to be said. The urgency of their mission was suddenly brought into new perspective. If ever the pressure was on, it was now. Daniel almost physically felt a noose being drawn tighter and tighter around them and the Romanovs. The weight of their undertaking was suddenly crushing. But he strode away from that barn with resolve and purpose, forcefully banishing the sense of defeat that threatened him from all sides.

———

Talia was mixing ingredients for bread when Tatiana and Anastasia Romanov wandered into the kitchen. She smiled at them. This wasn't their first visit to the kitchen. They had indicated an interest in learning to cook and had received permission to do so. The other day they had helped make soup, but they really wanted to learn how to make bread, so the cook had informed them when the bread was usually prepared and welcomed them back.

"May we watch?" Tatiana asked politely.

"Of course," said Talia. "If I had known you were coming, I would have waited to mix the ingredients. But it is just flour and water and a bit of sugar, and of course the yeast."

"Sugar?" questioned Anastasia. "But the bread doesn't seem sweet."

"There is only enough for the yeast to feed on."

"It sounds alive."

"In a way it is—the yeast, at least. That's what makes the bread dough rise." Talia stirred the mixture until it was the right consistency, then turned it out on the board. "Now it must be kneaded."

"Why is that?" asked Tatiana.

"So it will have a nice, smooth texture, and so the yeast is worked throughout. Would you like to give it a try?"

The girls nodded eagerly, and Talia divided up the dough so each could have a part.

"We've already washed up," said Tatiana.

"Good, then go right ahead."

At that moment one of the guards came into the kitchen with a box of groceries.

"Where do you want these?" he asked, then stopped, a bit embarrassed when he saw the girls. Talia wasn't certain if his reaction was because he suddenly found himself in the presence of grand duchesses, or if it was just because they were two pretty young women about his own age.

"Thank you, Yevgeny," Talia said. "Just put them over there."

He placed the box where indicated but lingered a moment watching the girls. "Don't tell me you are making the prisoners cook, Talia?" he said a bit brashly, probably to offset his shyness.

"We want to," said Anastasia.

"We have always wanted to learn to cook," added Tatiana. "We get so bored doing nothing."

"Yes, I suppose it would be boring." He watched a moment longer, then continued, "Don't slap the dough like that. Use the heel of your palm." He looked at Talia. "You're not much of a teacher, Talia," he said good-naturedly.

"And how did you get to be such an expert?" Talia said, half-mocking. This was one of the nicer guards of the new batch, a young man no older than twenty.

"My father was a baker," Yevgeny replied. "I'd show you the proper way myself, but my hands are dirty." He paused and watched the girls attempt to knead the dough as he had instructed. "Not so hard," he said. "You don't want to kill the yeast. Firm, but at the same time gently. That's it."

With a friendly exchange of conversation and banter, they continued the task for several minutes. It was like any group of young people anywhere having a good time. Talia nearly forgot the nature of their tragic circumstances. However, with sudden force, reality intruded upon them as a gunshot exploded nearby.

The girls screamed. Yevgeny raced from the kitchen to the yard to investigate. Talia put a calming arm around the girls and encouraged them to stay put until Yevgeny returned. In a few moments the young guard came back.

"One of the guards claims he saw someone poke his head from a window upstairs, so he fired," explained Yevgeny. Seeing the grand duchesses' shocked looks, he added quickly, "No one was hurt. He only fired in the air."

"We must find our parents," said Tatiana urgently.

The two girls started to leave but paused at the kitchen door to thank Talia and Yevgeny.

When they were gone, the guard shook his head. "They shouldn't be treated like common criminals."

"I know," sighed Talia.

"They haven't done anything. I think they should let them go."

"Yevgeny, be careful what you say."

"Will you turn me in, Talia?"

"Not I, but you never know who might be listening."

"I don't care. I'd prefer to be assigned elsewhere. I didn't join the revolution to harm innocents."

Talia lowered her voice. "Yevgeny, I think you ought to try to stay here as long as possible. Imagine what it would be like for them if there wasn't at least one or two sympathetic guards."

Later, Talia told Andrei about the encounter. It didn't surprise him.

"Most of the outside guards—of which Yevgeny is one—tend to be more sympathetic," he said. "Not enough to conspire to rescue the prisoners—I've tried to subtly feel them out. They don't like the duty, but they won't disobey orders either."

"Should I work on Yevgeny a bit more and try to turn him to our side?" suggested Talia.

"Too risky for the good it will do. But I have talked to Yevgeny myself, and if the need arose, I think we could count on him. What we really need are some allies among the inside guards. But they are Cheka and of the Urals besides—as hard core as they come."

"What can we do, then?"

"Keep closely apprised of the health of the tsarevich and tsaritsa. As soon as they seem able, we may just have to attempt a break when they are out in the garden. At least there we will only have the outside guard to contend with at first, and they might be counted upon not to fire on women and children. Not that the Cheka won't be hot on us the minute we make an attempt."

"They are such nice girls, Andrei," Talia said sadly of the grand duchesses. "Even in the midst of the excitement today, they stopped to thank me for showing them how to make bread."

"We'll do everything we can for them," assured Andrei.

"I know, but I am afraid it won't be enough. The odds seem so much against them."

43

Nicholas did not like the look of the new flock of guards to take command a week later. He'd heard they were Cheka—what those Bolsheviks were calling their secret police. Their commander was Yakov Yurovsky.

"He's the worst we've had yet," he murmured one night to Dr. Botkin, noting the commander's sinister appearance, his cold dark eyes, and thin, hard mouth.

Nicholas, however, said nothing of his misgivings to Alix. When she came into the room, they talked about rumors of the approach of the White Army. The distant sounds of artillery boosted their hopes.

Andrei saw the replacement of the inside guard with Yakov Yurovsky and his Cheka troops as nothing more or less than what it was—an execution squad. But even more alarming was the news that a VIP was arriving from Moscow. Could this man be there to oversee the imminent execution of the tsar? What else could it be? Yet wouldn't Moscow be more likely to play down their involvement in the execution? Perhaps, then, the man was here in an unofficial capacity. Moscow could keep tabs on the operation without appearing to be involved.

Regardless, the replacement of the guards and the arrival of the VIP could only mean that time had run out. The original date of their rescue attempt was already twenty-four hours past, and still Andrei had not been able to come up with a way to get the family out of the Ipatiev House.

The money for the skipper had arrived from Moscow, and the boat was fully provisioned and waiting. Andrei had been fervently praying for an escape opportunity to present itself. When they had decided to postpone the attempt yesterday, Daniel had laid no blame on Andrei. No one could have wrenched the captives from their prison. Still Andrei felt as if he had failed because this part of the rescue had rested solely on his shoulders.

He now had to find Daniel and inform him of this new, unwelcome development. Perhaps if they put their heads together once more they could come up with something. Before leaving he managed a few words with Talia behind the house as she carried out a bag of trash.

"Andrei, you can't go directly to the hotel."

"There isn't time to arrange anything else. For all we know this thing may take place tonight."

"Maybe we could overtake the guards when they move the tsar to some place of execution?" she said hopefully.

"It's a thought," Andrei said, trying to match her optimism. "We've got to think of something and quickly."

"You will be careful."

"Of course. Anyway, the Cheka headquaters is in the Hotel America, so there is little chance of running into any of them at the Palais."

"Is there anything I can do?"

"Get a message to the tsar telling him to be prepared to fly at any given moment."

"Oh, dear Lord," Talia breathed, "please help us."

Andrei wanted so much to hold her. Anything could happen now. They might never see each other again. Who could say? But he had already talked to her much too long. An embrace at this point might be fatal. So, with a mere nod, he walked away.

A half hour later he walked into the Palais Royal Hotel. He strode up to the front desk wearing his most arrogant Cheka attitude, given further credance by his intimidating size. He hardly had to say a word to the clerk to command his instant obedience.

"I am here to investigate reports of seditious activities centering in this hotel," he growled.

"Here, comrade? You must be mistaken. We are loyal Bolsheviks."

"Not you, fool! You have guests I must question."

"Tell me the names. I will give you the room numbers."

"I have the room numbers, idiot! What do you take me for? But rather than disrupt the hotel, I want to take care of this outside the hotel."

"Thank you very much, I greatly appreciate—"

"Shut up and listen to me. The room number is two-fourteen. You will take this message there. Are they in?"

"I believe so."

Andrei grabbed a sheet of hotel paper and a hotel envelope, then quickly scrawled the message: "Fifteen minutes, Murmsk's Tavern. A." He slipped it into the envelope, sealed it, and handed it to the clerk.

Andrei watched as the clerk hurried toward the stairs. He could not have been more surprised than the clerk when the object of his search appeared on the stairs.

"Ah, Mr. Sergiev, what a coincidence!" the clerk said to Daniel.

"You wish to see me?" said Daniel.

"Well . . . uh . . . well . . . um . . ." Suddenly the clerk realized the delicacy of his predicament. He glanced helplessly toward Andrei, whose eyes met with Daniel's instead. Daniel paled, obviously understanding that there must be bad tidings if Andrei would risk coming directly to the hotel.

There now seemed no other recourse but to play out the ruse. Andrei marched up to Daniel. "I have orders to take you in for questioning, Mr. Sergiev."

"But this is outrageous! I have done nothing!" Daniel protested.

"You will come!" Andrei grabbed Daniel's arm, and only a fool would have resisted further, so Daniel allowed himself to be led away.

They were within three feet of the door when it burst open, and they were suddenly face-to-face with the last person either of them expected to see.

Stephan Kaminsky.

Even Andrei would never have guessed that the VIP from Moscow would be Stephan, yet it made perfect sense. Who else would Lenin assign his dirty work?

"What's this?" said Stephan as he quickly recovered from his own surprise at the unexpected meeting. It had been a long time since he'd seen Daniel Trent, his one-time rival for the affections of Mariana, but there was no way he would not recognize him.

Andrei could think of nothing else but to keep up the ruse. "I've just arrested this man for acts of sedition."

"This is rather interesting, isn't it?" said Stephan dryly. Three other Cheka soldiers were right behind him.

Andrei sensed then that he was backed into a corner from which there was no escape, but he had to keep trying. "Haven't I convinced you yet, Stephan, that I won't allow anything to interfere with my duty to the revolution?"

Daniel jumped in and, glaring first at Stephan then at Andrei, exclaimed, "You can't think I'm working with this dog! Ha! We disowned him from the family long ago." He spat, very convincingly Andrei thought, in Andrei's face.

"I don't know what to think," admitted Stephan.

Just then, the clerk decided he ought to protect his own flank. He came forward and in an ingratiating tone said to Stephan, "Commissar Kaminsky, is this man not working for you?"

"What did he tell you?" questioned Stephan.

"That he was here on Cheka business—" The clerk stopped, suddenly remembering the note still in his hand. "He gave me this to give to Sergiev." He gave the note to

Stephan, and Andrei knew it was over then.

Kaminsky ripped open the envelope, read the note, and smiled. "You will both come with me." He drew his side arm and, backed up by his men, prodded Andrei and Daniel from the hotel.

After an hour of interrogation, they were locked up in separate cells. All hope for rescue of the tsar—by them, at least—appeared to be over. Stephan had learned nothing from Andrei, and he was certain nothing from Daniel either, though they had been interrogated separately. But Stephan had made his own assumptions. The note alone was incriminating enough for a conviction in any court. But the case was unlikely to reach the courtroom.

That evening the final blow came. Plautin, the steamboat skipper, was arrested—and he had no reason for heroism. He told Stephan everything about Daniel's proposition. This did not necessarily implicate Andrei, but it was bad enough. And Stephan knew how to best use the information to his advantage. He brought Andrei back into the interrogation room.

"I have just received conclusive evidence that your brother-in-law was involved in a plot to rescue the Romanovs," Stephan said. "I have in my custody the skipper of a steamer who will testify he made a deal with Trent to carry important passengers away from here."

"That doesn't surprise me," Andrei replied. He was still trying to keep up the earlier ruse—perhaps if he could get released, something still might be accomplished. But he was getting more and more disheartened. He hated this double game and wanted to admit to it all.

"How did you learn of this plot?" Stephan demanded.

"I heard talk in a tavern."

"Who else is involved?"

"I don't know."

"Come now, you must have had some conclusive proof in order to attempt an arrest?"

"I'd seen him in town and heard rumors that he was talking to suspicious people."

"Then you rushed to arrest your own brother-in-law?" Stephan chuckled dryly. "I don't believe you, comrade. You are, remember, the man who vomited when he watched an enemy being shot. You simply don't have it in you to betray a member of your family. And I tell you, I am almost ready to have Trent shot as a spy."

"Shot?" Somehow Andrei had always let himself believe Daniel, as a foreigner, would be in no such danger.

"Does that bother you, comrade?"

Andrei shook his head wearily. What good was the game? Why keep it up? They couldn't save the tsar. And it was probably useless to try to save himself. But there still might be a chance to spare Daniel.

"All right, Stephan, I'm going to tell you everything. It doesn't matter anymore. We can't save the tsar. That's what you're here for, isn't it? You're going to supervise the execution."

"Not at all. I am here to visit my sick mother."

Stephan smiled and Andrei knew now that Moscow didn't plan to have any official part in the executions. However, they did want to make certain all came off in an efficient manner.

"Nevertheless," Andrei continued, "why should any of us die for a plan that has failed? But Daniel only came here to try to stop me."

"To stop you? You mean you are the organizer of this attempt at rescue?" Stephan shook his head incredulously. "Again, I am at a complete loss at what to believe."

"Well, believe this: you have captured the skipper, so our plan has failed. What else do you need to know?"

"Who were your accomplices?" Andrei had hoped to avoid this question.

"Look around, Stephan. There are monarchists everywhere in this town. You can't arrest all of them."

"I might try."

"You've got me where you've always wanted me, Stephan. Isn't that enough?"

"You are wrong, Andrei. What I always wanted was to believe you to be a loyal Bolshevik."

"I was until I saw what it was really all about. To Lenin it is more about power than freedom—"

"You are in no position to preach at me, Andrei. I am ready to have you summarily shot as a traitor. I need no trial, do you understand?"

"Then get on with it. I am not about to reveal any accomplices."

Towering over the seated Andrei, Stephan glared down at him with a mixture of fury and disappointment on his face. Finally, in a tone that belied the emotion in his eyes, he said calmly, "I will trade your brother-in-law's life for the names of accomplices."

"Russia can no more afford to murder a prominent American citizen than it can afford to put bread on the table of the masses." And for a brief moment, as he saw the truth of his words in Stephan's eyes, Andrei felt a sense of victory. The fact that Russia could easily afford to shoot *him* was something he'd already accepted.

"I have pressing business to attend to," said Stephan. "When I am done, I will deal with you and that American."

Kaminsky called in a guard to take Andrei away. Andrei could only wonder and fear what Stephan's "pressing business" might be.

Bruce heard about the arrests a short time later. He was amazed that he, too, had not been caught in the net. But then he had always kept a rather low profile. Apparently, Plautin, the boat skipper, had been arrested and had incriminated Daniel but, no doubt thinking Bruce nothing but an unimportant flunky, had failed to implicate him. Nevertheless, Bruce was completely powerless to do anything about his friends save make some noise at the British consulate where he was lying low until the heat of the present events cooled.

And the worst of it was that the arrests signaled the failure of their rescue plan.

Assuming the British "stiff upper lip," Bruce tried to convince himself that there would be another day, another plan. He could not accept complete failure. He sent a message to Talia.

They met later in the deserted barn. Talia was holding up quite well, considering the danger her fiancé was in, but her face was extremly pale and her voice trembled as she spoke. Bruce convinced her to remain in the House for a few more days. He might be able to join forces with other rescue groups in town and still mount an attempt.

He also told her not to try, under any circumstances, to contact Andrei in prison. That would only place her in extreme danger. Moreover she could do more good continuing to do what she had been doing. She agreed reluctantly.

44

Talia could barely concentrate on the menial tasks in the kitchen of the Ipatiev House. Her only comfort was that she had heard no rumors of executions at the jail. Surely the guards would talk if a fellow guard had been executed.

It was the evening following the day of the arrests, and events in the House had become disturbing. Since yesterday, most of the staff had been dismissed. After dinner the cook came in wearing her coat.

"You are leaving, Alla?" Talia asked.

"I was let go. You are to finish cleaning up the dinner

things, then you must leave also."

"Are they closing the house?"

"I ask no questions. We are dismissed. That's all I know. Perhaps I will see you at the trade union hall."

Talia took her time washing the dishes and scrubbing the pots. Somehow she must find out more about what was happening. If they were going to move the family, it might be the only opportunity they would get for escape. She wondered if Bruce had been successful in recruiting help from the other monarchists.

A guard strode into the kitchen. "I'm hungry. Have you anything left from dinner?"

He was one of the inside guards, a brutish sort whom Talia had tried not to have much to do with. Now, however, she thought it might be prudent to be a bit more friendly.

"With the thin rations?" Talia chuckled humorously. "You are dreaming."

"Oh, come on . . ." The guard ambled close to Talia and placed his arm around her. "There must be something."

Talia slipped adroitly away from him but with a teasing laugh so as not to offend him. She went to the icebox and took out a covered dish.

"The cook was hoarding this pirogi, but since she has been dismissed . . ." With a friendly smile she held the dish out to the guard. "Perhaps you can do something for me in return?"

"Anything at all!" Taking the dish from her, he gave her a quick kiss on the cheek, then sat at the table.

"I just have a question. Cook tells me I am to be let go, but I desperately need this job. Isn't there some way I could keep it?"

"There won't be any work here after tomorrow." The guard took a large bite from the meat pie.

"Are they moving the Romanovs?"

"I don't know," he said around the mouthful of food. "I only know the house is to be closed."

"I'd be willing to travel with them. I really need the money."

"Bah! They have too many servants as it is. Maybe we'll make the old woman do the cooking."

Talia knew the guards often referred to the empress as the "old woman," and in a derogatory manner.

"Are you sure you want her to do the cooking? I'll bet she has never even seen the inside of the kitchen."

"Well, there is nothing I can do for you, Talia. Take it up with Yurovsky."

Talia knew that would be a lost cause even if she dared approach the commander. For one thing, he was such a hard character he would probably see right through her query. He could not be as easily cajoled as some of the young guards under his command.

When she finished the dishes, she left the House in search of Bruce. He was not in the hotel or in two or three other places she thought likely. She decided to return to the House. Of course, since she had been officially dismissed, she could not go into the House itself, but she found a secluded place across the street where she could watch undetected. If the royals were moved, at least she could observe the direction in which they were being taken.

————

Anastasia was awakened at midnight by the noise of stirring in the bed next to her. Tatiana was bent over Maria's bed.

"Come, we must get up," Tatiana was saying.

Maria's reply was muffled and groggy.

"What is it?" asked Anastasia. She had not been sleeping soundly and so came more quickly awake.

"Papa came to tell us to dress quickly and pack a few belongings," said Tatiana.

Anastasia could see Olga slipping a dress over her head at the other end of the room. "We are being rescued?" The seventeen-year-old girl could not help the hope rising in her. There had been so many disappointments, but perhaps at last the moment had come.

"Papa will explain. Now hurry!"

Now fully awake, Anastasia and Maria jumped out of bed.

"Mama says to wear these," said Tatiana, handing her sisters the corsets they had been sewing for weeks now. Sewn into the fabic of the corsets, and cleverly concealed, was a fortune in precious stones. This was how they would support themselves once they were free.

Soon, fully dressed and carrying small valises, the girls hurried out into the corridor. Anastasia paused to scoop up her spaniel, Jimmy, who had remained with her throughout the captivity. Downstairs she found Papa already there holding a sleepy Alexis in his arms. Both were dressed in plain military uniforms. Mama was leaning heavily on her cane with her maid Demidova beside her clutching a pillow against her body. Anastasia knew Mama had told Demidova to guard the pillow closely because it contained a fortune in jewels. Also with the little group was the faithful Dr. Botkin, Papa's valet Trupp, and the footman Kharitonov.

Anastasia went to her papa and put her arm around him. Nicholas bent down and kissed her forehead.

"Be brave, Stasia," he said, then was interrupted by the appearance of that awful commander Yurovsky.

"Because the fighting is getting closer to the town," Yurovsky said civilly enough, "I have been ordered to move you to a safer place."

He motioned for them to follow, while other guards took up the rear and led them across a small courtyard at the back of the house to a semi-basement attached to the corner of the house. Yurovsky led them inside while the other guards remained outside.

"You will wait here until a truck arrives," said Yurovsky.

The room was bare of furnishings and Papa asked, "Are there not even chairs for my wife and son?"

The commander poked his head out the door. In a few moments two chairs were brought and Mama and Alexis were seated. Tenderly Olga placed a pillow she had been holding behind her mother's head. The family and their loyal servants clustered around the two chairs. Anastasia stood close to her papa. She did not understand when ten armed men entered the room.

Yurovsky faced the group. "Citizen Nicholas Romanov, your relatives and followers have tried to rescue you but they have failed. And now we must shoot you."

"What—!" Nicholas began, but that was the last word he would speak.

Yurovsky quickly raised his revolver, aimed, and fired. Anastasia screamed as her papa crumbled to the ground, a bloody wound in his head. But she had no time to even feel her grief, for that single shot was a signal to the other guards who instantly raised their weapons, mostly hand-guns, and began firing into the group. From the corner of her eye, Anastasia saw her mama cross herself before slumping over in her chair. That was too much for the seventeen-year-old girl. She swooned into a faint, hearing, as unconsciousness engulfed her, the terrified yelping of little Jimmy as he scurried from her arms, mingled with the screams of her sisters and the others as they were massacred.

———

The tiny room was so filled with gunsmoke the shooters could hardly see their targets any longer, but still they fired at anything that moved. They had not planned on this horrible chaos. Each man had been assigned a target, and thus it should have been a simple matter. They simply had not thought the thing through. They had not considered missed shots and those bullets ricocheting off the stone walls, nor the screaming and frantic flailing of the targets. The bullets actually seemed to bounce off the female targets. It was unnerving.

Nicholas, who had died instantly from the first shot, received at least two dozen more shots. When the killers saw that Anastasia had only fainted, they finished her off with another volley of shots. When the tsarevich quivered in the throws of death, Yurovsky fired two shots into the boy's head. The maid was the last to die. The box of jewels in her pillow had repelled several bullets. She ran around the death-filled room screaming until she was brought down with a bayonet.

Yurovsky could not take a step in the room without encountering blood. He nearly slipped once as he supervised the wrapping of the bodies in sheets.

At first, Talia mistook the sounds as the distant artillery she had been hearing for days. The racing engine of the two four-ton military trucks had also obscured the sounds. Then she realized that the shots were much too close at hand. In fact, as she oriented herself, she could tell they were indeed coming from across the street at the Ipatiev House itself.

"Dear God! Don't let it be. . . ."

But there could be no other explanation.

After a while—it seemed to go on forever—the firing ceased. But the silence was nearly as unnerving as the horrible noise.

Talia's legs were so shaky she had to lean against the tree she had been hiding behind. If only her legs could carry her, she wanted more than anything to run away. But before she could tell anyone about what she was nearly certain had just transpired, she had to be certain. Willing herself to be steady, she crept from the cover of the tree, crossing the road to the perimeter of the house. She then inched along the outside of the fence to the back of the house until she had a view of the courtyard. She knew she was taking a terrible risk. If caught she might be able to plead that she had forgotten something at the house, yet even if they believed her, they might still shoot her to eliminate any possible witness.

She noted the two trucks she had watched earlier pull into the courtyard. She waited, still praying, still hoping that the shots she had heard were nothing but the guards target-shooting. Then came the procession of guards carrying bundles wrapped in sheets. Even in the gloaming she could see stains on the sheets. She felt sick inside. Yet she swallowed back the waves of nausea, for she was close enough to be heard should she lose control.

Only when the trucks with their grim cargo drove away did she turn away from the "House of Special Purpose" in order to seek the only person she could go to for comfort. How desperately she wished that person could be Andrei, but he was out of her reach, so she would have to find Bruce.

As she turned, she gasped at what she beheld. A guard was approaching, with his rifle aimed directly at her.

"What're you up to?" he asked gruffly.

"I . . . I . . ." But she was so startled she could not think of an answer.

"Poking your head where it doesn't belong can get you killed."

"I . . . work here."

"I know that."

"I forgot—"

"I don't care. You've had it now. Yurovsky isn't gonna like this." Prodding her with the barrel of the rifle, he added, "Get moving."

45

Stephan Kaminsky, though he did not take part in the shooting itself, verified the body count as each corpse was loaded into one of the vehicles. There was blood everywhere. In the basement room where the shooting had taken place, there was so much blood it had leaked through the floorboards to the ground below. Before leaving he set some men to the gruesome task of cleanup, but it would take days to do a thorough job. No doubt only a thick coat of paint would even begin to hide what had occurred there that night.

He sent the trucks away as dawn began to tinge the sky, satisfied that the job had been properly completed. Earlier the previous day Stephan and Yurovsky had scouted out a "burial" site for the bodies, an abandoned mine shaft at what had once been called the Four Brothers' Mine. It was about twelve miles north of Ekaterinburg.

Stephan was going to return to the jail and finish the business there, but he needed a drink first—even his strong stomach had found the task that night difficult. In one of the taverns the guards frequented, he ordered a vodka. The glass was barely set before him when he began to hear disturbing talk.

"I tell you it's done. The bloodsucker is dead," said a man Stephan recognized as one of the outside guards at the Ipatiev House.

"You saw this?"

"I heard the shots with my own ears. The bodies are being carried even now to the Four Brothers' Mine."

Stephan jumped up, strode to the guard, grabbed him by the front of his coat, and fairly shoved him from the tavern. Outside, he threw him up against the wall.

"Has no one taught you how to keep your mouth shut?" he railed at the guard.

"I . . . I . . . didn't Comrade Kaminsky."

"You fool! Go back in there and say you are drunk and don't know what you are saying. And if I hear you have talked more about this, I will have you shot."

Unable to trust the security of their plans, Stephan had to get to the mine and have the bodies moved. He spoke with some of the leaders of the local Soviet and learned of another mine that would serve his purposes.

He quickly comandeered a truck and raced as fast as the poor roads would allow to the Four Brothers' Mine. He might as well not have been in such haste, for he got stuck several times and it was late in the evening before he arrived.

There, he learned that Yurovsky was having troubles of his own. His group had also had problems getting stuck on the rutted roads, and they had gotten lost once as well. Finally, they broke an axle and had to haul their cargo the rest of the way to the mine in carts. Then there had been the difficulty of keeping curious locals away. Needless to say, they were not happy about having to fish the bodies from the mine and relocate them. But the need was obvious even to Yurovsky, for this place was no longer much of a secret.

Yurovsky was also having problems among the guards with stealing. Once the bodies were stripped, the fortune in jewels was discovered—thirty pounds or so, by his estimation! This and other trinkets found among the dead proved a huge temptation to the men.

More than a whole day had passed since the murders by the time they were ready to move to the new location. They also learned from some passing Bolsheviks that the White Army was getting closer. Stephan urged the driver to go faster and faster. Twice they had to spend time pushing the truck out of ruts. Finally, when the driver took a curve too quickly, the truck veered off the road into a deep, muddy hole from which there was no way to free it.

They decided to dispose of the bodies right there.

"I have some sulfuric acid," offered Yurovsky. "At least we can blot out the identities."

"It would take too long to burn them," said Stephan. "Start digging. We'll bury nine of them. Set aside the boy and the old woman, and we'll burn them so that if the grave is discovered it can't be connected with the prisoners."

A few minutes later, Yurovsky took Stephan aside. "We have a problem. There are only ten corpses."

"What?"

"I counted them myself. One of the females is missing. I think one of the girls, but it is hard to tell which one because they have already doused them with acid."

"You must have left one behind at the mine."

"I was certain—"

"Obviously, not certain enough!" Stephan made his own count and came up with only ten. "Curse you, Yurovsky! How are we going to explain this?"

"Continue with the original plan. Burn the boy—but the official report will read that two bodies were burned."

Stephan could think of no better plan and gave the orders, but it irked him that things had gone so poorly. That's what came of dealing with provincials. No doubt he would be taken to task by Moscow for usurping as large a role in the executions as he had. But there had been no choice in the matter. He would just make sure no official reports mentioned his name. He had been careful to make it appear as if Yurovsky had been in complete command.

Later, after they had managed to free the truck and were on their way back to town, it did continue to bother Stephan about the missing body. He debated returning to the Four Brothers' Mine to search, but he was anxious to be done with this job and return to Moscow. And he still had to deal with his other prisoner, the young Andrei Christinin.

46

Andrei sat in his cell, in no way believing that no news was good news. He did not know what had become of Daniel. It had been twenty-four hours since his arrest and a good ten hours since he had last seen Stephan. Anything could have happened in that time.

He first began to believe his prayers were being answered when a new guard brought his breakfast to him.

"Yevgeny, what are you doing here?" he asked the young guard who slipped the tray of food through the cubby hole designed for that purpose. They talked to each other through the small barred window in the thick wooden cell door.

"They didn't need me anymore at the House, so I was sent here. I expect this is temporary until they need me for the defense of the town. What happened to you, Andrei? I heard you had been arrested but no one would say why."

"I suppose it was because I didn't see eye to eye with my superiors on how they were running things at the House." Andrei had nothing to lose now in telling the truth. And he might just be able to use Yevgeny's obvious sympathy to his benefit.

"What do you mean?"

"Like you, comrade, I don't want to see harm come to the family. I don't care what they have done. They don't deserve to die."

"Then you don't know?"

"What?"

"They were executed."

"Dear God, no! That can't be!" Andrei's knees suddenly felt weak. He grasped a hand around a window bar to steady himself.

"I was not there at the time, but I spoke with a guard

who was there and saw the bodies carried from the house. I'm not ashamed to admit that I wept when I heard. Even the children, Andrei! What kind of animals would do that? I didn't become a Bolshevik for this! And the hypocrites also killed good proletarians, too. It is so senseless."

"What do you mean, proletarians?"

"Several servants were killed also—"

"Servants! What servants?"

"I don't know."

"What about the kitchen girl? Talia? You know who I mean."

"I just don't know. But they weren't going to leave witnesses, that is for sure."

"Did you see her?"

"She was there in the evening when I left—the evening of the, you know, murders. You and she . . . was there something?"

"Yevgeny, I must know if she is all right."

"But how—"

"Let me out, Yevgeny! You can do it. You can get a key—"

"I'd be shot."

Andrei grabbed the bars with both hands and shook mightily, though the effort did nothing. In frustration he kicked the tray of food that still sat untouched on the floor.

"I have to find her. I have to make sure she is all right," Andrei said, but mostly to himself, for he had already lost hope that the young guard would help him. And why should he take such a risk? He *would* be shot for helping a prisoner escape.

"If they have hurt her . . ." Yevgeny said. "But they couldn't have. She was completely innocent—"

"They murdered children!" Andrei cried. "Do you think a kitchen girl would matter to them?"

Slowly, as if it hurt physically to make the admission, Yevgeny replied, "You are right, of course . . ."

Hope returning, Andrei begged—he would have dropped to his knees if the window hadn't been so high—"Please, help me, Yevgeny! Please!"

There was only silence in response and Andrei despaired again. Finally he crumbled to the floor, his head drooped in his hands. There seemed no logical reason why Talia should have been harmed, but he knew better than anyone that the Reds often made little sense in what they did. Yurovsky might kill her just for the pleasure of watching her die—

But the thought caused a stab of pain to shoot through him. Suddenly he remembered that he was learning a way not to bear his pain alone.

"Dear God, please protect Talia. Don't let the horrors of these times touch her. I would gladly give my own life to spare her if that is what it must take."

Then he heard the sound of metal against metal. He glanced toward the door as it opened a crack.

"Hurry!" came Yevgeny's voice.

Without another thought, Andrei jumped up. When he was in the corridor, Yevgeny relocked the cell door and motioned Andrei to follow him. He replaced the key in an attempt to delay discovery of the escape, then led Andrei to a back door.

Outside, Yevgeny said, "I'd go with you, but you'd probably do better on your own."

"Thank you, Yevgeny. You did the right thing. But what will you do now?"

"Maybe I'll join the Whites. I can no longer be associated with this new regime."

Andrei was about to turn when he realized he had forgotten all about Daniel. "Yevgeny, I can't leave without the American prisoner."

"If you go back inside you are sure to be caught. But the foreigner is gone anyway. They took him away by guard a few hours ago. I think they are going to deport him if they can get him past the Whites."

Trusting Daniel into God's hands, Andrei raced away to search for Talia.

First, he went to the Palais Hotel. He had some difficulty getting past the clerk—the same one he'd encountered before. Slipping upstairs, he found a maid and, after giving her a small bribe, learned that the "mute" fur trader had checked out of the hotel.

What could have happened? Had Bruce been discovered and deported also? And still he was no closer to finding Talia. He went to the boardinghouse where Talia had been staying, but she was not there either. He was told she had not been back in quite some time. Next, he went to the trade union hall, but again, no luck. Same with the deserted barn.

Frantic now, and perhaps not thinking clearly, he went to the only other place he could think of. The Ipatiev House. It was a foolish move. Talia would not be there, but perhaps he could find some clue as to her whereabouts. He also needed to see for himself if Yevgeny's news about the Romanovs was true.

The last time he had been there, a full contingent of guards had circled the grounds. Now it was ominously deserted. Heart pounding, he strode up to the front gate, hardly aware of the risk he was taking. The gate was locked, so he went around toward the back where he knew of an opening in the fence. Slipping through the breech, he found the yard, too, was deserted.

He ran into the house, looking through all the rooms. It all had the disordered appearance of a hasty departure. On the upper floor where the Romanovs had dwelt, many personal items still lay about. Andrei's foot stumbled over something and, bending down, he picked up a hairbrush that bore the engraved initials, A.F. Alexandra Fedorovna?

He raced down the stairs.

"Talia, where can you be?"

Back in the courtyard, he noticed for the first time the dark splotches on the ground. These he followed to the semi-basement that had been used for supplies. Hand trembling, he opened the door and descended the handful of steps. The splotches were worse now and his stomach began to churn.

In utter horror, Andrei stepped into his worst nightmare. How he managed to last as long as he did, he could not say. The room reeked with the stench of blood and death. Some attempt had been made to clean it, but it would take much more to scrub away the stains. It was still so fresh he could almost hear the screams of the victims echo off the wall of the tiny room.

As he viewed more blood than anyone could have tolerated, he began to sway on his feet, his own blood draining from his head.

"Dear God, not now! Please, not now!"

His legs could barely hold him, but there was nothing to grasp for support. Then his foot slipped and, looking down, realized he had stepped in a splotch of blood that had not yet dried.

His stomach lurched as he fled from the room, barely making it to the courtyard before it emptied of its contents. In complete despair, he sank to the ground, and paralyzed with nausea and fear, he wept. A sense of failure stronger than he had ever felt before overwhelmed him. Not only were all hopes of rescuing the royal family now obliterated, but had he failed Talia as well? Was her blood also mingled with those stains in that room?

He had to know. He had to find her.

He tried to get up, but fresh waves of nausea assaulted him and all strength seemed to be sucked from his legs. Experience told him he was on the verge of passing out. Then he truly would be useless to anyone.

"Curse you, Andrei!" he railed at himself. "You are weak and worthless!"

He took a breath. "God, help me!"

He forced himself to his feet. The yard spun around for a moment, but eventually it stopped and he willed his feet into motion. He had no idea what to do or where to go, but he could not allow defeat to consume him. And with each step he felt his stamina return. Vaguely he heard the sound of an approaching engine, but his mind was so full of other concerns he did not give it a thought.

He turned a corner, glad just to be walking and forgetting to be wary as well. He nearly ran headlong into Stephan. They stared at each other, equal expressions of shock on their faces.

Stephan regained his composure first. "So you have flown the coop. You were a fool to come here."

"You murderer!"

"More correctly, executioner."

"I don't care about that. Tell me where she is!"

"What are you talking about?"

"Where is Talia—the kitchen girl. What have you done with her?"

"What is this, Andrei Sergeiovich? Did you fall in love with the kitchen girl?" Stephan laughed. "The kitchen girl? Ha! Ha! And now you think she went the way of the Romanovs." He laughed even harder. "This is rich. Priceless."

"Tell me, you murderous dog!" Andrei advanced a step, his earlier weakness now all but forgotten in his rage. He did not wonder why Stephan was alone, or if others were close-by.

"All the guilty are dead!" Stephan retorted with enough arrogance to balance his sudden sense of aloneness. "Was she guilty, Andrei? Was she helping to free the bloodsucker? She deserved to die then." Suddenly, Stephan drew his side arm. "But you will soon join—"

But Andrei neither heard Stephan's final words, nor did he see the pistol, for he had already thrown himself into the attack. It probably wouldn't have mattered anyway. He had gone well beyond rational thought.

Though Stephan must surely have been expecting the attack, Andrei's force was daunting. He was slammed up against the wall of the house with such stunning force, he dropped the pistol. Andrei continued his offensive, smashing his large fist into Stephan's jaw. Stephan dodged one blow, and Andrei's fist painfully struck the wall, but still Andrei pummeled him. And Andrei had seen so much blood that day it hardly fazed him when streams of red oozed down his adversary's face. He heard the cartilage in Stephan's nose crack and vaguely remembered when, as a boy in Katyk, he had watched Stephan fight another boy and get his nose broken for the first time.

But soon Andrei had to let up his barrage, at least momentarily, as his fist cramped. Stephan seized the opportunity, dodging to the left with a deft sidestep even as he used the momentum to smash his left fist into the side of Andrei's head.

Andrei was thrown off-balance only a moment before he steadied himself and threw a right uppercut. Stephan blocked this, and for several minutes the fight swung back and forth. Stephan tried to make a couple of lunges for the pistol, but Andrei managed to kick it out of reach.

Stephan landed a blow that sent Andrei sprawling to the ground. The fight might have ended then, but Stephan was too full of rage to do the logical thing. Instead he dove at Andrei, fists striking blows from both sides. They tussled on the ground, one minute Stephan taking the advantage, the next Andrei.

At first Andrei wanted to kill Stephan, yet as the fight progressed he realized this would not help him find Talia—or bring her back if she was dead. He didn't want to kill. There had already been too much death.

It was then, as he attempted to dodge another blow by rolling away from Stephan, who was now on top, that Andrei's shoulder pressed against something hard. The pistol. It was the only way to end this thing. He hoped he would not have to use it, but it would give him the advantage he needed. If only Stephan had not also realized the gun was near. Andrei gave Stephan a hard shove. He then twisted around and grabbed the pistol. When Stephan turned back for another attack, he found himself facing his pistol.

"It's over, Stephan!" Andrei aimed the weapon at Stephan's heart.

"I don't think you have the guts to kill me," sneered Stephan.

"No," Andrei agreed, "but I can hurt you." He cocked the weapon, aimed the gun at Stephan's head, and prompted him to start walking.

"Where are we going?"

"You have a vehicle out front that should come in handy."

They walked around to the front of the house. There were two or three guards standing by a truck. They gaped in surprise at the pair as they approached, obviously helpless to do anything lest the important commissar from Moscow get a bullet in the head.

Andrei made Stephan get into the driver's seat, continuing to hold the pistol on him, and they drove away from the House of Special Purpose. Andrei would never see it again except in his nightmares.

47

A mile north of town, Andrei made Stephan stop the truck and get out.

"You won't get away, Andrei."

"I'm already away."

"For now. But I'll find you. I'll get you."

Drained now of practically all emotion, Andrei wearily shook his head. "We'll see."

"The only way for you to get away from me is to leave

the country, and even then, you'll have to keep looking over your shoulder."

Instead of a response, Andrei slid into the driver's seat, shifted into gear, and drove off. What did it matter anyway, if he couldn't find Talia? Still, even in his despair, he could not give up. Stephan had never actually *said* Talia had been hurt. There was still a chance. There *must* be a chance.

He circled around the town toward the south. The Whites and the Czechs were strongest there, and if there was a way of escape, it would be in this direction. It might also be that Bruce, realizing it was only a matter of time before he was captured too, had gone to the Whites. Perhaps he had found Talia and taken her also. Maybe Daniel was there—

Andrei knew he was dreaming. Even if he could hook up with the Whites, he wasn't about to leave this area until he was certain Talia was gone. He wondered if he could risk another visit to town. Perhaps he had missed her before and she would be there now.

After driving five miles, he stopped the truck near a steep canyon, jumped out and, putting the vehicle into gear, sent it over the edge of the road into the canyon. That might throw off pursuit for a short time at least. He was so completely exhausted and hungry that he could hardly think straight, much less continue his search. He had to find a place to rest for a few minutes, and he thought the old deserted barn was not far—at least that had been his plan when he ditched the truck. He would be in trouble if he had miscalculated.

He walked for a half mile, across fields, scrambling through brush and vaulting fences. By the time he caught sight of the barn, he could barely drag his tired body there. Once inside, he threw himself onto a mound of hay in a corner, and though he had not intended to do so, he fell instantly asleep.

It had to be several hours later when he awoke, for the

broad light of day no longer splintered through the cracks in the walls. But that was not the first thing he saw. When he rolled over, there was a figure, hidden in the evening shadows, seated beside him in the hay. He rubbed his eyes and looked up, wondering if he was still dreaming. But this was a sweet dream, and it made him forget all the horror that had so recently been haunting his sleep.

She reached a hand to brush straw from his tangled hair, but he took her hand and knew that the soft, tender feel of her was very real.

"Talia . . . you are alive!" He nudged her to him, and she came into his arms. He now knew for certain that she was indeed a dream, but one from which he would never awake.

"Of course I am, my love. We yet have a life to be lived together."

His lips sought hers in hungry passion for what he feared he had lost, and what he hoped for the future.

A timid sound interrupted from a short distance away. When Andrei glanced in its direction, he saw Bruce, his back turned politely toward the couple.

"I do hate to be a wet blanket," Bruce said, full of apology, "but we really ought not to linger here very long."

Andrei sat up. "Is there a minute to fill me in on what has been happening? Talia, what happened to you? Why couldn't I find you?" Andrei spoke in English and the conversation continued in that language. Talia, who had a better mastery of English than Andrei, had to help occasionally with interpretation.

"Had I known you had been released from jail I would have come here immediately," she said.

"I wasn't exactly released."

Deeming it safe to do so, Bruce turned and faced the pair seated in the hay. "You escaped? What?" As Andrei nodded, he continued, "Then they are after you?"

"With a vengeance, I fear," said Andrei. "Commissar Kaminsky is an old adversary, and I'm certain he won't rest until I'm caught. But I looked everywhere for you. What happened? And do you know what is going on now?"

"Do you know what became of the Romanovs?" Talia asked, and when Andrei nodded grimly, she went on, "I had been let go from my job in the kitchen. I heard they were going to move the family, so I decided to hide outside the house in hopes of getting some idea of where they might go, or something. I heard the shooting of the executioners. I saw the . . . bodies being carried out. Then one of the guards caught me. They held me in the jail—"

"We must have been there at the same time then," said Andrei. "Were you still there this morning when I escaped?"

"They released me last night. I finally convinced them I knew nothing. It was hard knowing you were in the jail, but I dared not say anything about you—"

"That was wise, Talia, otherwise they would never have let you go."

"I didn't care for my protection, but I knew it would help nothing if we were both locked up—and Daniel, too."

"Did you know they took him away early this morning, apparently to deport him?" asked Andrei.

"I've been at the British Consul for hours trying to get him released," said Bruce. "And those blackguard Reds had already deported him and said nothing! The first chance I get, I will create an international incident over this. See how far Lenin will get without foreign aid."

"I pray Daniel is safe," said Talia.

"I have no doubt he can take care of himself," said Bruce. "But now we must concentrate on getting ourselves away from here."

"You and Talia should have no difficulty—" Andrei began.

But Talia broke in. "We will stay together. On that point there will be no debate!" She folded her arms together adamantly and with her eyes dared him to dispute her.

Andrei smiled with pride and deep affection. She was indeed a treasure in which each moment he seemed to discover a new and more precious gem.

"Our best chance then would be to try to hook up with the White Army." Andrei glanced down at his jacket with its Red Army insignias and immediately stripped it off, tossing it into a corner. "Will I pass as a good monarchist?" he asked wryly.

"Why not?" Talia replied. "You *are* a Russian prince."

Andrei was saved pondering that sobering thought as Bruce began to suggest a plan.

"I believe Captain Sedov might help us with that," explained Bruce. "He's the officer who helped Daniel on his first trip to Siberia and who has been in contact with us since our arrival in Ekaterinburg. I believe he is still in town. I doubt he even knows about what happened to the Romanovs, since it has hardly been made public knowledge. At any rate, I can slip into town in order to enlist his aid. He has also been in contact with the Whites, so I am certain he could get us through the lines."

"That might take time," said Andrei.

"Would you feel safe staying here?"

"As far as I know, no one suspects this barn as a rendezvous point."

"Then I'll go now and be back in a couple of hours, should all go well."

"Do be careful, Lord Findochty," said Talia.

"I only hope no one tries to talk to me." A wry grin bent the Brit's lips.

As Bruce started to leave, Andrei called after him, "Would it be possible for you to bring back some food? I am nearly starved enough to try the taste of roots and insects."

Bruce nodded, then exited the barn, leaving Andrei and Talia to a long, uncertain wait.

Bruce did not return to the barn until after midnight, but Captain Sedov was with him. They brought with them disguises for each. An hour later, dressed as peasants, the little group of fugitives left the barn and trekked by foot south across the countryside, avoiding roads and populous areas. They encountered the first outpost of Whites the following evening. The password Sedov knew had been changed, and there had been a tense moment before an acquaintance of the captain appeared and vouched for them.

Without conclusive proof, the commanders refused to give up hope that the Romanovs had survived. And regardless, they were determined to fight on against the Bolshevik menace. If they could not put Nicholas back on the throne, they could surely find a far better leader than the usurper, Lenin.

After a night in the White camp, Andrei, Talia, and Bruce were helped on their return journey to Petrograd. They traveled by train when it was safe to do so, but also by truck or even horse cart. It took them about a week.

As the three fugitives were viewing their first welcome glimpse of Petrograd, many miles away to the east the White Army pushed into Ekaterinburg and captured the city. A contingent of Whites rushed immediately to the Ipatiev House, only to find their worst fears realized. Their beloved tsar was dead, along with his entire family.

48

Andrei and Talia bid Bruce good-bye at the British embassy. The Brit's papers were still in good order, and there was no reason for him to be denied departure. No government officials were aware of his part in the rescue attempt. Still, he decided wisely to waste no time in leaving.

Even as Andrei bid his new friend farewell, he realized that he himself could not remain in Russia either. He and Talia had discussed that possibility and now it was a reality. Stephan had come to Petrograd and had stormed into Anna's home with his Cheka goons in search of Andrei. Luckily, Andrei had anticipated this and had been in hiding in various safe places around the city. Stephan had also arrested Rudy and interrogated him thoroughly before releasing him. Thus far, Kaminsky had made no other threats against Andrei's family, but they all realized that such was an ever present possibility. The only way to lessen that threat was for Andrei to put himself completely out of reach of the Cheka.

He had discussed this with Yuri and had come to the logical conclusion. What he had not considered was how difficult it would be to tell his mother. Arranging to meet Anna in the Alexander Gardens he tried to broach the subject. The light of the afternoon sun reflecting in her eyes made her seem younger than her fifty-eight years. Somehow that made it a little easier for Andrei. He did not have the sense that he was leaving a frail old woman to fend for herself.

"So, Andrushka, this must be a very serious discussion you have in mind!" Anna smiled, not in a patronizing way, but rather with affection. "You have gone to a great deal of trouble to arrange this meeting." She obviously was referring to the disguise he had donned of an old man.

"Yes, Mama, I'm afraid it is. I have been home a week now, and you must realize that I cannot keep up this life of hiding much longer."

She nodded.

"Unfortunately, it would be different for me than it was for Papa. No one was ever specifically after him, and he was able to easily blend into society in a backwater peasant village. I fear Stephan Kaminsky will be relentless in his pursuit."

"I don't know what went wrong with that boy," Anna sighed.

"Well, anyway, Mama, I fear the time has come for me to leave Russia."

"I expected it might come to that. And I must admit I'd rather you leave than be mixed up with those Bolsheviks again. I'd be afraid that the same thing would happen to you that happened to Stephan."

"I was afraid of that, too, Mama. That is partly why I did quit."

"Where will you go Andrushka?"

"Talia and I will go to America."

"That is good. At least you will have family there."

Andrei was glad there was something in the situation to help ease his mother's mind. When word reached the American Embassy of Daniel's deportation, they had moved quickly to take Mariana and the children into their protectorate, essentially giving them assylum. The Soviet government had at first insisted that as a Russian citizen, Mariana could not leave the country without proper documents—and they quickly revoked her previous travel papers. Because of the children, and the new baby she had recently announced was on the way, a clandestine escape was deemed imprudent. Either she would leave the country legally or not at all. Then Trent Industries became involved and began pulling contracts with various business concerns in Russia. It did not take long for Lenin to see that one puny woman was not worth the loss of desperately needed revenue from the contracts. Papers were issued, but Mariana had to leave immediately lest the volatile Soviet government change its mind. She had but fifteen minutes to say good-bye to her family before her train departed.

"Mama, it won't be too hard for you to lose us both all

at once?" Andrei asked, his attention returning to the present moment.

"Of course it will be hard, but not more than I can bear. It helps that God in His grace has brought Misha back to me."

"And you will soon have a new grandchild to dote upon?"

"It will be Yuri's job now to fill my home again." Anna paused, then took a package from her coat pocket. She held the familiar leather pouch out to Andrei. "I guessed that the purpose of this meeting might be to announce your travel plans. I wanted to be prepared."

"Oh, Mama!" It was the old Burenin family Bible. It was at least a hundred years old.

"As you know, I gave it to Mariana years ago when she left Katyk for the first time. Before she left the country yesterday, she suggested I pass it on to you."

He took the leather pouch, opened the flap, and carefully removed the worn old book. He knew it was not meant for everyday reading, and no doubt it had not been opened more than two or three times since it had come into Mariana's possession. But Andrei well knew the tradition that went with the Bible. He opened it to the Book of Proverbs.

"It's funny that this should come to me now," he said reverently. "When I left before to join Lenin—although I slipped away without telling anyone and you had no chance to give it to me—it would not have meant very much except as a family tradition. But now, Mama, my heart is truly open to the things of God."

"I know, son. And perhaps that is why my heart isn't filled with as much sorrow as before."

"Shall I read, Mama?"

"You know I have not heard you read from God's Word since you were a boy."

"I'm sorry I made you wait so long."

"I learned long ago to allow God His own time. Now, go ahead and read."

He turned a brittle page:

"'My son, if thou wilt receive my words, and hide my commandments with thee; so that thou incline thine ear unto wisdom, and apply thine heart to understanding; yea, if thou criest after knowledge, and liftest up thy voice for understanding; if thou seekest her as silver, and searchest for her as for hid treasures; then shalt thou understand the fear of the Lord, and find the knowledge of God. For the Lord giveth wisdom: out of his mouth cometh knowledge and understanding. He layeth up sound wisdom for the righteous: he is a buckler to them that walk uprightly. He keepeth the paths of judgment, and preserveth the way of his saints. Then shalt thou understand righteousness, and judgment, and equity; yea, every good path. When wisdom entereth into thine heart, and knowledge is pleasant unto thy soul; descretion shall preserve thee, understanding shall keep thee.'"

Pausing, he glanced up to find tears trailing down his mother's cheeks. He reached out and took her hand, then he found the passage that he knew was his grandfather Yevno's favorite:

"'My son, forget not my law; but let thine heart keep my commandments: for length of days, and long life, and peace, shall they add to thee. Let not mercy and truth forsake thee: bind them about thy neck; write them upon the table of thine heart: so shalt thou find favor and good understanding in the sight of God and man. Trust in the Lord with all thine heart; and lean not unto thine own understanding. In all thy ways acknowledge him, and he shall direct thy paths.'"

Tears also welled up in Andrei's eyes, and the Scripture reminded him of the rich family heritage that was his. How ironic that now that he was able to truly appreciate it, he must leave. Yet he saw it was the kind of spiritual irony only God could create. For only now, with the—how did the verse go?—"buckler" of his faith and loving support of his family was he truly prepared to face an uncertain future in a new land.

Anna embraced her son.

"I don't know when, or if, we will see each other again," Andrei said, trying to be manly and strong, but feeling so very like a child in his mother's arms.

"Who knows what the future will bring, my Andrushka? Remember what I said about God's timing. So let's trust Him."

———————

Two days later, the time came for Andrei and Talia to leave. Anna and Raisa and Misha took the risk of seeing them off at the train station. In the crowd, no one would notice the presence of two Russian babushkas and an old war veteran. And though they all meant and understood the words about trusting God, Anna and Raisa wept freely at the departure. There were even tears in Misha's tough old visage, for he thought of both young people practically as his own children also.

Yuri was more stoic. He would have a little more time with them and had to keep a clear head because it had fallen to him to organize an escape for his brother. He saw himself as nothing but a simple doctor, not some secret agent. But when the escape idea came to him, he knew it had to be his responsibility to see it through to the end.

There was a large contingent of officers and monarchists in and around Petrograd who were at the time in various stages of hiding, hoping somehow to get to the south and join the White Army. The wife of one of these men, who was a nurse at Yuri's hospital, had come up with a rather creative plan to transport the men. There were still regular trains carrying wounded home from the Front and to various medical facilities in Russia. It would not be at all unusual for one such train to travel from

Petrograd to some point in the south.

Talia was easily transformed into a nurse. Andrei, along with about fifty of the White officers, was made up with all manner of wounds complete with appropriate bandages. Andrei's included a thick bandage obscuring a large portion of his face. Yuri made up a concoction that perfectly resembled blood, which he sprinkled liberally over many of the fake bandages. Oddly, this did not bother Andrei, and he hoped his horrible experience in Ekaterinburg had cured him of his phobia. But he learned otherwise when shortly after boarding the train he cut himself on a broken glass and nearly fainted.

"I guess I'll never be perfect," he told Talia, just a little disappointed at how true his words were.

Yuri, who was bandaging his hand, laughed. "Let me respond to that, Talia, all right? You will have many opportunities to do so when you marry this man."

Talia smiled and nodded for Yuri to continue.

"Well, Andrei, that never stopped us from loving you in the past, now did it?" Yuri said. "In fact, the more imperfect you have been, the more we loved you."

"Is that so? Had I known, I wouldn't have worried so about it."

Now Talia and Yuri laughed together and Andrei joined them. Suddenly all three, at the same instant, were struck with how much like old times that exchange was. There was a moment of sobering, then Yuri was called away to tend one of the real wounded on the train. And nothing more was said just then. None of them wanted to face the inevitable any sooner than they had to.

After a very tense inspection by the authorities, the train departed Petrograd. Each stop along the way presented dangers. If just one patrolman chose to actually look under one of the fake bandages, all would have been lost. But Yuri made sure his "patients" looked as authentic as possible. In reality there was so much confusion in the south with the civil war raging, and so many real wounded to be dealt with, the train, bearing its large red cross, was usually waved through without incident.

They reached Rostov near the Black Sea in four days. The city was held by the Whites at the time. Andrei was able to buy passage for himself and Talia on a friendly vessel.

And finally, the day they had all been dreading came. Yuri went with them to the dock. It was dark and an evening mist drifted around them as they stood in silence facing each other on the gangplank of the ship. A lonely ship's bell clanged in the distance, muffled by the fog, and then the horn of the ship Talia and Andrei would board blasted.

"I guess this is it," said Andrei, unable to stand the tension a moment longer. "Thanks for everything you have done for us." Andrei held out his hand.

Yuri was about to take it when Talia said, "Just a minute! When we were young I used to referee you two; now I must do so again, but in a different way. Andrei, you know you want to do more than shake your brother's hand. There will be a good Russian embrace, or we are going nowhere."

"I fear what will happen if I do more," said Andrei, his voice now starting to break. "Dear Lord—! I'm going to miss you, Yuri. . . !" His voice broke completely as he stepped forward and threw his arms around his brother.

Yuri opened his mouth but no words would come. Instead, a sob escaped his lips as he returned the embrace. But he did not forget Talia. He held out an arm and drew her into the embrace also.

"As it should be," he said brokenly.

"I don't know if I can do this," said Andrei. "I feel I'll never see you again. And you almost a father. I'll never know my niece or nephew."

"And what of you two?" said Yuri. "I'll not be best man at your wedding, nor see your little ones—" But his emotion overcame him and he could say no more.

346

"Don't say that," Talia scolded, her own voice practically obliterated by her emotion. "I firmly believe this parting is only temporary. Once, we pledged to always be friends—and I believe that means more than merely friends in spirit." She held up her hand, showing the finger with the faint scar from their childhood ceremony.

Andrei and Yuri did the same. They brought their fingers together and touched. Then in unison, through their tears, said the words that would always define the depth of their bond:

"A threefold cord is not quickly broken!"

Now, more than ever, the words represented hope, desire, and prayer all together.

DASVIDANIYA...

I wish to take this final page to thank my loyal readers for sticking with it through the length and breadth of this series. When Mike Phillips and I first envisioned *The Russians* we never imagined—and we have very active imaginations!—that it would take eight years and seven books before we bid a farewell to the Burenin and Fedorcenko clans. Even now I cannot say with complete certainty that I am ready for that parting. I feel more like Anna when she said good-bye to her son. Who knows what will happen in the future? But for now it is time to leave *The Russians*—for a season at least. There is so much more to be told in the story of Russia, and my heart is so deeply tied to that country that I know I will return there one day—via my pen, if not via an airplane. I hope when the time comes you, the reader, will wish to come along on the journey once more.

In the meantime, you may wish to explore more deeply the history of Russia, and so I list below a few sources you might find of interest. In the course of producing this series, well over a hundred sources have crossed my desk to aid my research. Some became well-worn friends that I will miss as much as my fictitious characters. Many are too obscure for the casual seeker to find by normal methods, others are perhaps too specific in their content for many. But there are several that I feel the average reader would find not only informative, but readable and even entertaining.

Judith Pella
Eureka, California
1998

Nicholas and Alexandra, Robert K. Massie, Dell Publishing Co., Inc., New York. 1967.

The Shadow of the Winter Palace, Edward Crankshaw, Penguin Books, Ltd., England, New York. 1976.

Russia on the Eve of War and Revolution, Sir Donald Mackenzie Wallace, Vintage books, Random House, New York. 1961 (reprint).

Black Night, White Snow, Russia's Revolutions 1905–1917, Harrison E. Salisbury, Doubleday & Co., Inc., Garden City, New York. 1977.

In War's Dark Shadow, W. Bruce Lincoln, The Dial Press, New York. 1983.

Passage Through Armageddon, W. Bruce Lincoln, Simon and Schuster, New York. 1986.

The Russian Revolution, Alan Moorehead, Harper & Brothers, New York. 1958.

Nicholas II (Last of the Tsars), Marc Ferro, Oxford University Press, New York. 1993.

Years of the Golden Cockerel, Sidney Harcave, MacMillan, 1968.

My St. Petersburg, E.M. Almedingen, W.W. Norton & Co., Inc. New York. 1970.